Graced

Other books by Amanda

Captive: A Graced Story
Survivor: A Graced Story
Bitten

The Graced Series

GRACED

Book One

AMANDA PILLAR

Published by Maatkare Books
www.amandapillar.com

Editor: Julia Knapman

ISBN: 978-0-6480295-0-2

Cover Design: Amanda Pillar © 2016
Internal Layout: Amanda Pillar © 2016

First Published February 2015

For Liz Pentland, English teacher extraordinaire, who told the 13 year old me the revolutionary phrase: "a novel starts with a single sentence."
Thank you.

PROLOGUE

The familiar, warm weight pressing against Elle's legs vanished.

"Elle!"

Elle spun toward the sound of her sister's frightened voice. A man – a vampire by his purple eyes – was holding her sister aloft in the air, like a sack of potatoes. Emmie did a rather excellent job of imitating said sack, her body limp, a dead weight in the stranger's arms. But she would weigh next to nothing for someone like him.

Elle took a step toward the vampire, her hand instantly searching for the baton that was normally strapped to her side. But it wasn't there. She was off-duty. No City Guard uniform, no steel baton. "Put my sister down."

She had nothing but her bare hands to reduce the leech to pulp for touching her sister.

The vampire didn't even glance at Elle; his eyes were focused on Emmie. He wore expensive clothing and looked like an aristo, but Elle had never seen him before. And she'd gotten to know the faces of the nearby vampires. Better to know your enemy and all.

"What interesting eyes you have, little human."

Inside, Elle flinched. She should never have brought Emmie here – but she'd thought it was safe. They were in a human neighborhood, and it was a general store. Sacks of flour, bags of candy, pickled vegetables and scales were the standard items decking the glass counter and shelves. Most vampires wouldn't be caught dead near such a boring and non-flamboyant place.

"I repeat," Elle said, taking a menacing step forward, "put my sister *down*."

That finally caught the vampire's attention. His eyes flicked to her, scanned her up and down and then dismissed her. "She doesn't look anything like you. I don't believe she is your sister."

A sick feeling began to pulse through Elle. If he took Emmie, she might not be able to get her back for weeks. Or ever.

"She's my sister. If you don't put her down in five seconds, you'll wish you were never born." It wasn't a hollow threat. Elle would do anything to protect her four-year-old sibling. Their age gap made Elle feel more like a mother than sister, anyway.

The vampire's fingers visibly tightened on Emmie's ribs, and the girl gave a small squeak. "I think I will take her with me. She will make an excellent addition to my collection."

Elle's fists clenched. "Put. Her. Down."

The vampire looked around the room, suddenly seeming to notice the audience. A mixed assortment of humans stared back at the him. Women and men, some tall, some short, some in tough calico work clothes, others in prim suits. Their Brown eyes were stony though, locked on the vampire and his human prize. While Elle watched, the store clerk's arm disappeared under the counter.

"Yes," the vampire said. "I think I'll take this child. She clearly has no relations and is a street urchin in need of a home."

Blood turned to fire in Elle's veins. "Try and leave. I'll have you on so many charges for abduction you'll be stuck in court for years."

The vampire laughed. "Who's going to listen to you over me?"

"I'm a city guard."

"Again, who will listen?"

Emmie craned her head around and stared at Elle, waiting for her big sister to do something heroic. Elle was within reaching distance of Emmie. If she could snatch the child back…

The vampire's eyes were cold, calculating. "I will break the girl's neck if you come any closer."

Elle believed him. "She's no good to you dead."

"I can have her preserved. She'll still look good in my

collection."

The urge to vomit was overpowering. Elle doubted she'd ever get over the mental images of what her sister would look like dead and "preserved."

Emmie screamed, "You're a bad man! Put me *down*!"

The vampire, startled, loosened his grip on the child. He could have easily caught Emmie again, but Elle jerked forward and wrenched Emmie free. Her arms tightened around Emmie like steel bands, and then she set her down behind the store clerk, who stood holding out a wooden bat. Elle smiled.

The vampire wasn't laughing half an hour later, when the city coroner was called. Unfortunately for the vampire's family, when the other city guards arrived to check out the scene, no one in the store could remember who had landed the death blow; there'd been too many people involved in the fight.

But Elle knew.

No one touched her sister.

Ever.

PART I

May you come to the attention of those in authority

Chapter One

Three years later

"I'll suck your cock."

Dante raised one eyebrow as he looked down at the woman kneeling on the packed dirt between his feet. He hadn't even noticed she was there, until now. She was grimy, ragged and had bruises the size of fingers running up and down her arms. Her breath frosted in the air between them. She was shivering, but he doubted she knew she was cold. He looked past her and at their surroundings; no one else was in the enclosed exercise area, bordered on three sides by tall, stone walls. That didn't mean much, though. A handful of glass windows stared out onto the yard; the passageway that had led him here was fed by a series of corridors that wound back inside his father's estate, to the slave pens. While they were alone now, that situation could change in oh, say, two seconds.

She started to reach for his fly with grubby, nail-bitten hands. He took a step backward, placing a protective hand over his crotch. "That isn't exactly the grand offer you make it sound."

Raising sunken eyes, she gripped his leg with enough force to leave a temporary mark. "Please, I'll do anything."

Dante knew that some vampires would love an offer like that; they'd have her on her knees in the courtyard, fangs and cock buried deep. But he wasn't one of them. She was bit-ridden, a vampire bite addict, for blood's sake. Not to mention she was way too thin – her blonde hair looked like it hadn't seen water in months – and worst of all, she was a normal human. A normal *brown-eyed* human, and for him, that was the distinction.

"I'm not interested." Dante tried to shake her loose without hurting her, but the pesky rat wouldn't let go. He started walking backward, both hands cupping his groin, but she was still gripping his leg.

"I'll let you stick it in any hole you want." She followed belly-first across the hard ground. Dante could smell her blood as the thin skin on her legs gave way with his movement.

"I don't want to stick it anywhere near you." Dante stopped walking. "Will you just leave me alone?"

The slave looked up at him then, actually met him eye-to-eye, and he could see the desperation in her expression. She didn't care that she was lying in the dirt, that her one and only sackcloth dress had just obtained a few more holes; she didn't care she was bleeding in front of a vampire or that people had started filing into the exercise yard and were staring at her as she clung to his leg. By the blood, she probably *wanted* to bleed in front of him. But he wasn't a fledgling, and he was more than capable of smelling dinner and not devouring it without thinking of where it came from.

"Let go of my leg," Dante said when she didn't say anything in reply.

"I can't." Her voice broke as her grip tightened.

Dante searched for a fleck of blue in those brown eyes, a smidgen of green, a dollop of gray. But there was nothing other than brown. And there was no sense of self there, no flicker of intelligence; just need driven by addiction.

"I am not going to bite you."

She stared blindly at him, not really seeing *him*, just the hit she needed for her habit.

He tapped his teeth, shook his head and then said slowly, as if talking to a child, "Not. Going. To. Bite."

She threw herself on him, and the surprise sent him back a

step. She was clawing and hitting, her fingernails trying to scratch the skin from his face. Not that they made contact, he was a lot stronger than her, even bit-ridden as she was. He tried to be gentle, holding her hands away, but she kicked him in the shin, tried to knee him in the groin. There was nothing left to do, nothing in her eye color that made him *want* to try and help her.

For once in his life, he decided to do the kind thing.

♦

A low-pitched moan came muffled through the soundproof door of his father's study. Dante stopped walking down the bluestone corridor and glared at the metal door. Yes, he'd heard right; there were definitely sounds coming from within the study. Even though dull sodium lamps lit the corridor and he didn't really need their light to see – they were for the slaves' benefit – he squinted at the entrance and sighed.

Soundproof door, he thought and snorted as another moan reached his ears. It was soundproof for humans – and most vampires, he supposed – but not for him. "Sensitive," that's what the countess called him. "Delicate" was his father's term. "Unlucky," that was Dante's.

He *could* ignore the noise, but if his father found out that Dante had been walking by the study – and someone had been in there without authorization – and that Dante *had known* about it…

Shaking his head, he tried the door and found it unlocked. He raised an eyebrow almost to his hairline and pushed the heavy, reinforced steel slab inward. He grimaced at the sight that greeted him. His sister, blonde head thrown back, was sprawled over their father's hardwood desk, her skirt clumped around her waist. She seemed to be focused on the male human who was pumping between her legs, but with his sister, well, she was probably enjoying being caught more than the physical act itself.

The human's eyes were shut in concentration, the muscles on his neck corded up to his dark hairline. He probably didn't realize they'd been disturbed. Blood trickled down his throat from two puncture marks; the scent was clean, aromatic. This slave hadn't succumbed to addiction yet.

Dante knew Misty was aware of his presence. Her moans had gotten louder – and not just because the door was now open. She'd always had a sixth sense about whether or not she was alone, vampire hearing notwithstanding. If he backed away now, she'd simply confront him about it later. Call him a pervert or something equally ridiculous, but something his father might hear about and believe. Apparently "delicate" was close enough to "unhinged" for his father to care.

May as well get the confrontation over with, Dante thought. For some reason, his sister could never let anything go, even if she was in the wrong. Like now.

She moaned again. Dante cleared his throat under the pretext of politeness. Although, he didn't think there was a way to determine the appropriate level of courtesy required when one's sibling was screwing a slave on their parent's desk. Dante was fairly certain there wasn't an etiquette rule designed for that situation, but he couldn't be sure. It wasn't like he'd ever bothered to study manners, much to the countess' disgust.

The human stopped moving, staring like a mouse caught in lamplight. He grunted when Misty dug her fingernails into his ass as punishment. The smell of blood became stronger. The poor slave looked tormented, caught between his need to continue his activity and fear at being discovered by the master's son.

"I doubt Father would appreciate you using his desk that way," Dante said, taking pity on the creature. His sister, sure as anything, wasn't going to.

Misty exhaled slowly, and let go of the human. The man stumbled back a step and tugged his homespun pants back to his waist, pulling the drawstring tight. The material was having a hard time covering everything. From the muscular torso down to the tented material, Dante could see why his sister had chosen this particular slave to dabble with. Head down, skin flushed, the human stumbled from the room without a backward glance.

Dante heard the sound of ruffled silk as Misty swung off their father's desk. He didn't want to watch her settle into a more appropriate level of dress, so he moved over to one of the bookstands. As he always did when in his father's study, he stared at the three skulls that sat side by side on the top row of the shelf. They were brown-tinged with age, the bone shiny, like it had been covered in some sort of resin. Since his father wasn't here, he could look at them to his heart's content, without having his parent breathing down his neck.

"You ruined a very pleasant interlude," Misty said while Dante studied the skulls.

"So, you're back to being heterosexual?" Dante asked. He couldn't keep track of her lovers. The last time she'd been caught by someone, there'd been two other women involved and possibly a guy, but he hadn't been the one to discover her on that occasion. Thankfully. "It stinks of sex in here." Dante flicked a glance back at her.

Misty tossed her hair over one shoulder and shrugged. "Father won't care. And I'm bisexual. I don't have to have a preference either way."

Dante tilted his head in acknowledgment as he turned back to the shelf. "I'd make sure Father's desk is cleaned before he returns."

His eyes locked on the human skull. Picking it up, he twisted it around in his hands. It was cool to the touch, slippery almost. It was the same size as the other two – *Typical brain capacity is the same as a were's or vampire's*, the small yellowed note tucked under the skull read – but there were differences. The bone was thin, fragile in touch and appearance. If he tightened his grasp, he'd crush it. Dante had read about the bone density difference, of course, but feeling the skull and seeing it in real life, without the flesh, was different.

No wonder they broke so easily.

"Okay, Father might care," Misty said into the quiet.

Dante flicked another glance at her. She had a one-track mind. "He might care you were fucking someone on his prized desk? Just a tad."

He turned his attention back to the bookshelf and replaced the human skull. The ledge it sat on was made of wood – something that his father would call reckless if anyone else had one – and it gleamed. Just like the desk his father loved to sit behind, as if he were some all-powerful lord, rather than just a regular "lord." Although, as far as Dante and the estate slaves were concerned, the former was true.

Dante ran his fingers over the shelf's surface; it was smooth to touch, almost warm, unlike the metal and stone that adorned every other part of the property. The only wood on the entire estate was in his father's study.

Misty had come to stand next to him, and he felt the rush of air as she re-flicked her hair back over one shoulder. "Well, he would care, but he would admire me for my daring."

Dante reached for the were skull. "True."

There were five simple facts in Dante's life: One, his father thought that Dante was an over-educated twat incapable of even the barest of vampire duties (he thought that feeding was almost beyond Dante's prowess); two, his sister was a maniacal bitch who constantly pushed the boundaries in order to gain their father's approval, and it usually worked; three, their father liked Misty more than Dante as a result; four, the countess treated the Kipling children with fond neglect, which meant that five, Dante had found life was better when he avoided being on the edge of his father's attention.

There were more, but these were the most fundamental and unchanging.

Misty's finger poked him in the arm. "Why are you so interested in those things?"

Dante glanced at her. "The skulls?"

She rolled lavender-colored eyes at him. "What else are you looking at?"

He turned the were – wolf in this case – skull over in his hands. It also felt cool and smooth, but its surface was grainier, even with the resin coating. And it was heavier than the human's. Much heavier.

"It says the werewolf skull has the same cranial capacity as a human's," Dante said.

"So? That just shows wolves are as stupid as humans."

The corner of Dante's mouth lifted slightly. Holding the wolf head in one hand, he lifted the vampire skull and peered at the yellowed note underneath. He carefully sat it back down, while noticing that it was lighter than the wolf skull, but heavier than the human's. "They have the same capacity as we do."

Misty snorted, but her arm snaked out and lifted the vampire skull to check for herself. "Fancy that."

"We're all as dumb as each other, then."

"There is no way a human is as intelligent as we are – the same goes for fleabags."

Dante had never really had much to do with wolves – or any other were – so he couldn't vouch for their mental acumen or their flea status, but he had to agree that he'd never really met a human who was anything other than pathetic. At least wolves – and weres in general – couldn't get bit-ridden.

"The human skull is fragile, the bone thin and delicate." He ignored Misty's chuckle. "But the wolf skull is heavy, the bone dense. Check out these suture marks." He ran his finger over the zigzagging lines that crisscrossed their way over the bone, far more than on the human's. "They're all over. And see here? This ridge on the top of the skull?"

He held it up, with his finger resting on the aforementioned ridge. Misty obediently looked, and for once he could tell that she was humoring him. "This is the gap between the jaw muscles. They were huge."

"So?"

"So? It explains why they can bite almost through bone, even when they're in human form."

"In a way, I can see why these bones interest you so much, but, Dante, they're skulls. It's not like you can talk to them; you can't have a chat to their owners. You need another interest, one that people can survive."

Dante turned to her. "These skulls are interesting because they show just how different we are from each other; humans, weres, vampires. But we're all essentially the same. Did you know there are theories that say we all came from the same source?"

Misty frowned. "Source?"

"We were all human once."

"Not possible." She waved a dismissive hand through the air. "Look at that vampire skull. It's clearly different."

Dante reluctantly put the wolf skull back. The eye sockets looked slightly smaller than the human's, but he couldn't say with certainty that this was the case. Not without his measuring tools. It wasn't a noticeable difference when the flesh was there, anyway.

Misty handed the vampire skull to him. "It's different, see?"

She really didn't seem to like the idea that vampires might have been related to humans or weres. He turned the skull over in his hands, running his fingers over the mandible and temporal bones. "The bone is thicker than the human's – but that probably means the vampire was old. All that constant regeneration tends to leave a calcium build-up. The skull isn't really that different."

"Apart from the fact that there is a calcium build-up. You know…the whole longevity thing. Humans die a lot. How old is old?" Misty asked.

Dante squinted as he thought. He guessed, "Maybe two thousand years?"

"That's not that old. Father is a thousand, and he's still got three more to go."

"So? It's not like you've had a look at Father's skull." Although Dante had thought about it, probably more often than would be considered healthy in a loving, dutiful son.

"True. But knowing Father, it's probably thicker than a werewolf's." She chuckled.

He quirked a half smile and turned the head around so it was on its side, facing Misty. "See here?" He ran his fingers over the maxilla, where the incisors met the bone. Tilting the skull again, he saw the thin pieces of the wire that bound the two teeth there. Muscle normally held them in place.

"Our teeth go that far up?" Misty asked. She was running a

finger over one of her own fangs.

"Yeah, they do." And then they dropped down, but she'd know that already. He placed the skull back on the shelf.

"You're a freak, you know that, right?" Misty said.

Dante took a step back from the bookcase and examined the display. It looked exactly as he had found it. "Because I like to know how my body works? About where we might have come from?"

"No," she said, turning around. He heard the sound of rustling silk; she must be smoothing her dress. "I can understand wanting to know how something works. But you don't *like* the things that live inside the casings you find so interesting. *And* you like to know about humans and dogs, too."

He slashed a glance at her. "You fuck them, what's the difference?"

She blinked. "I'd *never* fuck a dog. Or any were. Plus, what I do is *fun*."

"And what I do isn't?"

"As I said," she flounced her hair again, "you're a freak."

Dante shook his head and started walking across the thick, blood-red rug toward the soundproof door that wasn't soundproof.

"So why do you smell like death, but you don't have the accompanying aroma of yummy yummy blood?" Misty asked his back.

Dante shook his head, not bothering to turn around. "One of the bit-ridden slaves attacked me."

He pictured her eyebrow arching high onto her forehead. "So you killed them?"

He shrugged, almost at the door. "It did it in front of a group of slaves. What else was I to do?"

"Bite them?"

"That's what the slave wanted."

"I see." Her voice was thoughtful.

Maybe Misty saw something, but it probably wasn't Dante's point. He stepped through the doorway and into the corridor. She would think that he'd decided to be perverse – something she was good at – and that he'd given the slave the opposite of what it had wanted. But he'd thought that ending the bit-ridden creature's existence was…the kinder option.

To live for the bite; to want nothing more out of life other than the euphoria induced by vampire saliva? He shook his head as he walked down the corridor toward his chamber. It was hard for him to think of how a life like that would be worth living.

CHAPTER TWO

"Keep your head down, Emmie," Elle said. She tightened her grip on her sister's hand. The small fingers, a deep olive in comparison to her white, were wriggling in protest.

Emmie stopped moving down the sidewalk and tilted her face toward Elle, careful to keep her eyes away from the strangers who bumped into them as they passed by. Even downturned, that rich, unique Teal seemed like a beacon. "I just want to look around."

"We walk by here every day." Elle sighed and halted, quickly drawing Emmie out of the way of strangers. They seemed to have this argument every time they went out. And sometimes she gave in, but not today, not right now. Large bluestone walls towered on their right side and a street full of carriages rushed by to their left, with rows of fashionable shops past them. The icy smell of vampires seemed to permeate the air.

"People will see you." Or, more accurately, a vampire or werewolf who was strolling down Pittbrough Street – the city's main shopping strip – might notice Emmie's eyes and decide they wanted her for a "pet."

It wasn't dusk yet, which meant that it was mostly humans out, but Elle never liked to take chances. Not with Emmie. With her free hand, Elle touched her fingers to her sister's chin. Small, pointy and stubborn, that's what that chin was. "You're special, sweet."

Emmie pulled her face away and frowned at the cobblestone street. "I don't want to be special."

Nobody wants to be special, Elle thought. Well, nobody who had any sense. To be unique was like painting "food" on one's forehead and walking into a vampire's or wolf's estate. Like the one they were standing next to, those cold stone walls looming, a silent warning.

"Let's go," Elle said and started walking, half-dragging Emmie behind her.

"Do we have to go to Gran's?" Emmie asked.

Elle couldn't stop the edges of her lips rising. "Unfortunately, yes, we do."

"She's not very nice."

Elle looked down at her sister; the weak sunlight caught the golden lights in Emmie's normally brown hair. Their breaths were misting, but Emmie didn't seem cold. Elle tugged the collar up on her sister's jacket and made sure it was buttoned over her dress of pale green cotton, sturdy and washable. It hung a good two inches above the ground, and her brown walking boots were visible. She'd had another growth spurt. Did children ever stop? Elle noticed that Emmie had tied a dark green ribbon around her waist; a dusky green tail hung below the hem of her jacket. Their grandmother would not approve; but then, Gran never approved of much.

"Gran is old; old people tend to get crotchety."

Serious Teal eyes met hers. "I've met other old people, you know, and none of them are like Gran."

"*Nobody* is like Gran." Elle chuckled, a low sound that caught a passing vampire's attention. She shut her mouth quickly and took in his dark hair, which was tied back in a queue, and his eyes, which were a piercing violet. He seemed to search her face for…something. He was standing next to a blonde, icy vampire who wore a white gown that looked utterly ridiculous on her.

Elle looked away, her fingers tightening on Emmie's. Elle didn't like the way the vampire was staring at her, from the tips of her short red curls to the scuffed boots of her City Guard uniform.

Time to get moving, she thought, *before he or the ice bitch he's with notices Emmie.*

Elle's fingers closed spasmodically around Emmie's as she hauled her sister away.

♦

"Dante, what are you doing?"

Misty's voice pierced through Dante's mental haze. He blinked, shook himself, and turned his attention away from the human girl who wore trousers like a man, and had her flame red hair cropped to frame a face that was highlighted by hazel eyes.

Hazel.

"Dante?" A finger prodded his arm. Hard.

He hissed and turned to his sibling. "What?"

It was difficult for him, to stand there and not follow the human girl, but it would raise too many eyebrows. His father was due back in town within the week, and the less public attention he garnered, the better.

Misty's eyes were narrowed and her pale face was pinched in irritation. "You stopped walking and stood there like a fool, staring into space. We're being looked at."

"I thought you liked being watched," Dante muttered, searching for the telltale short hair of the human girl, but she'd vanished into the flow of people moving up and down the opposite side of the street.

Hawkers were shouting information about their wares from the shop fronts that lined the sides of the pavement, and coachmen were yelling at each other from the cobbled street. He didn't even want to think about the smells that were assaulting him. Too many unwashed humans. "I was looking at someone."

"My dress is getting dirty!"

The sidewalk wasn't really that dusty, he thought. It was paved and had been swept by each storefront owner in the early hours of the evening. He glanced at the hem of Misty's muslin dress. It had very faint smudges of dust decorating the lace. "Why did you wear white when you knew we were going to be walking?"

Other vampires were strolling by them, and as he watched, dry specks of dirt were kicked up into the air and danced their way onto the lace of her dress.

"Don't be dense."

Dante blinked. Dense? Freak, yes. Weirdo, he'd accept that, but *dense*?

"White makes me look innocent."

He laughed; it was a rusty sound. He saw that Misty had pursed her lips. At least she hadn't painted them with rouge, he thought, but being a vampire who fed regularly, her lips seemed to stay a bright berry color. She looked ridiculous enough as it was.

"Innocent?" he asked, his laugh having died down to a smirk.

"It *does*."

"Sister, *nothing* you wear could make you appear innocent." Some people just had vibes, he thought, and "harlot" was his sister's.

She rolled her eyes. "Fine, don't believe me. But I *always* wear white. So why were you standing there looking at someone? And since when are you even interested in other people? Aren't you still a virgin?"

Dante shook his head and held out his arm, waiting for his sister to place her hand on it. For a culture that didn't care about who hopped into bed with whom – gender and race not being important – they sure cared about someone who *wasn't* having sex.

Dante began walking again, forcing Misty to follow. The sea of people who had avoided them when they stood still now parted, as if royalty strolled through. From the smile on Misty's face, she seemed to appreciate the preference they were given. He had no idea why they moved out of his way so fast. Maybe he looked scary.

Remembering what she said, he muttered, "I am always interested in other people."

Misty smiled as an acquaintance nodded a greeting. The young man's cravat was set so high it nearly obliterated any sign that he possessed a chin. But his eyes didn't seem to suffer from the overly enthusiastic garment, and they stared at Dante just as much as they did his sister.

"You mean you like experimenting on humans," Misty said out of the side of her smile. "Humans aren't people."

"They're people enough."

"Try to smile, brother, people are looking at us."

They continued down Pittbrough Street, even though it was now called Park Road – what type of idiot changed a street name halfway down? – and turned into King's Park, the place for vampire aristos to see and be seen in Pinton.

He hadn't wanted to come, but Misty had proved sufficiently irritating. Like the weak-spined fool his father thought him, he'd given in. And she'd had a point – if he was seen trying to be sociable, their father wouldn't carp on so much about having such a disappointing excuse for an offspring. He'd still be annoyed at Dante for some reason, but at least it wouldn't be about that. As for why Misty had specifically wanted him to go with her, he wasn't sure, but he had a feeling it was because some aristos thought he was intriguing. Social hermits were fascinating like that; he guessed Misty wanted some of that attention focused on her.

He raised an eyebrow. "But if I smiled, wouldn't I appear less mysterious?"

Misty opened the parasol he'd forgotten she was carrying. Lacy shadow fell over them. As they moved farther into the park, the air smelled less like unwashed human bodies and more like flowers, metal and vampires. She didn't reply.

"I don't know why they bother to have trees that aren't trees," Dante said as he looked at the contorted sculptures designed to represent the plants. He'd failed to recall how utterly ridiculous they were. Curling around metal branches were twisting vines; the scent of honeysuckle, jasmine and ivy wafting through the air. They were beautiful, but pointless.

Like most of society.

"The landscapers didn't want any real wood here. Wanted it

to be a vampire haven." Misty rolled her lavender eyes at him.

Dante snorted. "And who, tell me, would come into a park filled with vampires, break a branch *off a tree* and then stake someone in full view of everyone else?"

Misty stared at him. "It's the principle," she said slowly.

"No, it's idiocy. Humans have access to wood – they build with it, they burn it, they use it daily – if they were going to try and kill one of us, they'd do it in a much safer environment."

"Safer?"

"For them."

"Your mind is a strange place, Dante."

He gave her a genuine smile, letting her words flow over him. "Thank you."

Chapter Three

Olive Brown stared at the messenger standing nervously before her. He was sweaty, grimy and tired, she knew that, but she wasn't going to offer him a chair. People didn't get to sit in her presence; it was a privilege to be treated as if someone was on equal terms with her. Most people weren't even close.

"He should be arriving any day now," the messenger – Trent – said.

Olive nodded. "That is good news."

The messenger seemed to sway on his feet. Trent's Green eyes flickered over Olive's face, never meeting her own sharp glare. But Trent was smart enough to not look at the floor. That would have spelled weakness, and weakness was something Olive would not – could not – tolerate. Olive and Trent may have the same eye color, but Trent was to Olive like a rat was to a bear. She would destroy anything threatening her, or her people. Like a mother protecting her cubs. And if some of her own kind were lost along the way, well, battles always ended in casualties from both sides.

"Is there anything else?" Olive asked.

"No."

"Then you may go."

Olive watched him leave. She frowned at the dirty footprints he'd left on the green carpet. She'd have to get it cleaned. Maybe she'd make one of her granddaughters do it the next time they visited.

Only after he'd shut the door behind him did she allow herself to smile.

Chapter Four

The city reeked of vampires. Icy cool; like chilled, bloody water. It clung to the insides of his nostrils and made his skin itch – from the inside. He didn't like it, liked it even less than the stench of the tanners and dyers that pervaded the other side of the Thyme River, but that meant little. What he liked wasn't exactly important, not anymore.

Clay tried to breathe through his mouth, but the iciness clung to his tongue. Vampires were like a plague, worse than the weres who'd come after him. At least they were honest in their brutality; they didn't hide behind pretty smiles and pretty clothes. No, they were blunt and humans knew to be wary. If a were wanted a human it was for one of three things: sex, food or life. And the latter was more a curse than a blessing.

Not like here, in this city coated with coal dust, the stench of human waste – despite the sewer system he knew was there – and the cold bite of vampires. Here, the leeches kept humans as slaves, and the humans didn't seem to care. Here, humans *liked* being Chosen.

It was nauseating.

From the other side of the twilight-darkened street, he noticed a vampire staring at him, its nose crinkled with distaste at his scent. He raised an eyebrow and deliberately swept his gaze over the long, tied-back brown hair, the cravat that seemed to obscure any sign of a chin, and the ridiculous pink waistcoat. Clay smirked. Clay wasn't the oddity here – there were few if any places that were entirely free of weres or vampires – but he stood out. In cowhide buckskins, a leather vest and white shirt, he looked like someone from another world – the *real* world – when compared to the primped and preened leeches of Pinton.

Shaking his head in disgust, he turned off Pittbrough Street and onto Bridge Road. Half a day in the city and he'd already had enough. Walking quickly, he decided to go and find a pub near the docks. Earlier, he had wanted to go straight into the heart of the city and find his apartment, but now he needed a drink first. Maybe more than one. He had to wash the taste of vampire from his mouth.

◆

Elle's fist tightened on the baton strapped to her side. She didn't really like this part of her job as a city guard. Pub brawls were always dangerous for the humans who had to break them up, and her partner, Kyle, didn't seem in the best of moods. That never boded well for those on the receiving end of his temper, or her, because she usually had to step in and prevent him from beating some poor drunken sod even more senseless.

The pub in question was the Tipsy Lantern, near the docks. The metal sign that swung over the door had a buxom wench holding out two flagons of foaming ale painted across it. What the sign had to do with lanterns – and a drunk one at that – was beyond her. The stench of stagnant water intermingled with that of old vomit and stale piss, and it was slightly off-putting, to put it mildly.

Shouts and yells could be heard from within, and the unmistakeable sound of breaking glass echoed through the night.

"Great. A bar fight is never complete without shattered glass," Elle muttered.

"Let's get this over with," Kyle said.

"Let's wait for backup." Elle raised the whistle that hung around her neck on a leather cord.

"We can take care of this." Kyle strode toward the door, baton loose.

"We haven't even seen the situation in there," Elle called at his back. "Don't just charge in there, baton waving. What if it's aristos?" She'd learned her lesson about taking on aristos in fights. It came with suspensions, interviews and a shitload of paperwork.

Kyle turned back to her, hand on the pub's door. He rolled his eyes. "In a place like this? Then we won't hit them quite so hard. Let's go."

He pushed the door open and Elle muttered some rather unflattering phrases about men, but she followed. The inside was almost as dim as outside, but the stench of tobacco, old body odor and fresh vomit wafted on the air. The scent of sex was probably mixed in too, but Elle didn't really want to consider that. Whoring in a "service oriented" establishment was legal, so she didn't have to add that to her list of issues with this pub.

Near one of the smoke-laden corners, a group of men were screaming and yelling, their movements chaotic and jerky. Narrowing her eyes on them, she could see the fists flying and hear the slapping sound of flesh against flesh. One man picked up a chair and brought it down on another's head. The clobbered drunkard then grabbed a broken leg from the dismembered chair and jabbed it at his attacker.

It only took her a few seconds to work out that all the drunk idiots were humans.

A barmaid was cleaning up a broken glass near Kyle. She seemed unconcerned with the fight taking place mere steps away. Elle hoped there was no more glass near the group of thugs.

"We can handle this," Kyle said. "Let's go bash some heads."

Sighing, Elle followed.

"City Guard!" Kyle yelled. His towering height and sheer size made those on the edge of the group pause. The men in the middle kept pounding away.

"Whass the prob'm?" one of the drunks at the group's edge slurred.

"You're making a public nuisance of yourselves. Get out." Kyle thwacked his metal baton against his other hand.

Great, she thought. *Just taunt them next time.*

"We're just having a chat," another said, then threw himself back into the fray.

"With your fists?" Elle snapped. *Dang,* she thought, *should've kept my mouth shut.*

"Just settlin' sumthink. No need to get involved."

Kyle met each non-fighting man's wild-eyed look. "Get. Out."

One man moved, as if he was going to leave, but swung around and threw a blind punch at Kyle's head. It never made it, but Kyle's baton certainly made contact with the idiot's face.

Before she could blink, the other drunks were throwing themselves on Kyle, and the big man was batting them away as if they were flies. He was grinning, white teeth a bright slash against dark skin.

The fool.

"Need a hand?" a voice murmured near her ear.

Turning her head, but keeping her body facing the action in case Kyle needed her – for once, he seemed to be keeping his temper in check – her eyes met a muscled chest, partly covered by a white shirt. Raising her eyes from that interesting sight, she met an amused yellow gaze.

Yellow.

Were. Most probably wolf, since she'd never met any other kind of were before, and the lands around Pinton were their "territory."

Elle quirked an eyebrow. "Do I look like I need help?"

The wolf grinned, showing a set of even white teeth. "Well, not yet. But you might."

"Really." It wasn't a question.

"Well, pretty thing like you, waltzing around a pub. A man could get ideas." His accent was strange; a mixture to the point where there wasn't one.

Both her eyebrows nearly hit her hairline. "Waltzing? Do you see me dancing, wolf?" She ignored the other, stupider comment. He didn't refute her claim regarding his animal type, so she guessed she was right.

"Well, you are tapping your foot. That's musical."

"To a drunk."

Kyle let out a roar. Elle swung her head back to the fight and saw that one of the drunks had landed a hit on the guard's kidney.

"Oh, that's not good." Shaking her head, she walked into the melee, snapping her baton out and connecting with elbows and knees. Grunts of pain followed her. She ducked a badly aimed fist at her head, and then reached Kyle, who was now pounding the life out of the moron who'd tried to stop the guard from ever urinating again.

"Kyle, quit it. The guy was dumb to begin with. He's brainless now." Kyle didn't look at her. She reached out to grab his arm, but felt herself being picked up.

Squealing in surprise, she kicked her foot back and slammed it into her captor's knee. He grunted.

Her cry must have caught Kyle's interest, because he paused in his meting of justice. He looked over at her and charged. She held up her hand and he stopped mid-step, blinking. "Why are you being held by a were? Was he even involved in the fight?" Now Kyle was thinking again, he knew better than to try and "save" her.

"No, he wasn't part of the fight and he should be putting me down any second," Elle said, teeth grinding.

The wolf spoke, breath teasing the hair at the nape of her neck. "You shouldn't approach hulking guards who are beating the life out of someone. You could have been hit. One of his fists could have killed you, human."

Elle tried to turn around to look at the wolf holding her. "I'm a guard, in case you didn't notice. The hulking guy over there is my *partner*."

Slowly, the wolf set her down, sliding her down his front. Did he have an–? "You pervert!"

"Did he just touch you?" Kyle growled.

Oh, shit.

The hulking guard began approaching the wolf standing behind her. "Did you just touch her?"

"I was holding her, so the answer to that is yes."

"By the blood," Elle muttered. She turned to Kyle. "Charge these idiots for disturbing the peace, okay?"

Her partner looked from the wolf to her and back, then nodded slowly. "You touch her again, I'll rip your arm off." He turned to the drunks. "Get your asses off the floor you pieces of drunken slime! Time to pay up!"

Elle turned to the wolf, tapping her baton against her leg. "Next time, keep your hands and head out of a bar fight that has nothing to do with you."

"Or what, you'll spank me?" He wiggled his eyebrows. In the dim light, he looked like a frontiersman who'd just wandered in off the plains.

"Or I'll throw you in the cells. Now get out."

He grinned, chucked her under the chin and left, whistling. She was too slow to stop him.

Elle gritted her teeth. Dogs, who'd ever understand them?

♦

The next day, Clay was wandering down Pittbrough Street, nursing a sore head. It took a lot to get a werewolf drunk, but he'd managed it. He also had a vague memory of accosting a female guard. Well, picking her up when he'd thought she'd been about to be flattened by her "partner." That man had been psychotic.

He grinned. She'd been a feisty one. Normally he kept his hands and thoughts to himself, but from the minute she'd stepped inside the Lantern, he'd wanted to make sure she was okay. She hadn't been like the other women in the bar; she hadn't seemed hard enough to survive in a place like that. The booze must have made him sentimental; she was a bloody city guard – they didn't come much tougher than that.

Coming to a stop, he realized he'd forgotten where he was going. Stupid hangover.

"Are you lost, sir?"

Clay looked down and blinked.

A little girl stood at his elbow, her hand raised as if to touch his arm. She had the most glorious pair of blue-green eyes he'd ever seen, set in a dark, serious face. He should have heard her approaching, but his bloody pounding head was distracting him. Clay's eyes took in her dress, noting that it was speckled with dust.

"Why do you ask that, little human?"

Over the years, Clay had met more than his fair share of humans. Around ninety-five percent of them, he reasoned, had Brown eyes. It'd been much the same when he was young, a long, long time ago. Despite his years, and seeing enough Blue, Green and Gray eyes, he'd never seen that shade of Teal before on a human. The little mite was unique with her strange irises, and that was something that could attract a vampire's notice. They liked unusual "prizes." The fact that she appeared to be free from vampire attention caught his interest. Which was too bad for her.

"Emmie!"

Clay looked up and saw a woman wearing breeches and a City Guard shirt running toward the girl. Her red hair was cut severely around her face and she didn't glance up at him as she grabbed hold of the little girl's still-raised arm. She wasn't panting, but he could see that her pupils were dilated; shock, he decided.

The little girl blinked up at the redhead. "I was just help–"

"What did I say? No talking to strangers!" The young woman's knuckles were white around the girl's arm.

Clay stared at the woman's legs. Those trousers really should be illegal, he thought, eyes locked on the curve of her hips. Was she *trying* to attract attention? Mission accomplished. Attention certainly attracted.

Ah. That was how he'd noticed the female guard last night.

"But–" the little girl started.

Carriages passed alongside them, throwing up muck he'd rather not think about – but could smell all too clearly – over the curb. He took a step backward. Humans moved by him, mostly ignoring him, but giving him a wide berth without realizing it.

"But we're not strangers," Clay said and crossed his arms over his chest. He even cracked a smile, a lazy, cocky expression that had earned him a reputation over the years.

The guard flicked a glance at him then narrowed her eyes. Hazel. "What do you mean?"

He wondered what her name was. She didn't seem to have a single freckle, which was unusual for a redhead. He speculated whether the rest of her was as pale and smooth-looking. Then Clay thought about how long it would take him to achieve such a survey. Seeing the narrowed Hazel eyes, probably too long. Plus, she was violent. His knee didn't hurt anymore, thanks to his regenerative abilities, but she'd kicked it well and good. And, he thought, somewhat disappointed, she probably wouldn't be worth it; they almost never were.

"Oh, the little human and I have known each other for practically forever." He winked one bright yellow eye.

The woman was a half-blood. One human (or Brown-eyed) parent, one Graced parent. Not that he was meant to know that, but he knew a whole lot he wasn't meant to know. Kept his life interesting. He hadn't realized she was a half-blood last night, if he had, he might have kept his hands to himself. But then, maybe he wouldn't have. Those legs would have probably been his downfall, no matter what.

The redhead pulled the girl behind her. She didn't move her eyes away from him, or his shiny white teeth on display. "Emmie?"

"He looked lost." The little girl's – Emmie's – voice cracked.

"She just wanted to help," Clay said slowly, taking pity on the child.

"You don't look like you need help to me." She tilted her head to the side. "How's your head?"

"Sore." Clay laid a hand over his heart. "Can't you see how helpless I am?" He saw Emmie's eyes widen before she covered a smile with one small hand. She was smart enough not to giggle. The redhead continued to glare. Hers was a sour nature, from the appearance of things. Definitely not worth the effort it would take to get her out of those trousers.

Unfortunately.

He leaned closer, and found his senses overwhelmed by the scent of her and the girl. Fresh, clean. Soap, with a hint of violets from the redhead, and strawberries from the mite. They were a little unsoiled-smelling oasis in the stench of Pinton.

"I can see what big white teeth you have," the woman snapped. "Time to go." She started dragging the child after her.

Folding his arms over his chest, Clay watched them leave. He thought about following them, but decided against it. He had an appointment, and anyway, *if* he decided it would be worth the effort of charming the redhead out of her pants, he'd be able to pick out their scent easily enough, even in this stinkhole of a city.

Chapter Five

"How could you *do* that?" Elle hissed to her sister. Her fingers were bruising Emmie's arm, but she didn't care.

"Do what?"

"Approach *him*." She was so angry she barely managed to get the words out through her gritted teeth. What was *wrong* with her sister? What was she thinking, approaching a muscle-bound wolf who may have been the handsomest man Elle'd ever seen – not that that meant anything – in broad daylight?

"He looked lost."

Elle groaned. Today was just not a good day. And they still had to visit the dragon lady that was their grandmother. They visited her almost every day, unfortunately. For Emmie's "lessons." It was Elle's penance. *Although, Elle had never worked out what it was penance for.*

"Just hurry up," Elle said gruffly and eased her grip.

◆

"Eleanor," Gran Brown said.

Elle stopped walking and stood facing the door at the end of the room, its handle gleaming a brassy promise in the dim light of her gran's "meeting room." Ten steps, she thought, that's all it would take to escape. There was even a track of muddy footprints that led the way. Her feet were rooted to the ground though, and the yellow glow from the oil lamp cast her shadow forward, stretching it toward freedom.

"Yes, Gran?" Elle didn't turn around, just kept staring hopefully at the door.

"Where do you think you're going?" The voice was crackly with age; rusty like it didn't talk much, which was a blatant lie.

"Training?" She hadn't meant it to sound like a question. But when Gran used that voice…

"And since when is training to use your non-existent abilities more important than spending time with your only grandmother? And why are you staring at the bloody door? Turn around, girl!"

Elle turned. Her grandmother sat in a wing chair that was overstuffed and upholstered in an olive green color that matched her irises. Everything in this room was a shade of green, and it wasn't just because it was her gran's favorite color.

It was the color of Gran's eyes.

It was the color of Gran's magic.

Not that it *was* magic; magic didn't exist according to Gran. It was about bloodlines and genes and inherited traits and eye color, and blood knows what else. Most of the words didn't even have *meaning* anymore, they were so old. But whatever it was, it always came back to eye color. And Elle's lack of it.

"There you go, stand tall, girl!"

Elle straightened her shoulders and looked her gran in the eye. Well, down at her gran, anyway. Gran was short; she barely made it to Elle's shoulder, and Elle could clearly see the thinning thatch of gray hair that topped her pale, crinkly scalp in the dim light. Gran also smelled faintly of copper-scented lavender, which had always bothered Elle, as it reminded her of blood-stained petals.

"I really do need to go to training," Elle said.

"Bosh! You're a half-blood, Elle; you aren't going to suddenly learn how to do TK."

TK. Telekinesis.

Not that you can do that either, Elle thought. Green meant that Gran could read people's minds. She was strong, there was no doubt about that, she ruled over the Graceds in Pinton with an iron fist – easy to do when you knew what almost everyone was thinking. Thankfully though, Greens couldn't read other Greens, and Elle had enough Green in her Hazel to make her safe. Just like she had some Gray, which meant that one day she *might* develop telekinesis. And pigs might fly.

"No, but the mental training helps my guard work," Elle said and smiled, a curving of the mouth that didn't expose any teeth. Gran didn't like openmouthed smiles – she said teeth-baring was for leeches and dogs.

Gran narrowed her eyes and pursed her lips. "If you must go, then go." She waved a hand dismissively and then focused her attention on Emmie. Emmie turned to look at Elle with an expression akin to panic, before it smoothed into a thin-lipped smile.

"Why are you smiling, girl? Have you started reading people's minds yet? Can you move things around without touching them? Manipulate emotions? What can you do? What good *are* you?" The rapid-fire questions left no time for Emmie to answer.

Elle opened her mouth to say something – anything – but Gran snapped a look at her. "What are you standing there for? You said you had to leave, so leave!"

Feeling sorry for her sister, Elle left. *If I was stronger*, she thought, *I would have stayed to help Emmie.* But she wasn't. She was weak and human and scared to death of her grandmother.

Chapter Six

Dante laid the scalpel on the stone benchtop carefully, trying not to spread blood anywhere it didn't need to be. Picking up a glass slide and a pipette, he turned to the naked human. She was lying strapped to a metal table that was positioned in the middle of the room. She was shivering, with fear or lust, he guessed, but he wasn't entirely sure. Human emotions were a bit of a mystery to him – mostly because they didn't matter and partly because he couldn't see what all the fuss was about.

The scent of blood wreathed around his senses, but he kept the hunger in check. This wasn't dinner time; it was study time. His father had sent a messenger to Kipling House saying he wasn't coming home for another week, which meant that Dante had time to work.

The cut on the human's arm was bleeding freely, so Dante carefully took a small sample of the fluid in the pipette before placing a droplet on the glass slide. He walked back to the bench and laid the utensil next to the scalpel, before inserting the slide into the microscope's slot. A groan reached his ears.

Frowning, Dante looked up at the bluestone wall in front of him before turning toward the human. Strapped down to the table, leather manacles held her firm, but shivers seemed to make the human quiver. Her skin had taken on a series of bumps and she was chewing on the gag. Blood had pooled into a large puddle on the side of the bench and had begun to drip onto the floor.

He stared at it.

Shaking his head, Dante snapped himself out of the blood-trance, walked over to one of the cupboards and hunted on the shelves for some bandages. He kept forgetting about the delayed clotting in humans' blood. If he didn't put some pressure on the cut, then the human would bleed to death, and it would serve no purpose whatsoever. Returning to the prone form, he quickly tied a bandage around the wound and fastened it with a firm knot. Another groan emanated from the creature. He removed the gag. "What's the matter?"

The sound of chattering teeth rose. "I'm cold."

More forceful shivers were wracking the human's body, and he could see now that it was goosebumps rippling on the skin. He was about to shove the gag back in the human's mouth when he remembered something about humans dying from the cold. There were so many possible ways to cause death, he had trouble keeping track of them. He went back to the cupboard and found a blanket which he threw over her.

"Better?"

"Uh–"

"Great." Dante shoved the gag back in place.

He turned back to his workbench and frowned into the yellow glow that was produced by the dozen lamps he'd placed around the room. He didn't need the light, but it was polite to keep the room illuminated for his guest. Deciding that more light wouldn't hurt either way, he turned the flame up on the oil lamp sitting on his workbench, and looked through the microscope at the spot of blood. It looked like normal human blood. *But why wouldn't it?* he wondered. It had been bloody difficult to find a human with eyes a color other than brown – a human he could take and not get into trouble for – and now he had one, their blood was just the same.

It made sense, but at the same time, it *didn't* make sense.

Pulling up a stool, Dante sat on it and stared at the human as her shivers slowed. Female, maybe twenty years old – he wasn't sure, he could never tell humans' ages (apart from if they were young or old, they all looked the same to him) – with blue eyes. He *knew* that humans with different colored eyes weren't like the brown-eyed humans, he just knew it. But how could he prove it?

Their blood looked the same and it tasted the same.

Both his father and sister said his theory was crazy.

But he *wasn't*, and his theory *wasn't*.

Humans with non-brown eyes never acted differently to their brown-eyed counterparts when in front of him. But there *were* differences. He'd only ever seen brown-eyed humans as slaves, never ones with blue or green or gray eyes. And they always avoided him, as if they knew they shouldn't spend time with a vampire. Even Misty said she'd never taken a non-brown-eyed lover. And she'd screwed more than her fair share of humans.

And the most compelling thing he'd found – he'd only ever met brown-eyed humans who had been changed into vampires. Not that many humans were allowed to make the transition. He'd asked the few Chosen he'd met what their original eye color had been, and they'd all been brown. After the change, their eyes had become a deep violet, darker than those belonging to born vampires. More red.

He wondered what happened to the non-browns when they were Chosen by a vampire. It reminded him of the human tied to his worktable.

"You're a whore, aren't you?" he asked.

A muffled sound reached his ears. The gag, he thought, right. He quickly stood and pulled it out.

"You're a whore, aren't you?" he repeated.

A small pink tongue emerged from her mouth and she licked dry, cracked lips. "I'm anything you want me to be, sugar."

He looked at her, trying to determine what would attract a vampire to her, to encourage one to *pay* her for her sexual services, but he just couldn't see it. Maybe his sister was right, maybe he was…different.

"You sell your body for money, don't you?"

She seemed to be searching for something in his face. She was frowning when she said, "Yes, that's why I'm here. Although this wasn't what I was expecting; Madam Venus is meant to tell me if the client is into bondage and playacting."

No, he admitted to himself, he couldn't imagine she would have expected this particular scenario when she arrived at his father's estate. Not unless she could see the future.

"This isn't playacting," Dante said.

She blinked and then her eyes filled with water. Tears, he discovered. "You mean you've tied me down to…experiment on me?"

Dante ran a finger over the bandage. She was clever. That was good. "Yes."

Her breathing and heart rate accelerated. "Won't you let me go?"

She was looking at him again, like she was expecting something from him.

"No."

"But I'm afraid."

"That's too bad."

The tears dried up and she was frowning again. Were humans normally this mercurial?

"You don't feel any remorse for what you're going to do?"

Dante looked at her askance. "Why would I?"

She didn't say anything in reply.

He ran a finger over the smooth skin of her neck, and he could feel tiny marks from previous bites. "You aren't bit-ridden." It was a statement, he didn't need to see her shake her head. Maybe she thought that would save her from whatever it was he intended.

"Madam Venus knows I'm here."

"Why aren't you bit-ridden? You let your clients bite you, yes?"

"Some people don't get addicted to the saliva."

He could sense she wasn't telling him the whole truth. By the blood, he'd never met a human who *wasn't* addicted after half a dozen or more bites. She was a whore; she'd had to have been bitten far more than that.

"My madam knows I'm here."

"You already said that."

"You can't hurt me." Her voice was trembling and she was tugging at her restraints, trying to break free.

"I don't intend to hurt you."

She raised her blue eyes to his. "I don't understand."

He shoved the gag back into her mouth, tired of talking. "You don't have to."

◆

Dante scrubbed the blood from his hands, watching the dark color seep from the white lines in his skin, glaring at it as it swirled down the sink in a wash of crimson-tinted water. He didn't bother looking at the corpse that was lying cold on the stainless steel table of his workroom. Gripping the edge of the sink with both hands, he hung his head.

It hadn't worked.

He'd done it right, he knew he had. Choosing someone wasn't really all that hard – drink their blood, give them your blood. Do this three times in three days. On the third day after that, they woke up a vampire.

But the whore had died moments after the final blood transfer.

"Since when did you get into bondage?" Misty's voice echoed in the quiet room.

Dante looked over his shoulder at his sister. Her pale hair was tied back in a chignon and her gown was white. It was very plain for her normally…frilly…tastes. With a sudden swipe, he jerked off the taps and turned away from the sink. He grabbed a nearby towel and dried his hands.

He saw Misty take a few careful steps toward the corpse. "She's dead."

"I know," Dante said. He leaned his hip against the stone bench and folded his arms across his chest, the towel dangling from one fist.

"Who is she?"

"Her name was Sandy."

"Why'd you kill her?" Misty walked around the table, inspecting the naked body. The limbs were touched with a blue tinge.

Dante shrugged. "I didn't mean to."

Misty leaned forward and considered the bite marks, before pointing to the smear of red around the human's mouth. "You *Chose* her?"

"Tried to, yes."

Misty flicked a frown his way. "Didn't you do it right?"

"I did it by the book."

She stared at him. "I didn't know they had a book about this."

Dante rolled his eyes. "It was a metaphor."

"Right."

He was quickly growing sick of the conversation. "Why are you here?"

Misty pursed her lips. "I was just popping by to say hello."

Dante shook his head. Misty never popped by to say hello. Popped by to be an annoying pain in his ass, yes. Dropped by to rub his face in her glory, yes. But hello? No, he had no familiarity with that. His eyes dropped down to the body and then he flicked them away. Such a disappointment. "Don't you have anything better to do? A human to screw? Aristos to preen in front of?"

Misty's eyes narrowed. "Don't you like my visits?"

"I've just never been…blessed…with so many of them."

She moved her arm in what appeared to be an attempt to fluff her hair, only to drop it when she remembered it was tied back. "Oh, well, things *are* a little boring at the moment."

Dante wasn't really sure what to do. He wanted to drive her off, but with their father due back to town so soon and the fact she was trying to be nice…

"No social intrigue?" he asked.

She visibly brightened, although she tried to pretend hauteur. "Well, not apart from the fact that Jeanette DeRoy was caught having sex with three humans by her father – at the same time, mind you – or that Markus Brune was caught peeping in the women's garderobe…"

Dante figured it would be safe if he tuned out. Guiding Misty from his workroom, he shut the door behind him with a distinct click. He'd have to get rid of the body before his father returned.

For now, he'd humor his sister.

Chapter Seven

Elle sighed and rubbed her shoulder. Her sort-of cousin, Bjorn, had thrown her against the wall and dislocated the joint. Bjorn and his brother Kevin were her gran's bodyguards. She'd been training with him at her gran's house; him testing if she could block his telekinetic power. The painful and obvious answer was no. Kendra, the sawbones, had popped it back in, but it still hurt like shit. As it was, actual guard work tonight was going to be a bitch with her shoulder out. She'd probably get stuck on desk duty. Boring.

Turning the corner, Elle began walking toward her grandmother's "meeting room" where she spotted Emmie waiting in front of the closed door. Her sister's dark face looked unnaturally pale and her Teal eyes glittered ominously, but no tear stains marred her cheeks.

Elle reached her sister's side. "Emmie?"

"Can we go home?" Emmie's voice was wobbly.

"Sure, kiddo." Elle held out her hand and Emmie took it without a murmur. Their gran must have really ripped into her, Elle thought. Together, they walked down the dark hallway and past another set of bodyguards at the front door.

They were halfway home, winding their way through the narrow, cobblestone-paved side streets, the cold air burning in Elle's lungs, when Emmie spoke. "I *hate* Gran."

Sometimes Elle felt more like Emmie's mother – their almost twenty-year age gap made Elle feel more protective than was probably healthy for a small child. But she couldn't save her from their grandparent. Wasn't strong enough.

Elle tightened her fingers around her sister's hand. "No, you don't."

Emmie tried to pull her hand free, but Elle spotted a couple of vampires nearby, heading inside a whorehouse, so Elle kept her grip strong.

"I do. I do. I hate her. She's so mean, Elle." Emmie looked up at her, and her eyes were awash with the tears Elle had expected outside their grandmother's door.

"She's just tough."

"She's *mean*."

Elle went to counter that, but she shut her mouth and sighed. The thing was, Gran *was* mean. Elle could remember saying the same things to their mother – and their mother replying much the same as Elle had. But at least Emmie had it easier; she didn't have to live with Gran.

"Come on," Elle said, walking faster. "Let's get home."

♦

Clay folded his arms and rocked back on one heel, smiling broadly. The old human woman seated in front of him looked like a grumpy old grandmother, with her deep frown lines and steel gray hair. She was flanked by two tall, muscle-bound men in black shirts and breeches, who wore their dark hair short and their faces expressionless. Flickering yellow lamplight cast shadows throughout the room, but he didn't really need their glow to see. Provided there was *some* light, wolves could see just as well, if not better, than their vampire cousins.

Filthy leeches.

The walls behind the grumpy old bat were covered with faded olive-green wallpaper that housed darker green patterns, all of which swirled together into what looked like a drawing. Tilting his head to one side, he tried to make some sense out of the patterns, but found none. He could feel the lackeys on either side of the old woman following his movement with their gazes. The flickering light cast shadows, but he could still see that they had Gray eyes. Even with their abilities, he thought, he could probably still take them. His smile broadened.

"You took your time getting here," Olive Brown said, her voice raspy and dry. He figured it was meant to give the impression of great age, but he'd met her a good forty years ago when she'd been traveling around the northern continent, and knew it was probably the result of too much tobacco.

Clay kept his arms folded and lifted one dark eyebrow. "I didn't realize that I was on a schedule."

"Don't get uppity with me."

He barked a laugh. "I was *born* uppity. Plus, I'm here as a favor; you shouldn't forget that."

The old woman frowned deeply at him. Yellow lamplight continued to cast wavering shadows over the room, exaggerating her expression. She was seated on a green overstuffed wing chair. The flunkies didn't move.

The raspy voice sounded again. "You're impertinent."

Clay smiled again and saw her blink. "Says the young to the old."

She didn't appear to like that, but Clay didn't care. She might *look* decades older than he was, but he was *millennia* older than her. He noticed another armchair, this one upholstered in a color that looked suspiciously like puce – the only non-green hue in the room. It was pushed up against the wall that boasted an empty fireplace. Unfolding his arms, he walked over and picked the chair up, before carrying it back to where the old bat was positioned. Setting it down in front of her, he took a seat and leaned back into the chair, crossing his feet at his ankles. He was tempted to clasp his hands behind his head, but decided against it when the old woman glowered at him. Clay refolded his arms.

"Don't like your guests to be comfortable?" he asked.

She smiled tightly, lips compressed. "It keeps things interesting if they're not."

"Quick, you mean."

"It apparently makes no difference to you."

"I'm not most people. So, why did you send your henchmen out to find me?"

Clay had been enjoying a rather boring existence out in the half-wild town of Gorke. It was werewolf run, so it was mostly built from wood and stone, and was surrounded by wilderness. The scent of fir trees and snow and woodsmoke, they're the things that make you feel alive, he thought. Not coal dust, bitter vampires and human waste. Gorke was a dangerous place for the humans who lived there, but they didn't stink up the place, and they were probably safer there than with the animals that prowled the outskirts of the town.

He'd spent most of his time in wolf form in Gorke, many of the wolves did, and it had taken her messengers a while to catch him. After spending the majority of the last two centuries as his animal, his curiosity had gotten the better of him. Two legs still felt a bit strange at times.

"I need your…help." She spat the last word, like it was a rotten piece of meat.

"Really?" He'd been able to figure out *that* much. It's why he'd bothered to come to Pinton in the first place; City of Stink and bad memories, but he didn't want to go there.

She flicked a glance at the flunkies. He didn't need to hear the command to know it had been given. The duo nodded and left the room, shutting the door quietly behind them.

He grinned again. "This must be very secret, to send out Muscle A and B." And they weren't just physical bodyguards; he knew what Gray eyes meant: telekinesis.

Clay noticed that Olive was staring at him in frustration. Her Green eyes meant she was a telepath, but thankfully, he was immune. Some genetic quirk – because he had a Graced ancestor. But then, most of the early weres and vamps did.

"I want you to give me a grandchild."

Clay laughed, he couldn't help himself. "Olive, I'm not your son, so that would be a bit impossible. You aren't even my very-great granddaughter."

"I have children." Her voice was frosty, almost defensive. He was surprised that ice didn't form in the air between them. But even the Graceds had their limits, and manipulating the elements was one of them.

"Congratulations?" Clay re-crossed his ankles, placing his right foot on top of his left.

"My surviving daughter–"

Which meant, the daughter she still had control over.

"Is of no interest to me," Clay said. He didn't move from his reclined pose, but he tensed. Something flashed in the old bat's eyes, and it wasn't annoyance. He'd met Melissande years ago, when she'd been sent out to Gorke on some "mission," and hadn't been impressed by her. He hadn't been *un*impressed by her either, but she wasn't really, well, remarkable. Just another Graced girl in a world that was freckled with Graced girls.

The grumpy bat's eyes narrowed and he could hear her teeth grinding. "She is beautiful."

He smiled, remembering another woman grinding her teeth. His smile locked in place. Yes, he could see it and smell it, now that he thought about it. Violets and strawberries, the violets a faint trace on the air, the strawberries stronger. In his mind's eye, he could see that the sharp angles of the redhead's face were reminiscent of the Melissande he remembered – and the shade of red hair he'd seen before, on the old grumpy bat in front of him before she'd gone gray – but there was little else to show the family resemblance.

"I don't care how beautiful Melissande is, she'd be nearing forty now, and I thought that was an unhealthful age for a woman to be bearing young. Especially Graceds."

Olive sucked air in sharply through her teeth when she heard him mention her closely guarded secret. Not the age of her daughter, but the name of her race.

"You–"

"Me what? I know what you are, you know what I am. I've known about your race for longer than you've been alive." Clay sat upright, resting his elbows on his knees.

She sighed. "That's why I asked you to come here."

"I thought you wanted me to sire a child on your daughter."

"I couldn't just ask any were to do it. They had to know what they were doing."

Clay coughed. "I'm sure there are many weres out there who know how to have sex, Olive. It's something that people tend to learn quickly, given the correct stimulation."

Her brows snapped together. "Don't play dumb with me."

"You do know it is against the rules to mix the bloodlines," Clay reminded her. He clasped his hands loosely together between his knees.

Not that they were *rules*, really, just guidelines. But then, most of the modern vampires and weres *couldn't* breed with the Graceds anyway. They were too distantly related to each other. Unlike him.

"Those rules are ridiculous; they serve only to protect your race and the leeches."

"I'm glad you think so highly of us all."

She made a noise that sounded rather like a kettle boiling over.

"You are immortal." Olive jabbed a finger in the air at him.

Clay shook his head. "No, I'm not."

The noise came again. "You will live for thousands of years unless an 'accident' happens. That's close enough to immortality for me."

"We still die, Olive. We can't be immortal *if we die*." But he knew what she was getting at. And he could see why she wanted him to father a grandchild for her. He was an old wolf, one who didn't give two figs about the established order and the vampires' choke-hold on society in this region of the world. She wouldn't think that he'd care about giving his genetic superiorities to her offspring, but she didn't understand one thing: he wasn't about to play *her* games. And he'd *never* abandon a child of his to her keeping.

But he'd let her think he would. For now, at least. "So, have you got any other candidates?" he asked.

He felt the hairs on the back of his neck rise. Olive seemed…pleased, at his question.

"I have a granddaughter."

Clay thought of the redhead. He couldn't picture her willingly submitting to his extraordinary good looks. Not easily, anyway.

"But she's young, we'll have to wait."

Clay blinked. "Sorry?"

"I don't condone pedophilia."

A sick strawberry feeling settled in his stomach. "How old is this granddaughter?"

"Seven."

"You have no others?"

"None…suitable."

Clay fell silent. He could see that Olive didn't want to talk about the half-Graced grandchild, and there was something strange about that, he decided, although he couldn't place why. *She* would think it better to merge his bloodline with a pure Graced, but what she didn't seem to understand was that his yellow eyes could mix with whatever color her granddaughter had – and he had a sinking feeling it was a bright Teal – and produce a Green, just a Green. Or even a Brown, or, another yellow. She may not get the immortal Graced great-grandchild she wanted.

"Well, I'll think about it," Clay said and stood.

"You'll *think* about it?" Olive's face scrunched into a strange wrinkly mass.

Clay shook his head, fighting the urge to roll his eyes. "You just said she's too young. It's not like I can go and do the job right now. Or, did you want to make sure that my merchandise is in order?" He put a hand on his belt buckle.

"That's enough!"

He smirked. "Scared to see a little bit of flesh?" Chuckling, he amended, "Well, a big bit of flesh."

The boiling kettle sounded again. "Get. Out."

He bowed. "Always happy to oblige."

Turning, he swaggered from the room, grinning. He winked at Muscle A and Muscle B on his way out. Now, he thought, time to go do something interesting.

CHAPTER EIGHT

Olive gritted her teeth at the shut door. She'd forgotten how objectionable that wolf was. But then, he was better than a lot of other weres, which wasn't saying much. However, Olive couldn't afford to be picky. Not in this. There were only a handful of weres – or vampires – left who would be able to sire a child on a Graced girl. Half of them were insane, sociopathic or stuck in their animal form. Clay was the best of a bad bunch. But she wasn't simply relying on him. She had time. Years even. If he didn't come to the table, then there were others she could contact.

Olive hoped she didn't have to, though. Clay's blood relatives had a proven record; his family had produced offspring with Graceds in times past. From him, Olive could have a potentially immortal Graced great-grandchild. It would be the start of a new era.

Olive tapped the arm of her chair. *"Is he gone?"* she asked Bjorn telepathically. She shot the query out like a barb, to create as little disturbance to her mental shields as possible. They were so reinforced that sometimes she felt as if the weight of them might crush her. It was fanciful and not worthy of her. But if she wasn't protected, then she could hear *everyone*. And people, she had learned long ago, were not worth listening to. Not unless she could gain something from the encounter.

While her bodyguard was not a Green – he was a Gray – she could hear his reply loud and clear. The wolf had left the building. She withdrew her probe.

There were very few people whose minds she couldn't read, even when she tried. Other Greens had shields too strong for her to listen through, unless they were projecting; but she *could* shatter them and break open their minds if she wanted the information enough to want them dead. And there'd been times when she had wanted that knowledge badly enough. Normally though, other Greens were like little islands of peace and tranquility in a sea of noise; the cacophony so loud at times she thought she'd go deaf from it. It's why she tended to run things from her house; why she sent lackeys to do the public work for her. Even her shields weren't strong enough when there was a mob of people nearby.

It wasn't a common ability, hers. But then, nothing about her was common. She was the strongest Green born in this city – probably on the continent – for two hundred years. There were only three shields she doubted she could shatter. Her two granddaughters and that wolf. That's why she knew Clay was an excellent choice. He already had some kind of latent ability.

Mixing the bloodlines wasn't allowed, the wolf was right about that. It had been unofficially banned, but that had been due to the Civil War, when weres and vampires had abducted Graceds and kept them prisoner, breeding with them to increase their numbers. The results had been interesting. Were-Graceds combinations without the ability to shift or vampires without the need to drink blood. Graceds that could live forever. There'd even been rumors of new colors; something other than Blue, Green or Gray. But a new color did not mean a new ability. Look at her useless granddaughter, Emmie. The child couldn't do a single psychic thing. That's why Olive knew she would be ideal for one thing: breeding. It was to be Emmie's sole purpose in life.

It was a shame that the half-breed Graceds had been destroyed. Olive could have learned much from them. As it was, her people barely made up five percent of the human population. There weren't enough of them to rise to their rightful place as rulers of this land. But it would happen. The vampires, weres – and even the pathetic humans – had had their time.

And when Olive was ready to strike, it would be too late for them. But for now, all she had to do was wait.

CHAPTER NINE

Baron Anton Greystoke felt another shudder wrack his body and he finally admitted to himself that there was something wrong. Something horribly, unaccountably wrong. Raising a shaking hand, he splayed his fingers, watching their tremors with a mounting panic. His bed felt lumpy and hard, pain spiking out from his back and legs, but he knew it wasn't the mattress – he'd had it made from the finest of goose down when he'd started to get serious about Annabel.

Sweat began to bead on his forehead and his legs went from painful to sluggish, numb.

"It's like withdrawal," he mumbled to himself and froze.

It was *exactly* like withdrawal.

But he hadn't been taking anything, hadn't done drugs for longer than he cared to think. Hadn't even taken a drop of opium since he'd recovered from his addiction, months after his shattered leg had healed. He barely even drank coffee. But he was addicted to *something*; he would bet on that, he just didn't know what it was.

He laughed to himself, a pained sound. He'd said jokingly, on more than one occasion, that he was addicted to Annabel, but you couldn't be addicted to a *person*. And he'd only been separated from her for a couple of days – she was away, visiting friends. She was the only thing – the only person – he'd ever needed, after he'd controlled and withdrawn from his drug addiction.

Thinking back over the past few months, he began analyzing

his behavior, a part of his mind ticking away an unseen checklist, while the other part, the addicted part, began screaming in mindless agony.

◆

Elle slumped against the entryway wall for a few moments. The cool stone was a blessed relief against her hot cheek. It had been one shit of a night. She'd had to go check out a human who'd had their throat ripped out by a vampire. Most humans were just drained to death if a vampire lost control. Two neat holes and a cold corpse afterward. But this vampire had been angry, and this human's head had been almost severed. And the vampire had shoved a hand through the human's abdomen. It had been disgusting. The smell had just been…well, Elle had taken her notes and gotten out fast. Then she'd had the coroner called. And been stuck working on paperwork for the rest of her shift.

Her shoulder still hurt like a bitch and her head felt like it had been stuffed with cotton wool. It always felt like that after an evening with the books. Stupid Bjorn. Stupid work. But most of all, stupid Bjorn. She was going to rip him a new asshole the next time she saw him. No, she'd shove his balls down his throat. That way, he'd never inconvenience another woman again.

Groaning, she shoved herself off the stone wall and headed down the slate-covered hall, past the sitting room and small kitchen toward the rear of the apartment. Sunlight was peeking through the curtains in the sitting room and she squinted at it. Her mother would have left for work already. Stupid guard duty. Why'd she apply for a job with the city? She was an idiot, that's why.

Shuffling down the hall, she remembered to kick her shoes off as she walked by the washroom.

"Elle?" The sleepy mumble came from Emmie's room.

She trudged over to the bedroom that was two doors down from her own and poked her head inside. "Yeah?"

A small body was curled up on the bed. Emmie's head was covered by the blanket. A muffled, "You home?" emerged.

Elle smiled. "I'm here, aren't I?"

She went to shuffle away when she heard, "Do I have to go to Gran's today?"

Looking back into the room, she saw that Emmie had uncovered her head. Elle swore she could almost see the bright blue-green color of her sister's eyes in the dim light.

"No, you don't have to." It was sixth day, their day off.

"Good." Emmie rolled over, tucking the blankets over herself again.

Elle shook her head and walked over to her room. How her sister could sleep like that, well, it was beyond her. Tired, aching and wanting nothing more than to collapse on her bed, she opened the heavy wooden door to her room. Kicking it shut behind her, she threw her pack on the carpet. Without bothering to light a lamp, she dropped onto the mattress. *Feathery softness, here I come*, she thought.

"Ow!"

Elle snapped upright and jumped away from the bed, wrenching her sore shoulder. Turning around, she tried to scrabble for her pack, but couldn't see it in the dim light.

A wheezing voice filled the room. "You elbowed me in the gut."

She knew that voice, she thought. Her brain, already stuffed with wool, shut down. It couldn't be *him*. A match flared in the dark and a shadowy face emerged, one pinched with pain and too bloody handsome for its own good.

"*You*," she hissed.

He was lying half sprawled on her bed, white shirt unbuttoned to reveal a broad chest smattered with dark hair. His pants were still on, which was good, she told herself. Although, seeing him on her bed made her heart flutter in ways she didn't like. By the blood, there was a *werewolf* on her bed. Just feet from Emmie.

"Me." He grinned, showing a mouthful of white. Although he was still wheezing slightly.

Good.

"What are you *doing* here?" she demanded. How had he found

her?

"Thought I'd pop by, see how you're doing, chat about the weather…" He leaned over and used the match to light the lamp that sat on the small wooden table propped next to her bed.

Her jaw was starting to ache. "I'm annoyed and the weather sucks. *Now get out,* you stalking bastard."

The wolf frowned and twitched the curtain aside. Gray storm clouds hung menacingly in the small patch of sky that was visible through the window. "I thought you said the weather was nice."

"I *said* it sucked." She wanted to kick him. Hard.

"I generally find that a good thing."

"Get out!" she whisper-screamed, not wanting to disturb Emmie.

He stood and walked over to her, smiling. He was barely a foot away from her when he stopped. She could feel the heat emanating from him.

"You don't want me to leave." His voice was a deep rumble.

"Yes, I do." Her shoulder was making her feel dizzy. She just wanted to lie down and go to sleep, but she had to make sure he left, that he wasn't after Emmie.

He frowned. "You're in pain."

"Wow, you're a bloody genius. Get out." She tried to step around him, so she could get behind him and shove him out the door. She froze mid-step. "Wait, how did you get *in*?"

He shrugged. "The window."

"The *window*?" Moving faster than she thought she could – what with the pain and the wool – she jerked the curtain aside and stared at the small glass pane. Opening it, she peered down the four-story drop. There were no stairs or rails nearby. "You climbed the wall?"

"What? It's not that hard a wall to climb; plenty of handholds." He scratched his bare stomach.

She didn't need to stick her head out and have another look at the wall. It was dressed stone. *Not that hard my ass,* she thought. "How'd you know where we live?" Elle was going to strangle Emmie if she'd said anything…

His voice stirred the air next to her ear. "Followed my nose."

Elle spun around.

"You smell like violets."

"Right." She raised her eyebrow slowly.

His eyes were like molten gold. "You do."

"That's stupid." With him so close, it was the best she could come up with. Which said it all, really.

He took a step closer, his chest almost touching hers. "You didn't tell me to get out."

She was barely breathing. He touched her shoulder and she winced.

"What happened?" His touch turned, light, careful.

"I dislocated it."

He frowned. "How? Did you get in another bar fight? I told you to be careful."

She shook her head. "I'm a *guard*." It was her job to deliver the beatings, not receive them. Then she sighed. "My cousin, Bjorn, threw me against a wall. We were training."

Clay gently felt around her joint. "Well, it seems to be back in place. It still hurts?"

Elle shrugged out of his grasp and slumped onto her bed, rubbing her injured body part. "I'm human."

He grinned. "I *had* noticed that."

She stared at him with a feeling close to resentment. "We don't heal like you do." *We age, we die,* she thought.

"I forget about that."

She narrowed her eyes at him. "Oh, how fortunate for you."

"It can be annoying."

"Your memory problem? I imagine it could be at times."

He rolled his eyes. "You're a real handful, you know that?"

"First time I've heard it." She fought to keep the smile from her face. Why was she even talking to this guy? He'd stalked her!

You have serious issues, her mind said.

She told it to shut up.

He leaned back against the curtains, his body enfolded by azure material. "Oh? That surprises me."

She shrugged and then winced in pain. "Well, normally it's 'psycho bitch,' 'crazy fool' and things of that nature."

He folded his arms across his chest, his shirt wrinkling and bunching, leaving the dark trail of hair that marched down his stomach exposed. "That's not very nice."

"That's life." She thought back through their conversation. "So why do your super-healing problems rate as annoying?"

She would have thought they'd be pretty awesome.

He moved one of his arms, slashing it through the air. "Imagine breaking an arm and not setting it right, only to have to re-break it again."

"I thought that part of the super-healing powers meant you didn't need to have bones set – they had some type of ability to heal how they should." Elle absently rubbed her shoulder.

The wolf took a step closer to her and stopped when she tried to slink away from him. "I'm not going to bite."

She narrowed her eyes. "That's what they all say." She didn't move her eyes from his teeth.

He shook his head. "I won't." A grin flashed. "Not this time, anyway."

"Oh, I'm so relieved."

The grin turned wicked. "I only bite when I'm trying to keep the sound of my groans quiet."

She wanted to say something mocking, but her mind was caught on the idea of why he'd need to keep his groans silent. She shuddered and closed her eyes, picturing his body moving…What was *wrong* with her? He was a wolf and she was human. He was interesting, as much as he was annoying. She couldn't believe she was entertaining the thought of him naked. But she was, blood help her. Maybe it was because she was tired. And she hadn't had sex in a long time. She was attracted to strong men, and the only ones she spent time with were colleagues or relatives. Which meant they weren't options. Plus, thinking of Clay naked was a wonderful thought.

"What are you thinking?" His voice was a whisper next to her ear.

Opening her eyes, she noticed the wicked gleam in his eyes. "Get out." It was weak, her voice breathy.

"In a minute." His hands came up to cup her jaw and he leaned forward, his lips touching hers softly, their texture warm and firm. As they molded over hers, his tongue swept forward, sending tingles down her spine. Without thinking, she wound her arms around his neck, but broke away from the kiss when her shoulder protested. And logic descended.

Pain and reason returned. "What did you *do* to me?"

"Kissed you." He was still too close – she could smell him and it was *good*.

She stared at him.

"People have been doing it for thousands of years." He brushed some hair back from his face. "That wasn't your first kiss, was it?"

She jerked. "No!"

"Oh."

Irritation and embarrassment rushed through her. "What? Was it that bad?"

He laughed and she kicked him in the shin. He looked at her, mouth hanging open.

"Quiet!" she hissed.

"Get out?" he offered.

"That too."

He darted forward, too quickly for her to stop him, and kissed her firmly. "Until next time." Then he climbed out the window.

Chapter Ten

Anton flicked his arm outward, then grabbed the snowy white sleeve of his evening shirt and fastened the ends together with a ruby cufflink. He straightened the sleeve before reaching up and flipping over his collar. Turning to the mirror, he studied his reflection, straightening his simple black cravat as he did so.

He was thinner than he'd been two days ago, his cheekbones more pronounced. Beads of sweat were glistening on the caramel skin of his forehead. His normally short, wavy black hair hung lank over his head, despite the washing he'd given it. Shadows loomed under his brandy-colored eyes and he watched as the man in the mirror winced.

Anton wasn't well, but he wasn't suffering the agony he'd experienced for the last two days. He didn't know what had triggered it, but he doubted it would happen again. At least, he hoped not. He'd fired his cook, cleaned out the medicine cabinet and studied every inch of skin he could find to make sure there weren't any needle marks or vampire bites. He hadn't knowingly been with a vampire – he was faithful to Annabel, after all – but he'd heard stories where they could charm humans into doing whatever they wanted.

Deciding that he wasn't going to improve on his sickly appearance, he rang the bell for his valet, who arrived and helped Anton into his tailored black evening jacket. It was a little loose on him, not the second skin it had been designed to be. Running a hand over his lifeless hair, he thanked the servant, grabbed his silver-tipped walking cane and headed out to the marble entry, to wait for his carriage.

Black and white tiles spread out across the entrance, stretching from wall to wall and to the foot of the elaborate marble and wood staircase. Sculptures and vases sat in wall niches, their presence a statement of his family's wealth rather than the good taste that had selected them.

His home wasn't really a bachelor's residence, but it had become that this year, since he was the only Greystoke in town. He was always in town, unlike his family. They preferred country life, said the air was cleaner, the stench of vampires less apparent. Actually, those were his father's words. Anton was quietly positive his mother would be thrilled to spend time in town. He couldn't argue against his father's logic though, and he didn't really want to. His sister and mother were *safer* in the country with his father, the Earl of Maerton, who was also the local magistrate. There was only one aristocratic family in the area and they were wolves, more interested in breeding sheep and cattle for meal times than corrupting or eating the local humans.

The sound of carriage wheels on cobblestones grew louder and Anton assumed it was his vehicle's arrival. Walking toward the front door, he waited for the footman to open it before heading outside. The coachman had already lowered the steps on the carriage and opened the door, so Anton quickly climbed inside, careful of his bad leg.

Making sure the window was shut, he leaned back against the squabs. The smell of the city permeated the carriage despite the closed glass: coal dust and shit. Which was strange, considering the sewerage system. The muted sounds of music – from aristo parties, he assumed – reached his ears as they passed through Lord Row, and headed out toward Pittbrough Street. The call of hawkers became clearer as they headed toward Court Road. In this area, the city woke up at night, its patrons being blood drinkers rather than vegetable consumers.

Soon, the carriage rolled across the cobbles in front of his destination. The coachman let the stairs down, and Anton limped from the carriage. He stood in the brisk cold as he knocked on Annabel's door. He began walking on the spot, his breath misting in the air. His bad leg ached, and for the first time in two years, he found he actually needed the support of his walking stick. Restless, Anton knocked again and waited, his eyes locked on the brass knocker, which looked like a reclining, naked woman. Funny how he'd never noticed that before. Maybe he should point it out to Annabel? Let her know that it more suited a courtesan than a widow?

Eventually, the door opened and a sleepy-looking maid stood visible in the three-inch gap. She was wearing an old robe and a mob cap that rode low over her eyes. "Can I help, sir?"

"I'm here to see Annabel."

The maid peered at him through the small open space. "She's not here."

He blinked. "Did she already leave?" Anton was meant to be taking her to the theater, but maybe he'd remembered their plans wrong. He'd been out of his mind for two days, after all.

The door opened a little more, and he could see that the maid was wearing a pair of threadbare slippers in addition to her silly cap and dressing gown. "No, sir."

He frowned. "But you just said she wasn't home."

"She hasn't been home for days."

Worry began to beat a tattoo in his blood. "Did she send a note?"

The maid's lips puckered. "She doesn't normally send notes when she's working."

"Working?" Anton tried to keep the frown from his face. He could feel the tremors start again and his bad leg wobbled.

She was nodding. "Yes, at Madam Venus's."

Madam Venus's?

"I didn't think she worked." He thought she'd inherited money and was living quietly as a widow. But he could understand that she might not want to tell him she worked as a clerk or some such at the famous brothel – it would lead to awkward questions…

"Oh, not all the time. Just for special clients."

Just for special clients. Each word was like a knife in the gut. Clients. Clerks didn't have *clients*. Annabel – his Annabel – was a whore? But…no. Anton told himself that he wouldn't have cared if she had been a whore *before* they were together – well, he would have, but he loved her so much, it wouldn't have really mattered – but to still work as one?

Just for special clients.

The maid looked about to shut the door, so he blurted, "She doesn't come home when she's working?"

"Not when she's on a job; she has to go to the estates sometimes," the maid said.

Estates.

He felt his stomach drop to somewhere below the steps under his feet.

"I think I'll go over to Madam Venus's, see if she's forgotten our date." Anton turned to leave.

Just for special clients.

"I doubt she will be there…but, do you know where it is?" the maid called out as he headed down the path toward his carriage, leaning heavily on his cane, his body feeling heavier than ever.

Estates.

"Yes!" he shouted, without bothering to turn back. "Do I know where it is?" he muttered. More to the point, who *didn't* know where Madam Venus's was?

By the blood, he realized, *Annabel's a* vampire *whore.*

CHAPTER ELEVEN

Dante's father had returned.

He was warned of his parent's arrival from the subtle changes: the surge of vacant-eyed slaves roaming the halls, the flurry of panic amid the servants, the whispers. There was no sign of his father, though, or a summons to his side, but that was to be expected.

Further confirmation of his father's return was obtained when he walked past his parent's study and he heard voices within. His father's being the loudest. Mostly arguments, he thought, although he couldn't hear the conversations word-for-word, and since vampire hearing wasn't meant to be able to penetrate the soundproof doors, he kept walking.

Returning to his workroom, his eyes locked on the shiny table. Thankfully, he'd already gotten rid of the whore's body. Dante had taken care of it himself, despite the fact that he could have ordered a slave to do it. He had supposedly Chosen the woman because of an undying passion for her, after all. He was meant to display some level of emotional attachment to the corpse, so he had organized her funeral arrangements. Wooden coffin, lots of flowers, a service out at the human cemetery that was reserved but elegant. The funeral home had made most of the decisions, he'd just gone there wearing all black and trying to appear as mournful as he could.

There'd also been the interview with Madam Venus. That hadn't been pleasant, but he'd coughed up enough money to make her happy.

Despite the hassle he'd had with the dead human, and the fact it had been less than a week since his initial failure, he had tried to Choose another woman. He hadn't wanted to miss out on the opportunity, especially since it had walked right by him. She'd had green eyes, and had fought him from the moment he found her wandering down a side-alley, alone. He'd knocked her out and hired a hotel room under a fake name and attempted the transformation there. He'd followed the procedure to the letter, but he'd ended up with another corpse.

He'd gotten rid of that body too, although its funeral had been more of an ignominious river dive, rather than an elaborate ceremony. Dante thought disposing of dead bodies was a waste of his talents. But…humans got crotchety when too many failed Choosings occurred, which meant that his father might ask some uncomfortable questions, so he had cleaned up his messes.

The waste of time had been productive to a small extent: he'd decided that colored-eyed humans couldn't be Chosen. He'd paid close attention to the second woman, and he'd found that it was the third transfer of blood that did it. Within seconds of the critical, Change-occurring blood entering her system, she had expired. It was poison to them, he was convinced.

But, *why*?

He had a drop of the second woman's blood on a glass slide and was studying it when his father found him.

"Dante," his father said into the cold chamber.

Dante had heard his father's entrance, but had pretended to be absorbed in his task. Viktor liked to think that he was almost silent when walking, and Dante figured it was better to prolong his father's delusion.

"Father," Dante said and stood, pushing his chair back across the stone floor. He put the slide in a wooden box with care and shut the lid with a click, before turning to face his parent.

Dante's father was tall, had always seemed towering, but Dante now stood three inches higher. Like Dante, Viktor Kipling – the Earl of Wintermere – had dark hair, pale skin and aristocratic features, but his father had lines around his eyes and a thin mouth, which was pressed together in a perpetual scowl whenever he was in his son's presence.

"What are you doing?" Viktor asked.

Dante shrugged. "Just trying to work out why Sandy died."

His father straightened a sapphire cufflink. "Sandy?"

"I Chose her, but she didn't survive." Dante tried to look upset. He didn't know if it worked, but his father frowned and it seemed more thoughtful than annoyed.

"Misty mentioned something like that."

Dante wasn't sure what the appropriate response was, so he nodded.

"Did you bother to let Madam Venus know what happened to her employee?" Viktor asked.

Misty must have done more than just "mention" it for their father to know Sandy had been a whore.

"Yes." Dante frowned. "She wasn't...happy."

Viktor snorted. "I can't imagine why she would have been. Sandy was one of her most popular...staff."

Dante decided he didn't want to know how his father knew about Sandy's popularity.

His father walked forward and wrapped an arm around Dante's shoulders. It felt like a band of iron had settled against his back. Viktor led – although pushed would have been more accurate – Dante out of the room, kicking the door shut behind them. They walked down the hall to his study, yellow lamps illuminating the stony passage. Slaves walked by with downturned heads, their clothes little more than mended rags, their bones protruding.

Dante was stiff under his father's hand. Viktor *never* touched him. Dante thought back through his mental catalog of his father's behavior with Misty, and realized that he *did* hug her, so this must be a sign of parental affection.

His first ever.

Dante was suspicious, but decided that candor may be called for. He hated this, this not knowing what to do in social situations.

So he said, "After the meeting, I was sent a rather terse note – she insinuated there would be an investigation."

"She *what?*"

Dante figured his father probably already knew about the threat, but the apparent anger in his voice was real enough. "Yes. She seems to think that Sandy was unwilling."

The band of steel tightened on Dante's back. "Ridiculous." Flicking a glance at his father from the corner of his eye, Dante saw Viktor lift one imperious eyebrow. "Who would *not* want to be Chosen? What human would reject such an opportunity?" Disdain rumbled through his voice.

Dante guessed that the assumption would be true – most of the time. But he figured there would be a human *somewhere* who wouldn't want the perks of immortality. Living forever could be bloody boring.

And…what if they knew they wouldn't survive the Choosing?

Dante stopped walking and stood transfixed in the hallway.

"Dante?"

What if the whore and the green-eyed girl had *known* they wouldn't survive being Chosen? What if that was why the second girl had fought so hard? What if that was why the whore had been immune to a vampire's bite?

"Dante?"

He shook himself and looked at his father. The familiar sneer of contempt was teetering on return.

Dante thought quickly. "Sorry, Father. It just occurred to me that it was very strange for Madam Venus to assume that Sandy would not want to be Chosen. After all, Sandy made a living off working with vampires. Isn't that why humans work with us? In the hope they'll be Chosen? Do you think that reflects on something about the establishment Madam Venus runs? After all, she provides entertainment for vampires – does she have something against us? A hidden agenda?"

The flicker of scorn had vanished from his father's face. He looked thoughtful. "I hadn't considered that. Interesting."

Normally Viktor would have dismissed Dante's concerns out

of hand, so it was strange that his father had latched onto Dante's thrown-together theory. Stranger still that a look of something almost like pride had crossed Viktor's features.

"Come," his father said. They resumed walking toward Viktor's study, the cold of the hallway unnoticeable, except for the puffs of air that grew misty in front of the slaves' faces as they passed.

Dante waited while his father pushed open the study door, and followed him in. He couldn't stop his eyes flicking to the three skulls on their wooden shelf, but at least he was able to walk by them without wishing to stop and handle them.

"Misty said you showed her the differences in those skulls," Viktor said, almost conversationally.

Dante froze for a split second then walked over to one of the chairs positioned on the door-side of the large, hulking desk. "Yes."

So now the stake will fall, Dante thought.

"Why were you in my study without me?" His father sat in the huge, dark leather chair behind his desk. He clasped his hands together over his flat stomach and leaned back, apparently waiting, as if he was just having a normal conversation with his son.

"Misty didn't tell you?" Dante thought nonchalance might work.

"Tell me what?"

"I thought I heard someone in your study, so I went to check."

"You heard someone in my study?" His father's forehead crinkled.

"Yes."

"Through a shut door?" Viktor's eyebrows almost reached his hairline.

"Yes." Although Dante hadn't said the door was closed.

"The door is soundproof." His father folded his arms, eyebrows returning to their normal level, which was still raised.

Dante shrugged and studied his nails.

"Your hearing is that acute?" Rather than annoyed, Dante

thought his father looked pleased, but then, Dante didn't understand facial expressions all that well.

"Sometimes." Dante didn't want his father to think that he was some super-hearing freak and put him to use accordingly. Whatever that would be. Spying, probably. He gave an inward shudder – having to be *nice* to people. Having to *socialize*. Ugh.

"And what did you find? Was anyone in my study?" Viktor leaned forward on his elbows, across the desk.

Diplomacy or hard truth? Misty could do no wrong as far as their father was concerned, and she'd already gone babbling to Viktor with half-truths... "Misty was having sex with one of the slaves on your desk." Dante took some enjoyment from seeing his father start, briefly look at where his elbows were resting and then look back at his son.

"The little bitch." But there was admiration in Viktor's voice. Misty, it appeared, could still do no wrong.

"She didn't tell you?" Dante leaned back in his seat, enjoying the way the red leather cushioned his back. It was a novelty.

"No, she said she'd found a slave in here. That you stumbled across them as she was punishing him for trespassing."

"'Punishing' may have been a rather accurate term to use." Dante forced a smile.

"I thought she hadn't punished him enough." Viktor shrugged.

"Oh?" He didn't know why he bothered to ask, because he knew what the answer would be. There was only ever *one* answer when his father thought his privacy had been invaded.

"I put it down," Viktor said then frowned. "It may have been a waste. And Misty seemed rather...irritated at me for it."

"From what I could see," Dante said, "she seemed pretty pleased with the slave's, ah, attention to detail."

But the dead slave explained why his father was in such a good mood. Being able to suck a human dry always seemed to cheer up his relatives, and they had to be careful about doing it, because slaves were a somewhat limited stock. Only debts or illegal activities could turn a freeman into a slave. That, or being kidnapped from another country. It was quite an industry. Lots of death, though.

"Well, that should teach Misty a lesson for lying to me," Viktor said.

Dante didn't want to know how euthanizing a temporarily favored pet would do anything to teach her a lesson, but he wasn't about to criticize his father's disciplinary skills.

"For the next week or so," Dante said, deciding that brotherly spite was called for.

Viktor chuckled. He *chuckled*. What was going on here?

"Misty is never one to dwell on things." There was pride there, and amusement.

Dwell? It was lucky if she could focus enough to remember the days of the week sometimes. "No."

Footsteps, four sets, came up the hallway. Dante frowned in concentration. Two were slaves, he'd bet, one was a servant and the other, well, those heavy steps suggested a limp and high-quality boots. Flicking a glance down at his fob watch, he read the time: 4.18 p.m. Very early – or very late – in the vampire day for such domesticity.

"Dante?"

Glancing up at his father, he gathered that was probably the third or fourth time his parent had called his name.

"Sorry, Father. Someone is about to knock."

Viktor glared, but he wasn't staring at Dante anymore, it was at the door. Was he trying to hear the commotion himself?

A few seconds later, the door was pushed open ever so slightly and Jenkins, the butler, appeared in the small space. "Sorry to interrupt, my lord, but there is a gentleman here to see you. He is most insistent."

Viktor was still frowning, and Dante decided that he was glad to not be the idiot on the other side of the door.

"Who is this insistent gentleman?" Viktor's voice was smooth, calm, but Dante had a feeling his parent was not happy about the intrusion.

"Baron Greystoke," a new voice announced.

Dante twisted in his chair and felt his eyes widen in shock at the appearance of the speaker. A human aristo?

Here?

Most of them kept away from the city, rather than spend time with the vampires who had begun the class system. It worked well for both races; humans got to be part of the upper classes and vampires could say they didn't dominate the system, and best of all, they never really mingled. Apart from in the Counsel of Lords.

"Welcome," Viktor said. "Have a seat." His father moved a hand, indicating the empty chair next to Dante.

Greystoke began the walk toward the desk, leaning on a cane as he did so. The man was uncommonly attractive for a human, Dante realized, which surprised him. He didn't normally notice whether or not humans – or vampires, for that matter – were pleasing to look at. He was tall, although not as tall as Dante, with brown-black hair and dark olive skin. Most importantly, or least importantly, he had brown eyes. But they weren't the typical muddy color of most humans; they were almost a brandy hue, with warm highlights. You couldn't call them golden or anything like that, but they weren't *normal*.

Greystoke pulled the chair out next to Dante and sat, resting his gloved hands on the silver handle of his walking stick.

"Lord Wintermere, thank you for agreeing to see me at such short notice." The man's voice was smooth, warm, like his eyes, although even Dante could sense the irony in the statement.

"Greystoke, it is entirely my pleasure."

It probably would be too, if Greystoke was susceptible to mesmerization. The fact that he had made it past the butler seemed to indicate he was not.

"Greystoke, have you met my son before? The Honorable Dante Kipling?" There was a glimmer of something in his father's eyes, but Dante didn't understand the emotion.

Dante noticed that the hands on the cane tightened briefly, but Greystoke was polite in greeting him. "I have only met your daughter before, Wintermere. How is the viscountess?"

Being the eldest, and their father's favorite, Misty had

inherited the courtesy title that went along with the earldom; an estate that none of them, bar their father, ever saw.

"Mistique is doing wonderfully. A father's joy."

Greystoke smiled at that, but there was something strange about the expression. Dante shrugged mentally. Humans.

"To what do we owe the pleasure of your call?" Viktor asked.

Greystoke's face smoothed until it became devoid of expression. "I am here to find out information about my fiancée."

"Your fiancée?" Viktor was polite, but there was something in his voice that alerted Dante to his father's rising amusement. Which was strange.

"Yes, her name was Annabel White, but you may have known her as Sandy."

Dante flicked a quick glance at his father and felt a sinking feeling hit his stomach. Fiancée?

Ah, crap.

CHAPTER TWELVE

"How's the shoulder?" Mikael asked.

Elle looked up from the guard register she was annotating. "Better than yesterday."

No thanks to a particular werewolf. But she didn't want to think about *him*. She couldn't believe she'd let him kiss her. And that she'd been thinking about doing more with him.

"Your family has a strange way of showing affection," Mikael said. He was the night captain and her boss.

"It's my cousins," she said. "They can't handle losing."

Normally, she worked in a team of four, although they often split into pairs, and together they patrolled the streets wearing the black-brown outfits that showed they were city guards, rather than soldiers. Today, she was a desk jockey and they would be a team of three.

"But you're a trained guard." Mikael looked surprised.

"And they're bodyguards – ex-soldiers." Bjorn had spent a while in the army, fighting blood-knows-who over blood-knows-what. So had his brothers. They'd liked it. It was only because Elle's gran had called them back to protect the family that they'd done so.

You didn't say no to Gran.

"Tell them the next time they decide to beat on you for fun, they will answer to me." He smiled, but his eyes were cool. "I don't approve of my guards being put out of action so that your cousin can make himself feel like more of a man."

Elle nodded, cracked a close-mouthed smile in return and went back to her paperwork. But, covertly, she took a good look at Mikael. He was tall, over six feet in height and built of solid muscle. His skin was so dark he blended into the night perfectly. Only his teeth and eyes gave him away. He was easily bigger than Bjorn and spent a lot more time beating the crap out of people – it was his job, after all. And he used a steel baton rather than a wooden one like Bjorn did. But he had Brown eyes. All the muscle and dirty-fighting tricks in the world wouldn't help you if you couldn't actually land a finger on your opponent. Greens and Grays were formidable adversaries – one could tell what punch you were going to throw before you threw it, and the other could throw you clean across the room without lifting a finger.

Most of the city guards were non-Graceds, or Nons, as she and Emmie called them. Which was fine by Elle. It made her feel more…normal. Although the downside was that Emmie was as fascinated by Nons as she was by vampires and weres. Maybe more so. And Elle didn't want Emmie spending too much time with her colleagues. Kyle was not child-friendly.

The city clock chimed three times, signaling two hours to the end of Elle's shift. Rubbing her eyes, she leaned back in her chair and stretched her good arm. Desk work was boring; it gave her too much time to think. And it was strange working in the day, doing all the paperwork for her team from the night before. Double shifts were killers.

It wasn't long before a messenger came through the guard doors. Looking up, Elle took in the scrawny almost-teenager; the shifty way he looked around, the tattered clothes and the hungry air. But she decided he wasn't too much of a threat. The kid was probably just dropping off some information for some coin.

She met Mikael's steady gaze with raised eyebrows. He shrugged. She turned back to the kid. "Can I help you?"

"Dead body in the river," he blurted out.

Elle frowned. There were plenty of dead bodies in Pinton; barely a day went by when there wasn't some kind of paperwork to be filled out and a death tax ordered. Although, to be honest, most of the dead were slaves. And there wasn't a death tax for them, because legally, they weren't people. But for someone to dump the body, that was a little unusual. Meant it might be someone important. Most killers were vampires, and they didn't care to hide what they did, not unless they might get into trouble for it.

"Can you go?" Mikael asked her. "I need to get some stuff sorted here."

Elle nodded. She pulled her leather jacket on carefully over her bad shoulder, hitched her baton to her belt – although she hoped she wouldn't need to use it – and followed the kid out the door. "Can you call the coroner?" she asked Mikael.

"Sure, I'll get her to meet you at the river. Where was the body found, kid?"

"Near the White Tower Tannery."

On the southern side of the Thyme, Elle thought. Where it stank. Following the kid out the door, she waved down a hackney and climbed aboard, motioning for the messenger to follow her lead. The kid looked nervous, but took a seat next to her. He smoothed his dirty hand over grimy blond hair.

As it was still daylight, it didn't take long to reach the waterfront. The traffic congestion would hit later on, when the vampires came out to socialize. Stepping from the hackney, she told the driver to wait. He looked disgruntled, but bobbed his head in agreement anyway. She was clearly a guard, and it was a guaranteed fare.

She looked at the kid. "Where's the body?"

Following him, she walked down the slick cobblestone path that ran alongside the river.

"There!" A bony finger pointed toward a small jetty, jutting into the dirty river. People were milling about, some scratching their heads. They all wore rough-looking clothes, Elle noticed; they were probably laborers working in this area of the city. All human. As she got closer, she noticed they were all Nons.

Elle walked out onto the jetty. One of the men spotted her and waved her over. "Over here!"

"Can I go now, miss?" the kid asked. Nodding, Elle slipped him a coin. The boy vanished as quickly as the coin did. She headed toward the gesticulating man. The small group parted as she reached them. Behind the speaker's feet, she saw a hand lying palm up, the skin dark against the bright, wet blue of a shirt and the damp wood of the jetty. There was a gaping slash along the wrist. The fingers were stiff, and they belonged to a woman, Elle saw. Not too long dead, she thought. Although rigor would last for up to three days.

"We found her a little while ago," the speaker of the group said. "Dressed too nice to be a slave. Thought we should let someone know."

Elle nodded a greeting and hunched down over the woman. Black hair obscured her face and she was nicely dressed, as the workman had pointed out. Although the clothes had seen better days. Bloodstains splattered them, but that wasn't unusual considering the cut wrist. She checked the other arm. The woman was lying on her back on the jetty, clearly dumped there after being hauled out of the murky Thyme. Flicking the hair aside, she felt her heart stutter. Almond-shaped Green eyes looked upward, vacant. Elle had seen this woman before, but she didn't know her name. Gran would.

A voice intruded. "What have we got?"

Elle looked over her shoulder at the speaker. Alice Reive was the city's coroner. She was a sawbones of sorts, but preferred patients who couldn't talk. The woman sat her bag down next to the body and then knelt on the jetty. Alice was wearing black slacks and a red shirt that she filled out well enough to make Elle jealous. The other woman must have been working at one of the funeral homes she freelanced for. She provided death certificates to grieving families, so the death taxes could be sorted – if they were needed.

"Dead woman; looks to be mid-twenties, two cut wrists. Plenty of blood stains, body in rigor."

Alice nodded at Elle, auburn curls bouncing against her forehead. "Not bad." Then she started inspecting the corpse.

When Alice got to the woman's mouth, she started frowning. Her gloved hands froze on the dead woman's jaw.

"What's wrong?" Elle asked.

"She has small bits of dried blood around her mouth," Alice replied.

"That can't be good."

"It never is," Alice said. The coroner checked the slashed wrists again. She muttered something about potentially hiding bite marks. Elle figured she wasn't meant to have caught that.

Alice stood abruptly, grabbing her black leather bag in her right hand. "I'll take her back with me; I need to do an autopsy. I'll send you my report tomorrow."

Chapter Thirteen

To have said that Anton felt uncomfortable would have been a grave understatement. He felt thoroughly idiotic, but he'd had to come. He'd had to see the man that Annabel had chosen in preference to him – the *life* she had chosen in preference to the one she could have had with him.

"Yes," he said to the two vampires in the room, "her name was Annabel White, but you may have known her as Sandy."

And the man was, well, he was a very fine figure of a vampire. One of the prettiest men Anton had ever seen. At present, Kipling was slouching in the huge leather seat next to him, all loose-limbed grace. He was the younger version of the vampire sitting on the other side of the desk, although Kipling's eyes were violet rather than the mauve of Lord Wintermere's. And Kipling was far more handsome – a refined, purified version of Wintermere. Something that Anton couldn't see Wintermere liking.

From working with Wintermere in the Counsel of Lords, it had become clear to Anton that the earl always had to be the best; the most important, the richest. It was too bad that he kept failing at his objectives. Wintermere wasn't the most important man in the kingdom – King Johan was. He wasn't the foremost earl in the realm; there were even other *human* earls whose estates were more prosperous. And he wasn't the richest; the king once again took that title from him.

And now it was obvious that he wasn't even the best looking in his own house, either. Did that mean he wasn't the strongest or the most cunning? Anton had met Wintermere's daughter, Viscountess Kipling, so he had to wonder about the latter, as well.

"Sandy?" Wintermere asked, and mockery oozed from the word.

"Yes, I believe that was her working name." Anton smiled, showing his teeth. Kipling moved restlessly in his chair.

"I thought a baron could do better than a whore." Wintermere was smiling back, his fangs showing.

So, intimidation was the angle of attack, was it?

Anton shrugged and bit back the obvious retort, "She was going to quit" – from what he'd recently learned of Annabel, he privately questioned that statement – and said instead, "This was going to be her last job."

"It certainly was that." Wintermere was having fun, Anton discovered. He was *amused*.

Bastard.

No, that word wasn't strong enough for the rage that Anton was feeling.

"Yes," Anton said and decided to lie. "She *had* quit, but your son requested some very specific physical characteristics that only Annabel could meet. And so she went. Despite the fact that I have enough income to support her a hundred times over, she wanted her own money, and your son was offering a great deal of it."

Anton watched Kipling out of the corner of his eye. He saw the vampire swallow, but otherwise, his face remained impassive. Almost like it was carved from stone. This was the man who had fallen so passionately in love with Annabel that he'd Chosen her? He barely even blinked.

"She sounds positively mercenary. Are you sure she wasn't marrying you for your groats, while feeding her addiction on the side?" Wintermere had stopped smiling, but amusement was marked all over the snide bastard's face.

"She wasn't addicted to vampires, if that's what you're saying," Anton said. Despite the fact he hadn't known about her...career choice, he did know she hadn't been addicted to anything. That would have been something he could have spotted a mile off. Personal experience and all.

"Of course she was; all humans are if they're vampire whores." Wintermere waved a dismissive hand through the air.

"She wasn't addicted." It was the first time Kipling had spoken and his voice was soft, deep, and slightly…timid?

"Don't be ridiculous, Dante."

"She *wasn't*. It was one of the physical characteristics I wanted." Kipling shot Anton a look he couldn't decipher. Was the vampire warning him to not say anything else about why he'd wanted Annabel specifically?

"That's ridiculous." But there wasn't as much venom in Wintermere's voice. Doubt was creeping in.

"I don't like bit-ridden humans. Why would I want to try and Choose one?" Kipling was still slouching; he looked sullen.

Wintermere tapped his lip with one long finger. "Yes, you did put down one of the bit-ridden slaves when I was away, didn't you?" The earl shook his head. "You didn't even drink its blood."

"It tastes bad when they're addicted."

They'd just talked of murdering a human in front of him as if it were nothing. Anton fought the urge to clench his fists. Not that there was anything he could do about it. There was no law governing how a man treated his slaves. He could rape them, kill them, and even *eat* them. And there was nothing that could be done. Slaves weren't legally people.

"So, we have established your whor – fiancée wasn't bit-ridden. It's novel, but not really the issue at hand." Wintermere flicked a wrist through the air. "You want to know if she asked to be Chosen or if she was Chosen against her will. This is correct?"

One was legal, the other wasn't.

Anton blinked and nodded. Wintermere was trying to keep him on his toes; to maintain control of the conversation. Anton didn't really care. He figured that he was good at reading people's expressions and body language, and right now, Wintermere was vastly amused.

Kipling, on the other hand, was a closed book. No matter what answers Anton got today, he'd never know if they were true or not.

"Yes, I want to know if she was Chosen against her will or not," Anton replied.

"Well?" Wintermere said, nodding at his son.

Kipling started slightly. He uncrossed one of his legs and sat up straighter. "Sandy wanted to be Chosen."

That was it. No explanation; no reason for the life-altering decision. Just *"she'd wanted it."* Everything screamed in him that Kipling was lying, but his face was serious, and he was staring into Anton's eyes. Anton may not have known a lot about Annabel, but she hadn't really liked vampires. Or weres.

He couldn't see her ever wanting to become one.

"She wanted to be Chosen so badly she didn't even tell you her real name?" Anton blurted.

Kipling shrugged, and Anton noticed the vampire began to play with the armrest of his seat. "We didn't do much talking."

Wintermere let out a chuckle that he smothered with a cough.

"But enough to know she wanted to be Chosen," Anton said. It was rather like speaking to a wall, he thought. Actually, he'd probably get more out of that conversation than this one.

"Yes."

Deciding that coming here had been as foolish a choice as he'd feared it would be, Anton rose. He would get nothing useful out of these two. If he could interview the slaves, he might learn more, but he couldn't do that without bringing his own honor into question.

Blast them all.

CHAPTER FOURTEEN

"Much on for the rest of today?" Mikael asked.

A well-deserved sleep, Elle thought. Guard work really screwed with the internal clock. And she felt extra tired after seeing the blood around that dead woman's mouth… It was as if a vampire had tried to Choose her. She guessed that was what Alice had been thinking. Most dead humans didn't warrant autopsies. No Green would have agreed to be Chosen; so what could have happened? But Elle couldn't write that in her report, which was as finished as she could make it, without Alice's statement.

"Picking Emmie up from Gran's, that's about it. You?" Emmie had classes there every day after school. She hated them, but then, who wouldn't?

"Just have to go to a formal dinner being held at one of the estates. Rumor has it King Jo might be there." Mikael screwed up his face.

"King Johan?" Elle echoed. "He actually might leave the palace for a meal at an aristo's estate?" She shook her head. Elle wouldn't know what to do if she found herself in the room with the king. "That's why you're the guard captain, and I'm the grunt." Elle smirked. She didn't envy him. Dealing with aristos – vampires – was not high on her list of desires. Then again, it did rank higher than being bitten by a vampire or dealing with a certain werewolf who didn't understand the meaning of boundaries. Or windows.

She just wasn't sure she had enough self-control to deny her attraction to the wolf. And why should she? He'd move on, and she might be left a little happier.

He might be after Emmie, she thought. And that soured her mood. She'd kill him if he was. It wouldn't be the first time, after all.

She pulled on her leather jacket, careful of her sore shoulder, then buttoned it up mostly one-handed. "Well, you have fun with that dinner." She smiled lopsidedly at Mikael.

"Sure, as much fun as I would've had getting a hole in the head." Mikael grimaced.

Her expression turned sympathetic as she slung her satchel over her good arm. "Well, you could always force Dinya to go instead."

Dinya was the day captain and a grouchier, more taciturn woman Elle had yet to meet. Barring Gran, of course.

"Blood, imagine her in a room full of vampires! She has enough trouble when she bumps into the aristos on the streets as it is. That's why she's day shift. Most of the toffs just wander around King's Park and don't get in her way." Mikael was shaking his head.

"See you tomorrow, then!" Elle headed out of the room. She didn't want to wait around in case Mikael decided she should suffer with him.

Whistling to herself, she jogged down the stone stairs of the Guard House and out onto Bridge Road. The cold was like a physical sock to the jaw. It had cooled drastically in the last hour. Her breath instantly misted and her face soon felt numb. It was only third month. Winter wasn't due for another two.

Turning right, hands in her pockets, Elle wished she was wearing a scarf. She tucked her chin under her jacket collar and kept her eyes on the cobblestone sidewalk. Sodium lamps were beginning to glow in the dimming light and the streets were dominated by luxury carriages rather than work carts and hackneys.

It was early evening, and the city's vampires would be out and about now, preparing for their social activities. She may not look like Emmie, but she was different enough – with her red hair and semi-Brown eyes – that a vampire might take an interest in her. Even their mother, who was normally too placid to react to much, had always said to keep out of a vampire's, or were's, line of sight.

Elle was on the opposite side of the road from Gran's house when she saw him. The streets were emptying out, as it was a human neighborhood. Nightlife didn't really exist here. Tall stone buildings arched overhead and the smell of coal was thick, as it was used for cooking and was burned almost constantly to produce the hot water that serviced this area. Her eyes were drawn back to the werewolf. He was leaning against the wall on the other side of the road, still in buckskins and a white shirt, flagrantly unfeeling of the bitter cold that was seeping into her bones.

Ignoring him, she crossed the road and knocked on Gran's door. *Please make him leave,* she thought. Emmie must have been waiting on the other side, because she opened the door herself. Her normally nut-brown face was pale and set, but Elle couldn't see any sign of tears.

"How was it?" Elle asked as Emmie shut the door behind her. She was wearing an old jacket over a pale blue dress. She looked like a child from a lower-class family – old mended clothes and worn-out shoes. They certainly weren't rich, but they weren't poor. Gran was a wealthy and powerful cit; although she kept a tight rein on her finances. But she wouldn't begrudge buying Emmie some new clothes. Although she shouldn't need to. Elle's mother, Melissande, earned a good living working for Gran in her agency, which supplied all of the estates with their servants and many of their slaves. But since Melissande and Elle had moved into their own apartment, Gran had stopped helping them out financially. Despite that, Elle brought in a reasonable sum from her guard work. Surely Emmie could have some new dresses and shoes?

Elle held out her free hand, but Emmie ignored it. She was growing more independent every day and Elle wasn't sure she liked it.

"Not as bad as normal."

"No?" Elle tucked her hand in her jacket pocket and they began walking down the street. They were going to head down Court Road – it was a longer journey than walking straight up Pittbrough Street, but they wouldn't have to pass the rows of vampire estates. If she'd been on her own, she would have risked it.

There were plenty of humans wandering the streets next to them, and carriages rattled alongside. Horses nickered and coachmen cursed. Elle dodged the passersby and kept Emmie close. As they walked, they passed row after row of stone buildings, with cobbled pathways snaking between them. Her eyes on the path, she noticed a large shadow fall over them in the late afternoon light. Without thinking, Elle shoved Emmie behind her, up against the stone wall of the apartment block behind them. Her heart thudded and she realized she was acting strangely. She then looked up at the shadow caster and groaned.

Almost larger than life, the werewolf stood in their path, grinning like a loon. "Only me!"

Elle blinked, hoping that would wipe the image of the smiling werewolf from her vision.

"You scared me, sneaking up like that." Elle's voice was barely audible.

The wolf's grin grew wider. "Sneaking up on you by walking straight into your path?"

She couldn't fault him on that. If she hadn't been staring at the ground, then she wouldn't have been able to miss him. Flicking a glance at her sister, she could see Emmie staring at the man in something like amazement.

"Hello, little human." His voice softened when he addressed Emmie.

Elle pushed her sister further behind her, not that there was much room for her to be pushed to. "What are you doing here?"

The wolf looked around, raising his eyebrows mockingly. Elle's eyes followed his. "This is a public sidewalk."

And they were standing in the middle of it.

Elle could feel curious eyes on the three of them, so she started walking, keeping Emmie close to her side, hoping he'd leave. He didn't. "Why are you following us around?"

"I saw the little human go in there after school," he pointed backward down the street, "and I wanted to make sure she got home safely."

"So you were watching the house for hours?" Elle's heart was beating oddly and her skin tingled. They – Emmie – were being stalked.

"My name is Emmie. Esmeralda, actually, but I don't like it." Emmie was smiling her close-lipped smile, but there was a bounce in her step that hadn't been there in weeks. Her brown ponytails swung jauntily as she walked.

"Well, I can see why you prefer Emmie. You're much too small and lovely a girl to have such a big name." He had his hands in his pockets as he walked next to them. Trying to appear non-threatening, she thought. He was too bloody handsome for his own good. It was obviously why Emmie was so drawn to him; that and because he was different. Like her.

"You watched the house for hours?" Elle asked again.

He flicked a golden glance her way. "One hour, but yes."

Over Emmie's head, Elle glowered at him. Despite the gathering dusk, they were drawing curious glances from the vampires that had started entering this part of the city. They were all primped and pressed and nearly all of them had long hair. Tucking her chin further into her jacket, she wished that the wolf would just disappear.

"Go away," she hissed at him.

Emmie nearly tripped over her own feet. "What?"

"I told the wolf to go away." Elle pushed her onward down the street, wishing the encounter was over.

"The wolf is ignoring her, though," he said and he *winked* at Emmie. Elle wouldn't have been surprised if he had started whistling.

"What's your name?" Emmie asked him.

Elle made a sound that imitated a boiling kettle.

"Clay."

"Clay what?" Elle asked, unable to help herself.

He shot her a sidelong look. "I thought you wanted me to go away."

"I do."

"Clay Lovett," he offered.

"Will you just *go away*?" Elle hissed.

"Now you've learned my name, you just want to wash your hands of me?"

"*Yes.*"

CHAPTER FIFTEEN

They were home. Thankfully, they'd managed – or more accurately, Elle had managed – to drive the wolf off.

Clay.

Clay Lovett.

What a ridiculous name. She didn't believe for a second that was his real name; but then, most wolves had surnames like Lupu, Dire and Blaidd. Why not plain old Lovett?

Still, she wasn't about to believe that that was his name just because that's what he'd told them.

"When can we see Clay again?" Emmie asked.

Elle slung off her jacket and hung it on the metal hook behind the front door using her good arm. She walked over to the wooden bench that ran along the opposite wall of the entry hall, and dropped her satchel as she sat. She took off her boots one-handed and mentally sighed. Clay had certainly made a convert of her sister. It was disgusting and horrifying how easily he'd managed it.

"Hopefully never," Elle muttered.

"Elle!" Emmie stamped her foot.

"Take off your shoes."

Grumbling, Emmie did as she was told.

Elle shook her head and walked down the hall toward the kitchen in her socked feet. Emmie followed.

"What?"

"He's just being nice." Emmie's lower lip started to protrude.

"And did you ever wonder why?" Elle asked. She opened a white-painted cupboard and took out two glasses before going to the cold box and finding some milk. She poured them both a glass each.

"Why does there have to be a reason? Why are you so grouchy about everything?" Emmie sat at the petite, scuffed wooden table that was positioned in the middle of the small kitchen.

Elle plonked the glasses down and then pulled a chair out with her good arm. She sat opposite her sister and studied her. Weak sunlight filtered through the high windows and into the kitchen. Emmie had her hair tied back in a braid and it shone with red highlights. Elle hadn't noticed that it had a bit of auburn to it before, normally it hinted gold.

"I'm not grouchy about everything," Elle protested.

Emmie rolled her eyes.

"I just think there can't be a good reason why a werewolf is interested in you." Elle took a sip of milk; right now though, she could have done with something harder.

"Not me," Emmie said. "*Us.*"

"Great."

Emmie giggled. "He's very pretty."

"I hadn't noticed," Elle lied. She stood and took her glass to the sink, leaving it there. As she walked back to the table, she rubbed her shoulder.

"Does your shoulder still hurt?" Emmie was frowning.

"Bjorn dislocated it."

As Elle sat down again, Emmie reached out and touched her hand. It should have been a simple gesture; a physical expression of sympathy. But it wasn't simple. A frisson of *something* zapped up Elle's arm and she froze. Within a heartbeat, her shoulder felt like it had been dipped in ice cold water, needles of pain shooting through the joint before it suddenly went numb.

Then, no soreness.

Elle stared at Emmie in shock.

Her sister was looking pale, her eyes shadowed.

"What happened?" Elle asked, but she had a feeling she knew.

"Don't tell," Emmie whispered. "Please." Her grip tightened on Elle's hand. "Please don't tell anyone."

♦

"You knew about this – this ability?" Elle asked.

She rotated her shoulder and it felt good. Better than it ever had, really. In fact, overall, she felt fantastic. Like she could run a marathon. Emmie, however, was not looking so well. Elle tucked her sister into her bed and plied her with food and hot chocolate. Emmie's hair looked plain brown again, and it was tied back in two plaits running behind each ear. Her caramel-colored skin had recuperated some of its normal glow, but she was still pale. Emmie was holding a steaming mug between two somewhat shaky hands.

Elle was pacing the length of Emmie's bedroom. She ran a hand through her short hair as she did so, muttering to herself as she waited for Emmie's answer. Elle reached the small wooden bookshelf and turned back. Pink wallpaper decorated with flowers ran along the walls, making it feel like an army of petals was closing in on her. No toys scattered the floor. Emmie couldn't sleep with mess, she said. The small room was almost too neat for a child, Elle thought.

"I did it once before, but I thought it was an accident," Emmie replied. She was peeping out over the top of her pink blanket, which she'd pulled right up. It wasn't cold, but then, Elle didn't know what the effects of healing a person might do to someone.

Healing.

By the blood.

Healing.

"Who? When?" Elle was trying to think of who she would have to shut up – permanently, if necessary. She couldn't allow for anyone else to know about Emmie's ability, if that was what this really was. She couldn't let it be talked about.

Emmie mumbled something.

"Sorry?"

"A cat!"

Elle stopped pacing. Turning, she looked at her sister, who still had the blankets drawn to her chin. Protectively, Elle finally grasped. Feeling like a total bitch, and berating herself for being one, Elle walked over to her sister's bed and sat down.

"You healed a cat?" she asked, her voice softer. She met her sister's troubled gaze and kicked herself mentally again.

"It got run over by a cart," Emmie explained, "and it was hurt. I knew I wasn't meant to touch it, but something inside made me. So I touched it, and then it got better."

That simple. One life-changing event and all it had taken was a touch. And she hadn't told Elle about it. Hadn't even thought of saying something, Elle could tell.

"Why didn't you say anything to me?" Elle asked as she plucked at the little pieces of lint that stuck to Emmie's blanket.

"I didn't want to upset you. And I didn't know if it would work on *people*."

Elle stared at her sister, trying to gauge the honesty of her words. It hurt to think that they were true. Elle had worked hard to build the relationship she had with Emmie, one that had hopefully meant that Emmie could be comfortable with her; that she could tell her anything. It was the relationship Elle didn't have with their mother and certainly not with their grandmother. She'd wanted different for Emmie, and it looked like she'd failed.

"I'm sorry, Emmie. You must think me a bear." Elle found her sister's leg and gave it a squeeze.

"I didn't know if I could do it again. And I knew you would worry." Emmie lowered the blanket.

"*Of course* I'm going to worry," Elle said and tried to smile. "But I will worry about you anyway, no matter what."

"Promise me you won't tell anyone about what I can do?" Emmie reached down and grabbed Elle's hand in a pincer-like grip.

"I promise."

CHAPTER SIXTEEN

To say that Olive hated vampires would be an understatement. She smiled a tight-lipped smile at the one in front of her, to hide her unease about being in an estate. The stone walls and roof felt like it would envelop her, swallow her whole. And then there were the mental voices, from the hundred or so servants and slaves who lived and worked here. Her shields were struggling to keep their errant thoughts out.

It reminded her of her childhood, where she'd spent five years of her life living in an estate, her mother a slave. Her mother had been Graced, a Gray, but she'd also been a gambler. Olive had gotten her mother out of trouble more times than she could count; making people forget Garnet Martell had owed them any money at all. But she hadn't been there the last time; the time that a vampire had won so much that Garnet had been forced into slavery, taking a ten-year-old Olive with her.

And then, after five years of being beaten and bitten and touched in a way a child shouldn't be touched, Olive had walked in on her mother with a vampire. She was a slave; they were there to be food. But instead of the proud figure Olive had fantasized about in her mind, her mother had been nothing more than a moaning, panting whore, begging for the vampire to fuck her. For all four of the vampires in the room to use her.

Olive had suffered for her mother; been exposed to the bombardment of others' voices, to the point where sometimes she didn't know who she was. She'd had no childhood; knowing things far beyond her years. And all she had wanted to do was protect the woman who had failed her so many times. Hiding in the shadows, Olive had heard the vampires' and her mother's thoughts. Had seen how her mother had really just been a bit-ridden slut. Graceds couldn't get *physically* addicted, but they could still mentally crave the bite. Her mother had loved being bitten, loved the high. And she had suspected that one of the vampires was interfering with her daughter, but hadn't wanted it stopped, because it might have meant that she could get sent to a wolf estate where there would be no bite.

So Olive had watched. And when all four vampires had strangely lost control, draining her mother to death, ripping her apart in a frenzy, Olive hadn't shed a tear. Instead, she'd packed her bags and left. After all, you couldn't track a child who had a new surname and a face no one could ever remember.

"How are you, Olive?" Viktor Kipling asked, drawing her from her memories.

Viktor was an ally of sorts – she ran an employment agency for servants and sold slaves at horrendously expensive rates to vampire estates. But then again, slaves were never cheap. And Viktor was a somewhat prolific customer. He had a taste for death that was unusual for a city vampire. They normally tried to pretend they were more than just bloodsuckers, with their fancy clothes and social rules and regulations. They played at being human. At being humane.

Step outside the city and it was a completely different story.

"Well," Olive replied. "How may I help?"

"I need a personal servant for my son," Viktor said.

His desk was made of a dark, shiny wood that was clearly expensive. As were all the fixtures and fittings in this room. But the thing Olive coveted the most were the skulls on one of the bookshelves. They would not have been easy to come by – at least, not the vampire or were examples.

"I thought he was averse to having a personal servant," Olive replied. She had tried to hire out a Graced servant to Viktor for his son two times previously. As yet, she hadn't managed to secure a spy in the Wintermere household.

It wasn't for lack of trying.

"I have been thinking about your last proposition. All your servants are extremely well-trained. I think his protests will subside when he sees how much a personal servant can…assist in one's life."

Olive tried to not appear as pleased as she was. Viktor had asked for something she had been prepared to force on him.

She now had even more reason to want a spy living in this estate. Two Graced women were dead; both from being Chosen. One only just discovered yesterday. She knew without any doubt that Annabel had been killed by Dante Kipling, but the second girl had been dumped in the Thyme. She suspected he was behind that death, too. She wanted him watched. His fascination for Graced women could simply be a fetish, or something worse. After all, some vampires knew about Graceds, but not Viktor. He suspected she was more than she appeared, but there were only a handful of records that actually spoke of Graceds. And he wasn't powerful enough to own them.

"I have the perfect servant. However, I don't want them to become bit-ridden, so I would appreciate it if your son does not bite her. Or offer to Choose her – she has family obligations that she cannot shirk," Olive said.

"We could have a trial period. Can you guarantee she will work out?" Viktor asked.

"I will send a family member to attend to this. Say two weeks?" Olive suggested.

CHAPTER SEVENTEEN

"Your grandmother isn't very happy at the moment."

Elle looked up from the kitchen table and the sandwich she'd been eating. Her mother, Melissande Brown, was standing just inside the stone doorway. She was one of the most beautiful women Elle had ever seen. Naturally, Elle looked nothing like her. Oh, you could see the resemblance when they stood in exactly the same pose wearing the same expressions, but that was where it ended. Melissande's pale blonde hair was upswept in a bun, accentuating high cheekbones and a straight nose. Classic, Elle thought, that was what you would call her mother's appearance.

"Gran is rarely happy," Elle said in response. She took another bite of her cold meat and cheese concoction.

"That is true." Her mother cracked a thin smile.

Melissande was broken, Elle knew. Gran had long ago beaten and bent her spirit and no one could fix her.

Her mother took a few steps into the kitchen before she seemed to shake herself. Grabbing the kettle, she added some coals to the stove, filled the metal boiler with water and set it to heat.

"What is she *un*happy about this time?" Elle asked.

Her mother sat down at the table with a sigh and the scent of roses. It reminded Elle of Clay, the asshole. According to him, Elle smelled like violets. So her whole family stank like flowers, did they?

"Graceds are being murdered."

Elle jerked in her seat and nearly dropped her sandwich.

"What?"

She'd only heard about one Graced death. She'd seen the body herself.

People – humans – were always being murdered. They killed each other or vampires and weres killed them. Sometimes Graceds got caught in the crossfire, but normally the victims were just humans. Nons. There weren't any strict laws about murder – but there were huge death penalties to pay to the family, if the culprit was found. Most vampires thought they'd get away with it, and they did. For the humans who were stupid enough to kill, they generally ended up in the clink because they couldn't afford the death pension. And then they were sold off as slaves. Elle had only escaped the same fate because they hadn't known who had dealt the final death blow, when the vampire had tried to abduct Emmie.

The kettle let out a shrill whistle and Melissande stood. She made herself a cup of tea, the lemon scent strong in the still kitchen air. Sitting back down, her mother held the chipped mug between both hands. Elle found herself staring at the cup. They had plenty of mugs and cups that weren't chipped, but none of those had been made by a five-year-old Elle who had thought that bright colors meant better quality work. It touched her to see that her mother still used it; that she chose it in preference to all the others they had.

"Two women so far," Melissande said.

The heart-pounding worry subsided. "Just two?"

Her mother nodded, her face impassive. "Both by vampires."

"Really?" Graceds had hidden from vampires in plain sight for thousands of years. The two deaths were probably just coincidence. Although Elle had had her suspicions about the body from the river.

Anyway, it *had* to be coincidence. Their survival depended on it. Emmie's survival did.

Melissande nodded.

"How did they kill them? Who died?" Elle realized that she hadn't finished her sandwich, but she wasn't feeling hungry anymore.

"Annabel White and Mala Kite."

Elle frowned. "Annabel was a vampire whore."

She'd never liked Annabel, but she hadn't wished her dead. She might have hoped that the woman's hair might fall out or that she'd suddenly get ugly, sure, but never dead. Emotional blackmail had been a hobby for Annabel; being a full-time bitch had been normal. Elle figured the world was probably better off without her. She was guessing that Mala was the woman Elle had found at the Thyme.

"Annabel died during the Change."

Elle blinked. "She asked to be *Chosen*?"

"Your gran doesn't think so. That's why she thinks it was murder," Melissande said.

Elle shook her head. "Murder implies that the vampire would *know* that Annabel or Mala wouldn't make it."

Dreamy Blue eyes focused on Elle sharply and it made her wonder what her mother would have been capable of, had she not been born to Gran. "That's true."

"And if they *knew* Annabel or Mala couldn't survive the Change, then it means they might know that there's something different about Graceds." Elle began picking at her bread.

"That's what your gran is worried about."

"Do they think it was the same vampire who tried both Choosings?" Elle asked.

"Yes, and your gran thinks she knows who it was."

Elle winced. She wouldn't want to be on Gran's bad side – being on her good side was uncomfortable enough – and she almost felt sorry for the vampire who'd decided that Graceds were attractive potential friends.

"And," her mother said, "she wants you to look into it."

"Huh?"

"She says you're perfect for the job."

"Perfect? She thinks I'm useless."

Melissande shrugged.

CHAPTER EIGHTEEN

Dante pinched the bridge of his nose between his forefinger and thumb. He was the same as he was yesterday, and all the yesterdays before that, so why was it happening?

"So, you're coming to the ball?" Misty asked.

Why did his father suddenly *like* him?

Dante looked over at his sister, who was dressed in a white ball gown covered with yards and yards of handmade lace and little sparkling stones. He mentally shook his head at the sheer cost of the dress, then realized he'd temporarily forgotten about his plight.

"No, I'm not going. I just thought I'd dress up like a fool for the sake of it."

"What did Father threaten you with?" Misty chuckled and ran her hands over her gown. She seemed to be admiring the way the material felt, but she could just be doing it to see if she looked fat. He didn't know.

Dante turned toward the mirror on his dressing chamber's wall and examined his reflection. Everything was in place; his cravat was suitably snowy and his jacket was a deep black without a hint of lint; ready to attend the Baron of Gloster's annual ball. He looked moronic.

"Nothing," Dante admitted. He turned away from the mirror and then strode toward the door.

"Nothing?" Misty's face was a comical mask of confusion.

"Father *asked* me to go," Dante said.

Her hand went to flick her hair over her shoulder, but froze when she remembered that her hair was swept up in a pile of curls. "He just asked?"

"Yes." Dante opened the door.

"And you said yes?"

Dante held out his hand for her to follow. She took his arm, which wasn't his intention, but he shrugged to himself and shut the door behind them. The stone hallway was free of slaves, but plenty of servants quietly moved about their tasks.

"Was there another response to give?" Dante asked.

He led Misty down the hall and into the "family area," where the rough stone walls gave way to polished red marble floors, and white marble walls. Dante paused when they reached the top of the central staircase, and then led Misty down.

"Well?"

Misty started. "Sorry?"

"Was there another response to give Father when he asked if I was going to the ball?"

Ignoring the servants staring at them – as if they'd never seen Dante dressed for a ball before, which they probably hadn't – Dante continued down the stairs and toward his fate. Thinking back to his earlier annoyance, he sighed to himself. Why had his father suddenly taken an interest in him? Why? He was the same today as two years ago, when his father had declared that Dante was a waste of space and should have been strangled at birth. Either way, Dante was suddenly as popular as the skulls in his father's study and it was uncomfortable.

"I would have thought you'd try to come up with some excuse," Misty said.

Normally, he would have. But he was suspicious of his father's sudden interest in him – in his apparent acceptance of his eccentricities. It was true that Dante was trying harder than usual to be more satisfactory to his parent, but in times past when he'd done the same, he had received a cool response. *Now* it was adequate? He somewhat doubted that.

It may have something to do with Dante Choosing the whore,

but he wasn't entirely sure why that would have made a difference.

Forcing a smile, Dante handed his sister to a waiting footman, walked out the front door and climbed up the stairs of his waiting carriage.

◆

"Son," Viktor said and thumped a hand down on Dante's shoulder. "How are you?"

Dante fought the urge to shrug his father's hand off and attempted a small smile. How was he meant to respond to that? He had seen his father four hours ago at the town estate. It wasn't as if his health was delicate. He was a vampire, for blood's sake.

"Fine, and you?"

"Excellent!" With his free hand, the earl grabbed a glass of red wine from a tray being carried around by a passing waiter and took a sip.

Dante stood with his father uncomfortably, wishing he was elsewhere, but there was really nowhere else at a ball he'd rather be. He found cards too easy and billiards weren't exactly a titillating sport. Eyeing the other ball-goers provided some entertainment, but he didn't really understand their social interactions. Did the fact that the red-haired Countess Bothrey was hanging off the arm of some young human man indicate that she wanted to have sex with him? Or was she merely being polite? Or did she just want to eat him?

"Do you see anything you like?" his father asked.

Dante blinked. "Like?"

"To marry?" His father's smile was genial.

Dante swallowed. "Marry?"

"Isn't that why you Chose that girl?"

And now the stake falls, Dante thought. He hedged, "I had developed a special regard for her."

"Since you are finally growing up, I thought you might be willing to look more broadly for a wife. Choosing someone is all well and good, but they can't have children." Viktor removed his hand from Dante's shoulder.

"I don't need to have children." He hoped that his nearly choking on the word "children" hadn't been too obvious.

"No?" His father's voice was smooth and Dante flicked a glance at his face. Impassive. The slight arch of an eyebrow.

"Misty's children will inherit the earldom, won't they?" Dante asked.

Viktor finished his glass of wine and flicked his fingers in the direction of a servant. A man dressed in black and white appeared at the earl's side and held out a tray for Viktor to put his used glass on. His father did so and promptly ignored the man, who left without looking backward. The human was clearly used to dealing with vampires, and he wasn't really of any use to Dante. He had brown eyes.

"They will inherit the earldom, provided she has any. Although, the rate she is going," his father slanted a look at him, "she probably won't."

Dante looked across the ballroom at his sister, who was flirting with every male within a five-yard radius, and some females. She sparkled – thanks to the gown – and she seemed to draw eyes without having to try. Her admirers were a mix of human and vampire.

"Why don't you think she'll have children?" Dante asked. Misty may have the morals of an alley cat, but she understood responsibility.

Viktor shook his head. "She deliberately picks men to flirt with who are completely inappropriate."

"But she doesn't have to pick someone appropriate, unless she marries."

Vampire women didn't have to marry to produce legitimate offspring; any child they bore would be legitimate because there was no doubt that *her* blood ran through the child's veins. For a male, they had to have either a contract or a marriage to produce legitimate children; double standards, but there was still a possibility that male heirs could be cuckoos in the nest.

It contrasted with the fact that human women were expected

to marry or have a contract for legitimate offspring, just the same as for males. No double standard there, Dante thought, which was stupid in this instance. Although, the fact that humans and vampires could marry even though no children would ever be produced was just idiotic. Politics.

"I don't want some inferior vampire siring my grandchildren." Viktor glared at him.

Dante smothered the urge to chuckle. Then why did his father want *him* to have children?

Realizing he'd been quiet a little too long, Dante said, "But they will have your blood."

His father's glare lessoned in intensity. "True."

"And Misty isn't the type who could be comfortably...married." Not with the way she worked her way through the slaves, servants, visitors and strangers on the street. No man would tolerate the infidelity, no matter that she was the one with a title. Not even a human would. And she wouldn't be able to get rid of a husband without causing a scandal and a half.

Viktor raised an eyebrow. "Also true." The earl's eyes were still on his daughter, Dante saw. "You are both past your second century of life–"

Only just in my case, Dante thought. And Misty, well, she was four hundred years old.

"–and I want you to start thinking about the future. You may just be an Honorable, but your blood is my blood. You need to make a good alliance. Marriage is a must for you. You cannot expect that Misty will take care of you forever."

It suddenly fell into place, and it was all so simple, really. His father wanted him gone; if Dante married, he would become someone else's burden, someone else's financial rock to bear. Someone else's embarrassment. If Dante Chose someone, then they were *his* responsibility. His *family's* responsibility. The earl must want to prevent Dante from looking among humans for a mate; but he was clearly pleased that Dante had finally started to search. It meant that he could get rid of his son in a socially pleasant manner.

Although, Viktor didn't know that marriage wasn't what Dante had had in mind for the women he'd Chosen.

Love was a fable.

Sex was rather, well, messy.

And children were frightening.

Dante turned to his parent and smiled, one corner of his mouth turning upward. "I will start thinking, Father. I promise."

CHAPTER NINETEEN

"I just need you to have a look around," Elle muttered to herself. Those were the words that Gran had said to her earlier that morning.

Pausing in her perusal of the stone-walled room, Elle thought back to the conversation. After speaking with her mother, Elle had received a summons from Gran. She'd gone there, after checking on Emmie, to be told that she'd just had the most fortunate luck of being employed by the Earl of Wintermere, as a servant for his son, the Honorable Dante Kipling.

"No way, Gran," Elle had said.

"You're worried about Esmeralda." Gran hadn't been asking a question, Elle gathered. She was about to play her trump card. "Esmeralda won't have to come here while you're on this assignment. It's only for a couple of weeks. She'll be safe at home or at school. It isn't like I can do anything with the child anyway."

There'd been a lot of bitterness in the last sentence. Part of Elle wanted to tell Gran that Emmie did have talent – that she was special – that it didn't matter what Gran did, Emmie was never going to develop telepathy. But she couldn't betray Emmie's trust like that.

"But if you refuse to do this, I will make the child come here every day; rain, hail or shine, and I will make her life a misery. Is that clear?" There hadn't been any emotion in Gran's eyes. They'd been cold.

And Elle had truly hated her.

"Fine." Elle had turned to walk out, not waiting for Gran to dismiss her, but she'd spun around again, just before the exit. "I'm only doing it for two weeks, no more. I'm not quitting my job at the Guards, and it's all the time I can get off." She'd taken a step closer, her voice dropping. "If Emmie comes to any harm while I'm away – if any vampire or wolf takes her, or *you* hurt her – I'm going to hold you responsible. I don't care if we're blood; I will come after you and you *will* pay."

It had been rather melodramatic, Elle reflected, staring blankly at the stone wall in front of her. But she'd do it again, and she *would* hold Gran responsible. Gran must have believed Elle, because she hadn't said a word. She'd actually gone a little pale and had left her mouth hanging open like a fish. Elle had spun around, stormed out of the room and slammed the door behind her. She'd also punched Bjorn in the face on her way out.

Overall, she thought, rubbing red knuckles, it had been a productive morning. And now it was time to be productive here. Blinking away her thoughts, she returned to examining the room. A steel worktable stood poised in the center, looking more like something from a morgue than an apparatus in a science lab, which she supposed this room was meant to be.

A couple of steps forward took her to the stone bench that lined one wall. A cupboard was propped near the door, heavy steel and locked. She could pick the mechanism, but she didn't know if it would be worth it – or if she had the time.

The sound of the door grating made her jump. She grabbed the handle of the broom she'd kept close by and started industriously sweeping the floor, not that there was any dust on it. A man entered the room, rubbing his hands together while he appeared focused on something that wasn't in front of him. When he spotted her, he nearly shot to the roof in surprise. Literally. Elle had to admit she was a little envious of that ability.

Realizing that she was staring and that servants probably didn't stare at their vampire masters, she dropped her eyes to her broom and began thinking fast. She'd seen this vampire before, on the street. His eyes were a bright violet, so he was probably born, not made, because there wasn't a lot of red to the color. His black hair was tied back, but it would be long, she'd bet on it. He was also tall, taller than her, which didn't happen too often with humans; they rarely had the money to eat properly. And he was drop dead gorgeous; amazingly pretty – the most handsome guy she'd ever laid eyes on.

Although, if she had to pick, she'd choose Clay.

She froze. No, she didn't just think that.

"Are you quite done?" The voice was smooth and deep with no inflection.

Elle snapped her eyes up to the vampire standing in the room with her. His expression was unnerving, almost like being caught in the stare of a snake.

"Sorry…sir?" She only just managed to tack the title on afterward.

"You seem to have been sweeping that bit of floor for a while now. I am sure it is as dust free as possible."

It almost sounded like he was smiling at her, but when she flicked a glance at his face, there was no expression there whatsoever. Just blankness. *What a cold fish*, she thought.

"Sorry, sir." She held the broom close to her side, ducked around the stainless steel bench and out the door. She felt a blush dusting her cheeks and didn't know if it was real or not. Whether her maid persona was embarrassed or whether *she* was embarrassed – because she'd been comparing Mr. Too-Pretty with Mr. Drop-Dead-Gorgeous.

I'm an idiot, she thought.

She didn't see the vampire staring after her as she walked down the hall.

◆

Dante's eyes followed the servant as she ventured away from his workroom. She almost…strutted, with that broom hooked to her side. He shut the door and pressed his back to the heavy steel. It was the girl from the street, he was sure of it. The one who'd caught his interest. He'd forgotten about her; about the shock of red hair and those hazel eyes.

There had been too many failed experiments, and the uncomfortable navigation of social niceties since he'd spotted her. Dante liked to think he would have remembered her eventually, but he wouldn't have known how to find her when he did anyway. He couldn't afford to call attention to himself, not when his father was eyeing him with parental zeal.

The servant hadn't seemed at ease around him, nervous almost. Her pulse rate had accelerated and blood had rushed to her cheeks. But then, a lot of humans weren't comfortable around vampires. They were either excited or afraid. Dante could normally understand the latter; he could barely tolerate the former.

Could he take the servant as a "mistress"? Was it too soon after the whore? Was there an expected grieving period for vampires who lost a pet – a human? Why was everything so complicated?

And worst of all, how was he meant to convince the human girl he wanted to have sex with her?

CHAPTER TWENTY

"You positively *reek* of vampires."

Elle froze halfway through stripping off her homespun shirt in the darkness. Dropping her arms to her sides in surprise, her crappy shirt fell back into place. Warm breath tickled her neck, and she could hear someone *sniff* her. Panicking, she sent her fist sharply into the intruder's gut, before slamming the palm of her other hand into the man's face.

"Will you quit it?" Strong hands pinned her arms to her sides. "It's just me. Clay." He smiled; she could see the flash of white in the darkness.

"Oh, what big shiny teeth you have," Elle mumbled.

"Will you stop trying to do me bodily harm?"

"What are you doing here?" she demanded. When he didn't reply, she growled, "*Wolf.*"

"You stink."

"You already said that," she muttered.

"You calmer now?" he asked.

"Fine. Yes. Now go away."

"Come now, is that any way to treat a guest?" A match flared to life as Clay lit one of the lamps next to her bed. He looked good. The bastard always seemed to look good. He was wearing his buckskins and shirt again, and his hair was tied back, but he somehow managed to appear as handsome as any lord she'd ever seen, excepting Mr. Beauty.

"Most guests don't tend to break into their hosts' homes."

Clay ignored her jibe. "How's the shoulder? You didn't seem to have too much trouble just then." He rubbed his stomach.

By the blood, he was well built.

Tearing her eyes away from his body, Elle frowned and rubbed her shoulder in remembered pain. "It's feeling better."

"How…informative." Clay sat on her bed.

"Go away."

He tilted his head to the side, his eyes like molten gold. Why was it so hard to stay unaffected by him? Weres and vamps were generally good-looking. It was part of what they were; they needed to attract prey. She'd *seen* more than enough handsome examples of both races, but for some reason this irritating sod was the only one she couldn't get out of her mind. Or room.

She strode over to the window. "I swear I locked that."

"Oh, well, what's a lock between friends?"

Turning back, she saw Clay flick his ponytail over his shoulder. Like a girl. She huffed out a short laugh.

"What?" Eyes wide, he held a hand over his heart.

"You are utterly ridiculous, you know that?" Elle found herself sitting down on her bed next to him.

Clay frowned, all traces of affectation gone. "Why do you smell like a vampire?"

He keeps going on about that, Elle thought. She caught herself as she went to sniff the collar of her scratchy shirt. "No reason."

He leaned forward and sniffed her. "Thanks," she muttered, hunching down on herself.

Clay fingered the material of her shirt. His voice was sharp and intense. "You've been in one of their estates. Why would you do something so stupid?"

"Work."

"You have a job already; you don't have to work in one of those places."

Elle just shook her head. "Go away."

◆

Clay tried to fight the scowl he knew was coming, but lost. "Are you crazy?" He grabbed Elle by her shoulders. Too late, he remembered her injury and released his grip, but she looked more pissed off than hurt.

"Go away."

"You say that a lot," Clay sniped. Really, couldn't she get the hint that he wasn't going to go anywhere? Not when she was so bloody interesting. And he hadn't met an interesting woman – scratch that, *person* – in centuries. It's what made Elle so irresistible; she was a cranky puzzle he wanted to solve. And she had some of the sexiest legs he'd ever seen.

"That's because I'd like you to *go away*. It's not a hard concept to follow." One eyebrow was arched.

"I thought you worked with the City Guard. It's not exactly a brilliant career choice, but for someone with your temper, it's ideal. Why'd you quit that for an estate job?" He put a palm on her forehead, pretending to feel for a temperature. "You have a fever or something?"

She snorted and stood. "What do you know about my temper?"

"Far too much." He widened his eyes in mock alarm as he ducked the fist she sent at his head.

"Go flirt with someone else. I want to go to sleep."

Clay smiled, wickedly. "But I had so many other things planned."

"Out!"

Clay stood and backed toward the window. "I'm going, I'm going."

But I'll be back, he thought.

Chapter Twenty-One

Dante tried not to stare at the servant. She seemed to know he was looking at her though, because she kept sneaking peeks at him through her hideous mob cap's fringe whenever his gaze fell upon her. Which occurred all too frequently for the mere interest a master would show a servant.

It was rather like bad choreography.

The whole situation was just plain stupid. Curling his lip, Dante sat at his workbench and pretended to study a slide and its droplet of blood. The small label had cramped, spidery handwriting that said "Sample G, Pure." He had the lamps shining brightly, more for the servant's sake than his, but he didn't want her getting close enough to read his writing. Dante was *trying* to be courteous, but had the servant thanked him? No. So, in revenge, he'd asked her to polish the stainless steel bench. "I want it to shine," had been his instructions.

Why did he have to try and pretend he'd fallen in love with a human, anyway? Or that he lusted after one enough to Choose them? Why couldn't he just say that he wanted to? It wasn't like vampires had to *fear* what humans thought about them. There may be fewer vampires in the vampire to human ratio, but one vampire was the equivalent of ten humans. There wasn't any need to give a shit about them and their petty lives.

Father, however, insisted they must. "Humans make our clothes, mine our coal, and build our homes. We have to pretend we actually care about them and their lives."

Unfortunately, Dante couldn't find fault with the argument. But he didn't like it. Who would care if he did manage to turn a colored-eyed human into a vampire, anyway? Shouldn't the human be joyous? They'd be immortal, for blood's sake! And strong, and fast. Those perks should be enough to make anyone happy. He'd never met a Chosen human who wasn't satisfied with their lot in life.

Then again, he'd never met a human who could hold a decent conversation. Like now, with this servant; she hadn't said more than "Morning, sir." Even that had seemed a challenge. She hadn't even responded to his polite enquiry as to the state of her health. Wasn't that how humans greeted each other? It didn't bode well for her mental acumen, he decided, and she seemed, rather, well, muscular. She had short hair, features that could cut glass and she wasn't very feminine. Well, not feminine according to aristo standards. Maybe commoners had a different view. Maybe she only liked women? That would make things a little bit more difficult. Or maybe she was just one of those humans who was all about the physical side of life, rather than the intellectual. How was he meant to pretend love and lust for *that*?

So far, her packaging and personality seemed a rather large waste for such an extraordinarily interesting eye color.

"The bench is finished, sir."

Dante turned away from the microscope, swiveling slowly on his chair to face the girl. She stood by the bench, hands folded primly in front of her, head downturned. He focused on the object of her work. It was definitely shiny, not enough that he could see his reflection, but then, he hadn't asked for that. Maybe he should be more specific in future.

Pinching the bridge of his nose, he sighed. He'd never had a personal servant before. He wasn't really sure he knew what to do with one. He knew what *other* vampires did with their personal staff, and he knew he'd have to pretend interest in her because of it – and it would help his cause, after all – but why did his father have to hire one *now*?

Ugh.

"Excellent," Dante said and tried to smile in a pleasant manner. "Now come here."

◆

That guy gives me the creeps, Elle thought.

Walking back down the cold stone hallway, which was barely lit by yellow lamps, Elle clutched a few polishing rags and her cleaning products to her chest. She wanted to know why Gran hadn't assigned a Green to this case. They could have read the creepy bastard's mind in a few minutes flat and then Elle wouldn't have had to put up with his stupid orders and his even dumber attempts at seduction.

"Come here," she muttered sarcastically. Apparently that – and a toothy I'm-a-hunk smile – was all that a woman needed to get turned on. The idiot. She'd had to make some excuse about feeling faint due to human female problems, and almost bolted for it.

What Elle hadn't realized before, and what Gran hadn't bothered to tell her, was that personal servants were really low-paid whores. Half of the ones she'd seen here were low-paid *bit-ridden* whores, which was even worse. Of course, Elle thought, Gran wouldn't have bothered to mention *that*.

There's no way I would have agreed, Elle thought, *Emmie or no Emmie*. Elle would have found a way to protect her sister, without bothering with this farce, she knew it.

No point in crying over spilt milk, she told herself. Or spilt blood, as the case may be. Reaching the top of the servants' stairs, Elle carefully navigated her way down. If the halls were poorly lit, the stairs were even worse. It was almost as if the bloody leeches wanted someone to trip and break their neck. Freezing, her foot hovering over one stair, she blinked in comprehension. Two realizations in five minutes, she'd better be careful, she thought with a chuckle. Mirth disappearing, she frowned down at the stairs. She knew with a gut-churning certainty that the leeches wanted someone to trip and fall. Servants weren't free game when it came to dinner time – not draining-to-death free game, anyway. They could do that to their slaves, but slaves weren't as healthy, weren't as appetizing. At least not the ones kept on this estate, mangy bit-ridden creatures that they were.

Shaking her head, Elle continued her downward journey. Now, she just had to try and evade the Creep's advances.

♦

"I want you to keep an eye on my son," Lord Kipling said.

Elle was standing in his office, her eyes on the floor. When she'd first entered the masculine room – it was overly manly; dark colors, lots of wood, heavy furniture, almost like it was compensating for something, she thought – she'd realized that the man on the other side of the desk was an older, rougher replica of the Creep. But the Creep was prettier, much prettier.

"Yes, milord." Elle bobbed a curtsy. *I'm the Creep's bloody servant, isn't it my job to keep an eye on him?* And she'd already had this chat with the housekeeper. Why was it being rammed home? Was it even normal for the master of the house to want to speak to a servant?

"Your grandmother recommended you personally," Kipling continued as Elle fought the urge to jerk and glare at him. Barely. "And I don't want to regret hiring you, as I'm quite partial to Mrs. Brown and her agency always makes excellent recommendations."

It went unspoken that he was partial to her for a human. For now.

Gran *knew* Kipling?

Gran spoke to him *personally*?

A work relationship, it had to be. Although selling Nons to vampires wasn't exactly morally clean. But this was just getting stranger and stranger. Gran was meant to hate vampires and weres more than anyone else she knew. She'd taught Elle to hate them. Gran was a purist – she'd kicked Elle's mother out of home since she'd had her first child with a Non, and because that child hadn't grown out of her Hazel eyes. Now Gran was out socializing with a leech?

She was beginning to like her gran less than ever, which she hadn't thought possible. Hate, was, after all, hate.

"I will keep an eye on him, sir," Elle said into the quiet.

"Please tell me if he shows any preference for humans with…unusual features."

Was that his father's way of making sure that Dante wasn't into guys? Elle didn't think she was on the same page. A guy liking another guy wasn't exactly unusual.

"In what way, sir?" Elle asked.

In her peripheral vision she saw him slash a hand through the air. "Skin color, eye color…"

In other words, eye color. In Pinton, there was no such thing as "unusual colored skin," as everyone was varying hues of white or brown. Some, like Mikael, were so dark as to be a shade of night.

"I see."

"Excellent. I want you to report to me once a day." Kipling flicked a hand at her dismissively.

Elle turned to leave, but was forestalled by his voice. "Also, please tell me if he tries – or, in fact, does – have intercourse with you." *Personal* servant, she thought.

She nodded then quickly left the room.

What was going on in this house?

CHAPTER TWENTY-TWO

Clay was waiting for the human – Elle – to arrive home. He was stretched out comfortably on her bed, hands tucked behind his head, shirt half-buttoned and legs crossed at the ankles. She'd left the window locked again, silly chit. Even if she'd hammered it shut, he still would have worked out a way to get in. Just to piss her off. He smiled.

Clay wasn't really sure when he'd decided that seducing the girl would be a good idea – considering his first thought had been that it would be too much work – but he'd apparently made the choice without consulting his brain. Every time he thought about bedding her, he got hard; it was a little embarrassing. He hadn't been this keen on a woman in a century or three. Maybe even a millennium or three. To his shame, he couldn't get her out of his head.

Having sex with her was a terrible idea, really.

I mean, he thought, *screwing Olive Brown's eldest granddaughter?* The one who the grumpy old bitch clearly wanted him to keep clear of? Although, his plan hinged on Elle actually letting him seduce her, and that was still touch and go. Originally, he'd thought his extra interest in the redhead had been inspired by his need to irritate her grandmother, but he'd recognized that his desire for Elle had sprung up independently. The tent in his trousers attested to it.

He wasn't really sure *why* Olive didn't want him to know of this granddaughter; shame was at the top of his guess list, but that could change. A Hazel meant that someone had mated with an ordinary human – with a Brown. And that that someone had wanted to bear the child, would have ignored all advice to the contrary and given birth. It meant that Elle's mother, Melissande, had loved the father, something that Olive would have been furious about, he knew.

Why were humans so predictable?

He figured that was part of the reason why he liked the redhead so much. She left him guessing more often than not. Telling him to get out, and then kissing him back. Telling him to leave, and then talking to him like a friend. Hating him while liking him. Her contrariness just made him grin.

But Clay wasn't dumb. He knew that the only reason Elle tolerated him was because she wasn't entirely sure that he was interested in the little girl. But he wasn't. He was no pedophile, and while she had pretty eyes, she wasn't really his concern. No matter what her grandmother wanted him to do in a few years' time. Clay had seen plenty of people with nice eyes in his lifetime, and one child was just that, a child. He'd come to this stinkhole of a city to see what Olive Brown had been after; he didn't hold her in any great regard, but he'd been interested to hear what the Graced matriarch had wanted from a rogue like himself. And he'd found out.

He almost wished he hadn't.

Most Graceds couldn't breed with vampires or wolves. There needed to be a lot of luck – or an excellent knowledge of their genealogy – involved. Clay guessed that Olive had the latter. And most mixes didn't survive childhood; infant mortality was high, and so were the "accidental" deaths. Clay knew. He'd spent years hunting the half-breeds – or dhampirs – down and helping them, trying to find them a place in the world where they'd be accepted for who and what they were. But he hadn't seen a dhampir survive to adulthood in centuries. They'd been brutally wiped out, the hatred a remnant of the Civil War that had occurred thousands of years ago. The murderers probably didn't even realize *why* they were told to make the killings, just that they did.

But Clay knew why. And he used to return the favor.

The sound of the door opening jolted Clay out of his musings. He started to grin, a sleazy expression he knew would make Elle want to hit him.

"I know you're there," Elle said. Her voice was low and she sounded tired.

Clay's smile wilted as he lit the lamp next to the bed. He studied her, noting the wan face and droopy eyes. She also stank of vampire, more so than yesterday. It made his fingers itch.

"That vampire get handsy with you?" he asked, surprised at his own growled words.

Elle flicked a glance at him as she dumped her bag on the floor. "He tried to, but he wasn't very good at it."

Clay blinked, distracted. "A vampire who isn't good at getting into a human's pants?"

Elle slumped onto the end of the bed, rubbing her neck as she did so. "No. He really is rather bad at it. You can tell his heart's just not in it."

"His *heart* shouldn't be the organ involved in wanting to get into your pants." Clay waggled his eyebrows. Elle thumped him in the side.

Propping himself up on one elbow, he stared at her, serious. "Are you a *personal* servant?"

Elle's shoulders drooped. "Yes."

"And you didn't let him into your pants?"

"No."

"Why not?" Clay tried to tell himself that he wouldn't care if she slept with anyone, but the burning feeling in his gut told him that would be a lie.

"I don't like vampires."

"Or werewolves." Clay saw the lightning glance she shot his way.

"Most of them," she muttered.

"But I'm the exception to the rule?" He grinned at her and hooked his hands behind his head, leaning back to lie on her bed.

"Not really."

He loved her attitude. Tilting his head to the side, he frowned. She looked beyond tired. *Too bad*, he thought. *I'm not.*

He raised an eyebrow at her. "Just like my pretty face, huh?"

Clay meant it as a joke, but he felt a little uneasy when Elle looked at him. Her eyes were intense, more Green than Brown in the dim light.

"Yeah, I like your face." She moved closer to him then reached out a hand, touching the stubble on his cheek.

Clay shut his eyes, feeling her fingers move toward his mouth. She ran a gentle thumb over his lips. He reached a hand upward and grasped her wrist, pulling her toward him. Eyes now open, he used his other hand to cup her neck, pressing her face closer. He kissed her, tasting her soft lips, the sigh of air as she exhaled. She really was gorgeous, with her fierce face and luminous hair. It began gently, but it didn't take long for hunger to overcome sense, and he flipped her beneath him on the bed, hands roaming, mouth demanding.

She matched him though, her hunger as great as his own. As his fingers fisted in the material of her shirt, she pulled away from him. "Don't rip it."

Panting, lying on top of her, he nearly moaned. She had stopped him to tell him not to rip her crummy shirt? "I'll buy you a new one."

She chuckled, a breathy sound. "It's my work uniform."

"Just get rid of it," he groaned.

Thankfully, she complied. Her breastband quickly followed, and he was left staring at the two most perfect breasts he'd ever seen. Firm, high and tipped in a pale pink blush. He had to touch them, taste them. Leaning down, he ran the tip of his tongue around an erect nipple. By the blood, he was harder than a rock.

Elle arched beneath him, and he took the unspoken invitation. His hand closed over her left breast while he sucked on her right. Her head rolled back on the pillow and she sighed. After he'd treated her other breast to the same attention, she grabbed his hair in a tight grip and jerked his head up. She kissed him, openmouthed, hungry.

Clay growled and began kissing a line down her throat. "You had better not say no," he warned, "or tell me to get out."

"Don't worry," she gasped as his tongue traced her navel. "I won't."

CHAPTER TWENTY-THREE

She smelled like werewolf.

Dante didn't think any other vampire – or were – would be able to detect the odor, but they weren't cursed with his "delicate" senses. The overpowering scent of soap clung to the servant's skin, but it didn't quite erase the smell she was obviously trying to hide.

Dante was seated on the chair in his workroom. He'd been facing the bench and the microscope, but had turned around when the servant had entered, in an effort to be polite. But what was the point? She'd carefully rebuffed his attempt to have intercourse with her yesterday – something about female human troubles, whatever they were – not that he'd put much effort into it. But she'd then gone home to have sex with a wolf.

"Good morning," he said.

"Morning, sir." She bobbed him a curtsy.

For the first time, he comprehended that she didn't seem to like him very much. Because he was a vampire? Overnight, he had decided that his father had assigned her to him most likely to ensure he was sexually satisfied enough not to Choose any more humans. That deduction wasn't hard though; Viktor approved every servant to enter the house. Why he'd assumed that this human was Dante's "type," Dante wouldn't know. But Dante's attempts at coitus hadn't worked. Why would his father have picked a woman who would be immune to his charms? Dante almost laughed aloud at that thought. He'd never met a woman who even *liked* his charms.

"So, my father assigned you to me," Dante said. He was surprised at himself; why was he starting this conversation?

"The housekeeper assigned my role, sir." She kept her eyes on the floor, which was a shame, because they were the only interesting part about her. Her cleaning cloths were clutched in her hands.

"Look," Dante said as he stood, "I'm not in a very nice mood. Please dispense with the bullshit."

Startled, her eyes flew to meet his. *That's better*, he thought.

"My father assigned you to me, correct?"

She nodded, her cap bobbing with the movement.

"Did he tell you why?" Dante took a step closer to her and she backed away from him toward the door.

"No, sir."

Chatty, he thought. Normally he'd appreciate her muteness, but he was in the mood for answers. "What did he want you to tell him?"

She looked uneasy, but she kept quiet.

He rolled his eyes. He was going to have to get nasty. He didn't really want to, but then, what choice did he have? Maybe feeling like her life was in danger would loosen her tongue.

Another two steps took him within reaching distance, and he shot his arm out, grabbing her by the throat. Within seconds, he had her pinned to the heavy door, her feet still on the ground. He turned the key in the lock with his free hand and leaned his face in close to hers. He popped the key in his pocket.

He hoped he looked scary. "What did my father want you to tell him about me?"

Her face was turning red. "He wanted to know if we had sex."

Dante studied her; he didn't think she was telling the whole truth. She'd looked away from him as she answered. He hated not understanding how people communicated. "What else?"

She'd struggled to speak, and she'd gone a little purple in the face, so he eased his grip. She gasped, "If you were interested in people with certain physical characteristics."

Hmm, so his father hadn't been convinced by the story of love as his reason for Choosing Sandy. Dante *had* wondered why Viktor had bought that line; it appeared he hadn't. *No big loss*, he told himself. It just meant that his father wouldn't swallow the lie that Dante had managed to fall in love with his servant, either.

Time for a new plan.

"Characteristics such as eye color?" Dante asked and let go. He took a step backward.

The servant slumped down and rubbed her throat. She was staring at him like he was crazy, but there was something else there, some emotion he couldn't pinpoint. Not that he was any good at that.

"Yes, but I didn't understand why he wanted to know that."

"He didn't say anything?" Dante asked.

The girl shook her head.

"He didn't mention that I Chose anyone recently?"

Eyes wide, she shook her head again, mouth tightly closed. "No, sir."

"I wonder why?"

"Why did you Choose a human, sir? I didn't think it was very common."

Dante frowned at her question, but she was looking at the stones under her feet. "I loved her." There, that had been easy. He hadn't blinked or looked away from the girl, not that she glanced up from the floor.

"I'm sure she was beautiful."

Dante raised a brow. "Yes, she was. Did you know her? Her name was Sandy."

He saw the girl blink. "Did I know her?"

Didn't all the humans know each other? Weren't they all cousins or some such?

"Never mind."

"Did you pick your Sandy because of her eyes, sir? Is that why your father's worried?"

He resisted the urge to laugh wildly. How close this servant was to the truth! Did she know something, then?

"I just like interesting eye color, that's all." What a way to sum half a life's obsession in one sentence. Dante didn't know *why* they were different, those humans, but he knew in his gut that they were.

"So you like mine, then?" She stepped closer now; he could feel the heat emanating from her body.

"Sure." He wasn't going to tell her that he liked hers more than any other he'd found, because he thought she might be able to make the transition to vampire, and then he'd *know* why those humans were different. A thought struck him; was she trying to seduce him?

This close, the scent of werewolf was stronger. Yes, she'd definitely had sex with one. That, or they'd been wrestling without clothes on.

So why was she suddenly approaching him, when she'd rebuffed him yesterday? Uncertain, and feeling like he was missing something, he decided his first course of action was the best. Make her fearful for her life, and she might tell him what he wanted to know. Moving faster than she could follow, he picked her up and threw her down on the workbench, quickly chaining the manacles to her wrists. Her breath whooshed out and her head bounced hard off the metal benchtop. She blinked up at him, stunned. After a second or so, she jerked against her restraints.

"I'm fast. Didn't my father tell you that?"

She just stared.

Maybe Viktor didn't know. It was entirely possible; he saw his son as delicate and weak. He wouldn't have bothered to learn that Dante's extra sensitivity had extended toward speed, dexterity and strength.

"Now, I have a problem. You clearly aren't a normal *personal* servant. You were hired by my father to keep an eye on me and keep me sated, but you refuse to have sex with me and yet you put out for a werewolf." He saw her eyes widen at the last statement. "What is going on?"

"Nothing."

"Look, I have no problem killing you. It would be a waste, but

I'll do it. I'll pay the death tax to your family and that will be that."

Her eyes narrowed. "I'm a servant, I'm not a *slave*."

Dante shrugged. "Hence the death tax. Accidents happen."

"What, I tripped over and fell on your fangs?" Sarcasm dripped from each word. He realized that she was beginning to show some fire. He liked that. Perhaps she was genuinely worth his interest.

"It's been known to happen before." And he smiled a big, openmouthed smile that showed his fangs.

She swallowed and shut her eyes.

"Be careful, you don't want to hurt yourself, thinking too hard." He turned around and walked over to his stool. He dragged it closer to the bench and sat on it.

She didn't open her eyes while she spoke. "I swear I'm just a maid. Why are you convinced this is some kind of conspiracy?"

"Let me tell you a few facts about my life. One, my father hates me, but after I tried to Choose a human recently, he discovered an affection for me. I thought at first it was because he wanted to marry me off, make me someone else's burden, but now I think it's because he thought he could trick me into revealing something to him."

"Into revealing what?" She was looking at him now, her eyes wide in a pale face.

He thought about answering her. There was no harm, he decided. He was either going to kill her, or Choose her and see what happened with those interesting eyes of hers, so it didn't matter. She probably wasn't going to survive the night. Or the third night, anyway.

"This is the second fact: I'm obsessed with humans who have eye colors other than brown." There, he'd said it. The Great Shame of his life.

Her eyes opened wide. "But *why*?"

"I think they're – you're – different. I've never been able to work out how or why, as your blood is the same as any other human's, but I just *know* there's something odd. When I tried Choosing the blue-eyed human, she was quite calm, until she realized my full intention. She tried to fight me, manipulate me, but it didn't work. I wanted to try and turn her, because no one else has ever managed to. Choose a human with non-brown eyes, that is."

"That's illegal, Choosing someone against their will."

"Who are you going to tell?" Dante asked.

"Why do you even care about eye color?" she said in a strangled voice.

"Why do people study flowers or birds or anything? *Because I want to know.*"

"Why didn't you just ask?"

He laughed. "I've been asking for *years.* I'm over two centuries old, and no one has ever told me anything other than, 'You're crazy, Dante.' You think someone will suddenly agree with me, that there's some kind of…of human sub-race?"

She was so white she could pass for a corpse. "Why are you telling me all this?"

"Why are you asking?"

She stayed silent.

"You want to know." He answered for her. "I'm telling *you* because I'm going to try to Choose you."

She started fighting the bonds.

"I have a theory. I don't think non-browns can survive being Chosen, but I think *you* will, with your hazel eyes."

"If you Choose me, I'll fight you! I will kill you." The green in her eyes was glowing.

He chuckled. "That's the beauty of it. You can't. Some sort of bond springs up between the Chosen and their Chooser, and it becomes almost physically impossible for one to hurt the other. That's why it's normally lovers who Choose, because the bond sometimes ties them emotionally as well. It's not something that's advertised, and it goes beyond logic, but it's true."

"People will miss me if I don't go home."

"Who? Your werewolf lover? He won't come here looking for you; they don't like our estates. And your family? Well, we'll see."

"Fuck you!"

Dante shook his head and tsked. "Such language."

She began fighting the bonds in earnest and he chuckled. This was going to be fun – well, as much fun as he ever had. Moving closer to her, he struck, quick as a snake, and bit into her neck. She gasped, and her struggles grew weaker and weaker as he drained the blood from her, and soon she was close to unconsciousness.

He opened a gash on his wrist with a scalpel from his workbench. Holding her jaw, he dripped his blood into her open mouth. She didn't swallow, and the blood spilled, running down her cheeks. He pinched her nose and she gasped for air before choking down mouthful after mouthful of his blood.

"Good girl," he crooned. "Two more times and then we'll see if you make it."

CHAPTER TWENTY-FOUR

Clay had a bad feeling.

His gut was churning and he had a coppery taste in his mouth, which wasn't blood, but something like fear. He could almost feel trouble in the air, as if a storm was about to break. Tucking his hands back behind his head, he settled onto Elle's bed. He hadn't bothered to unbutton his shirt or attempt to look sexy. Not that he did sexy very well, not in his mind, but women seemed to think that if you sprawled over their bed, then you were trying to be sexy. He could see why they would; he *was* unfairly good-looking.

Clay grinned suddenly. No doubt Elle had adjectives other than "sexy" to describe him; "annoying" was probably at the top of the list. Although, if he was honest, the list of words that Elle would use to describe him wasn't really of concern to Clay at the moment. What *was* important was the fact that Elle hadn't locked the window. Not for two nights – well, days, but they were nights for Elle – in a row. There also happened to be the rather minor problem of her not coming home on either of those days. He could smell her absence.

Rolling over, he breathed against the pillow. It was a cold scent, one of abandonment, despite the fact that the linens still held his and Elle's odors. He had a feeling that Elle would've changed the sheets if she'd had to sleep here since their bout of passion; the smell of soap and starch should have greeted him upon his clandestine entrance.

Clay also knew that Elle hadn't come back in the early hours during the last two days, to just get changed or eat or do something, because he'd been here. He'd only left when he'd heard the others in the house stirring.

It meant that Elle was probably still at the estate.

That's what he was hoping for, anyway. Better that than her lying dead on the street, although he had the feeling that if someone was stupid enough to corner her, they'd probably end up battered and bruised, rather than the opposite way around.

The door opened suddenly and a burst of light hit him in the face, almost like a physical punch. Clay jolted upright. He mentally cursed at himself, because he hadn't heard the approaching footsteps, but then, he'd been too busy lolling around sniffing the sheets. Sitting on the edge of the bed, he shoved his hair out of his face and looked at the little girl standing silhouetted in the door frame. She carefully held a candle up and squinted into the room. Her eyes widened when she spotted him.

"You're not Elle."

Give the child a sweet, Clay thought, but he kept his mouth shut.

"Where is Elle?"

He stared at the girl – Emmie. Why wasn't she screaming, or crying out in fear at his presence in her sister's room? Was the child used to finding strange men in Elle's chamber? Used to seeing great hulking werewolves propped on her sister's bed like they belonged there?

He bloody hoped not.

He was going to have a talk to Elle when he next saw her. If he saw her. Scrap that, he thought, *when* he saw her. Clay would also have a few points to discuss with her about her just up and vanishing as well.

Emmie walked into the room, pushing the door almost closed behind her. She set the candle down on the bedside table, making sure it was well away from the edge, and hopped up onto the bed next to him. She started swinging her legs. "Your name's Clay? Elle said she wasn't sure if it was."

He nodded.

She looked down at her moving feet. Left first, then right. "I'm worried about Elle."

He didn't know what to say. "Why?"

"Because she was meant to come home." Emmie turned to look at him, her eyes bright in the dim light. She would be a beauty when she was older, he thought, once she grew into those sharp features. Just like her sister.

"Usually people stay at the estates when they work there," Clay offered. Although, he didn't believe that in this case; he just couldn't see Elle sleeping under the same roof as a vampire, not willingly. The fact that she'd had sex with him was way out of the normal behavior for her character, he knew.

Ah, his feisty redheaded racist.

"Not Elle, she asked for permission to come home. To look after me." Emmie scowled at her swinging feet.

"You don't seem to need too much looking after," Clay said. He was lying through his teeth, of course. A young child in a town full of stinky vampires? A young, *interesting* child? Hah! She'd need an army to protect her when she got older. He'd stashed his own sister on an island in the Turquoise Sea. But that wasn't what Emmie wanted – or needed – to hear.

"Elle took the job for me," Emmie blurted. Her feet stopped moving.

Clay stared at the girl. "What?"

He really wanted to know why Emmie wasn't asking him about his presence; why she just accepted him being in her house, but he knew he shouldn't interrupt her. Kids were like that; they got to the places they were going in their own time. Plus, he decided, she might just be too caught up in her concern for her sibling. It was pretty clear they loved each other; Clay would be the same over his. Blood, he *had* been. Still was, to the extent she let him.

"Elle didn't say it, but I think Gran said something mean to her about me, because I know that Elle didn't want to go to the estate and Gran really wanted her to go, but I said don't worry, it was okay, but Elle said she had to go, and I didn't want her to go–" Emmie bit back a sob.

Clay blinked and placed a hand awkwardly on the girl's shoulder. Within seconds, she had climbed onto his lap and was crying in earnest. He looked at the child in his arms bemusedly.

From stranger to comforter, Clay thought. His brief stay in this city had just gotten way more complicated than he'd thought it could get. *You should have known better than to try and climb between a half-blood's legs*, his mind said. *You* did *know better.*

"This isn't your fault," he said to the little girl and patted her on the back.

She cried harder.

"Sssh." He smoothed the hair back on her forehead. "Elle will be okay."

Emmie looked up at him, her face splotchy, eyes still running. "You don't know that."

He tried to grin then failed. "It's Elle," he said. Emmie kept her gaze on him. "She's too stubborn for something really bad to happen to her."

Chapter Twenty-Five

Dante rolled down the arm of his white shirt, careful not to get blood on it. Seeing the still-oozing gash on his arm, he decided to leave the sleeve partway up his forearm; better to be on the safe side. He'd had one too many notes from the laundress threatening to make him wash his own shirts of late; just because she'd gotten sick of cleaning the blood from his – as if he was any worse than any of the other vampires here.

Sighing, he walked over to the workbench and felt the pulse at the servant's wrist.

Nothing.

Maybe he hadn't pressed hard enough. He undid the manacle and then decided to undo them all. It wasn't like she was going to jump up and run around now, was she? He picked up her other wrist and tried again.

Nothing.

Quickly, he ripped open her cheap shirt and pressed his ear to her chest. Her skin was cold, and he couldn't feel her ribcage rising or falling. But… Ah, there it was. Very, very faint, but there.

Thump…thump…

He rocked back on his heels with a sigh of relief. She was still alive. Just, from the sounds of it, but alive anyway – that was what was important. The other two girls had been dead as soon as the third blood transfer had taken place. As long as her heart kept beating and she was breathing for the next three days, then the transformation could still take place.

Turning away from the girl, he walked over to the sink and washed his hands and face. He could feel his skin pulling at the corners of his mouth, so he figured there was dried blood there. He rubbed wet fingers against the skin, before rinsing the newer blood from his wrist. When he couldn't smell the blood as strongly, he turned off the faucet and faced the room again.

She looked dead. Dante wasn't sure that she would make it. He hoped she would.

"What in the name of–!"

Dante looked up from the girl and into his father's furious gaze. *Ah, crap.*

"Hello, Father."

Viktor took two angry strides into the room and came to an abrupt halt before the table and its occupant. He was dressed in formal attire, like he'd been preparing to go to a ball. His knee-high boots were so shiny Dante could see his face in them. His cravat was a deep red color, like the fresh blood that had just wound its way down the plughole, and was adorned with a ruby pin. He looked totally out of place.

"What in the name of blood have you done?" Viktor's eyes were glued to the girl on the table.

"I Chose her." Dante shrugged. He half-turned around and picked up a towel that was next to the sink, and began to dry his hands.

"She's dead!"

Dante focused on the servant. Objectively, he had to admit that she looked terrible. Even *he* thought she hadn't made it. Dried blood was crusted around her mouth, rusty stains adorned her throat like a macabre necklace, and her skin had the pallor of death.

"She's not dead." Dante dropped the towel back next to the sink.

His father ran a hand through his long hair, his eyes riveted on the girl. "You idiot, of *course* she's dead!"

"Of course?" There was no of course about it, Dante thought, not unless you knew she wouldn't survive. A sinking feeling took weight in his gut, but he ignored it.

"Well," his father blustered, "you can hear her heart isn't beating."

"But it is."

Viktor looked in disbelief from Dante to the servant. *He's worried*, Dante grasped, hearing his father's accelerated heartbeat. *He's actually worried the servant is dead.*

Why did his father give a single drop of blood about this human being Chosen? Especially when Viktor supposedly didn't care about humans? Dante would have to think about that later – along with the fact that his father believed that the servant wouldn't survive being Chosen. Had assumed she was dead *before* he'd taken the time to listen for a heartbeat.

Viktor grabbed one of her wrists. "No pulse." His face was paler than normal. He dropped the cold limb and it made a thwacking sound as it hit the bench. Hopefully the impact hadn't damaged anything. Dante wasn't sure how much the human body could take, and he didn't want the transformation to be more difficult than it had to be, since she was already struggling.

Dante inclined his head. "It's there; you need to listen on her chest."

Bending down, Viktor pressed his ear to the exposed body part in question. "Nothing."

"It's there," Dante insisted.

Viktor jerked upright. "This is beyond enough!" He slammed a hand down against the bench, next to the servant. The metal buckled and her hand flopped over the edge.

Dante took an involuntary step backward.

"This time you have gone too far." His father was seething; it didn't take a degree in body language to work that one out. Dante wouldn't have been surprised if steam had emerged from his father's ears.

Dante straightened. "She agreed to be Chosen; it's not my fault she didn't make it."

"That is preposterous. She would never have agreed."

Dante blinked. Not the response he had expected. "Another

one?" or "It is your fault" or "I said to find a born vampire bride," but not "She never would have agreed."

He folded his arms across his chest. "You just told me the other day that no human would refuse being Chosen. And now you're saying that you know the mind of a *servant*? *This* servant? And that their answer would have been no?"

"You dare to talk back to me?" Viktor's hands tightened into fists at his sides. His nails must have cut skin, because the smell of vampire blood reached Dante's nostrils.

Dante thought about it. "I thought the answer was pretty clear."

"You will pay her death tax out of your allowance, do you hear me?" His father's expression was gaunt, intense.

"I keep telling you, she isn't dead." Dante rolled his eyes.

"There is no heartbeat."

"Well, there is one, I can hear it."

"What? With your *special* hearing abilities?" Viktor sliced a hand through the air when he saw Dante was about to speak. "I have had enough!"

Viktor turned to face the hall and shouted, "You!"

A servant appeared in the doorway. She was all but cowering in her lord's presence. It was pathetic. "Yes, sir?"

"Bring me two men and some new clothes." The servant bobbed a quick curtsy and then dashed away.

Dante watched as Viktor turned back to him, his features twisted in rage. "I've had enough of your obsession. I thought giving you a servant with a non-brown eye color would contain your curiosity; make you realize they are no different. But what happened? You fucked up – again!"

"She isn't dead!"

"She is dead. And now I have to explain this to her grandmother." He rubbed a hand over his eyes.

Her grandmother? *What the–*

"I don't want you to leave this estate, do you hear? You are to stay here and *not* attempt to Choose any more humans. If I hear a cross word about you, I will make you sorry you were ever born."

Two burly footmen hurried into the room and the female servant returned with an armful of clothing.

"Dress her and clean the blood off of her," Viktor snapped at the servants.

"She's not dead," Dante insisted.

Viktor flicked his fingers at Dante. "I don't want to see you for a decade."

"You just said I can't leave the estate."

Dante thought his father's head would explode. His face flushed a deep red and his lips disappeared. He turned away from him and addressed the servants. "Leave her down in the cold room. Her family will arrive to collect her later."

They nodded, wide eyes focused on the floor.

She wasn't dead, Dante wanted to shout.

His father stalked out of the room.

Dante wanted to stop them from moving the body, but he knew his father would snap whatever control he had left. Dante just hoped that they wouldn't cremate her or bury her. He'd have to try and work out a way to sneak out and be there when she awoke.

If she woke.

PART II

May you live in interesting times

CHAPTER TWENTY-SIX

"She's *what*?"

Melissande felt as if her heart had been ripped from her. Her hand groped her chest and it clutched the soft material of her shirt as she slumped down on one of the plush green armchairs that littered her mother's salon.

"Dead, Mel." Her mother sat opposite her, on her "throne" as Elle called it. Olive's face was impassive; Green eyes with cold flints that reflected the lamplight in imitation sentiment.

Melissande's fingers tightened on her shirt. *Why aren't I crying?* she wondered. *Where are the tears?*

"How?"

"She was Chosen."

By the blood, *no*.

Melissande unclenched her hand and raised it, shaking, to her eyes. Not Elle, not her baby. Not Simeon's daughter. "Elle would never have agreed!"

"*He* says she did." Olive spat the first word of her sentence.

"He?" Melissande stared at her mother, her hand tangling in her hair, tugging, pulling strands out. She didn't feel it.

"Viktor Kipling's son."

"Who?"

"The Earl of Wintermere's son."

The name meant nothing to her. But then, she'd never been interested in the aristocracy; that had been her mother's obsession. All Melissande cared about was that this earl was the father of her daughter's murderer.

"I am to collect her body later on tonight," Olive said.

Melissande jerked her hand away from her face and glared at the blonde threads of hair caught in her fingers. "You *left* her there?"

"I only just received notice."

Oh yes, sure you did, Melissande thought. *You probably found out three hours ago and finally got around to "passing the message on."* She didn't care that her mother could probably hear those thoughts. She hoped to blood she did.

Melissande clenched her fist around the hair caught there. "I want her back home, now."

Her mother sighed. "She won't be going home; she'll be going to the funeral parlor."

"No, she'll be coming back to my house. I will prepare her body for the funeral." Melissande's fingernails bit into her palm, and blood seeped from where her nails had bitten into flesh. She dropped the mental barriers that shielded her from other people's emotions and irritation swamped her, but it wasn't hers, it was Olive's.

"She will go to the funeral home."

Melissande jerked her head up. "She will *not*."

Her mother's Green eyes flared. "Do not argue with me, child."

"Don't talk to me like that!" Melissande fought for calm, but it was hard. She wasn't a calm person; it was too hard to be when you could feel everything that everyone else felt. And it was especially difficult when all the emotion that radiated from her mother was relief, irritation and yes – a little bit of pleasure. "This is *my* daughter we're talking about. You never cared one whit about her, but I do – did. You are *not* going to let her final preparation be handled by strangers."

"You are overwrought. Graceds don't do the care of their dead. Only Browns do that."

"What I *am*, Mother, is angry. You forced Elle to go on this mission – you think I didn't know? – and then you tell me a couple of days after she's gone that she's dead! I am her *mother*!"

"It is a deep shame, but you should let the professionals handle the arrangements." Cold, frosty Green.

"Really? You think it's a shame? Because all you *feel* is annoyance and relief."

"You are so upset that you can't read emotions properly," Olive insisted. She waved a hand and her two bodyguards appeared from the shadows.

Melissande stood. "Oh, I'm reading them fine." She stalked toward her parent and leaned down over her "throne." "Know this; I'm the best empath in this country and you're as emotionally barren as a desert. You can pretend sympathy, but you can't fake it, not here." Melissande thumped her chest.

With that, she turned on her heel and stormed from the room.

Tears were pouring down her cheeks, but she didn't feel them. Couldn't feel anything other than her own emotions. Once, she would've thought that to be a blessing.

More tears welled; her chest was broken and her heart shattered.

Again.

My poor baby.

♦

Olive breathed in the aromatic steam of her tea. She nodded her thanks at Kevin, Bjorn's brother, who left the room with the empty teapot. The scent of lemongrass and willow bark surrounded her. She settled back in her green chair. The tea wasn't like the expensive stuff that came all the way from Bangkor, but it made her bones ache a little less. And that was something in this bitter weather. Especially since she'd had to go out in it to check Elle's body.

Thinking of her granddaughter reminded her of Melissande and the debacle Olive had had to endure. Sending out a mental probe to check on Mel, she found her daughter's mind mired in turmoil. It made her draw back. Melissande was at her apartment in the city, with Bjorn on his way back to Olive's house. Mel was fuelled by emotion, to the point where Olive had trouble grasping

Mel's thoughts at times. Whether her daughter had developed it as a defense against her mother or whether it was just part of her strength as a Blue, Olive didn't know.

But she didn't like it.

Aside from the Green daughter Olive had had, Mel was the only child of hers that had been able to block Olive from entering her mind whenever she wanted. Four children, Olive had had. One Hazel, one Blue, one Green and one Gray. All four colors, which was abnormal for a Green-eyed mother to produce. But then, Olive had deliberately picked different fathers for each pregnancy.

Unsurprisingly, Olive's favorite child had been the Green, Jenny. Whoever claimed that people shouldn't have favorite children was a fool. Olive *knew* that there were very few people who loved their children equally. Children, after all, were a commodity. They helped you get ahead in life. Children were about you, not them. Too bad her granddaughters hadn't quite grasped that yet.

But her Jenny had been strong, and had shown signs of intelligence. But like her Hazel brother Yale, she had died young of a fever. Yale hadn't been much of a loss; he'd only been two and not much of anything at that point. But he may have been worth something later in life. And so that one virus had cost her two children, two futures. And that had left Mel and Brock, her Gray-eyed son. Who had been too stupid to live.

And after he'd died, there'd just been Mel. Who was strong-willed when it came to her children, which was a problem Olive wished she didn't have. It had taken her almost twenty years to "convince" Mel to have another baby. And it had produced Emmie. Useless, unusual Emmie.

But Mel had been right. Olive *was* relieved that Elle was dead. It meant that Olive wouldn't have to kill the girl. Because if Elle had survived being Chosen, that's exactly what Olive would have done. The bond between a new vampire and their Chooser was a strong one, and in a Graced's case, psychic. Olive could not afford for Elle to be tied irrevocably to a vampire; to give away the

Graceds' secrets to a weak-minded blood-sucker. Vampires should bow to Graceds, not the other way around.

That was why Olive wanted an immortal Graced great-grandchild. It would move her closer to the dynasty she dreamed about. The child would be Graced; wouldn't be forced into doing anything by their Chooser, or have an overpowering need for blood or meat. Whatever power they had would be Olive's.

No, it was lucky that Elle was dead. Elle would have been a puppet pulled by a vampire's strings and that was an abomination.

Chapter Twenty-Seven

Clay didn't believe that Elle was dead. *Couldn't* accept that she was, despite the news, the evidence; he'd seen her body. Emmie had shown it to him, when he'd come the next night to see if Elle had returned. It had been cold, devoid of life.

Even though he hadn't known Elle for long, she'd made bulls look like pansies when it came to stubbornness. He just couldn't admit that Elle was dead. Especially from being Chosen.

He just hadn't thought it could happen.

Blood, it *shouldn't* have happened. Elle was a Hazel; she had enough Brown – non-Graced blood – in her to make the transition. She could have survived as a vampire *or* a werewolf. Blood, in his darkest hours over the past few days, he'd even thought about Biting her once or twice. The only way she could have died was if the vampire Choosing her had been a complete and utter imbecile.

Clay folded his arms across his chest and leaned his shoulders against the back wall of the funeral home. Cool brick dug into his skin through his shirt. Vampires and weres didn't go in for funerals, but humans did. As a result, so did Graceds. Not because they thought there was something to go to after death, but because it was a human tradition; mourning their dead in public displays of affection. And Graceds liked to blend in, even if they didn't share the beliefs that inspired the ritual.

The funeral home was filled with people. Most of the guests sat on the rows of benches that faced the wooden coffin, which was positioned at the front of the large room. There were a few others like him, standing at the rear of the chamber. Flowers were draped over the coffin's lid in artistic disarray and the wood was shiny in the daylight. He thought the blooms may have been orchids, they certainly smelled like it, but he didn't really pay much attention to plants as a general rule. If he couldn't eat it, he didn't give a shit about it.

A small hand suddenly fastened around one of his larger ones. Glancing down, he noticed Emmie's bright eyes looking back at him. She was dressed from head to toe in a deep mourning red.

"You lied to me." She didn't appear angry, though. In fact, her eyes weren't even red or swollen. Not like that night when she'd shown him Elle's body.

Which was odd.

"Hello, imp."

"Hey, Clay." Her nut brown fingers tightened on his.

"Should you be talking to me?" He looked up and saw the pale face of Melissande staring at the two of them. *She's aged*, was his first thought. *Well duh*, was his second. The last time he'd seen her was when she'd been a teen. She was still beautiful though, but in a pretty, breakable sort of way. Not like either of her daughters. They must have gotten their strength from their grandmother or their fathers. Clay couldn't read her expression, but she didn't seem irritated at seeing him with her daughter. Just... blank.

"No, I shouldn't be talking to you *at all*." Emmie smiled at him then, a slight smirk.

The conversation struck him as decidedly strange.

He tried to shake his fingers loose. "Shouldn't you be with your family?"

"Yes." She clung to him like a limpet.

He wasn't sure how to take that. Children he mostly understood, but Graced kids – no, he lied – *this* Graced kid was a whole new world of bizarre. "I'm sorry for lying. I'm sorry Elle is dead," Clay said.

Emmie looked at him for a long minute. "I got to touch her before they had to bring her here for the funeral."

He shut his eyes. Clay could just picture how Emmie would

have looked at seeing Elle again, pale with death. He hadn't gone back after his first sighting, maybe he should have. Maybe he should have kept an eye on the imp. Clay tightened his fingers in sympathy.

Emmie tugged on his hand. Clay opened his eyes and looked down at her.

"You lied when you said something really bad wouldn't happen to her." Emmie brushed some hair from her face and let go of his hand. "But you didn't say she wouldn't die."

Emmie walked away from him then, her face taking on a mask of pain and sadness, eyes growing swollen with unshed tears. And it was a mask, Clay realized, he'd seen it slide into place alongside the rise of tears.

Clay refolded his arms and stared broodingly at the family side of the church. Olive Brown was glaring in his direction while one gnarled hand rested on a wooden cane. As she leaned down and whispered an admonition to Emmie, the old woman's eyes locked with his. Emmie appeared to ignore her grandmother. The little girl took a seat next to her mother and reached out, taking one of Melissande's pale, limp hands in a firm grip.

Voices rose and fell in the room. There were lots of tears and handkerchiefs being used. It seemed that Elle was popular despite her starchy ways. There was also a reasonable crowd of city guards in attendance. He'd had more than a few belligerent glares sent his way. From her partner, especially.

He wondered where her Chooser was. Perhaps he hadn't thought it would work, that's why he'd abandoned her?

Clay's attention was distracted by the funeral director, who took a step toward the podium, and cleared his throat.

◆

Elle woke up dead.

She'd always thought it was a stupid phrase. How could you wake up dead? You were *dead*. That wasn't something you just woke up from. Although, Elle hadn't understood she was dead. She thought she was hungover.

Majorly hungover.

Elle opened her eyes to velvety darkness and strained to find light, any light. She tried to roll over, to light the bedside lamp, to see if Clay was there or not, but she came up against resistance. Reaching out, her hands slid against walls that were covered in something soft and slippery and which smelled faintly of dye and soap. Satin. Frowning, she pointed her toes and felt them hit another cool barrier. Worry began to kick in. She lifted her hands, only to flatten them against the roof of her prison. Cool, smooth wood slid underneath them as they began to move more rapidly, feeling for a latch, anything.

Elle shut her eyes in the blackness. There was only one thing she could think of that was lined with satin and that was made exactly to fit around a person. A scream began to build from deep inside as blood rushed to her ears and then she realized something else.

Elle couldn't hear her heartbeat.

Not at first. No pounding to accompany the blood rush. Then, faintly, *thud*. Breath held, she waited for another thirty or more seconds before there was another *thud*.

That was when she grasped she didn't need to breathe. Not like before, anyway. She suspected she could now hold her breath for minutes, since there was no sense of urgency, no need to inhale, no constricting, horrible urge to take a gulp of air.

Hands dropping to her sides, Elle tried to think back, to remember what had happened. Why she'd ended up in a coffin. Eventually there were flickers of light behind her eyelids, then faint images, pale and watery, as if they belonged to someone else.

Slowly, one formed, the brightest so far, and it was awash with red-tinged, fiery pain.

That *bastard*!

♦

Clay heard when Elle woke up. He'd been waiting for it, ever since he'd managed to piece Emmie's hints together. How the girl had known that Elle was undergoing the transformation when no one else had realized, he didn't know. And he wasn't going to ask.

Her heartbeat was slow, really slow, but that was normal for Chosen vampires. They weren't like born vampires whose heart rates were faster – but then, non-Chosen vampires could age. He may have heard that she was "alive" earlier, if he'd been standing as close to the coffin as he was now – which was right next to it, with a hand resting on the smooth wood.

It was actually a very attractive coffin, and from the smell of it, it was also made out of Mirama hardwood – which was nearly impossible for a vampire to break due to their "allergy."

How…convenient.

Clay just hoped Elle would stay where she was. He didn't think the people in the room would react well if she started banging on the inside of the coffin, or if by some fluke, she flicked the lid open and announced her undead existence. The city guards would probably try and restrain her, thinking she would fall into a bloodlust, and her family would no doubt try to stake her.

Especially her grandmother.

Clay bit back an audible sigh. When had his life become so complicated? He should have stayed in Gorke. He began tapping his fingers on the wood, gently, but loud enough that Elle should hear him.

Graceds – or more accurately, half-bloods, with Hazel eyes – did not become Chosen or Bitten. When they did, and if they were discovered, they were hunted down and eliminated. The hunters liked to say it was because Graceds became unstable; dangerous. After all, they could not predict what would happen to their "abilities" when the change took over. But Clay knew it was a thinly veiled excuse. Most Hazels didn't *have* any abilities; being Chosen shouldn't change that. The Graceds were just trying to protect their secret and their powers. They didn't like the idea of a vampire Graced who could be controlled by their Chooser. They also didn't want the vampires to learn about their existence; that it was possible – difficult but possible – to breed vampire offspring off them.

After all, Graceds had been part of the reason for the Civil War, almost thirty thousand years ago. Breeding and food; that is what had driven the vampires and weres to fight. First, there'd been wars over their favorite food source: humans. Then, when the skirmishes had brought vampire and were numbers dangerously low, they'd begun capturing Graceds to repopulate their numbers. Back then, the bloodlines had been less diluted and Graceds could breed easily with weres and vampires. After all, vampires and weres *were* descended from Graceds.

Since then, the Graceds had been protecting themselves by slowly killing off all the old wolves and vampires and preventing anyone from knowing they had any abilities. They'd destroyed cities, wiped out towns. So much had been lost in their purging.

Despite that, their secret was badly kept.

Clay knew about them, and he was pretty sure the king of this stupid little country did too, and from that, who knew how many aristocratic vampires as well. But it wasn't his problem – correction, hadn't been his problem. Now, because of Elle and the kid, it was.

Clay stopped tapping and resumed stroking his hand over the wood.

"What are you doing here?"

Clay looked over his shoulder at Elle's grandmother, who stood to his right with both hands resting on her cane. She looked like a wrinkly, ugly bird, with her head tilted to the side. She even had a brooch with a feather pinned on it to complement the whimsy.

"Paying my respects." Clay smiled and showed his teeth, just to annoy the old crone.

"You don't even know the girl." Her eyes narrowed and he felt a little tickle inside his skull.

Blood, he hated it when she attempted to read his mind. She couldn't, but it didn't stop her from trying. His hand stopped moving on the coffin. Elle had had some Green in her Hazel…could it be…perhaps it was *her* who was trying to read his mind? He wasn't sure if she could, wasn't sure if it was even possible for her to; he began to think about her staying still and him coming to help her later.

This is what her Chooser should be doing, he thought, and blocked the anger he felt. He sure hoped her grandmother couldn't hear Elle's mind; otherwise his plan would be in shreds.

Now he just had to stop her from climbing out of her coffin and onto a stake.

Easy.

Chapter Twenty-Eight

Elle was going to *kill* that idiot vampire when she got out of her coffin. She was going to find the sharpest, hardest and meanest stake she could find and then she'd end him.

How *dare* he try and Choose her.

He hadn't tried, her mind whispered, *he had succeeded.* Why else would she be in this box?

Oh, go and sit on a pole, she snapped back.

Suddenly, she had to control the urge to laugh hysterically. Here she was, trapped in a bloody coffin after having been Chosen, and she was arguing with *herself?*

Crazy is as crazy does, her mind said.

Oh, shut *up.*

She dropped her hands back to her sides and began to listen for noise outside the coffin. Maybe, just maybe, she hadn't been buried yet. Elle *really* didn't want to have to dig her way out of the grave.

Now she was paying attention, voices began to trickle through the wood:

"She'll be dearly missed–"

"Can't believe Elle's gone–"

"The vampire must have really mucked up. That's twice he's failed to Choose someone–"

"What are you doing here?"

Wait, the last had been Gran.

"Paying my respects."

And that was Clay, she'd bet her last paycheck on it. Literally. Last. Paycheck. She felt like laughing and crying.

Wait – I'm at my own funeral. She started trying to hear what people were saying, but Gran's voice was the loudest. Elle figured it meant that Gran was standing near the coffin.

"You don't know my granddaughter, so there's no point in wasting your time here." Good old Gran, Elle thought, hating weres without reason. *Just like I used to do.*

Something made a rasping noise over her head. Elle realized it was the sound of a hand running over wood. Was Clay or Gran leaning on the coffin? Maybe she should say something…

"I don't know if you can hear me or not, but if you can, keep your mouth shut and stay in the bloody coffin."

The words couldn't have been louder if Clay had been in the coffin with her. Startled, she jerked a little and heard his fingers start drumming on the wooden lid.

He's…he's thinking *at me. How does he know I can hear him?* she wondered.

"I don't know if you can hear me or not, but if you can, keep your mouth shut and stay in the bloody coffin."

He was set on repeat, she thought. *He doesn't know I can hear him.* Hopefully Gran couldn't hear him, either.

Clay spoke aloud, "Is it wrong to want to pay my respects to your family then? We do go way back."

Elle froze. Clay and Gran went way back. What did that mean?

"I want you out of here."

"Hello." That voice had to belong to Emmie, high and sweet and full of trouble.

Elle felt tears well in her eyes. How would her little sister have coped, thinking that she was dead? Elle had promised Emmie she would look after her; she'd *lied.*

"Emmie, go away," Gran snapped.

Please Emmie, Elle thought, *pretend you don't know* Clay. *Listen to Gran for once.* The last thing they needed was Gran poking around people's heads, trying to sort out what was going on. Blood, Elle didn't know half of what was going on, that was growing clearer by the minute.

"How do you know Gran?" Emmie asked Clay.

Clay's internal monologue stopped for a moment. "I met her when she was a lot younger."

"My sister is in there." Her voice sounded a little wet, so Elle figured that Emmie was crying. It broke her slow-beating heart.

"Emmie, go back to your mother," Gran said.

"Did you know Elle?" Emmie asked, ignoring Gran.

So, Emmie wasn't going to pretend she didn't know Clay – but she *was* going to pretend that Elle hadn't known him. It made her head hurt.

Elle could hear a rustle of cloth moving in the direction of the coffin. She could hear the whole room, breathing, talking, crying, farting; it would have driven her nuts if she wasn't concentrating so hard on the conversation taking place next to her coffin.

"I met her once or twice," Clay said.

Elle thought, *He's just put me in the shit. Good thing I'm dead.*

"Did you think she was funny? I think she's funny."

Gran made a moaning noise.

"Y-yes." Clay had hesitated. The bastard. She was perfectly hilarious. She had a great sense of humor.

"Did you think she was pretty?"

Of course she was… Wait. What was her sister doing?

"Of course." Clay was tapping on the coffin again.

Then she heard Clay think, *"I think you're pretty hot without your clothes on, but I don't want to say that to your sister."*

She wanted to hit Clay, and ask him how in the blood he knew Gran. And why he was *thinking* at her. Ask him why he hadn't told her about it all before.

"I don't know if you can hear me or not, but if you can, keep your mouth shut and stay in the bloody coffin."

"Oh will you just shut up already," she thought, *"I can hear you and I haven't said a bloody thing."*

She thought she heard a snort which turned into a cough.

Had Clay been able to hear her?

"I think Elle is pretty," Emmie continued.

Elle concentrated a thought at Clay. *"What in the name of blood is going on out there?"*

"Your gran looks ready to strangle Emmie. And me."

"So it's my funeral, right? You, I can understand Gran wanting to strangle, but why Emmie?" Elle hadn't appreciated that Greens could talk to each other, mind-to-mind. She might have, if she ever thought about it, because it sort of made sense. Greens were locked to other Greens, but if they focused a thought *out*, well then, it might work. But she hadn't thought that Greens could chat back and forth with Nons or weres.

"Emmie, your mother wants you." Gran again.

"Because Emmie keeps avoiding Olive's, ah, subtle, hints to go away."

"I can hear that," and she could, Gran was chiding Emmie again to step away from the coffin, *"but why does she want Emmie to go?"*

Emmie's voice came smoothly through the wood. *"No Gran, Mother doesn't want me, because she's talking to Captain Mikael."*

"I'd say it's because she doesn't want me to notice the imp's eye color, but she's already pointed the girl out to me before."

Elle's heart stopped beating entirely. *"WHAT?"*

"Ow, loud much?" She heard him take his hand away from the coffin entirely.

"We need to move the coffin, and you're in the way." Gran's voice was growing brittle with exasperation.

"What do you mean? When did she point out Emmie? How do you know Gran? How do you know about Graceds?" Elle asked, ignoring his complaint.

"Where are you taking Elle?" Emmie's voice was strained. Elle could picture her sister's expression.

"Look, there's a lot to explain and not really the time to do it here. Just accept that I know. I'm going to help get you out of the coffin without Olive knowing."

"Why?"

"What, is that your word of the day? Because she'd bloody well stake you if you announced your newfound undead life. And you know it."

"The coffin has to go into the next room to await the cremation."

Cremation?

Oh, no.

One billion times *no*.

Gran was going to burn her alive?

"I'll give you one guess why she's going against Graced custom and cremating you."

She stretched her mind out to her gran's, but shied away at the last minute from the green, glittering swirl. She wanted to see what was in her grandmother's thoughts, but she didn't want to risk letting her gran know that she was awake.

"I'm guessing she's worried that I really was *Chosen."*

"Really? I wouldn't have guessed."

"No!" Emmie shouted.

"You don't have a say in it, young lady."

Emmie started crying then, in earnest. She was hiccoughing and spluttering.

"Maybe she just needs to say good-bye," Clay said.

Gran snorted. "She needs a good spanking."

You bitch, Elle thought.

"When the coffin is taken into the next room, you should let her say good-bye properly. Maybe that will help." Clay sounded reasonable, calm, as if he couldn't give a crap about Emmie or her.

And maybe he didn't. No, she thought, he didn't. No maybe about it.

"What do you think this funeral has been for?" Elle could almost hear her gran roll her eyes.

Emmie started wailing. "You can't burn her. She's my sister!"

"She's *dead*." Gran hissed the words, but Elle heard them and she didn't doubt that Clay had, too.

The coffin moved slightly as something was thrown against it before thuds echoed in her prison.

"No! No!"

"By the blood," Gran muttered, "you're causing a scene. Step away from the coffin."

"Come on," Clay said and the thumping stopped. The coffin started moving, but Elle couldn't tell which way.

"We're going into the back room," Clay thought at her. *"You will have all of one minute to get out of the coffin and get hidden."*

"Leave the child here," Gran said, her voice still close by.

"Look, Olive, you're not exactly the grandmotherly type. Give the kid a chance to say good-bye."

"Fine. She will have two minutes."

"Your grandmother is sure in a rush to burn you."

"Yeah, she's a real gem. Wanna keep her?" Elle thought back.

"Blood no. She's all yours."

"Yay."

CHAPTER TWENTY-NINE

Clay had decided to push the coffin himself. Thankfully, it had been set on a bier with wheels, which made this ruse a whole lot easier. The funeral director was huffing in annoyance behind him, but sometimes being a hulking wolf had its benefits. The flowers on the casket were really over the top and made him want to sneeze, but he kept control of his nose. Barely. Unlike Emmie, who had ruined his best handkerchief by blowing a bucketload of tears and snot onto its once pristine glory. She was keeping up with his steps and was almost glued to his buckskin-covered leg.

It was a shame that Emmie had acted familiar with him – even though it was true. He was sure that Olive's mind was spinning now, trying to work out when he'd met Emmie. But Clay figured she'd decide that he had wanted to meet the girl who would be the future mother of his offspring. The fact he had no interest in siring anything was beside the point. Hopefully, his professing to know Elle had been taken by Olive as an annoyance, rather than a truth. Either way, he could always say he'd seen her at a bar fight. It was true, after all.

Ah well. Thank the blood Olive couldn't read his mind. He loved his quirky genes. Although, it was odd that Elle could hear him and Olive couldn't. Maybe it was because she was no longer human. He'd have to think on it, later, when he wasn't trying to sneak a newly woken vampire from her own funeral.

As he moved the coffin slowly, he caught the eye of the funeral director, who had moved in front of him and stood before the rear doors to the room. The man's black suit was still immaculate, but his bushy brown sideburns looked a little ridiculous next to the shiny plate of his bald head. At least the director didn't stare at him like the other humans in the room did – both the Graceds and the Nons – as though he was going to steal the body and do horrible things to it. Or maybe they were just sad that this was the last time they'd be in Elle's company.

He was betting on the former. Elle's guard partner, the big guy – Kyle, was it? – was staring at him with a kind of intensity Clay found disturbing. *Being a werewolf sucks sometimes*, he thought. Sure, he *did* plan on stealing the body, but he wasn't going to do horrible things to it, just naughty things. And he didn't think that Elle would protest too much. Not after he'd saved her newly dead hide.

Over his shoulder, he said to Elle's grandmother, "Look, Olive, you're not exactly the grandmotherly type. Give the kid a chance to say good-bye."

The wrinkly face scrunched alarmingly and she thumped her cane on the polished wooden floor, her green dress swishing with the motion. The funeral director winced at her action; the cane had come close to Clay's foot.

"Fine," Olive said. "She will have two minutes."

Probably more like one minute thirty, Clay thought, and kept pushing. "Where do you want me to leave this?"

"This" meaning Elle.

The director wiped a cloth over his shiny head and said, "Just take it into the next room. The furnace entrance is through there."

Clay nodded. "Will do. Come on, little human."

The director held open one of the wooden doors and Clay pushed the coffin through the opening. The door swung shut after him and Emmie, and Clay pushed the casket and bier forward, toward the end of the room.

This chamber didn't have the bright, airy ambience of the funeral hall; rather it was dim and clustered with extra tables and chairs. Empty vases stood poised around the room like waiting flytraps, and there were spare drapes and cloths hanging over trestle tables in the far corner of the room. He made a mental note of those.

Making sure the door was definitely shut, Clay quickly moved the coffin toward the door marked "furnace room" and set the flowers on the floor. Then he began snapping open the clasps that held the lid down.

"We have to hurry," Clay said to Emmie, whose tears had dried with remarkable speed.

"Where can she go?" Emmie asked. "Will she be okay?"

The last clasp undone, Clay flicked the lid open and looked at Elle. She looked different, really different, but he didn't have time to focus on the changes. He had to make sure she was out of the coffin, and safe.

He reached in and hauled Elle out, propping her up next to him. Her eyes were wide and she was breathing fast for a Chosen. Clay thought at her, *"Ignore how Emmie and I smell. I know we smell nice."*

Out loud, he said, "Quick, see that rear table and the drapes? Hide under them."

Moving faster than she'd ever been able to before, Elle was gone from his side. It hadn't taken her long to work out how to use that vampire agility, he thought. Not turning to see if she'd done as told, he shut the coffin lid and flicked the clasps shut then dumped the flowers back on top. He could hear footsteps coming toward the doors. Then he knelt down in front of Emmie.

"Cry some more."

Emmie nodded and started sobbing into the used hanky. Gross. She could definitely keep it.

"Are you ready now?" The funeral director stepped into the room and rapidly approached the coffin, looking rather like a shiny turtle after one too many cups of coffee. Behind him, and with a clickety-click of her cane, came Olive.

Clay nodded and stood.

"Let's check everything is in order and then head home," Olive said. She hobbled her way over to the casket and paused, staring hard at the wood. As if she could see through it and into the emptiness inside.

The director walked around the coffin and nodded his head a few times. "It all looks good; I'll just push the coffin on through."

Olive looked at Clay and Emmie and then snarled, "Open it."

Clay folded his arms across his chest and tried to appear bored. Emmie cried harder.

"Sorry, ma'am?" The poor funeral director looked like he was about to faint.

"Open the coffin," Olive snapped.

The director was sweating, a lot. Then again, Clay thought, the room was a little close to the furnace. The portly man's chins jiggled as he said, "I'm sorry, but that's against policy. There are disease problems to consider."

"Policy? Don't be ridiculous; she's my granddaughter. Plus, I don't care; I want to make sure she's in there before she goes through."

The director drew himself up to his full height and dabbed the cloth onto his sweating brow with renewed vigor. He opened his mouth to speak, but was cut off.

"Mother, of course Elle's body is in the coffin. Where else would it be?" Melissande had walked quietly up to Emmie's side and had taken the small girl's hand in one of her own. Her long blonde hair was swept upward in an elegant bun and her dress was red. Melissande's expression was fierce, but broken. Clay rather thought the dress reflected the blood that was pouring from the woman's shattered heart.

A tear-stained face looked up at Melissande. Emmie should be an actor, Clay thought. She could traipse the boards with ease.

Clay noticed for the first time that Olive didn't wear a speck of red in her entire outfit. Not even a garnet winked in her jewelry. No mourning to be seen in any shape or form.

"I can assure you," the director said, "we are not in the habit of losing bodies."

"Amuse me."

"Mother, no. You are going beyond the bounds of sane behavior." Melissande was shaking her head, her face so white she could have masqueraded as a vampire. "Elle is dead and we brought her body here yesterday. I prepared her for the funeral myself – she has not been embalmed or anything." She leaned away from Emmie and whispered to her mother, "She will smell and Emmie has been through enough."

"But–"

"Have you lost your mind, Olive?" Clay decided he should hurry this along. "Your granddaughter is dead. Unless you think the vampire who Chose her has stolen her corpse, why in the name of blood do you want to see it again after it has been sitting out for a day? Didn't you see it yesterday?"

Clay could see Olive's eyes flicker as she tried – and failed – to think of an acceptable excuse to look inside the coffin. She was either going to have to accuse Clay of stealing the body, which he would hardly have had time for, or admit that Elle really had been Chosen. And that she wanted to kill her for it.

Olive slashed a hand through the air. "Fine. Do it."

The director nodded and exhaled deeply in a sign of profound relief. He then pushed the coffin through to the next room while dabbing his forehead with a free hand. Clay caught a glimpse of a large furnace before the door swung shut behind the man.

"Come on, let's go," Melissande said gently to Emmie.

The little girl nodded and followed her mother from the room, still clutching the disgusting hanky. Olive stared hard at Clay, but he knew she wouldn't say anything, not without giving herself away – just in case Clay hadn't done anything to help her Chosen granddaughter escape.

"Can you stay hidden in here for a couple hours?" Clay thought at the corner of the room.

"Yeah, but I'm pretty hungry."

"So," Olive said, her Green eyes narrowed and focused on him. "What did you think of my granddaughter?"

"Elle? She was feisty. Met her by accident." Clay grabbed hold of Olive's elbow and "helped" her from the room.

Olive sounded exasperated. "No, what did you think of Emmie?"

Clay pushed Olive out of the room and shut the door behind him. "Nice kid."

"Don't eat anyone," he thought at Elle.

He thought he heard a snort in reply.

CHAPTER THIRTY

Dante was trying to sleep. Despite the plush, satin-covered cushions and the warmth beneath the sheepskin cover, he just couldn't manage it. He'd even tried counting humans, but it had done no good. Sleep was elusive, especially when all he could hear in his mind were the words, *"I don't want to see you for a decade."*

He hadn't realized how much his father's temporary affection had mattered to him. The awkward one-armed hugs, the pleased attitude, even the simple questions about his day. They'd meant something to him, which was something he couldn't understand because Dante had *known* they would all be fleeting. And very few things actually meant *anything* to him at all.

He adjusted the red-dyed sheepskin over his stomach and crossed his arms. The curtains that hung either side of the four-poster bed were heavy black velvet, but they were open to let the weak sunlight through. He was such a bloody disappointment – to himself, as much as his father.

He'd failed on so many levels.

Oh, there was the surface issue of his killing a human who was related to an acquaintance of his father's. Then you went one deeper and hit the thorny issue of Dante not being able to Choose someone properly. How else could he explain that no one had realized the servant was still alive when the body was removed? Moving on, there was the fact that no matter how much Viktor had tried, he hadn't been able to rid Dante of his obsession. And an obsession it was, Dante could admit that much to himself. But he knew he was right. There *was* something different about those humans and he would one day prove it. Although, he was smart enough to leave it for another century or so while his father calmed down and he was – hopefully – no longer under the control of his parent's purse strings. How he'd achieve that miraculous feat, Dante wasn't sure.

Shutting his eyes again, he hoped for sleep. For several minutes he lay there, corpse-like, arms across his chest, breathing slow and even, trying to lure sleep into his web.

The door to the outer chamber opened and footsteps click-clicked across the stone toward his bedchamber. Part of Dante wished that it would be the maid – until he remembered that he'd apparently "killed" her – but the scent of sex and blood wafted through the air and he knew it was someone he'd rather not see.

"You're really in the cesspool this time," Misty said.

Dante opened his eyes and looked across the length of the bed at his sister. She stood at the foot of the mattress, arms crossed over her chest and one foot tapping against the floor. Her white sarcenet gown left little to the imagination – with her arms positioned where they were – and her hair tumbled down her back in a length of coitus-messed waves.

Blood, he resented her sometimes. Or thought he did. The feeling never seemed to last. None of them ever did.

"You think?" Dante muttered, propping himself up against the headboard.

Misty sighed and walked over to the far side of the bed. She carefully climbed on top of the sheepskin and leaned back against the headboard next to him. Pulling her knees up and tucking them under her chin, Dante had to wonder how on earth that position could be comfortable with all the undergarments that went with the ensemble. But he wasn't about to ask.

"Why'd you Choose another human?" Misty propped her chin on her knees, but her eyes were watching him.

Dante lifted a hand and then let it drop to his side. Maybe honesty would be a better option right now. Misty seemed in a...practical mood. "I thought it would work; I wanted to see if I could do it right."

"But you Chose your *servant*." Misty moved her chin from left to right.

Dante's hand turned into a fist next to his leg. "I didn't think anybody would care. The girl worked for vampires, for blood's sake; I thought she wouldn't mind being Chosen."

"You didn't ask?"

"Of course I did," Dante snapped.

Misty frowned. "Father is furious. He says the girl never would have agreed – despite the fact he's told me a hundred and one times that no human would ever refuse – and that her family are up in arms."

"What does it matter?" Dante asked. "They're humans."

"Yes, but these humans are apparently powerful cits."

Ahh, cits, Dante thought. The bane of an aristocratic society; wealthy merchants who wanted in on the few titles there were around, and could afford to buy their way into one.

"Shouldn't they have been happy then? If I was keen on the servant enough to Choose her, wouldn't it follow from that that I would have married her?" That had been the argument he'd been planning on spouting. Plan B had had its definite drawbacks.

"Didn't Father have his little marriage chat with you?" Misty asked.

Dante thought back. "Yes, he wanted the noose – as in, me – gone from his neck. I think that he thought he might have a chance at grandchildren if he married me off."

"What, you're saying I'm infertile?" Misty's chin jerked up and her eyes flashed at him.

"No." He shook his head with a sigh. "Just that you aren't the marrying type."

"I don't need to marry to have an heir. In case you hadn't noticed, I'm a *girl*."

"Sorry, no, hadn't picked up on that before." Dante tried to smile and Misty returned the expression, although hers was hard to read apart from the flashing of teeth.

"Why did you Choose that servant in particular, Dante?" Her voice was serious and without a lot of the girliness she often used when around him or any male. In fact, this whole conversation felt entirely too mature for his older sister.

He didn't know what to do. Should he admit his ongoing obsession to Misty? She already knew about it from the past, but maybe she thought he'd put it behind him? *Don't be an idiot*, his mind grated, *she's your bloody sister. She remembers how you obsessed for sixty years on learning how to play the pianoforte when you had no talent.* And she'd suffered for it – everyone who had been in the house within earshot of the music room had.

"Because she had interesting eyes," Dante admitted.

Misty groaned. "I knew it!" She flicked some hair over her shoulder and then stretched her legs out on the bed while tugging her bodice up with her other hand.

"What? Knew what?" Dante said.

Misty rolled her eyes at him. "That you weren't over your obsession."

"Well, I'm right. There *is* something going on with them." Dante folded his arms across his chest.

"Really?" Misty raised her eyebrows.

"Really."

"I was being sarcastic," Misty said.

"Look, the first girl I Chose was a whore, all right?"

"Yeah, we all know that. Tell me something new." Misty began rearranging the cushions behind her back. First a yellow satin one, then a red damask one.

"But she had blue eyes."

"Yeah?" Misty was starting to look bored.

"She died when I Chose her. So I Chose someone else." Dante felt heat rising to his face.

"The servant, right." Misty leaned back against all her cushions – she'd added a purple one to her pile.

"Wrong."

She sat up a little and met his eyes. "Wrong?"

"Sarcasm?" he asked.

"No."

"Oh, well yes, wrong. It was a woman I found in the street. She had green eyes. It was like she knew what I wanted and she fought me. But I overpowered her easily enough. I then hired a hotel room in the dock area around Bridge Road and tried to Choose her."

"You're bloody crazy!" Misty said. "What happened?"

"She died, within seconds of the third transfusion." Dante watched as Misty sank back against the cushions.

"What do you think it means? That you're doing it wrong?"

He briefly wondered why she wasn't angry at him for breaking basically the *only* law of their kind. And why he was telling her any of this. But it wasn't like there was anyone else he could tell. And she wouldn't let anyone else know; it would mire the family in scandal. "No, I think I'm doing it perfectly fine."

Misty snorted.

Dante inhaled and tried to keep his frustration with his sibling on a simmering level. "I think that it means they can't make the transition. Whether they have green, blue or gray eyes; I don't think they can become one of us or a were, for that matter."

"No loss on the last point. We've enough fleabags around as it is."

Dante was about to point out that Pinton had a rather low were population – and that it only comprised wolves – but stopped himself in time. Misty wouldn't care. One werewolf was one too many, in her mind. He'd have to ask her about her aversion one day.

Misty was quiet for a few seconds, appearing to think. "What color eyes did the servant have?"

Dante smiled a little, the right corner of his mouth rising. "Hazel."

"Hazel?"

"Hazel." He nodded.

She exhaled, seemed to pause for a moment, then asked, "What's hazel?"

"Mostly it's brown, but it has bits of green, blue or gray mixed in. I thought that since her eye color was mostly brown, the human could be Chosen, since it appears that brown eyes *can* make the change."

"Seems like you were wrong."

"I don't think so," Dante said. "She was still breathing when they took her."

"Father couldn't hear a heartbeat; I heard the servants talking. They're all convinced you're going to maul them next."

Dante picked some lint off the sheepskin blanket. "Yeah, well, Father's hearing isn't as acute as mine."

"No one's is," Misty said. He couldn't tell if she was teasing him or not.

"Either way, Father won't let me go and see her. I heard the servants talking in the hall; they said that her family was going to cremate the body because they were worried she'd turn into a ghoul or something."

"Ghouls don't exist," Misty scoffed.

"No, but a lot of humans think so, from what I can hear. A Chosen person who doesn't rise within the proper time may one day rise, without a brain, to suck the blood from the living without knowledge or reason."

Misty started laughing. "That's hilarious!"

Dante shrugged. "It doesn't really matter if it's funny or not. If they burn her before she wakes, then she's dead. If they burn her after she wakes, but she's stuck in her coffin, she's dead. I won't know if my experiment really worked or not."

"You aren't going to try again, are you?" Misty's mirth had vanished.

"Not for a long time," Dante answered.

"Thank the blood for small mercies."

CHAPTER THIRTY-ONE

Anton stared at his father with his mouth hanging open in shock. He shut his jaw slowly and watched as Reginald Greystoke settled back into the large, brown leather chair opposite Anton. They were in the library at the Pinton townhouse and Anton felt like he'd been hit by a brick. He tried to ignore the groan his father made as the leather stretched around Reginald's frame, and the sound of his popping bones. His father was growing *old*. Had age muddled his parent's mind?

Reginald had once been a man of stature, but age had shrunk and withered his athletic frame. White hair had largely replaced the original black, and his father's eyes were a troubled deep brown. Anton and his father didn't really look anything alike. Anton took after his mother's side.

"You're to marry," his father repeated.

"No." He couldn't seem to get past that word, that single uttered *no*.

How could his father have done this to him? Agreed on his behalf *without* consultation?

A fire crackled in the grate, adding warmth to Anton's numbed body, but he barely noticed it. He hardly recognized the room – the hundreds of books that usually made him feel welcome like long forgotten friends; the leather chairs for easing a man's aches, and the air of love and friendship that clung to the very walls – he was so wrapped up in the horror of his father's news.

Marriage.

Not even a child-bearing contract, but *marriage*. Anton could have performed stud duties had they been required, provided he got at least one heir out of the bargain, but this?

"Son, I've arranged the dowry and contracts."

Anton choked on air. "Dowry?"

"Your partner is to have one, being immortal. It's the law."

Being immortal?

"You're marrying me off to a *vampire* or *werewolf*?" Anton couldn't believe it. And it probably wouldn't be a werewolf, this being Pinton and as such, leech infested. "I was just engaged," Anton said, "but she died. I'm in mourning." He dropped his head into his hands, one foot tapping a continual and erratic beat against the carpeted floor.

His father scratched his white hair and frowned. "Always found that business a bit odd myself."

Anton looked up. "Mourning?"

"No, you being in a relationship with that hussy."

Anger bubbled up through his chest. "What?"

Annabel had been *perfect*.

Okay, he thought to himself, maybe she hadn't been *perfect*. But she'd been his. And she would have quit being a whore, he knew it. Once she'd told him about her profession, they would have discussed it and she would have gathered she didn't need to do it anymore. She would have become a baroness.

How would you feel though, his mind whispered, *when you kept meeting other aristos that she'd fucked?* Anton brushed the thought away. It wouldn't matter – couldn't matter now. She was gone.

Frowning, he thought back to what his father had said. He hadn't told Reginald about Annabel's profession; had never seen the point, since she'd been dead when he'd learned about it.

His father shrugged, seeming to watch the thoughts flitter across Anton's face. "She was a whore."

Anton's jaw sagged again.

"Don't look so surprised. I had her checked out. Couldn't understand your instant infatuation with her. Always thought you preferred boys."

Anton's eyes went wide. "*Boys*? You thought I was a *pedophile*?"

His father waved a hand through the air. "Men. I didn't mean to imply you were a kiddie fiddler."

Anton slumped back in his chair, feeling rather like oozing onto the floor in a puddle of woe. "I've always liked both; men *and* women."

But he'd only ever been in love with a woman.

"Well, I just remember your sister finding you with that stable hand. You'd gone for a man, rather than a girl, for the first time. Seemed to show a preference."

"Father!" Anton felt heat rising into his cheeks.

Red also tinged his father's face and he muttered, "Just saying."

It wasn't that Anton preferred men to women, or women to men. It was as he said, he *liked* both. Could have sex with both, provided he found them physically appealing. And he hadn't really found anyone appealing for a long time. Not since he'd met Annabel and she'd swept him away with a tide of longing, lust and love so strong that it was like he'd never *felt* before.

Well, he amended, ever honest with himself, he hadn't found anyone attractive except for one person. And he didn't even want to go there. *Couldn't* go there, because that bastard had taken Annabel from him.

"Why marry me off, Father? Couldn't you have gotten the heir from Darla?"

Reginald coughed into his hand and looked uncomfortable.

Anton sat back and eyed his parent, thinking over their conversation. "You're marrying me off to another *man*?"

Men marrying men wasn't uncommon. Anton wouldn't have blinked if he'd been told a friend was marrying another member of the same sex. But those marriages occurred when someone was solely orientated that way, or when they were in love. Anton wasn't either.

Reginald tugged at his loosely tied cravat. "As I said, I thought you preferred boys, I mean, men."

"So you're marrying me to one? A *vampire* or *werewolf* one?" It wasn't like he was a racist. He wasn't. But when you were born into the upper echelons of society and you were a minority even there, it left you feeling bitter toward the majority. And that meant he didn't really like vampires – *before* that bastard had killed Annabel.

"The family offered the marriage contract – I didn't approach them."

"It's not the only time I've been proposed to." And it wasn't. He had come to accept that he was attractive to women and men – he had enough bed offers, which he normally declined, to show that. But he'd never said yes to marriage, because he'd wanted love or something like it. He'd wanted what he thought he'd have with Annabel.

He'd also wanted children.

"As I said, they offered."

"And just like that, you accepted? It had better have been a bloody good offer." Like for a new title, or a life free of debt, or for something that was worth more than a gold ring on his third finger.

His father didn't reply.

"Did you at least make a clause that says I can have a child-bearing contract?" Anton asked.

"Of course! There is one for both of you. He is his father's only son as well, but like you, there is a sister." Which meant there wasn't really any *need* to produce offspring, not unless their sisters failed to do so.

An uneasy feeling settled in his stomach. "So what *was* the offer?"

Reginald sighed, the sound coming as if from the very depths of his being. "They're going to clear the debt."

"Debt?" He knew that the estate owed some coin, but that was normal. Nothing a good season couldn't fix.

"Of fifty thousand groats."

"*Fifty thousand?*" His stomach hit somewhere below the rugs under his feet. Maybe even the bedrock.

His father's leathery face flushed.

"*How?*" Anton's voice was strangled.

"A bad investment."

He thrust a hand through his hair. "On what?"

"There was a shipping enterprise, but the ship sank. We owed a lot of money to the Kiplings, and–"

"Wait. Did you just say Kipling?"

His father nodded.

No.

Chapter Thirty-Two

Don't eat anyone.

That was the last thing Clay had said – no, thought – to Elle, and he sure hoped she kept her fangs to herself. But who knew with Chosen vampires? They were a bloodthirsty lot; they weren't like their makers. Well, they weren't supposed to be like their Choosers. Vampires nowadays weren't like how they used to be; they drank blood every day because they wanted to, not because they actually needed it. But that was another story.

Clay knew.

Just like weres weren't like they once were; but they were closer to their original ideal than the vampires. Scratching his head, Clay settled back into the booth of the stinking bar he'd taken refuge in after the funeral. Cloying smoke hung low in the air and the less than pleasant odor of unwashed bodies permeated the walls, tables and booths. Ale wenches zigzagged through the taproom, their breasts more exposed than not, their eyes flashing and their bodies adding to the unwashed smell, but this time, with a hint of sex.

Clay winced at the stench of a particularly smelly customer and sighed to himself. He'd wanted to go straight back to the parlor for Elle, but he knew he couldn't. Olive was already suspicious of him, and he hadn't *done* anything suspicious. Yet. No doubt she was having him followed. It's what he'd do.

"Wolf."

Clay looked up at the hulking mound of humanity that stood

in front of the scarred wooden table. He was dressed from head to toe in black, with a red armband tied with a no-nonsense knot.

Clay raised an eyebrow in acknowledgment. "Human."

He wanted to say "Graced," but from the look of those cold Gray eyes, he probably shouldn't.

The hulking idiot – who did look rather like Muscle B, come to think of it – took a seat at the other side of the table, uninvited. He caught the arm of a passing waitress and, after eyeing her exposed chest, ordered himself a tankard of ale. *More fool him*, Clay thought, carefully avoiding taking a swig of his own. It tasted like a sick horse's piss, or what he thought it would taste like, anyway.

"Well," Clay said, folding his hands over his stomach, "what do you want?"

"The Green Lady isn't too happy with you right now."

"Who?"

Muscle B's newly arrived ale hit the table with a careless *thunk*, as the waitress appeared to be distracted by Muscle B's hand up her skirt. Idiot. Between the ale and the wench, Clay would take the ale. It might have more resemblance to urine than mead, but it would be fresher than the wench – she'd already had at least five customers that had bought more than beer from the smell of her.

"The Green Lady." The man withdrew his hand from the barmaid's skirt and focused on Clay.

"I obviously don't know who you're talking about." Clay shoved his tankard back and forth across the wooden table, careful not to knock it over on the bumps and grooves that scored the surface.

"You do so; I've seen you speaking to her." The man's dark hair curled high on his forehead, contrasting with his light eyes.

Ah, so he *was* Muscle B.

"Are you talking about Olive Brown?"

"Who else?" The man shrugged.

"Who knows? 'Green Lady' is a bit of a generalized term."

"There is only *one* Green Lady, and Olive Brown is it."

Clay had a feeling he was about to step into something he

didn't want to – worse than trodding into a pile of shit someone had just thrown out of their window.

"I don't want to know," Clay said.

"Fair enough." The man took a swig of his drink, and to his credit, he didn't flinch at the flavor. Maybe that's what he thought mead should taste like. Poor bastard.

"So, are you ever going to get to a point or are you just gonna sit there?" Clay asked.

"The Green Lady–"

"Just say 'Olive,' it's quicker and that way I won't forget who you're talking about."

"–Olive wants to know how you met her granddaughter."

Clay squinted through the smoke at Muscle B, and noticed some emotion flash through the human's eyes. "No, she doesn't."

Clay was good at reading people – he had to be after the millennia he'd spent wandering around – and he knew Muscle B was lying. Olive didn't want to know squat about how he knew Elle. She probably figured he'd bumped into her during his efforts to find and meet Emmie. The only thing Olive wanted to know was that her granddaughter was well and truly dead.

"Yes, Olive wants to know," Muscle B insisted.

"No, she doesn't."

Muscle B pokered up.

"So why do *you* want to know?" Clay smiled then, showing his teeth. He saw Muscle B's eyes drop down to his pearly whites.

That seemed to stump his interrogator, so Muscle B went back to his main issue. "Olive wants to know how you met Elle."

Clay took a sip of ale and swore mentally when the sour taste hit his tongue. He'd briefly forgotten about not drinking the swill.

Feeling less charitable due to the taste in his mouth, Clay snapped, "Cut the bullshit. *You* want to know, not Olive."

"I swear, it's Olive–"

Clay leaned forward. "I don't have to be a telepath to know when someone's lying."

He saw Muscle B swallow.

"She was meant for me," the man blurted.

"Who was? Meant for you how?" The idea of Elle with this muscle-bound freak made Clay's stomach churn.

"Elle. She's my cousin."

"That doesn't explain anything." Clay snorted.

"Well, she's sort of a cousin." Muscle B shrugged.

"Sort of? That only tells me you want to have sex with your cousin. How was she meant for you?"

Werewolves liked to breed outside the pack, to spread their genes. Although nowadays, wolves thought the sole reason was to prevent inbreeding. It was almost an anathema to want to marry within your own family. There were good reasons for that.

Muscle B's hand clenched around his tankard. "Not have sex with. Marry. Have children."

"But she's a half-blood," Clay protested without thinking.

"Yes, but she has a good line. I kept hoping she'd develop some...ability...but it never seemed to happen. I trained with her a lot."

"Wait – you're Bjorn?"

The man's eyes seemed to brighten. "She spoke about me?"

Clay didn't like that light. "Not really. She seemed pissed at you, to be truthful."

Bjorn looked away. "I was tough on her, but I needed to know she was strong. For our sons."

Something like jealousy reared its ugly head within Clay. "Sons that you would never have had; I can't see her agreeing to have children with her *cousin*."

Bjorn's hand was clenching tighter and tighter around his tankard. "You only met her once or twice, so what would you know about her?"

A little evil rose up from within that jealous beast. "I know plenty. We got along *really* well."

Bjorn's face blanched. "She would have never, *never* gotten to know a werewolf *well*."

"Whatever you say, bucko." Clay grinned again. He began sliding to the side of the booth. "As much fun as this pointless conversation has been, I must be off."

"But–"

Clay stood, decided his earlier response was foolish. "But what? You wanted to know how I met Elle. It was in a bar fight. Then I bumped into her on the street. We talked. I figured out who she was from chatting with Olive. I noticed she had a busted shoulder. Asked how she was. End of story."

"Right. I'm going to keep an eye on you."

"Do that. But bear in mind, I've got a lot of time on my hands. You don't."

With that, Clay walked away. Now he knew he was being watched, he was going to have to be more careful. He just didn't know how he was going to help Elle.

CHAPTER THIRTY-THREE

Don't eat anyone.

It had seemed laughable when Clay had thought it at her an hour ago. Eating people – as if she would *do* something like that. She may have woken up a little different, okay, a lot different, but she'd never been tempted to hurt someone, not unless they deserved it.

And there'd been plenty of people who'd deserved it.

But now his instruction just seemed cruel.

Her stomach was clenching in a way it never had before, and her skin felt too tight, like it was stretched for tanning. Elle also couldn't stop staring at her hands, which were fisted in her lap. The skin was so white it was translucent; she could see the little blue veins running beneath the surface and each and every pore on her skin. Her nails also seemed different; stronger, sharper. She'd managed to cut herself when she'd scrabbled into her hiding space, and the smell of her blood had caused her stomach to do an odd flip-flop. But it hadn't been an appealing smell, not really. It was a very different odor to that of human blood, at least, how she remembered it, anyway – not as metallic, sweeter.

Still, she'd sucked the wound out of reflex. It had tasted different, too; not like copper, almost like an exotic fruit she'd never eaten before, but could somehow imagine. It wasn't filling, like a piece of candy that tasted great but left the hunger pangs behind. Elle tried to compare the flavor to her memory of the Creep's blood, but it was a red haze. Mostly of anger, but also of fear and pain.

She'd always been taught that Graceds couldn't survive being Chosen, but she had. Did that mean it was only purebloods that couldn't make the transition? And if so, what had happened to all the other Hazels who'd been Chosen or Bitten before? There would have had to have been plenty. Most Hazels weren't recognized by their Graced ancestors; they wouldn't know it was a real danger to agree to being Chosen. So if other Hazels had been Bitten or Chosen, then where were they? What had happened to them?

Elle wasn't sure she wanted to know the answers to those questions. Suddenly, her hiding space under a cluster of unused tables and cloths seemed flimsy. All it would take was for a vampire or wolf to walk into the room and she'd be undone. What would they do if they found her? Hand her back to Gran – who had been suspicious at best – or just eliminate her anyway, because she was different?

Elle didn't like the answer that formed in her mind.

Or maybe she was just being paranoid.

And why would the vampires or weres care? A part of her mind wanted to know. *Gran insists they don't know about Graceds, so why would your previous eye color matter?*

Although, Clay obviously *did* know about Graceds. Otherwise, how would he have known she could hear him *think*?

Elle frowned and shook her head. Why was she worrying about some vampire or wolf finding her when she didn't even know if she was going to make it out of here alive? Or if Clay would even come for her?

Elle looked up from her fisted hands and at the tiny woven threads of the red cloth that covered her sanctuary. Her mind was starting to grow a bit fuzzy around the edges.

Why, that annoying part of her brain intruded again, hadn't Gran realized she was awake? And how hadn't Gran "heard" the conversation between her and Clay?

Unable to answer the questions, and too distracted to think about them more, Elle felt her stomach's hollowness turn to gnawing pain. Her teeth began to extend, so far that they pricked her lower lip. She licked it, to see if she could taste blood, but thankfully, there was none. She began to grow light-headed, her skin overly sensitive. Worst of all, she felt so incredibly *empty*; it was unlike anything she'd ever experienced before.

This is what it means to be a leech, she thought.

She didn't like it.

Elle had thought Clay would come back for her – would help her – but he hadn't shown head nor tail since he'd told her to hide. Maybe he wouldn't come at all. *He likes me*, she thought, *enough to have sex with me at least. He'll come back.* Sure, that other part of her replied, they'd had sex, but he might have just done that to get closer to Emmie.

She groaned, her thoughts so turbulent she didn't like any of them.

Then there was Emmie. Sweet, human Emmie who had smelled almost good enough to eat earlier, when Elle had escaped her coffin.

Coffin.

Dead.

Food.

By the blood, she *hurt*.

Breathing was becoming a chore, each inhalation like burning knives raining down her throat. She hadn't heard any stories about this – that the hunger could be so strong that it even made existing a challenge.

Elle fought back hysterical laughter.

She wasn't sure how much longer she could last before she *did* eat someone.

♦

Clay was whistling a jaunty tune as he walked down a side alley. He could feel Bjorn following him – hear him, too – so he made a few quick detours; over a wall, under a fence and through someone's vacant living room. Detours that only a fellow were would be able to pursue. Grays were good, but not *that* good.

Within minutes, he was standing outside the funeral parlor's side entrance, half the city traversed behind him.

Now, how to gain entry without raising suspicion?

He eyed the side of the building and walked around the corner, into an alley. He couldn't hear or see anyone nearby. He spotted a window that was partially open. *Piece of cake*, he thought. Quickly, he walked over to the area underneath the window then leaped. He gripped the frame and looked around again to make sure he was unobserved. Then he hoisted himself up and pressed his ear to the glass. No sounds within. Perfect. Within seconds, he'd pried the window open the rest of the way and swung himself inside.

He was in an office. Clay ignored the wooden desk – human owned – and its associated paperwork and headed toward the door. Prying it open, he listened for the sounds of anyone approaching or talking, but heard nothing.

Just rapid breathing coming from down the hall.

Walking toward the sound of crackling fire from the crematorium, he found himself outside a plain door. Blood, he didn't like this place. It wasn't so bad when he'd been surrounded by people, but burning furnaces and the heat of flames reminded him of the past, back when cities had crumbled and people were burned alive. Trying to banish the memories, Clay opened the door and stepped into the storeroom that sat between the parlor and furnace room. *See*, he told himself, *no bombs, no screams*. Just a room. Plus, bombs didn't exist anymore. His eyes scanned over the tables, chairs and cloths, as he walked toward the corner where he'd told Elle to hide. All he could hear were those rapid breaths, which was odd for a vampire. He hoped she'd kept to his final instruction.

Bending down, he lifted the drooping red cloth that covered her assigned sanctuary. He barely had time to blink before he was thrown onto his back. He thrust his forearms up to protect his face as a pair of hands latched onto his upper arms. Sharp teeth snapped the air in front of him.

Looking up around his arms, he saw Elle's face contorted in

pain. Her pupils were so dilated the red-purple of her irises was barely visible. Stretching his arms out, he tried to push her away, but she was strong, so he gripped her shoulders and held her at arm's length.

Something like sanity seemed to flicker in her wild eyes and she moaned, "Hungry."

I'm an idiot, Clay thought and slowly let go of one of her shoulders. Instantly, she tried to swoop down and latch onto his neck, but he shoved her away. She landed on the floor with a thump and he threw himself at her, pinning her down. Her eyes had grown wild and there was no sense of Elle left within them, just pupil-huge hunger. He was going to have to allow her to feed from him.

The idea gave him the creeps.

Slowly, like working with a wounded animal, he waved food – in this case, the veins on his wrist – in front of her mouth. Needing no more encouragement, she struck like a snake, her fangs piercing his wrist. He could feel her greedily sucking on the wound she'd made, but because he healed so fast, she had to bite him again and again to keep the blood flowing. He grunted and tried to pull away, but that made her bite harder.

It fucking hurt.

A lot.

After she'd drunk her fill, she fell back from his wrist like a sated tick. He rocked back on his heels and squatted before he looked down at his wrist. The wounds were already closed, but there was blood smeared over the skin around them, and he felt a little light-headed. It was too bad weres were immune to the toxin in vampire venom; it would have made the feeding less horrible.

"Sorry," Elle muttered, wiping her mouth with the back of her hand. She seemed like she was in control of herself again, but he wasn't sure. New vampires were blood-hungry, but he'd never really had to deal with one before. Everything he knew was hearsay.

This is what her bloody Chooser is for, he thought.

Running his eyes over her as she half lay on the floor, Clay tried to convince himself that she was still Elle – his Elle – and her bloodlust was gone. For now. When his eyes reached her face, he dropped onto his ass in shock. He hadn't really *looked* at her since she was Chosen. He'd been hurrying her to a hiding space and then he'd been prying her off his arm. But he was looking now.

"What?" Elle raised her other hand to her face and touched her cheek.

She was like an ancient princess, he first thought. Her short red hair had grown over the last day or so and now hung like a blood-colored curtain down her back, the darker color accentuating her pale skin. Her cheekbones, which had been sharp before, were now matched by the clean, forceful lines of her forehead and chin.

He'd seen her body before, when she'd been "dead," and she hadn't looked any different. But then, the external changes were usually the last stage of the transformation. The first two days were when the internal organs adapted, the muscles grew stronger, the blood systems reworked. The final day was when the outside was made over; hair grew longer, skin became clearer, features sharpened, teeth grew and the body became the perfect hunting machine. Faster to catch prey, more attractive to lure it in.

Shaking his head, he met her eyes and froze. He'd never seen anything like it. The unique color was stunning. Even Clay's sister's weren't like this.

"What?" Her hand had moved from her cheek and was now rubbing at her nose, as if it was dirty.

Her eyes. They were a deep red-purple color with slashes of glowing Green and luminous Gray.

"You're beautiful," Clay managed to choke out.

"*What?*"

He'd thought her lovely before, no doubt about it, but this was different. It was like seeing a refined version of Elle – as if her personality was now showcased by her appearance.

"You're beautiful," he repeated. Shaking his head, he forced himself to focus on what was happening in front of him, which was Elle's disbelief.

Elle stopped rubbing her nose. "Tell me another story."

Clay just shook his head. Again. Until Elle saw herself in a mirror, she wasn't going to be able to reconcile what he was saying to what she thought of herself. Now wasn't the time anyway, he had to get her out of here.

"How are you feeling?" he asked, which was a dumb question, but he needed to know that her hunger was gone.

"Better."

Clay nodded and then quickly scanned the room. "We need to make you look less like a vampire and more like a werewolf."

"Why?"

"Because your grandmother is having me followed," Clay answered.

Elle just watched him with her amazing new eyes.

He ran a hand through his hair. "Have you forgotten she'll want you dead?"

Elle sighed and stood. "No." She seemed to think for a moment. "Fine, let's make me look more wolfy." She barked a quick laugh. "Never thought I'd ever say that phrase."

CHAPTER THIRTY-FOUR

Dante stared at his father, too stupefied to say anything. His fingers were clenched on the arms of his leather chair and his body was coiled, ready to launch away from his father's words. The walls of the study, normally a place that Dante enjoyed visiting, seemed to close in on him. He didn't even want to look at the skulls.

Deep down though, he had *known* something like this would happen. Not the particulars – Dante had never really been able to predict what his father would do next – but he'd *known* some punishment would be meted out for his Choosing that girl. Misty had even hinted as much.

Viktor glanced up from the paperwork spread out on the desk in front of him and tapped his chin. The papers had been sorted into three methodical piles, one of which seemed to hold the most interest. "The marriage is to take place shortly."

Dante looked at the yellowy paper; he could see the swirling letters and make out his name, which was mentioned over and over: Dante Daemon Ernest Romanov Kipling.

"What is the settlement?" Dante asked.

His father's inky eyebrow slashed upward. "I didn't realize you needed to know anything about this, other than the time and place."

"In case you hadn't noticed, Father, *I* am the one getting married." He didn't even bother to cloak the sarcasm in sycophancy.

Dante wasn't interested in pleasing his parent anymore. This was about trying to determine how much his father had handed out to get rid of him. And who he'd handed him to. That little gem had yet to be announced. His stomach started to churn uncomfortably, making him restless. Maybe the blood he'd had this morning had been polluted by drugs?

"Enough to clear your groom's debt."

Groom. So Dante was being married off to some financial idiot, who happened to have a cock. Part of him hoped that his prospective husband didn't like men sexually, because then it meant Dante wouldn't have to have sex with him. It would just be a dry union on paper. Not that they *had* to have sex. There was nothing that said they had to, and there seemed to be plenty of couples who didn't copulate – it seemed to be the one common theme of marriage, Dante had noticed – but it was expected.

Dante, however, assumed that the man *would* like men; it wouldn't have been a punishment otherwise. What Viktor didn't understand was that it wouldn't bother Dante that he was being married off to a man. Gender wasn't important. It was sex that was the problem.

Any type of sex.

It was just, well, not for him. People talked about sex drives and libido, but he didn't have one.

The uncomfortable feeling in his stomach built, and he was feeling…antsy. Was that the word for it? Pretending calm – which was in itself strange, since Dante seemed to be perpetually calm – he leaned back in his chair and folded his hands across his stomach. "How much is my groom's debt?"

"Fifty thousand groats." His father picked up a pen and began signing the paperwork from the middle pile.

Dante deliberately kept his expression blank. Fifty thousand groats. What kind of an idiot was he marrying? "Well, you really must have wanted me out of your house."

"That's all you can say?"

Dante raised an eyebrow of his own. "I wasn't aware you cared about what I had to say."

Viktor shrugged.

Now, Dante thought, who would be in that much debt? He racked his brains, but couldn't think of a vampire family that needed so much coin. Then again, he didn't really know much about the financial situations of other families; although he may have heard something about *that*. Misty would know, but she had been barred from this meeting.

His father signed the final page with a flourish. "Here is the situation in a nutshell: You are going to marry Anton Greystoke, and you aren't going to complain. Not once." His hard voice didn't match the gentleness with which Viktor placed the pen in its small holder. His father steepled his hands.

Dante blinked and racked his brain. Why did he know that name? His stomach did an uncomfortable flip-flop, and were his hands sweating? His hands *never* sweated. But he was sure he'd only met the person recently… "The one who came looking for the 'fiancée' I had Chosen?"

Viktor nodded.

That pretty boy? But he was *human*. The levels of punishment were just piling on top of each other. Hopefully, Dante thought, Anton may not like having sex with men, seeing as he had been engaged to a woman. He definitely wished it was so, and he dried his palms a little.

"You both have clauses in the marriage contract that will allow you to father heirs, if neither of your sisters do so. Is that clear?" Viktor's eyes turned to a frosty mauve.

"Sure." When his father stared at him, Dante added, "Become a stud if Misty doesn't perform her duties, I understand."

His father flicked a hand dismissively through the air. "It isn't stud duty; it is *family* duty, which you seem unable to grasp. And you will do it if it is required. Do I make myself clear?"

Dante fought the urge to roll his eyes. "Crystal."

Although, he had to mentally scoff at his supposedly not understanding "family duty." His whole life had been dictated by it. If not for that, he would have been following his suspicions about the colored-eyed humans more. A *whole* lot more.

"There are some rules, however." Viktor tapped the paper.

Of course there are rules, Dante thought. *I can't have something easy, can I?*

"You are *not* to bite your husband and you are not to Choose him without written consent from his family. In fact, you will not Choose any more humans. Is that clear?"

"Not to bite him?" Dante blinked. Most humans liked being bitten during…well. At least, that was what he'd been told. Dante wasn't really sure he wanted to think about that.

"Those two points are clauses of the marriage contract. If you do either of these actions, the marriage will be terminated, but the debt will remain paid." The tapping became more forceful. "I will be *very* unhappy if that happens and there will be consequences."

"What happens if I refuse to go through with this marriage?" Dante asked, more out of curiosity than any desire to disobey. He was sure that whatever it was would be worse than marriage to a potentially man-loving, brown-eyed human.

"The paperwork I have here," Viktor tapped the pile of yellow parchment on his left, "are forms which will allow me to place you in Pinton's Insane Asylum."

The insane asylum. Dante repressed a shudder.

Curiosity killed the cat. He could now see why.

"I see."

"No, I'm not sure that you do. If you refuse to go ahead with this marriage, I *will* have you confined to the asylum. If you violate the clauses of the marriage and it is terminated as a result, I will confine you to the asylum. I would prefer not to risk the earldom's succession, and this way there is still the hope that we could obtain an heir from you, if necessary."

Dante's heart seemed to kick up a gear, and his palms went back to sweating. He'd never had this physical reaction before. What was going on? He'd *known* something like this was going to happen. And anyway, why couldn't his father sire another child, why did Dante have to?

"Not if I refuse to play stud," Dante snapped.

His father snorted. "If a man is given the right stimulation, then he can perform."

Dante wasn't so sure that his father's plan would work. Dante didn't exactly respond to the "right stimulation," or any stimulation for that matter. Not without a lot of effort on his *and* his partner's part. And even then it was hit and miss.

"I *do* have another contingency plan as well, just in case you do prove stubborn; another letter I can use to gain your obedience."

Dante didn't like the sound of that; he was even feeling a bit light-headed. There was something *worse* than being committed?

"A death warrant?" Dante quipped, trying to discreetly wipe his palms on his jacket.

His father froze, hand hovering over the final pile of papers. Viktor appeared to give himself a shake before he clasped his hands together. "Yes."

Dante shrugged, pretending he wasn't shocked. Pretending he wasn't feeling…anxious. That was it! He was feeling worried, for himself. He'd never experienced that before. Was something wrong with him?

Thinking about his father's words, about the threats, he figured, *Well, it probably* is *okay to be anxious when your father is threatening to have you executed.*

And really, his mind said, why are you even surprised?

CHAPTER THIRTY-FIVE

Elle hadn't felt so bereft in her entire life.

She couldn't see Emmie, couldn't steal a quick, hard hug off her mother, and she couldn't even be told off by Gran. Although, to be fair, the latter was no hardship. It was just different. Everything was different.

Now that her stomach had stopped asserting itself and her head was clear, she felt mortified. She'd attacked Clay without provocation. Just jumped him and tried to bite him. Elle figured she would probably *still* be trying, if he hadn't given in and let her have her head and his blood.

She felt dirty, like she had violated him.

Hugging her knees to her chest, Elle propped her chin on them. The mattress was soft under her – Clay must have some coin; most people couldn't afford that kind of feathered luxury. She looked contemplatively across the room at Clay, who had just come out of the small bathroom, which was attached to the bedroom of his apartment. He had a towel draped around his neck and a pair of buckskins on and nothing else. It was enough to make her mouth water again, although this time for a different reason.

She wondered when he had stopped being a stalker and an enemy. Elle's eyes ran over his bare chest, which was all hard planes and muscle. *About the time you jumped in the sack with him,* another part of her replied. Looking at him, she wondered if anyone but Gran could really blame her.

She still couldn't believe that she'd slept with a werewolf, but then, she still couldn't really believe that she was sitting on a stupidly soft bed in a foreign apartment as a member of the undead. She'd hated vampires and weres for so long that it seemed strange to not care about having had sex with one. Although, that was nowhere near as bad as being one.

And she didn't really care too much about that, either. Oh, she had already admitted her embarrassment and horror at what she'd done to Clay, but other than that, she felt strangely content.

Calm.

Not that she'd had a choice in the matter. She'd always thought approval from the human in question was required – blood, it was meant to be a law – but the Creep had just gone and done what he wanted. Since she had survived, most people would assume she'd wanted to be Chosen. And if she were to say she hadn't, would that mean that she'd get her head lopped off, along with her Chooser's?

Elle somewhat doubted that Gran would care if it had been consensual or not. None of her family would give a shit, Clay was right about that; they would probably want to stick a stake in her quick smart. After all, Gran was a purist and Elle was defying the natural order: the one according to Gran. She didn't need her newfound telepathy to tell her that.

Clay picked up one end of the white towel hanging over his shoulders and scrubbed his hair. "Have you looked in the mirror yet?"

Elle shook her head. She wasn't really sure she wanted to. The way that Clay looked at her – as if she were a princess come to sweep him off his feet – made her feel uncomfortable. He'd never looked at her like that before; did she really want to know what had caused such a big difference in his regard?

He dropped the towel. "You should."

"Why?" Elle jutted her chin forward.

"Because you need to get to know the new you. You're a vampire now, you aren't human. You need to accept that; there's no point fighting what you've become."

Elle wasn't so sure about that. Sure, she was calm about the change, for now. Why risk a hissy fit, when said fit had taken on a whole new level of danger?

"What? So I shouldn't fight my urge to bite every neck I see?"

Unfortunately, that wasn't an exaggeration. The trip to Clay's apartment had been horrible. She'd been covered from head to toe in a ridiculous amount of clothing, and he'd managed to smear soot all over her face. She'd looked like a chimney sweep who had decided to wear everything in their closet. Nobody had noticed her – that part of their plan had worked. What she hadn't counted on was *her* noticing everyone else. She could *hear* what everyone was thinking and most of it wasn't pleasant. Rage at lovers, lots of thoughts about sex and naked bodies, worries about children, hungry stomachs and the desperate need to feel safe. So she'd *known* beyond a shadow of doubt that no one had noticed her, but plenty of women *had* noticed Clay. She'd had to really work on strengthening her mental shield, especially when some of those women had thought very…explicit things about Clay. The jealousy had been harsh and swift and shocking.

It hadn't helped that she'd also found herself considering everyone in a food or non-food type of way.

Blood pumping in veins, heartbeats…the sheer smell of blood. Blood. Blood. Blood. It had been a cornucopia of edible scents. Even the stink of unwashed human flesh hadn't been off-putting like normal, because there was blood underneath the surface. Her fangs lengthened just thinking of it.

She tried to distract herself by remembering the other vampires she'd walked past. They had smelled different. It had been an almost icy, burning smell, and even though she knew the exotic flavor that ran through their veins, they hadn't smelled tasty at all.

Then there'd been Clay, who next to a human smelled a bit like a furry dog, but still good. Compared to a vampire though, he'd been appealing in a food *and* non-food way.

"Why don't vampires feed off weres more often, since you can't get addicted to vampire bites?" Elle asked into the silence.

Clay sighed and dropped his towel onto what appeared to be

his dirty laundry chair. "Can you really imagine one of us agreeing to it if we didn't have to?"

Elle tilted her head to the side. "Why not?" A little part of her felt even more guilty about what she'd done.

Clay walked over to his closet – which was really a pile of clothes on the floor – and began rifling through it. "It hurts."

Elle frowned at his response. She lowered her mental shield just enough so that she could focus on Clay's glittering amber mind. Perhaps she could see how much she had hurt him during her tick-like activities? It didn't take long for her to realize that she couldn't hear his thoughts, not like when she'd been in the coffin.

"Why can't I hear your thoughts now, when I could before? How do you *know* about Graceds?" Elle asked. Other mental voices began working their way into her mind:

"I can't pay the rent. Why the fuck did I bet on that stupid horse? A fucking donkey could have run faster. I'll have to suck that bastard landlord's cock again."

"I hate them both. I should have never had children."

"I just love John so much. I couldn't live without him. I really couldn't."

Elle slammed the shield back into place.

Clay was staring at her, eyes intense. "I was thinking them *at* you. And I just know."

Elle blinked. She guessed he must be right. She hadn't heard a single peep from his mind, although she could somehow *see* it when her shield was down. And he clearly didn't want to tell her how he knew about her race. Since she hadn't told him anything, either, she couldn't really fault him for not elaborating.

Clay slid a white shirt on and then walked over to the bed. He sat down next to her, causing the mattress to tip her upward. He began buttoning his shirt, which was a bit of a downer.

"I don't get it," Elle said, when she figured he wasn't going to say anything else.

"Normally, I am resistant to Greens."

That was interesting. She didn't know any were or vampire who was, not when a Green *wanted* to hear them. "So Gran can't hear you at all?" Elle asked.

Clay shook his head. "No, not even if I try thinking at her. She can't hear squat."

"But…she can hear everyone. Wolves and vampires, as well as humans and other Graceds – except Greens."

"Not me," Clay said. "But I am a bit of an oddity; something kooky in my genetic makeup."

Elle began tapping her fingers against her shins. For some reason, she didn't think the explanation was really that simple. "What exactly *are* genes? It's something to do with blood, but the word doesn't exist anymore. Not in any dictionary I could find. Gran talks about them a lot. Apart from you, she's the only person I've heard use the word."

"Really simply, they're a code that makes you, well, you. Everyone has a code and everyone's is slightly different. But there are bigger differences race to race."

"Right," Elle said, although she wasn't sure she really got it. How does someone have a code? Can you see it? "You have genes that mean I can't hear you unless you think loudly at me?" Elle frowned. "I can't hear anyone else at the moment either, but that's because I put up a shield, to stop the thoughts coming in. I think though, if I relaxed it, they'd seep in. Gran can hear everyone all the time, even shielded – I think – to some extent, unless they are other Greens."

"Some people can turn it on and off, from what I've seen. I think it would be more of a hindrance to be able to hear every little thought that runs through a person's brain. Most people are idiots. Or boring. Or worse, they're both." Clay shrugged.

Elle laughed. "True." She thought for a moment. "So, why don't wolves let vampires feed off them? I mean, you taste okay."

Clay finished doing up the last button on his shirt. "I taste good, do I?"

Elle just stared at him.

Clay ran a hand through his hair. "As I said, it hurts."

Elle raised an eyebrow.

"We heal, really fast."

"Tell me something new." Everybody knew weres mended fast. It was the most basic thing about them, other than the fact they had furry little tails every other night.

"We heal a lot faster than vampires do; it's part of being able to shapeshift. When you bit me, I healed almost as fast as you bit. So you had to bite me again and again – I'm not sure if you realized you were even doing it. And just because I heal fast, it doesn't mean I can't feel pain. I do."

Elle winced.

"The long and short of it: we don't like being bitten by vampires because it's painful. But here's the science lesson most people don't know: vampires and werewolves produce oxygen in their blood. But not enough. We need that and the platelets and a few other chemicals from human or animal blood to sustain our rapid healing and alleged immortality. Hence why you don't need to breathe as much – although you still do need to breathe, your blood gets enough oxygen from your food. Weres adapted to produce more oxygen, so we don't need to drink human blood much, if at all; a sufficiently bloody steak will suffice. Vampires didn't evolve as much, so when they drink our blood, they get most of what they need, but it's strong. Too strong for many of them, and they can't use it all. It's wasteful. It can feel like being kicked by a team of draft horses from the inside out."

All this talk of oxygen and platelets was beyond her knowledge. Gran would understand, though.

"Is that why they don't like weres?" Elle asked. She'd noticed – *everyone* had noticed – that Pinton had a low wolf population and figured it was because the city was vampire-run. She'd been happy that there'd only really been one group of freaks to deal with, now she wasn't so sure. Weres seemed better, somehow. After all, they were just as happy to munch on cow liver as human.

"It's more why *we* don't like *them*. They think of us as food – undesirable food, but food nonetheless. We don't like being thought of as an after-dinner snack. Plus, they're bigots."

Elle let go of her legs and leaned back on the bed, so she was lying down. "So why are there so few wolves here?"

"We don't generally like vampires and this town reeks of them." Clay lay down next to her on his side. He propped his head on his hand. "Competition for food and all that. Plus, they think we're lower class; even worse than humans, sometimes. Why would we want to work with people like that?"

Elle snorted. "Vampires don't work. Not unless they have to."

"That's another difference between our races. We aren't afraid of a bit of labor. Vampires like things being done for them. They're soft, weak. How they live in their cities and their aristo societies, that isn't what they were designed for."

"Designed for?" Elle asked with a frown.

Clay rolled off the bed. "Enough of this. Time for you to see the new you." He walked over to a set of drawers that were propped in the corner next to the bathroom door. Opening the top drawer, he withdrew an object the size of a small plate and then turned and walked back toward her. It was a mirror.

Dread filled the pit of her stomach and she wanted to spring up and run away. Precisely because she felt like that, she took the mirror from Clay. She wasn't a coward and she wasn't about to become one just because she now had fangs. And super strength, and really fast reflexes.

Taking a deep breath, she lifted the mirror up to her face level and tried to keep her expression blank, but the first thing she noticed was her hair. It was just as bad as she'd feared. It was *long*. And still curly. The color was different, and she wished it had become blonde or brown or something. But it hadn't. It wasn't so metallic anymore, so coppery; rather, it now looked like her head had been dipped in a vat of blood. She'd known it was longer though, because she'd had to keep brushing it away, but she hadn't looked at it, never really taken into account just how bloody long it was. It was down to her freaking ass! She was going to have to cut it.

Staring at the rest of her reflection, she felt shock sizzle through her, along with irritation. She still looked like her, there was no doubt about it, but she wasn't some princess from a fairy tale. Her face seemed sharper, all the lines more well-defined, her lips a deep berry red and her skin paler, almost toneless. Elle thought the shock of her new appearance would have been equivalent to the one she might have experienced if she'd dyed her hair black, painted her face in cosmetics, and decided to parade in front of a mirror.

That feeling lasted until she met her stare in the mirror.

Her eyes. Her *eyes*. The Brown was now a deep purple, which was strange, but she'd expected that. The major differences were the Green and Gray flecks; they were bright, brilliant shards of color. It gave her eyes an opalescent appearance.

"I look *mostly* the same," Elle said, trying to sound nonchalant as she lowered the mirror.

"What?" Clay's eyebrows shot to his hairline.

"I mean, yeah, my face is thinner and my hair is darker. Dark red rather than copper; but I could have got that from a dye job." All of what she'd said was true. She looked like her, but she didn't look like *her*. It would take some getting used to, and she needed to cut her hair. "But my eyes *are* kind of freaky."

CHAPTER THIRTY-SIX

Anton's cravat felt like it was choking him. Tugging at the snowy white cotton, he tried to loosen its grip on his neck, but only succeeded in making himself look uncomfortable. Which he was, but he didn't want everyone at the blasted ball knowing it. They were already staring at him enough as it was. Imagine the stories they'd tell: *Choked to death by white satin*. He fought a smirk.

He hadn't wanted to go to the Baron of Liverly's ball, but he hadn't had much choice. "Go and have fun," had been his father's words.

Anton had translated those to, "Go to the ball, pretend to have fun, but keep up the impression that we are happy with this match."

The ball was the biggest event of the week, so he couldn't fault his father's logic. It was just that Liverly was a pompous fool who'd married a conniving bitch. Every year they hosted their "Winter Ball," each more ridiculously decorated than the last. He really hadn't wanted to go; one, because he hadn't wanted to be chased by the baroness the whole night and two, he hated having to pretend happiness.

So far, his first concern thankfully hadn't happened, probably because the engagement announcement had been printed in the papers that morning. His sister and mother had come to town the night before, and they'd been so excited for him that he knew his father hadn't told them the truth: that he was sacrificing his only son for the sake of the family's coffers.

His sister, Darla, had been especially pleased; she hadn't debuted yet and didn't understand how the world really worked. She was full of romantic dreams; he'd met his soon-to-be vampire husband at a ball and they'd fallen instantly in love, so much so that the vampire wanted to marry him and eschew all others. Maybe the vampire would even *Choose* him.

Anton couldn't help but shake his head. He wondered if he'd ever been so foolish. Oh, he was well aware he'd made an idiot of himself over Annabel, but those emotions had been so intense. He couldn't have resisted following their urges and he doubted he'd ever be that in love again. Before he'd met her, he certainly hadn't wanted to get married this young and he'd never thought he'd settle for one person unless they were his perfect match. Funny how fate worked.

From the looks he'd been receiving ever since setting his polished boot inside Liverly's door, everyone knew about his engagement as well. And they weren't sure what to make of it. Most of the guests were vampires, and he could see the indecision on their faces when they greeted him. Should they laugh at him, or should they welcome him? After all, one day he may well become one of them.

It was ridiculous; he was still the same person, the same *baron*, as yesterday. But he hadn't been a threat then; he'd been a human they could tolerate or ignore. There hadn't even been the remotest possibility that he would join their ranks. Now, well, he might be Chosen at any moment by his vampire husband. A baron who was only going to be alive for a hundred years could be tolerated with a little hand waving – but one that could be around for centuries? That bore thinking about.

Anton took a step forward and plastered a smile on his face. He gave a short bow and greeted the bored wife of another baron. She looked at him like he was a sweetmeat she'd like to nibble on. Which was probably accurate, since her fangs were out. He moved on quickly, feeling the looks following him. Why was his upcoming marriage such a shock? Had he been considered that unwanted?

On his way through the crowd, the thousands of white roses that bedecked the ballroom caught his eye. So did the ice statues that stood poised on tables above glittering crystal glasses. They all cost money. Everyone wore ridiculously expensive satins, silks and velvets; their diamonds and rubies glittering on silver and gold settings. Everything they wore – even the flowers and feathers in their primped hair – cost money. And he was being married to it. Why that necessitated whispers and titters as he walked through the crowd, he didn't know. It was what most aristos married for, anyway. It was how they could afford to throw these ridiculous parties. He guessed though that most aristos married within their own races to achieve that wealth.

Well, their confusion wasn't his problem.

Anton walked toward the double glass doors at the end of the ballroom. They were open to the cool night air and a darkened terrace, but he couldn't feel the breeze from his position in the center of the room, surrounded by false well-wishers. Pushing past a vampire woman, Anton limped his way to the door. As he moved, he overheard snippets of conversation.

"Hadn't thought he liked men."

"Why is food marrying one of *us*?"

"Kipling is just too pretty to waste in marriage. Not that he ever socializes, anyway. Although, that human *is* a tasty-looking morsel."

"Hope he bites him."

No one seemed to have an original thought to say.

Anton made it to the terrace, where the cool breeze danced with damp tendrils of hair that had drooped low on his forehead. He limped to the rail and clasped the cool metal in one hand, leaning his cane against the ornate bars with the other. Candles in red and yellow paper lanterns lit the area, casting a flickering glow out onto the gardens below. The scent of roses and honeysuckle wreathed through the air. Finally, he was alone.

"So, you're the little boy set to marry my brother."

Of course, he thought. Someone would *have* to come and bother him in the five seconds he'd managed to think he'd found silence.

Anton let go of the rail and turned around. A woman was standing with her back to the doors, her blonde hair catching the light cast from inside, giving her a halo. She wore a white dress, cut so low he could almost see her nipples, and her skin was like alabaster. Vampire. Although, the fangs alone would have given her away.

She looked like a whore. Not even a well-paid one. He should know, he'd almost married one of those. And he'd met the viscountess before.

Anton gripped the rail. "Little boy here, at your service."

"You…"

"Me?" he said.

"You–"

"Do you suffer from a speech impediment?" Anton asked. He reached behind his leg and picked up his cane.

She shut her mouth with a click.

"So, I assume I have other such wonderful welcomes to expect?" he asked when she kept staring at him.

He'd met her father, for blood's sake, and he couldn't imagine being given a warm welcome there, either. He couldn't really work out *why* Wintermere had agreed to marry his precious little son to a human. To him, in particular.

"For a human, you're ruder than normal." She sniffed the air, tilting her chin up.

"Says the girl who came out here to make snide comments to her future brother-in-law." Anton crossed his arms, his cane leaning back against the rails again.

Her eyes flashed. "You are barely out of leading strings; it's ridiculous that you're marrying someone almost five times your age."

He couldn't help it, he grinned. "Ouch, you wound me with your harsh comments on my age."

She flicked her hair over a bare shoulder. "Says the child."

"Oh dear, you terrify me." Anton pretended to wince. He picked his cane up and bowed. "Viscountess Kipling, it was a pleasure."

Anton managed to make two steps before the vampire was at his side.

"So, you met Dante and then asked for his hand? Because you were so smitten?"

Anton sidled away. He didn't like being close to vampires. They made him feel uncomfortable, like prey. How he was going to stand being married to one, he didn't know. Maybe they could have a "fashionable" marriage and live in separate houses.

"That's the story Kipling told you?" Anton asked.

She took another step closer to him, forcing him to back further away. Soon they were out of the candlelight's glow. He had to fight the urge to tug at his cravat again. The cool air seemed like the hot winds of summer.

Blonde eyebrows shot high on the viscountess' forehead. "Dante?"

"Yes, did Kipling tell you I met him and then fell for him so badly I wanted to marry him?" Anton couldn't keep the incredulity out of his voice.

"Well, no." She tapped her chin. "That was what Father said. Dante didn't seem to have much to say on the subject at all."

Great, Anton thought. His fiancé hadn't even bothered to tell his sister about the marriage. Why would he have agreed to it if he wasn't even interested enough to tell his sister?

Anton's stomach had a sinking sensation.

"Let me guess. Your father said Kipling and I met somewhere socially?" Anton's fingers tightened around the head of his cane.

"At a ball, which I found strange, to be honest."

"Oh?"

"Dante doesn't…well, socialize."

He'd heard that in the whispered ballroom titters.

"I try not to, either," Anton said.

"Really?" She had a hopeful look on her face, which Anton found strange. This whole conversation had gone way beyond the pale a few hundred heartbeats ago.

Anton wasn't sure if he would be able to sneak away from her, so he might as well try blunt trauma. In a non-physical way. "I think most aristos are idiots."

Her pale eyes seemed to glow, he thought, with amusement. "You mean vampires?"

"Well, yes."

"That's wonderful!"

Anton began to wonder if she was a little backward.

"Dante doesn't like most people, either."

That did sound...wonderful, Anton thought. What kind of lunatic family was he marrying into? Did his father know that the Kiplings were freaks?

"I didn't meet your brother in a social setting." Anton tugged on his cravat.

"I didn't think so," the viscountess said. She flicked more hair over her shoulder.

"I met him because I forced an audience with your father, and he happened to be in the room." Anton's knuckles turned white as he gripped his cane.

"Why did you need to force an audience?"

"Because I wanted to know what had happened to my fiancée." Anton stared at her, hard. He wanted to see what her reaction was. Mild surprise flitted across her face and then her eyes narrowed.

"Which one was your fiancée?" she asked.

"Which *one*?" His fingers loosened on his cane.

"Uh, I mean, which one did Dante seduce?"

Anton felt his draw drop. She really wasn't very good at dissembling. "Which one he *Chose*, I think you meant."

"I know perfectly well what I meant."

How many women had Kipling attacked?

"Your fiancée was the whore?" The viscountess leaned forward, her breath wafting across his face. It smelled oddly of clove.

"*Was* being the operative word there. Yes."

She was frowning. "Why would you have gotten engaged to a whore? Are you a bit simple? You could have just paid her for sex." She really was talking to him like he was five years old.

He raised both eyebrows. He didn't feel he should have to reply to that; it wasn't any of her business by a long stretch, but he felt like being honest. "Because I loved her."

"Oh. And you don't love Dante?"

Anton snorted. "Far from it."

She flicked her hair over her shoulder again and began tapping her chin with her index finger. "I'm not sure I like this idea."

"What idea?" Anton wasn't sure his future sister-in-law was entirely sane.

"Of you marrying my brother."

"Good," Anton said.

She raised an eyebrow at him.

He sighed. "That makes two of us."

CHAPTER THIRTY-SEVEN

"So," Clay said into the quiet. "What do you want to do?"

"Do?" Elle let the mirror drop to her lap and she looked at him, eyes wide.

Clay ran a hand through his hair and leaned against the wall. He was still reeling slightly from her pronouncement that she didn't look too different. He guessed that she might not see so many changes, because it was still the same canvas, just a differently hued one. Maybe she'd always thought she looked like she did now; that the outside had always reflected the complexity and sharpness of her character.

He didn't know why it even mattered to him.

"Yes, what do you want to do now you're a member of the undead?" Clay asked. Not that vampires were undead, but legends are legends.

He wanted to walk over and sit down next to her, maybe hold her hand, but he wasn't sure it would be a good idea. He didn't know what she was thinking or how she might react to some of his suggestions about what she should do now. That's why he needed to hear her ideas. He doubted she'd thought far beyond her next meal, and he didn't want to feature as her next course.

"See Emmie."

"You want to see Emmie?" He crossed his arms.

She was looking at him as if he were an idiot. "Yes. Well, take her away."

"And how do you plan on doing this?"

"I will…well… I'll–"

"They all sound like great ideas," Clay said.

The Green in her eyes flashed. "I don't know. But I can't leave Emmie with Gran. I just can't."

"I can understand that." *More than you know*, he thought, but he tried to keep that one to himself.

"Will you help me?" Elle asked.

"Help you what?"

"Get Emmie." Her fingers clenched around the mirror and with a crack, the handle broke off.

He took a few steps forward and retrieved the now two-piece mirror set. "Thanks."

"Sorry." She looked sheepish.

He didn't say anything, just set the mirror down on the vanity. *Maybe this will make her understand that she isn't herself anymore*, he thought. Staring at the mirror, he amended, *That's if she hasn't already made a habit of snapping people's accessories.*

"So, are you going to help me or not?"

He guessed she hadn't worked it out.

When he turned around, she'd risen from the bed and was now standing with her arms crossed, chin pointed out stubbornly.

"It depends," Clay hedged.

Her eyes darkened. "On what?"

By the blood, he thought, jaw hanging. She looked sexy when she was riled. *Time to sit*, he decided, *I need to adjust the pressure on my crotch*. The movement also might turn his mind from his cock, which was important, because Elle didn't look like she was interested in him or his appendage. He walked past her to the bed and sat. He swung his legs up, crossing them at the ankles as he leaned back against the headboard.

"It depends on your plan," Clay said.

"My plan?" Her arms dropped to her sides.

"Well, I assume you've got one? Or were you just thinking about knocking on your mother's door and asking for Emmie?"

From the look on her face, he guessed that was what she *had* been planning.

He groaned.

"What!"

"You can't seriously think that your mother will hand Emmie over to you?"

Elle sat on the foot of the bed. Her finger began tracing over the circular patterns that covered his bedspread. "My mother loves me."

"She loved you, yes."

Her eyes snapped to his.

"You've been Chosen. You aren't the same person you were a week ago."

"How can you say that? I *feel* the same."

Clay wanted to make a smart crack about how she might *feel* now, but decided against it. Instead, he looked down at his wrist, not that there was any evidence of her feeding there now, but he figured she'd get the point. When Clay looked back at her, her pale skin had a faint pink flush to it.

"I said I'm sorry."

"Look, you're still you. Still prickly, adorable Elle. But what happens if you get hungry and I'm not around as a convenient chew toy? What if it's just you and Emmie?"

"I'd control myself."

He tried not to look as skeptical as he felt. He didn't seem to do a very good job.

"I just want to make sure she's safe!"

"So do I, but you taking her now isn't."

"But if you were with me, you could make sure I didn't...hurt her." Her whole face shone with hope.

"I can't be around you twenty-four hours a day. And where would we go? A vampire, a werewolf and a little human girl?"

"Somewhere far away. I hear that there are islands in the Turquoise Sea without vampires or weres."

Well, she was right about that, mostly. There were some weres that lived in the sea.

"And how would we get there?" He ran a hand through his hair. He didn't like being a naysayer, but she couldn't seem to grasp her situation.

"By boat."

"And we'd have to stop at ports. Lots of ports."

She was looking at him like he had a mental problem. "So?"

"So? Your gran is a Green, a very powerful one. All she needs to do is reach out to another Green a few hundred leagues away. They reach another…"

Understanding shot through her with a flinch. "And by the time we get to each port, there's a chance a Graced there will know about us."

"And try to get Emmie back."

He didn't have to add that their deaths would probably be a bonus.

Agony contorted Elle's face. "But I can't leave her with Gran."

Clay had to admire her passion, but he wasn't sure she was getting it. "You need to get out of here. Get away. I can keep an eye on Emmie for you."

"No, you don't understand." Her fingers were plucking at the bedsheet and he was worried she'd tear it. He only owned one.

"Understand what? You can no longer live without me?" He grinned, but it faded when she didn't say anything for a while.

"Emmie is different."

He'd already worked that one out. The both of them were. "I know."

"No, she's *really* different."

Clay thought about someone else he knew who was Graced and *really* different. He'd done everything in his power to protect them, and he could understand that Elle would want to do the same for her sister. At least he knew what Emmie's power wasn't – wrong eye color – but he didn't want to go there. He shook himself.

"How is she different?" Clay asked.

Elle's mouth formed a stubborn line.

"Do you want me to help or not?" He tried to look stern, but he didn't know what he'd do if he was in her position. Actually, he did know. Tell someone he barely knew, from a race he normally wouldn't share bread with, a confidence? Blood no.

"Emmie has ability; but it's not one that is normal for Graceds."

"So she can do something other than read minds, move stuff and manipulate emotions?"

Elle locked her eyes with his. "Yes."

He wanted to ask what it was, but that might be – blood, it would be – pushing the boundaries a little too far. And really, did he need to know? He wasn't going to tell Elle all of his secrets – plus, many weren't his to tell, anyway. Especially not the important ones.

Clay ran another hand through his hair, before tying it back with a small piece of leather he fished from a pocket. "And you don't trust your gran with Emmie? Not to exploit her?"

"Gran doesn't know about Emmie, about what she can do. She thinks Emmie is a latent, and that one day she'll develop telepathy or empathy or something. In the meantime, she's cruel to Emmie about it. Makes her feel useless."

It was sad that he could easily believe that. Look at what her grandmother had planned for Emmie already; bidding for potential "special" great-grandchildren, with Emmie as a mere vessel.

And why were the great-grandchildren that important? How could the old dragon achieve immortality – which Clay was sure was her main goal – from a half-wolf child?

"Look," Clay said, "there isn't much you can do. If you take Emmie, we will be hunted down. Maybe not straight away, but eventually, they'll find us." Especially since it seemed Olive had big plans for her "useless" granddaughter.

"I can't just leave her."

Clay tapped his thigh, thinking. "You might not have to."

CHAPTER THIRTY-EIGHT

"I like him."

Dante glanced up from his reflection and stared at his sister. She was wearing a blood-red dress that draped around her figure in a way that should have been decent, but wasn't.

"Why are you wearing red?" Dante asked, distracted.

Misty smiled at him and patted her blonde hair, which she'd piled on her head in a riot of curls that were speckled with carnelian beads. "It's your wedding day; I needed something a little more ceremonial."

Well, she'd certainly achieved that. Red was *the* vampire color, after all. It represented mourning for humans; life for vampires. Dante turned back to his reflection and his valet, who was struggling to maintain his temper. The man was a vampire – Dante wasn't allowed to have human servants anymore, in case he was tempted to Choose one – and he was wound so tight Dante wondered how it was possible the man could crap, let alone do something so outrageous as smile.

Which he wasn't.

Smiling, that was.

In fact, his valet looked as if he had just chewed on a pox-infested, bit-ridden whore. Although, Dante wasn't sure he liked thinking of himself in those terms, since his valet was aiming that disgusted look at him.

"What?" Dante asked the fussy man.

"You just look–" His valet seemed at a loss for words. He

waved a hand through the air, in what Dante assumed was the physical expression of his mental discomfort.

"Rumpled?" Misty offered. She came further into the room to stand by Dante's side.

"Exactly!" The skinny valet threw his hands up in the air. "I just took the clothes from the hanger and dressed him and he still looks like he fell out of bed."

"Unfortunately," Misty said, seeming to fight a smile, "that's just Dante."

Dante wasn't sure if he should be insulted or not. He turned back to the mirror, the valet's hands waving between him and the glass, and checked his appearance. He looked perfectly presentable; he didn't know what their issue was. His hair was slicked back in a queue, and his face was freshly shaved, without even a nick. His white shirt had a collar so high he was worried that it might strangle him, especially when added to the fact that a red cravat was tied tightly around his throat. His jacket and breeches were black and looked fine to him. He couldn't even see that many wrinkles – the clothing was stretched tight over his shoulders and thighs.

"I look fine," Dante announced.

The valet hovered around him, brushing this, flicking that.

"Thank you; that will be all," Dante said and stared hard at the man. With a sniff, the valet took himself off.

"Pompous little fool," Misty said after the door shut behind the fussy man.

Dante just shook his head.

"So, did you hear what I said when I came in?" Misty asked. She walked away from the mirror and toward the chairs in his suite. She took the one closest to the empty fire grate.

Realizing that he was going to have a little brother-sister chat, whether he wanted one or not, he followed her to the chairs and sat down, careful to try to keep himself neat. Although, he was apparently already rumpled beyond repair.

Idiot.

"No, sorry, what did you say? I was too busy being a dummy

for the valet." Dante tried to smile.

"I said I like him."

"Who? The valet?" Dante raised an eyebrow.

"No, you idiot. I like your fiancé." She lifted a hand to flick her hair, but recalled it was up, so she patted it instead.

"Greystoke?"

"Do you have another?" she asked.

"No." Dante crossed one leg over the other, then thought better of it when he saw the material stretch.

"I met him a week ago, at Liverly's ball. Well, I'd met him before that, but never bothered to pay any attention to him. Although he is handsome, for a human."

"Good for you. Liverly's an idiot." More so than most other vampires.

Misty was staring at him. "Greystoke seems to feel the same way about Liverly."

"He'd have to be brain dead not to."

That made her smile. He'd seen her smile a lot in the last few days. More than she normally did, anyway, but not around their father. She only smiled when it was just the two of them. Like when they were children, and she'd been happier and he'd been less awkward. He hadn't known he was so different back then. Dante wondered if it was because he was leaving the estate – maybe she was trying to bond with him? He wasn't sure. Misty had never really seemed to enjoy doing anything other than annoying him.

"And your fiancé doesn't seem to want to marry you."

Dante didn't even bother to raise his eyebrows. He'd already worked that little gem out for himself. "You don't seem too surprised. Should I be hurt?"

"I thought Father's story was too good to be true." Misty tapped her chin.

"I can't believe you even thought it *was* true."

Misty's finger stopped. "I try to give Father the benefit of the doubt."

"How nice for him."

Her eyes narrowed. "You seem even less charitably inclined to him than normal."

"Let's just say that you thought Father would want me off his hands and you were right. He had to give up fifty thousand groats to do it, but he did it. He also ensured that I would agree to this marriage with more than just the threat of being sent off to one of his remote estates."

Dante wouldn't actually have minded that.

Her lavender eyes glittered. "What else did he threaten you with?"

Dante shrugged. He wasn't sure he wanted Misty to know. What if she got angry at him one day and found the papers? No, he wouldn't take that risk.

She seemed to accept his reluctance to speak more about it. "I wondered why Greystoke would agree to marry you when you'd killed his fiancée."

"I wasn't *trying* to kill her. It was an accident," Dante muttered.

"I'm sure your soon-to-be husband really cares about that." She rolled her eyes at him.

Dante stood. "Well, let's hope he doesn't have a stake ready for me tonight."

◆

Dante was no longer a Kipling. From the moment he'd signed his name on the marriage certificate, he had become a Greystoke. Which was rather stupid, considering he would more than likely outlive his husband, provided that said husband didn't have a stake stashed anywhere. From the look in Greystoke's eyes, Dante wasn't entirely sure that wouldn't be the case.

"A toast," Viktor said, raising a champagne flute, "to the married couple!"

Dante and Greystoke were standing in the ballroom at Kipling House, surrounded by three hundred of their "closest" friends. Most of whom Dante couldn't even remember meeting, let alone liking. Tables laden with food were propped in the corners and servants wove their way through the crowd of guests, handing out glasses of sparkling wine.

The tinkling of hundreds of crystal glasses sounded amidst a cheer of "Hear, hear!"

Forcing a smile, Dante tried to look pleased with his new lot in life. From the corner of his eye, he could see Greystoke doing the same, although the man's knuckles were clenched white around his cane. Not only had Viktor married him to a human with brown eyes, he'd married Dante off to a cripple. Then again, it wasn't as if Greystoke had gotten a great deal either, being married to the man who had killed his fiancée.

The toast seemed to start a procession. Their three hundred guests swarmed forward, trying to be the first to congratulate them. Reds and blacks were the predominate colors worn by their "friends," and jewels and feathers glittered in various shades of hair. But Dante couldn't remember any of their names. And he doubted that any of the well-wishers were sincere.

After what seemed like an indeterminable amount of kisses and handshakes and coy smiles, the crowd thinned. Part of him was itching to get out of the room; he couldn't stand being around so many people. Listening to their chatter – and with his hearing, it was hard not to – just made him even more convinced of their idiocy.

"Have you ever seen two such handsome men?"

"Why did they have to marry Greystoke to *him*?"

"Food marrying one of us. It isn't *right*."

"I've heard he doesn't even *like* men."

"Greystoke was engaged and there's a rumor that Kipling *killed* her so he could have him."

That caught his attention. Interesting. He hadn't thought of that possible spin on the scenario. *Kudos to them*, he thought, looking around for the speaker.

"Kipling," Greystoke hissed.

Jerking his attention back to the few remaining well-wishers, Dante automatically smiled at whoever was standing in front of him.

Greystoke pinched Dante's arm, and Dante bit back a curse.

"Yes, dearest?"

He felt rather than heard Greystoke snort. "I'd like to introduce you to my mother and sister, the Countess of Maerton and the Honorable Darla Greystoke."

So, Dante was given their titles, rather than their names?

Dante bowed to them and took the countess' hand, raising it to his lips. "It is entirely my pleasure to meet my new mother and sister." He repeated the gesture on the girl.

The countess smiled at him warmly, and he had the feeling she was pleased by what he had said. The girl, Darla, seemed genuinely happy. Her face was flushed pink and her eyes sparkled. They were brown, not even the slightly more interesting shade of Greystoke's, but they seemed…kind. He wasn't used to seeing that in an aristo's eyes. In anyone's eyes, for that matter.

"It is so wonderful to have another son," the countess said. Her voice was smooth and soft, and he couldn't detect the lie in it. But then, he'd never been *that* good at reading people, and humans were sometimes harder to decipher.

"I'm looking forward to us all getting to know each other," Dante said, not really sure what else he *should* say. He could feel Greystoke's eyes boring into him.

"Aren't we all?" Greystoke muttered.

CHAPTER THIRTY-NINE

Anton drew off his gloves and threw them on the bed. There were no servants, no one to tell him off or take the gloves away for him; he'd asked them all to take the evening off. Alone in his room, he could finally let his shoulders slump. He felt uncomfortable, not right in his own skin. He'd pictured this moment months ago: a married man, in Greystoke House, on his wedding night.

But it was all wrong.

The person in the next room wasn't Annabel, wasn't anything *like* Annabel. It was worse than if it was just some other woman, someone who could be a mother to his heir. Instead, it was the murderer of all his dreams. Shutting his eyes, he rubbed his sore thigh and just tried to breathe. The reception had been a nightmare, so many people, far more than even he liked, wanting to pass judgment on his hasty wedding to one of Pinton's most reclusive vampires.

His father had only attended the service, and hadn't even bothered with the reception he'd forced Anton to arrange with Wintermere. Reginald had just made sure Anton had signed the contract, and then he'd returned to the country estate, where his dogs and port would be waiting for him.

Then there had been his mother and sister.

They'd been so happy for him. He'd seen Darla's eyes light up when she'd met Dante. Like there'd been stars in them, and not from infatuation, which he could have understood in a girl her age, when confronted with someone who looked like Dante did.

No, she'd just been so pleased for Anton.

"He's so handsome!" she'd gushed when she'd finally managed to get him alone.

"Yes." Because really, he wasn't about to deny what was right in front of his eyes.

"Oh Anton, I'm so happy for you. I knew you loved Annabel, but Dante is perfect for you!"

How she could determine that from a five-minute introduction, Anton wasn't sure and didn't want to know. Not when "perfect" was a freak.

A knock sounded on the door that connected his suite to Annabel's – no, Kipling's – rooms. Dread started to form in the pit of his stomach.

"Yes?" Anton called out, because he couldn't very well pretend to not be there. He watched, with moths in his stomach, as the brass handle turned slowly and Kipling appeared, dressed in a brocade robe the color of warm brandy. The vampire looked good. How could he? How could someone so evil look so appealing?

Kipling stood in the doorway, seemingly uncertain.

"I don't know what to do," he said.

Anton just looked at him.

Kipling ran a hand through his hair, knocking out the hair tie that held it back. Black silk cascaded over his shoulders and swept across one cheek. Something clenched down low in Anton's gut. Grunting, Kipling quickly bent down and scooped up the tie. The movement was so full of grace it made Anton feel like a clumsy oaf, just standing there, still decked out in his wedding finery.

"What do you mean?" Anton finally hedged. He limped over to the small sideboard positioned under a window. A silver tray set with liquor and glasses was perched carefully in the center of the sideboard. Next to it was a pair of chairs placed either side of a delicate, round table. Anton reached out and uncorked the whiskey decanter and poured two fingers of amber liquid into a small, square glass. He didn't normally drink spirits, apart from a nightcap here and there, but he took a deep swallow before taking a seat on one of the chairs. It was spindly, but cushioned. He sighed with relief. His poor leg wasn't up to being on his feet so much.

Seeing him sit, Kipling shrugged and took the spare chair.

"I don't know how to be married," Kipling said after a few moments of silence. Anton tried to savor his whiskey and pretend this wasn't his wedding night and that they weren't actually in his bedroom.

"Join the club."

Kipling eyed him. "You *wanted* to be married."

Anton nearly choked on a mouthful of golden burn. "Sorry?"

"You wanted to be married."

Feeling like he was no longer in danger of swallowing his way to death, he said, "Not to you."

"Well, no. But to Sandy."

Anton gritted his teeth, the familiar anger rising up at her whore's name. "Her name was Annabel."

"Sandy, Annabel." Kipling slashed a hand through the air. "Whatever she was called, you contemplated the concept of marriage."

"Well, yes. But marriage to *her*." He stood and poured himself another glass of whiskey. The first had disappeared awfully fast. Maybe he could get drunk on his wedding night? Then he wouldn't be expected to have sex, surely? Reaching over to grab the now-full glass, he had to stop and grip the sideboard to keep his balance. Bloody leg. He could feel the muscles trembling.

"Want some?" he asked, his back to Kipling, pretending that was why he was still at the window, not because his leg hurt too much to walk even those few steps.

"Why not?"

When he felt his leg would hold his weight again, Anton poured a couple of fingers of whiskey into another glass and headed back to the small table. He set Kipling's glass down on his side, before taking a seat.

Kipling took a sip of the drink and then wheezed. "You hate me."

"Whiskey a bit strong for you?" Anton asked.

The vampire cracked a half smile. "A little. But I meant, you hate me for taking Annabel from you. I didn't mean to kill her; I want you to know that."

"You just botched Choosing her. It's common among vampires." Anton rolled his eyes. They both knew that there were few fatalities from being Chosen. "I can't see her agreeing to being Chosen, despite the protestations from you and your father."

Something flickered in Kipling's eyes, but it was gone before Anton could decipher it.

"I did everything I was meant to, when I Chose her. I can't say why it didn't work."

Anton shrugged. He wasn't really sure he was drunk enough to be having this conversation. The one he'd wanted weeks ago.

"Either way, I just wanted you to know I'm sorry."

"Are you?" Anton asked, squinting at him.

"I just said I was." Kipling looked uncomfortable as he took another sip of amber fire.

"Most people say a lot they don't mean," Anton observed.

Kipling tilted his head to one side. "I'm sorry it upset you. If I could do it again, I probably still would have tried. Although, to be honest, if I'd known I would end up here because of it, it might have made me think twice."

Should he be happy that Kipling supposedly loved Annabel enough to Choose her? Maybe, if he'd actually believed it.

"So, why did you agree to marry me?" That question had been bothering Anton. He could see why *his* father had agreed to the wedding; there were fifty thousand reasons. But Kipling?

"My father made me."

Anton couldn't help the bark of laughter. "Oh, poor baby."

"You've met my father, right? You paid attention to him when you were there?" Both of Kipling's eyebrows were nearly in his hairline.

"Yeah, your father's an asshole." Actually, there were a whole host of other words he would have liked to use, but that one seemed polite enough given the context.

"Nice euphemism."

"Thanks, I tried."

"Anyway, you saw what my father was like when you came asking about San – Annabel. He sees a problem, he eradicates it. Crushes whoever is in his way."

"What's that got to do with the price of peas in Panzana?" He didn't want to say "you and me" or "our marriage." For some reason, that would make it feel real. Which was absurd, because the three hundred-odd well-wishes they'd received and the fact they were sitting in *his* room having this cozy little chat wasn't evidence enough?

"Well, I was a problem Father wanted to be rid of. Marrying you was my best option." From the look on Kipling's face, Anton wasn't sure he wanted to know what the alternatives were.

Anton took a sip of his drink and glared moodily at his feet. His leg wasn't in good shape, but he guessed that was a positive in this situation. He might be able to use it as an excuse to not consummate the marriage. Having sex with Kipling seemed wrong. But he didn't know if Kipling would want it. It wasn't necessary, but it might be expected. It just felt like the worst kind of betrayal he could do to Annabel's memory.

"So..." Kipling said.

Anton glanced up at him. "So?"

"Do we have to have sex?" Kipling blurted. His face was blank, utterly devoid of expression, which wasn't much of a feat, Anton thought, since he had decided that Kipling didn't emote at the best of times.

Anton's pulse kicked up a notch. Something about the word "sex" coming from Kipling's mouth made his gut churn, two parts dread and one part arousal. It made him feel sick. "No?"

Kipling seemed to sag into his seat. "Thank the blood."

Relief swamped through him only to be followed with something like disappointment as he processed Kipling's reaction. "You don't like men? I mean, you don't like men sexually?"

While he couldn't stomach the idea of fucking Kipling

now…Anton couldn't guarantee how he'd feel in ten years' time. He believed in honor, in keeping it. He wouldn't betray his vows, even to Annabel's murderer. But to have the option of no sexual relief for the rest of his life, other than from his own hand? It gave him a whole new feeling of dread.

"I don't really like anybody."

Anton frowned. "I don't understand."

A very faint pink tinge seemed to wash over Kipling's cheeks. "I don't really like…sex."

"Sorry?" Anton wasn't sure he'd heard correctly. Had someone said they didn't like sex?

Kipling seemed more than uncomfortable. He was picking invisible pieces of lint off his robe. "I'll do it, if you want it. But I don't like it."

He glanced up and must have seen some of the shock Anton was feeling.

Kipling pinched the bridge of his nose. "I just… This is awkward. I'm not like everyone else, I'm different."

"You like children?" Anton thought he'd throw up.

"No, I don't like *children*. That's disgusting." Kipling looked like he thought Anton was a deviant for even suggesting the idea.

"Then you just don't like sex?" Anton asked, feeling his nausea roll down a notch.

"Exactly." Kipling seemed relieved.

"With men *or* women?"

"No. I just don't like it."

"What about on your own?" Anton couldn't quite grasp the idea of someone not liking sex. He'd heard about it, and normally he would have no trouble accepting it. People were people and everyone was different. But he wouldn't have married someone like that, not if he'd been given a choice. Because Anton liked sex. A lot.

"What do you mean? You can't have sex on your own."

Anton couldn't believe he was having this conversation. "No, but you can masturbate."

"Oh. Well, no."

"No?"

"I don't do that."

By the blood. Anton was never going to get laid again.

"Greystoke?"

He'd married a murderer who didn't like sex. Anton wanted to cry. He started laughing.

"Greystoke?"

Anton was doubled over, laughing so hard he could barely breathe. But it wasn't funny. He didn't know why he was laughing, but he couldn't seem to stop.

"Greystoke?"

A hand touched his shoulder and Anton jerked mid-laugh. He looked up into Kipling's bright violet eyes, which seemed concerned. Surely that wasn't right, because Kipling was emotionless.

"Anton, are you okay?"

"No," Anton gasped.

It was the first time he'd heard Kipling speak his name, and it almost melted his bones. It shouldn't have sounded that good, it really shouldn't. Kipling gripped him under the arms and pulled him upright, almost without effort.

"You have had too much to drink," Kipling said.

Anton wheezed, "You think?" between hysterical bursts of laughter.

Kipling just shook his head and then hauled Anton over to his bed. Part of him panicked, and then he remembered their conversation and the laughter welled up again. No sex. No *sex*.

Somehow, Anton found himself lying on the bed, Kipling having already taken his shirt and jacket off. He was unbuttoning his fly when Anton came back to reality.

"I can do it," he snapped.

"Really?" Kipling asked, stepping back and folding his arms across his chest.

Glowering at the vampire, Anton shucked off his breeches. Next thing he knew, Kipling had him tucked under the covers.

"You had better not be a drunk."

"And you had better not murder any more of my friends," Anton growled.

"Done." Kipling seemed to smile, and it almost made Anton hard.

I'm in deep shit.

CHAPTER FORTY

"I look ridiculous," Elle said.

She stared at herself in the mirror and shook her head. Looking over her shoulder at Clay, she watched as he sucked the inside of his cheek while he studied her.

"I don't know," he said and strode forward. "You look pretty hot to me."

Elle turned back to the mirror and rolled her eyes. She was wearing a rusty red dress made from some type of shiny material – silk, according to Clay. The neckline was too low and edged in some expensive type of lace, but Clay said it was "the fashion." If she bent over, anyone looking at her would be able to see down to her navel. When she'd said that, Clay had just told her not to bend over.

Elle snorted.

"What?" Clay asked.

"Dressing me like an aristo won't *make* me an aristo," Elle said.

Her fingers itched to peel the long red gloves from her arms, but Clay had slapped at her hand when she'd tugged at one earlier. The color of her dress should have clashed with her hair, she thought. But it didn't. Maybe it was all that white skin on display; the paleness distracted from the hair Clay had piled on the top of her head in lazy curls. Where Clay had learned to dress women's hair…well, she wasn't about to ask.

And really, she didn't even want to think about her hair. She'd cut it, back to the short style she'd always preferred. Then she'd had a nap, and next thing she knew, she was awake and had a mane of the bloody stuff again. Not quite as long, but it brushed past her shoulders. She had wanted to cut it a second time, but Clay had prevented her; it wouldn't help their new plan, he said, it would grow back while she slept and vampires always had long hair. When she'd demanded why, he said it had something to do with their regenerative abilities and blah blah blah. It had become a bit of a lecture, so she'd tuned out. All she remembered was that she shouldn't stand out too much.

Bloody vampires.

"Remind me why I agreed to wear this abomination?" Elle asked.

Clay tutted.

She slashed a glare at him.

"You have to *look* the part," Clay said.

Elle turned back to face him, abandoning the mirror and the reflection that showed an aristo lady who didn't resemble her at all. Elegance and style were not the usual hallmarks of Elle's appearance. Rough and ready, those were more like it. That's how she *liked* it.

"I *look* like an aristo." Elle tried to keep the sneer from her voice. Clay had told her off for that earlier.

"Exactly. Vampires are normally aristo or *trying to be* aristos. If you look the part, it will make your life – uh, unlife – easier."

Elle sighed. She wasn't exactly sure about this plan. "I think this is going to get me killed."

Clay smiled and gently clasped her shoulders. "Trust me."

That's what she was worried about.

CHAPTER FORTY-ONE

The noise was deafening.

And it wasn't the chatter in the receiving room at the Crystal Palace that was causing her headache. The vampires' thoughts were doing that. It was like walking into a taproom during happy hour. Everyone was talking at once, except here, they were thinking. Taking a deep breath, she tried to picture her mental shield, the one she'd spent hours building for extra protection from Gran. It didn't stop the noise entirely, but it dimmed it, enough that she could take a deep breath and relax slightly.

Half clinging to Clay, she followed him as he walked down the receiving room's long expanse. Crystal chandeliers hung from the ceiling, casting rainbow glitters over the room and its hundred or so occupants. Mirrors hung on walls opposite each other, reflecting the sparkling structures and the jewel-gowned courtiers, replicating them into infinity.

At the end of the room, King Johan II, or King Jo as Elle's guard friends liked to call him, was seated on his throne and looked, well, bored. She hadn't thought he'd appear like that. Regal, yes; intimidating, probably – but not chronically bored. Not that she'd ever thought she'd get to see him this close. The City Guard rarely worked with the Palace Guard; the former generally employing humans and the latter vampires. And Elle had never gone to a formal dinner with Mikael. Not that the king showed up to all that many of them, from what Mikael had said.

The king was wearing a red silk suit that should have looked tacky – Elle would have called it that had it been on any other person – and a crisp white shirt. He had his chin propped on his hand and he was absently waving away an attendant who was hovering nearby.

As Clay "guided" her across the receiving room's floor, easily weaving them around curious courtiers, Elle tried not to tug on her gloves, trip on her dress or stare at the king. All were apparently bad. But it was hard to look away from him; the red suit highlighted the olive tone of his skin, which was unusual for a Pinton leech. His black hair swept away from sharp features and his light eyes seemed to glow. The king was one of the most handsome men she'd ever seen. Only Clay and the Creep were in his league, although the Creep was probably even prettier.

Thinking of Clay, she managed to turn her eyes away from the king and to her companion. He looked nice enough to eat, which wasn't necessarily a good thing anymore. Not for him, anyway. She hadn't ever seen him in formal clothes before, and his were certainly designed to highlight his assets. Which was everything about him, as far as she could see.

Elle hadn't thought she'd have much of a libido, not that she'd thought about it all that much. Since she'd woken up, she hadn't been interested in anything other than food and saving Emmie. Although, she had to admit, she hadn't been awake for that long. But as soon as she spied Clay in his fancy clothes, she'd tried to jump him. Literally. He'd had to fend her off and then gave her a lecture about leaping around in her new dress.

She still hadn't gotten laid.

"What?" Clay said.

Elle sent him a sidelong look. "Huh?"

"You started digging your fingers into my arm. What were you thinking?"

He was leaning close to her and she could smell him. By the blood, this wolf always smelled yummy. Her vampire hormones hadn't gotten over their rejection from earlier, so she felt her heart speed up and her blood rush to parts of her body that shouldn't be doing the thinking right now.

"About you." She didn't say anything more, but from the way his eyes seemed to darken to molten gold, she figured he'd understood.

He placed a warm hand over the one she had resting on his arm. "Later."

"Promise?"

He laughed.

Heads turned their way at the sound and the few courtiers in the room close to them tittered. They looked like overdressed cats, she thought; all glittering eyes and gems, furs and fangs. Cats were at least friendly.

Elle could hear their comments and they weren't flattering:

"There's a doggie in the room. Hope he's toilet trained."

"Who's his whore?"

"Who let the trash inside?"

Elle saw that Clay was smiling. Surely he'd heard what they were saying, too?

"Sir–"

Elle turned and looked at the nervous human who'd spoken to them. He was wearing royal livery and was obviously uncomfortable approaching a rather large were with a female vampire on his arm.

"Yes?" Clay said.

"Sir, may I ask your purpose here?"

Obviously one of the aristos had taken exception to the dog and his lady friend. She tamped down on the feeling of outrage, admitting to herself that a few weeks earlier, she'd have been saying the same things.

"I already gave my card at the entrance," Clay said.

Elle had tried to read what was on the card, but Clay had kept it out of her sight. The servant who had taken the card had gone a little pale, muttered something and ushered them on. Whatever it said, it was impressive. How had Clay managed that?

The servant looked wide-eyed at them.

"I'm here to have a meeting with the king," Clay said slowly.

The attendant appeared skeptical, then seemed to decide it

wasn't his job to eject them, and turned to lead them toward the throne, when a new voice said, "Dog, our king doesn't have time for you."

Clay let go of Elle's arm and turned to face the speaker. The man wore his hair long, down to his butt, and had a collar so high it poked him in the chin. He looked ridiculous, Elle thought, and familiar. She might have thrown him out of a brothel or three before.

"Why don't you let the king decide that for himself? Or are you making his mind up for him?"

As if he were a magnet, Elle felt her eyes drawn to Clay. The air about him crackled; gone was the buckskin-wearing backwoodsman, and here was the polished aristo wolf. It was as if he had shed part of himself like a winter coat.

"He doesn't need to make a decision. It's obvious." The man tilted his chin high in the air, which meant that Elle could see the marks the collar had left against the pasty flesh of his throat.

Idiot.

"What is obvious?" This new voice was deep and smooth; it sounded like how melted chocolate tasted.

Elle managed to stop her jaw from dropping by sheer willpower alone. The king was standing right behind the popinjay. Up close, he was even more breathtaking. For someone who didn't like leeches, she could fast see herself liking this one. *Does that make me shallow?*

The pompous vampire turned slowly on his heels, rocking back a little when he saw the king smiling at him. But it wasn't a warm expression.

"Your Majesty." The vampire dropped into a low bow.

Realizing that she should have done the same as soon as she spotted the king in their crowd, she dipped into a deep curtsy. One thing she had to say about her new vampire powers – she liked the fact that she was super coordinated now. She didn't even wobble.

Clay took hold of her elbow and slowly drew her upright. She frowned slightly when she realized he hadn't bowed at all.

Instead, she saw him tilt his head at the king, as if they were equals. She swallowed.

"I think the king asked you a question," a woman said, her wire-framed fan poking the collared vampire in the arm. From his wince, it must have been hard.

Elle decided, studying the woman, that the vampires in this city were all too attractive by half. Even the ugly ones, like the popinjay, were still good-looking. He was just ugly because he was stupid, and because he didn't have a lick of dress sense. The woman, on the other hand, seemed sharp, like a two-edged sword. She was wearing entirely white, from the ribbons in her hair down to the slippers on her feet, and her pale blonde tresses hung down over her shoulders like a silk scarf. She looked familiar too, for some reason.

"It was obvious that our king doesn't have time for this wolf." The man was struggling to speak, and his cheeks had a faint pink tinge. Elle worked out that a pink tinge was the equivalent of a human's full-body blush. The vampire shot Clay and Elle a glare, as if it was their fault he'd been caught making grand statements about the king's desires.

"Really? That's interesting, Jay."

Elle blinked. The man's name was Jay? That was too funny.

"Why is that?" Popinjay raised a hand as if to tug at his cravat, but lowered it quickly.

The woman's lavender eyes glinted. "Because I was talking with the king just as he spotted this lovely couple, and he said he simply must speak with them. Didn't you, Your Majesty?"

Cat with mouse, Elle thought. Cat one; mouse dead.

"Indeed," King Johan said. He turned to Clay. "It has been, what? Three centuries since I last saw your ugly face?"

Elle felt her eyes widen.

"Ha! Only when compared to you, pretty-boy." Clay was grinning.

Clay *knew* the king? He was on joking terms with him? And he hadn't *told* her about that *at all*?

Oh, she was going to kill him. Cut him into tiny chunks and

feed him to wild animals. No, she was going to bite him and bite him and bite him, and then when she was full, *then* she'd cut him into tiny chunks and feed him to wild animals.

"–Elle."

Elle jolted and then stared at the hand the king was holding out to her. When had that happened? He was murmuring something to her.

"S-sorry, Your Majesty?"

King Johan looked up then and met her eyes. His mouth parted slightly and he blinked rapidly. "Clay, where did you say you met this charming lady again?"

"I didn't."

The king took hold of her hand and placed it on his forearm. "Then she simply must tell me herself."

The king began leading her away from Clay, which was a bad idea. A really bad idea.

"Uh, I mean, sorry–"

"What my darling fiancée is trying to say, Johan, is that she isn't comfortable wandering around without me."

Elle froze. She almost mouthed the word "fiancée" at Clay. The king's arm tensed under her hand.

"What are you doing?" she mentally shouted at him.

"Play along."

"You didn't say anything about this before."

"I didn't think I'd have to say it."

"But…fiancée?"

"It means that I'm justified in my interest in you. In my proprietary interest."

She didn't like the sound of that, but she smiled at the king, teeth hidden.

Elle heard someone coughing, but since it was the popinjay who was doing it, she had to assume it was to hide some other emotion. Vampires didn't get colds.

"Fiancée?" he squawked finally. "Vampires aren't allowed to marry wolves."

"They are allowed to," the king said slowly, turning around to face Popinjay. "It is discouraged though, which you well know, Clay." That purple stare focused hard on her wolf.

My wolf?

Staring at him, she decided she didn't want to pursue that thought. Not now and not yet. It was just because he looked too bloody good, she thought. Purely physical.

"Is it my fault that she got Chosen by a vampire before I could Bite her?" Clay shrugged.

"I wasn't going to Bite you," Clay said telepathically. *"Well, I would've asked first."*

She tried not to grunt at him. He'd *thought* about it?

"You were engaged to a *human*?" This, surprisingly, wasn't from Popinjay. It was from the woman.

Clay raised both his eyebrows. "Yes. Wolves are happy to Bite our mates when we find them, if they aren't already our kind. I understand vampires tend to do the same."

Popinjay turned a sneer onto the woman, since he couldn't seem to ruffle Clay's hackles. "Isn't that what your brother did recently, Lady Kipling? Although now he's married to Greystoke. Such havey-cavey happenings."

Elle felt the floor drop out from under her. *This* was the Viscountess of Kipling? This was the Creep's *sister*?

"What? What's wrong?" Clay asked.

"How is it havey-cavey?" Viscountess Kipling asked.

"This is the sister of the vampire who Chose me," she replied mentally to Clay, not even looking at him. She was too busy watching the reactions of everyone around her.

She saw Clay turn to stare at the woman. Elle swore she could see the cogs turning behind his bland gaze. Part of her dreaded what insanity he would spout next. The other part of her looked forward to it.

Chapter Forty-Two

"Yes," Anton said into the sudden silence. "I would like to know how – and when – my marriage became classified as 'havey-cavey.'"

He'd been on his way to say a polite greeting to the king – since it was important to maintain appearances – when he'd overheard the conversation between the idiotic Jay Worthington and Anton's sister-in-law. Handy for Anton that their conversation was occurring next to King Johan's side; it meant he didn't have to limp across the room to greet his ruler afterward. With the king was a huge were – presumably a wolf – who easily crested six feet and beyond in height, and a tall, slim vampire woman. She was eye-catching, with her vibrant red hair and sharp features, but she wasn't beautiful. Not like his Annabel had been.

"Greystoke." The way Worthington said his name was almost like a sneer.

Anton didn't bother even inclining his head. The vampire was, after all, his social inferior. "Worthington. Please enlighten my sister-in-law and myself as to why my marriage is questionable?"

Out of the corner of his eye, he saw the king lean toward them, as if listening. The female vampire on his arm seemed totally absorbed in the conversation, her dark purple eyes burning into his neck.

"One minute your new husband was supposedly Choosing the love of his life, the next, he tries to Choose some servant, and then he marries you. You're in third place, by the looks of things."

Anton was surprised. Not many people knew of the servant.

He'd only just heard of the servant from Dante last night. He'd told Anton as a warning. "I feel like I should tell you that I recently tried to Choose a servant as well. After my failure with San – Annabel, I wanted to make sure I hadn't done anything wrong, but it didn't work either." His violet eyes had appeared solemn. "I don't make a habit of Choosing people, and I don't normally kill slaves, just so you know."

Anton had just raised his brows and rubbed the muscles in his sore leg, while sipping brandy.

"Well, you wanted me to stop killing people. I'm just letting you know I hadn't made a habit of it." Dante had sounded…defensive. As if Anton's opinion had mattered, which was astonishing.

"My brother only Chose the servant because she wanted it," the viscountess said now.

A sound almost like a hiss emanated from the female vampire on the king's arm. They all turned to look at her.

"That's fascinating." The werewolf crossed his arms and stared hard at Dante's sister. Anton wondered why the wolf was wading into this discussion.

The viscountess flicked her hair over her shoulder. "What do you care?"

"I care," the other female vampire said, the redhead. "Because it was me."

Anton's jaw dropped.

So did Worthington's and Misty's.

The king looked startled.

The viscountess was the first to recover. "What? That's not possible. She died."

The redhead cracked half a smile. "Well, yes, I assume that is part of the process." She tried to step toward the wolf, but the king had a firm grip on her hand.

"You were Chosen by Dante Kipling?" the king asked.

She turned toward him and nodded.

Please, Anton thought suddenly, fearing what would come

next. *Please, don't say you didn't want him to. I have enough scandal on my plate without adding this to it.*

Anton was starting to get a firm grasp of what had happened. Dante wasn't the sort to ask, and Choosing someone against their will was a crime. One of the few that was punishable by death. And it didn't just affect the vampire; their Chosen also suffered.

Looking up, Anton saw that the redheaded vampire was watching him closely.

The king spoke first. "From what I can gather from the viscountess, Dante thinks you're dead?"

"I don't know. I assume so. When I woke, I was about to be cremated." Her voice was flat, her accent distinctly Pintonite.

Everyone flinched, apart from the wolf. He seemed to be studying the blonde vampire.

The king tapped a finger on the redhead's hand and nodded at Anton. "Well, since you are newly Chosen, you need to be with your Chooser. You are very lucky your fiancé was there to save you, which I assume he was."

The wolf nodded.

Anton tried not to stare. The wolf was engaged to the redhead? Oh, this just got worse and worse.

The words, "be with your Chooser" suddenly replayed themselves in Anton's mind. Wait – had Anton just gained a step-vampire? He was still trying to deal with the one he had.

The wolf shook his head. "No, she can stay with me, she doesn't need her Chooser."

"Clay, she's a newly Chosen vampire," said the king. "She *has* to be with Kipling."

"Fine. She can be with Kipling with me there, too."

Anton opened his mouth to protest. Having that werewolf living under his roof? It would terrify his servants. It would worry *him*. Despite his finely-tailored court dress, there was still a definite feral edge to the man. Having Dante there was bad enough.

"You really still plan on marrying her?" Worthington asked.

The wolf stared at the courtier as if he were a bug that should be crushed beneath his shoe. "Not that it is remotely any of your business, but yes."

"That's—"

"Perfectly fine," the king said. "Provided Baron Greystoke's family agree."

"What has my marriage got to do with the baron?" the newly Chosen vampire asked.

The king patted her arm. Anton hadn't seen his ruler this friendly with anyone for a long time. "Baron Greystoke is your Chooser's husband, young one. Your human family no longer has any rights to your future, but your Chooser's family does. Until you marry Clay, that is. As such, you are now a member of the Greystoke family, and the baron's father is head of that family."

Anton blinked. He *had* just gained a step-vampire.

Great. Just bloody great.

His stomach sank. He really *could* wait to tell Dante.

Part III

May you get what you wish for

CHAPTER FORTY-THREE

If he could count on Elle for anything, Clay thought, it was to keep life interesting.

He really wished he could go back in time and re-do things. He *should* have told Elle that he already knew the King of Pinton, but he hadn't thought that Johan would greet him so openly. He *should* have warned her that he might have to pose as her fiancé, since her Chooser had more right to her than she did. And he *should* have told her to keep her mouth shut in public about her origins, although Clay probably should have known that it was the Kiplings who had done the deed. They always were an arrogant bunch and he'd heard the rumors.

Either way, there were a lot of "should haves" involved. But the actual events had put his vampire into a bit of a state. Clay hoped he'd given her enough time as he strode up the stairs to his apartment.

He rubbed his forehead and hoisted the paper bags full of shopping higher. Then, jamming them under his elbow, he used his free hand to fish the keys out of his pocket. He unlocked the door and walked inside, only to stop short at the sight.

Elle was on his bed, wearing nothing but one of his shirts. Feeling his pants growing a bit tight, he took a step forward, only to stop when he saw the small satchel next to her. It was packed full; probably with the clothes he'd bought her the day before. Looking over at the half-open closet, he saw the red dress hanging there like a swathe of blood.

"You're packed already?" he asked.

She shrugged. "I figured we'd be better off going sooner rather than later. Before Gran hears."

Clay sat the bags on the floor next to the set of drawers. "It wasn't the best idea to announce who Chose you in front of Worthington."

Elle looked at him. "No, I guess it wasn't."

He ran a hand through his hair. "Why did you?"

"I wasn't really thinking."

Clay sat down next to her. He picked up one of her hands and it was cold, so he began rubbing it. She pulled it from him. "I don't think I'm going to get much warmer again."

He felt his cheeks flush. "Are you hungry?"

She turned toward the wall and glared at it. "Yes."

Clay stood and walked toward the bags he'd dropped on the ground. He pulled out a skin from one of the paper packages. It was warm to touch.

Elle was eyeing the bloated container with a grimace.

"This is pig's blood."

She looked slightly queasy. "Yum."

"You should give it a try." *Before you bite me to shreds again*, he thought.

"I don't know."

"Go on." He handed it to her.

Elle opened the top of the skin and sniffed it tentatively. "It doesn't smell great."

"Hold your nose."

Wincing, she did just that. She upended the container and gulped the fluid down. She didn't gag, but she didn't seem too happy about it either. She thrust the skin back at him when she was done.

"How was it?" Clay asked.

"Not very nice, but better than nothing."

He had a feeling her reaction was more psychological than physical. From what he'd heard, pig blood was similar enough to human blood that you could transfuse it, back when the technology had been used. So it couldn't be *that* different. Either way, her cheeks were looking a little pinker, but she was still really pale. Then again, she'd probably always be one shade away from death from now on.

Clay stoppered the skin and popped it on the small kitchenette bench.

He felt Elle come up behind him. "Thanks. I know you didn't want me to bite you again."

"It's not just that," Clay said. "If you keep drinking my blood, any other type of blood will seem…weak."

She didn't look like she particularly believed him, but he wasn't lying. He turned back to grab a glass from the cupboard.

A sharp jab had him spinning around as pain shot through his lower back. Another punch hit his stomach and made him wince. He put the glass down.

"What?"

Her eyebrows were drawn low. "The first one was for not telling me about the king. The second was because you promoted me to fiancée without letting me know first."

He rubbed his back. "Sorry."

"Well?"

"Well what?"

"You said to trust you. It's a bit hard to do that when you don't tell me anything."

She had a point, especially when added to the fact that he doubted she'd ever trusted anyone but Emmie before. He reached out and placed his hands around her waist and drew her close. Resting his cheek on her head he said, "I'm sorry."

She snorted, but she wound her arms around his waist. It felt good.

"So, are you going to tell me how you know the king?" she asked against his chest.

Clay withdrew his arms and then walked over to the bed. He sat down and leaned back against the headboard, crossing his legs at the ankles. Elle sat next to him, crossing her legs underneath her.

"I knew Johan when he was a child," Clay said.

"You grew up together?"

He took a deep breath. "No."

"But, King Johan is at least two thousand years old..." Her expression was half-horrified and half-thoughtful.

"Yeah."

"You were an adult when you met him?" she asked.

"Well and truly." Clay gave her a crooked smile.

"How old *are* you?"

Clay paused. "Do you really want to know?"

He didn't really want to tell her, but he was meant to be inspiring trust. If he wanted her to believe in him, he should at least afford her the same courtesy. Even though trusting a newly Chosen vampire went against his instincts.

"I wouldn't have asked otherwise," she said dryly.

He winced. It sounded ridiculous when he said it aloud. "Just a touch over thirty thousand years."

"You...what?" Her jaw dropped. "That's not possible!"

He flicked a hand in the air. "Yes, it is. I'm living proof."

"But, vampires die after around four thousand, from old age! Aren't weres – werewolves – the same?"

Clay sighed. "Generally, yes. But my situation has to do with my blood. With genes."

"What do you mean?"

"How much do you know about the history of Graceds, vampires and weres?"

She looked at him out of the corner of her eye. "We've always been this way. The Graceds were always the rarest."

"Sort of," Clay said.

Elle frowned.

"There used to be Nons and Graceds, although the Graceds didn't always have abilities. That's why you'll get a Graced every now and then with no power at all.

"Scientists engineered the genes – the blood – so that the abilities manifested more often. Then they tried to make immortal Graceds. But they found that Blues, Greens and Grays just couldn't become immortal. So they made vampires – purples – and weres – yellows – which is a whole different story, and even I'm not sure of the particulars. But they were born to normal Graced parents."

"You said a gene is like a personal code. How can someone change it?"

Clay had to think for a moment. "Genes are the building blocks of life; people used to be able to see them – microscopes were much more advanced. And they could change them. Change the base of the structure, and you'd change the rest of the building."

Elle laughed, disbelief evident on her face. "Scientists could do that? Most of them don't even know what day of the week it is, let alone how to *make* a Graced. Dante – the Creep who Chose me – he likes to think he's a scientist. He just kills people."

"A scientist used to be a reputable job. It used to take years of schooling, and things were more advanced. I remember; I'm only third generation wolf."

"*What?*"

"My grandfather was one of the first werewolves."

"But..."

"Which means my *great*-grandfather was a Graced."

Her jaw had dropped again. "But, why do vampires and weres live only to four thousand years now?"

"Well, weres live longer than vampires, although not by a huge amount. As for the leeches; they're inbred. Those that *do* live longer are the ones whose parents were careful about who they procreated with. And a lot of them bred with Graceds; it shortened their life expectancies as Graceds are mortal."

Elle frowned. "That explains a few things. Could a Graced still have a child with a were or vampire?"

Clay winced. "Some could, yes. Most couldn't. They're too far removed from their Graced ancestors."

Elle stared at him.

"Think of it this way." Clay ran a hand over his hair. "You know dog breeds, how some of the most 'pure' breeds have lots of problems, like kidney disease and lung troubles? That's because of the inbreeding that was done to get them that way. A lot of vampires did the same thing, although there are stronger families than those in Pinton. This city is just one of the worst examples of vampire-kind."

"That kind of makes sense," she admitted. "So, I'm going to die at four thousand?"

"Probably not. Chosen vampires are different to born. They effectively stop aging the day they're changed. I don't know why, but it might be because the vamp blood mixes with Non blood and it becomes something similar to the old-fashioned vamps. Born vampires age, but at a dramatically slower rate than humans. Although, your life-expectancy might be tied to your Chooser's."

She seemed to accept that. "Why aren't there more of you around? Old ones, I mean."

Clay shrugged, but he felt a little hollow thinking about it. "There used to be. But we got hunted down. There was a huge war. Back in the day, the Nons thought we were abnormal and killed us because they were afraid. The Graceds killed us in revenge – a lot of older weres and vampires used to kidnap Graceds and breed with them, to keep the races going. Before that though, the weres had banded together for safety; we built our own cities. The vampires bred internally and quickly; hence their problems. Then vampires and weres fought over territories. Once things settled down, we let in the Nons that were left, and by then, they were used to us. Some of our own kind hunted the older ones down because they feared them – feared people like me. They were scared of what we know and remember."

She was frowning again.

"Remember, these things happened thousands of years ago. Long before Pinton was even a dot on a map." And he had summarized the absolute crap out of thousands of years of history. But then, he couldn't remember all the details; hadn't wanted to.

Elle scooted closer to him, tucking herself against his side, so he had to wrap an arm around her shoulders.

"How did you stay sane?" she asked.

Her question surprised him. "I spent a lot of time away from people," he admitted. "I normally live for decades, centuries even, out in border towns or alone in the forest."

She looked considering. "I guess I'll have to do that too, eventually."

Clay shrugged. "Maybe."

They were quiet. He tucked her closer.

"So, why did you say I was your fiancée?"

He ran a hand over her hair. "Because right now, you belong to the Kipling who Chose you. It was the only thing I could think of that would mean you still had someone around you could trust."

"Could have at least warned me." She tapped her head.

"That reminds me," he said. Using his free hand, he reached into his pocket and pulled out a small box.

"What is it?"

He watched her peer curiously at the little container. He flipped the lid open and she hissed. "A ring?"

"Engagement ring."

"But we're not really engaged!"

Clay shrugged.

"And it's not a Graced tradition." Elle shook her head.

"It *is* a were tradition," Clay countered.

He took the ring from the box and motioned for her to raise her hand. She lifted her left hand for him, and he slid it on her third finger. It glittered against her pale skin, a golden symbol that he'd never before put on a woman's finger, despite his years.

It made his gut clench.

"What stone is it?" she asked, moving her hand from side to side.

"It's a yellow topaz on gold," he said. "It's just for show, you know. To make it look sincere..."

Elle nodded, but her eyes were locked on the band around her finger. "Color of your eyes," she murmured.

CHAPTER FORTY-FOUR

"I heard an interesting rumor today," Olive said to Bjorn. Heard, spied, stolen from someone's mind. It was all the same to her.

The Gray-eyed male was standing in front of her chair. She had lost respect for him recently, after she'd picked from his mind that he'd confronted the wolf after the funeral. Making the yellow-eyed bastard angry at them would not further Olive's plans. But a TK as strong as Bjorn was useful. It's why she'd allowed him to pine after Elle. It kept him close. After all, strong Grays were few and far between, and half the time had no control over their abilities. A strong Gray could crush a person in a fit of rage. It's why Olive always kept a tight lock on Bjorn's mind. She had no intention of suffering an "accident."

"Really?" Bjorn asked. He sounded bored, but she knew he wasn't. He was hoping it had something to do with the wolf.

"Yes. I need you to go and do some surveillance for me."

CHAPTER FORTY-FIVE

Dante heard Anton's distinctive walk well before the human made it to his side of the townhouse. Dante had claimed the western wing of the home, or at least one room of that largely unused end of the house. The drawing rooms, bedrooms and ballroom were on the eastern side, and they smelled strongly of human. It wasn't unpleasant, not like back at the estate, but it did make him feel hungry a lot.

As the footsteps came closer, Dante looked up from the sheaf of notes he was reading from, and stared at the wooden door. He shuddered slightly. There was just so much wood in this house. It was like walking through a snake pit; at any given moment, there was the potential for disaster. Added to the constant temptation of dinner, Dante had started to live a little on the edge.

"Come in," Dante called, when he heard Anton stop outside the door.

The handle turned and Anton came inside, dressed in court finery, hand white-knuckled on his cane. He looked a little ridiculous, Dante thought, but better than most people who wore all that lace. Eyes traveling back to the cane, Dante stood abruptly and walked over to his husband. He still wasn't used to that term.

"You shouldn't walk that far. Your leg must be hurting." He grabbed Anton's elbow and hurried him over to Dante's now vacant chair.

He forced Anton to sit down and then moved his papers away. He wasn't really sure if he cared that the human might read his notes, but as Dante didn't plan on doing any more experimentation, at least not in Anton's lifetime, then it wasn't really necessary. And he didn't really need Anton to think that he was crazy. Well, crazier.

"It's pretty dark in here," Anton said.

Dante looked around and guessed that for a human, it was. He walked over to one of the lamps he'd set up on a table underneath the window and lit it. Turning the flame up, he brought it over to the bench where he'd sat Anton. The room was small, with only two tables, three chairs and a small curtain that covered a smaller window; the lamp seemed almost blindingly bright to Dante in the space.

"Thanks."

"Should you walk that far?" Dante had done a little research on human injuries after discovering Anton's. It seemed like it was a muscular problem, since Anton rubbed his thigh so much.

Anton straightened on his chair and laid his cane across the tabletop with a firm click. "I'm not an invalid."

"I didn't say you were." Dante wasn't sure how he'd done the wrong thing.

"I can walk a few hallways of my own house without a problem." Anton's tone was frosty.

"I'm sorry if I implied that you couldn't." Why did conversation have to be so difficult? He was just trying to be considerate. That was what husbands were meant to do – he'd researched it.

"You aren't very good at this, are you?" Anton said.

"Good at what?" Dante asked.

Anton rubbed his leg, but Dante wasn't sure that the human was aware he was doing it. "Interaction with people."

"No, not really," Dante admitted. Something seemed to flash in Anton's eyes, but he wasn't sure what it was, and he didn't know how to ask without insulting the human again.

Anton's hand dropped away from his thigh. "I came over here to tell you something you might find very important."

Dante pulled up one of the other stools and sat down. He

didn't like the sound of that. Very important? Nothing good was ever given that label.

"I'm not sure what you did to trigger your father wanting to marry you to another family, but I figure it might have something to do with what I heard today." Anton's brandy eyes were staring at him intensely.

Distracted, Dante wondered if Anton liked the drink because it reflected his eye color. It was something to think on. Thankfully, though, Anton wasn't the drunk Dante had feared he would be. He only seemed to drink when he was upset. Which happened a lot around Dante.

"Kipling?"

Dante shook his head and returned his mind to the conversation. "What did you hear today that may have something to do with my father's rage?" He couldn't really think of anything, apart from the servant, and that wasn't really a big deal, not unless Anton had business dealings with the girl's family.

"I met a girl today who was – apparently – a newly Chosen vampire."

Dante felt his gaze lock on Anton's cane.

"She was tall, not as tall as me, but tall for a woman. She had long red hair and was quite pretty, in a sharp way."

Dante felt something prickle in his stomach and sweat broke out on his forehead.

"*Long* red hair?" Dante asked.

"Color of blood," Anton said.

Dante shut his eyes, fingering the bridge of his nose. The hair wasn't the right length or color, but that didn't mean much. Human bodies changed as they were Chosen. "What color were her eyes?"

If she was Chosen, they should be a dark purple. No other hue. Not unless they'd been different to begin with.

"Why don't you ask me who Chose her?" Anton said instead.

Dante felt his breath quicken. "Her eyes first, please."

"Very unusual," Anton said, absently rubbing his thigh again. "The normal purple, but sometimes when she looked at me, I thought I saw green and gray."

Dante's gut clenched.

"You want to know who Chose her?" Anton asked again.

Something almost like an emotion surged through Dante, but all he recognized was the blood pounding through him. "I don't need to. It was me. They told me she was *dead*."

Anton was looking at him oddly. "A were apparently saved her from being cremated."

A were.

"He's her fiancé, apparently, and he's not too happy about her new situation."

The stench that had been all over her, that had prompted him to Choose her then and there. Fiancé. He hadn't thought it was that serious. Dante might be in deep shit – *more* deep shit.

"She survived," Dante said slowly.

There was silence.

"Did…did you love her?" Anton asked.

Dante blinked and looked at the human closely. Anton's mouth was pinched, but Dante wasn't sure what that expressed.

An impulse had him blurt, "No, she was an experiment."

"An *experiment*?"

Dante should have kept his mouth shut. How much should he say? Would Anton hand him over to the king?

"To work out why Sandy didn't survive being Chosen." Something twitched in Anton's face, but the human didn't say anything, although he began digging his fingers into his troubled leg again.

Standing, Dante walked over to Anton and shoved the other man's hands away, and began massaging the leg.

Anton jumped. "What are you doing?"

Dante flicked up a glance. "Even though you aren't an invalid, this gives you pain. You keep rubbing it. I thought I'd try and help. My hands are stronger than yours." Dante started working on the muscle with slow and firm strokes of his fingers.

Anton let out a groan.

"Am I hurting you?" Dante was trying not to press too hard,

but he didn't know what would be effective or not.

"No, it hurts in a good way."

Dante didn't know if he wanted to try and work that statement out.

"Where did you learn to do this?" Anton asked.

"I used to keep horses" – before his father had them all slaughtered as a lesson – "and they enjoyed being rubbed down after a hard ride."

Anton coughed.

Dante looked up. "What?"

"Nothing." Anton shook his head.

"So where did you see the new vampire? At court?" Dante asked.

"Yes, I was going to greet the king – try and keep up appearances – when I overheard a conversation taking place next to him. He had the new vampire on his arm."

Dante's hands stopped. "It came out that I Chose her?"

"Yes. So we're about to have a new family member arrive."

Frowning, he began massaging Anton's leg again, on the inside of the thigh. "Arrive?"

The sound of a servant's approaching footsteps reached Dante's ears. They were quick footsteps; servants didn't run, but this one was in a hurry to find him or Greystoke or both.

Anton grabbed Dante's hand and moved it away. "When you Choose someone, they become part of your family. You should know that."

Stepping away, Dante hoped he'd helped Anton's pain. It was what husbands were meant to do, wasn't it?

"Yes…"

"And your family is my family. So now I'm about to gain a step-daughter or something."

Slumping back on his seat, Dante pinched his nose. He hadn't thought about that. He hadn't thought she'd survived, so he hadn't planned ahead. If he'd known it from day one, his whole life would have been different. Viktor might not have married him off – although Dante wasn't going to assume that was by any means a certainty – and Dante could even now be in the possession of important knowledge. Knowledge as to why non-browns were different.

He looked at his notes.

"When is she coming here?" Dante asked. He was keen to see her, to ask her more. But now…he wasn't sure if he wanted to know. He was trying to put his obsession behind him. He had a husband to worry about, a mother and a sister who seemed to like him. Oh, and an execution threat if he didn't behave. He didn't know what to do as it was. This was just one more entanglement.

The servant Dante had heard approaching appeared in the doorway, looking slightly winded. "My lord, sir."

Anton nodded at the man, indicating he should speak.

"Viscountess Kipling is here to see Mr. Greystoke."

Like his life wasn't already complicated enough.

CHAPTER FORTY-SIX

Elle shifted from foot to foot, not that she needed to, but it was hard to break a nervous habit from when she'd been human. And she'd been human far longer than she'd been a blood drinker. She hitched her small bag higher on her shoulder.

"Why are we going around the back?" she asked.

Clay leaned down and picked up his last suitcase, waving off the hackney cab. He started heading down the small alley that lead around to the rear of Greystoke House. "We don't want everyone to remark upon our entrance."

"You mean, you don't want my gran to know we're here? I bet she does already," Elle muttered.

And that thought made her hunch her shoulder blades closer together, as if she could feel an invisible stake targeted there. Gran had already been monitoring Greystoke, not that Elle was about to tell Clay that. It hadn't been confirmed, just a suspicion she'd had, since Annabel had been involved. Annabel was only ever asked to be in on a project when they were desperate for information or control.

They strolled slowly between the stables and the rear stone fence before emerging through a wooden gate and into a small courtyard. It was pretty, with stone walls and benches, and flowers blooming in the crisp air. The smell of the city receded a little, hints of jasmine and honeysuckle cleansing the palate, like a crisp sorbet. The cobbled path led the way through to a large terrace, where a man was awaiting them, leaning on a cane.

It was the baron from yesterday.

Greystoke was handsome, with deep olive skin and pale Brown eyes, almost yellow in the sunshine, she thought. She wondered if there was some latent were blood there. Trying to smile, she walked forward, hand outstretched, but she froze when movement from inside caught her attention.

It was *him*.

The Creep.

She didn't even think. Dropping her pack, she darted forward. By the time his foot hit the first stone step on the terrace, she had him by the throat. "You asshole!"

He was tall; she'd forgotten that, so it was an awkward grip. She loosened her hand and then slammed her knee up, smashing it into his groin. As he doubled over, both hands hovering uselessly over his crotch, she threw an uppercut, which sent him flying back a couple of yards.

She leaped after him. "How could you leave me to be burned alive!"

Elle began punching, and the smell of his blood in the air made something in her snap. She didn't think the last hit she did was that hard, but he flew back across the courtyard, slamming into a stone wall over five yards away.

Arms grabbed her then, strong ones.

"Let me go!"

Clay's voice, warm and amused, sounded next to her ear. "You've already damaged the vampire enough for one day."

Greystoke moved in front of her vision as well. "It would please me greatly if you refrained from beating up my husband." She thought she heard him mutter, "That's *my* right," but she wasn't sure.

At the sound of a low groan, Elle went to spin around, but Clay had a firm grip on her arms.

Kipling came shuffling up then, one hand on his balls, the other on his skull. "My head."

"That's what you're worried about?" Clay asked with a laugh.

Kipling looked up and froze for a few moments, staring at

Clay. Elle moved back a step, closer to the wolf, protective.

Rubbing his skull, Kipling seemed to shake himself and muttered, "Typical dog to think more of his balls than his brains." There was no heat in the comment, though.

"Yeah, well, I didn't just have my ass handed to me by a week-old baby vampire."

"Stop the pissing contest," Elle snapped. She saw the baron's jaw drop out from the corner of her eye. She hoped he wasn't the sensitive type.

"I should kill you." She jabbed a finger in Kipling's chest.

"You can't," he said, but he looked a bit wide-eyed.

"I can *try*." She realized she'd started grinding her teeth.

"Enough!" A walking stick stabbed the ground between them.

Elle broke away and looked at Greystoke. He seemed to have a kind face, but he was standing up for Kipling. Why?

"We are going to take this...discussion inside. Where the neighbors can't see and the servants won't hear so easily." He looked at them all meaningfully.

Silently, they followed him in.

♦

"I don't like Kipling," Elle announced.

Clay looked at her. "And ten points goes to you for stating the obvious."

"What?"

"Points? As in, rewards for...never mind."

Elle was sitting on the massive bed in the room she'd been given to share with Clay, since he was her fiancé. Part of her had wanted to protest, on principle, but that would look odd, since he was a wolf. Werewolves didn't sleep in separate bedrooms from their wives, not like human cits and vampire aristos did. And since the story went that she was meant to have been Bitten, rather than Chosen as she was, then she'd have to go along with wolf tradition.

It was all doing her head in.

Flopping back on the bed, she crossed her arms behind her

head. "He's an idiot."

"All vampires are idiots, present company excluded," Clay said.

He was packing his things away in the drawers and closet, which was a room unto itself. He had a stupid amount of clothes for a man who barely spent any time in civilization. Plus, from the looks of the room, aristos sure knew how to live in a ridiculous amount of space. Although, some things they did right. She had squealed like a two-year-old girl when she'd spotted the adjoining bathroom: hot running water. Delicious. She was excited about taking her first bath in the huge bronze tub.

"Greystoke seems okay, though." She'd gotten over her resentment that the baron had interfered with her abusing Kipling. Kipling had deserved it, but she could see why he'd wanted it stopped.

Anyway, she really wanted that bath now. Elle felt a bit battered herself, even though Kipling hadn't laid a finger on her. Her head hurt and she was a bit tender in the stomach region.

"Why do I feel so sore?" she asked Clay suddenly.

He emerged from the closet and frowned at her. "What do you mean? Was I a bit rough last night?"

If she'd been able to blush properly, she would have. "No." Clay had been fantastic last night, better than when she'd been human. She had a feeling it was because he wasn't worried about breaking her anymore. Either way, she didn't care. As long as he did it again. And again.

"Maybe it's the link," Clay said.

Elle propped herself up on her elbows. "Link?"

"Between you and Kipling. There's some sort of psychic link between Chooser and Chosen, same with werewolves. Prevents the Chosen from attacking their maker, what with the bloodlust and rage and all."

"Aren't humans meant to *want* to be Chosen?"

"Consent wasn't part of the original goal, no."

"Kipling told me something about not being able to hurt him before he killed me," Elle said. "Are you meant to feel each other's pain?" She wasn't *that* sore, and she'd given Kipling a bit of a beating.

"Not normally, but you aren't a normal case." He went back to folding clothes.

She lay back on the bed and shut her eyes. "I don't see how any of this is going to help me get Emmie."

The mattress sighed as Clay sat down next to her. "It hasn't quite gone to plan, has it?"

She cracked one eyelid open and looked at him. "You think?"

"We needed to get the king's attention and support. I'm pretty sure he knows about Graceds and that he'd be happy to have you – a special case – watching over another special case, Emmie. With my backing. But now Greystoke and Kipling are involved? That isn't so easy to predict."

"But will the king give me Emmie? Gran is rich and has ties with the Kiplings and Anton. I can't say that they will help me get her away from Gran."

"What?" Clay looked surprised for a few seconds, but then he seemed thoughtful. "That shouldn't surprise me, but it did."

"I never had anything confirmed; I'm not high enough in the family to be actually *told* anything. But Annabel White was engaged to Greystoke, unofficially. She was working on getting him to publicly announce it. Although from what I hear now," she tapped her head, "everyone knows anyway."

Clay was frowning. "What purpose would that have served?"

"Gran likes to have her fingers in all the pies. Greystoke's family was rumored to be in financial difficulties, but they are well-respected. Lots of votes in the Counsel."

"This is getting overly complicated," Clay said.

"I have a feeling this is just the beginning."

CHAPTER FORTY-SEVEN

Clay wasn't sure that leaving Elle and Kipling in the same house – without him to supervise – was a great idea, but the king's summons had been clear, albeit very prettily worded. Clay had translated: Get your butt to the palace or watch out.

So he got his ass to the Crystal Palace.

Rather than his court gear, he'd decided on his buckskins and a flowing white shirt. Show Johan that he wasn't a civilized lapdog to do as he was bid. By the blood, he probably wouldn't have gone at all if it wasn't for Elle and the kid. Too many bitter memories about this place.

The door guard had sniffed when Clay had announced himself, but had let him into the white marble foyer, and organized for a page to show him the way. The Crystal Palace's entryway looked the same as it had the last time: gleaming walls, crimson rug running along the center of the foyer, crystal chandelier hanging low and heavy. And lots of priceless artifacts. Vases that had been ancient before the war sat in recessed niches; their bright colors preserved back when the technology had been available.

The boy barely waited for Clay to acknowledge him before marching off in the direction of Johan. The page held his back so stiff that Clay was surprised the lad could walk so fast. Clay followed. He figured he was meant to. Leaving the foyer, they entered an ornate hall, the ceilings high and covered with frescoes of purple-eyed folk dancing in the skies, all edged in gold.

Lowering his eyes, Clay thought that the page's red livery draped him like a bloody hug. They soon turned down another hall, then another. They were all marbled, with either frescoed or glass ceilings and plush rugs lining the floors. Soon, the boy stopped outside a set of double doors, these covered in gilt etchings. The boy knocked on a door with firm raps.

"Come!" a voice called from behind it.

The young lad opened one of the doors, and Clay wanted to offer help, since the lad struggled a little with the weight, but the stiff posture told him to leave well alone. Once Clay entered the room, the boy dragged the door shut, locking him in with the royal presence.

"Clay," the king acknowledged.

Clay looked around the highly decorated suite. The dome-shaped room had walls covered in red and gold silks, with priceless metals and gems glittering on tables, chairs and tapestries. A huge rug covered the floor, the wealth of which could have fed Elle's family for ten years or more.

"Johan," Clay said and forced a smile.

He had liked Johan, thought he was a great kid and had enjoyed spending time with him as he grew up. It had been during one of Clay's city periods, and since he was who he was, the old king had wanted Clay to stay in the palace. Old werewolves were better on side than not. Trust the dog you know was the saying.

"I hadn't expected to see you here again," Johan said. The vampire king waved a hand at a set of small, delicate metal chairs. Johan sat down on one of the padded seats and crossed a leg at the knee.

Clay followed the indication. He shrugged. "I received an invitation that I found rather interesting from a cit. I decided to check it out."

"What did they want?"

Clay shrugged. "Something I wasn't prepared to give."

The king studied him for a moment, and must have guessed that Clay wasn't going to elaborate any further. "You really are engaged?"

Raising an eyebrow, Clay said, "You believe that I'd announce something like that if I wasn't?"

Intense lavender eyes bored into him. "I always thought that you weren't interested in marriage or commitment."

"I just never met the right person, until now."

Only part of that was a lie.

Hurt flashed through the king's eyes. "No one was ever good enough? But what did you pick? A servant?"

Clay bit back a curse. He'd forgotten about Johan's infatuation with him. It was why he'd left. Why he'd been *forced* to leave.

"She's actually a city guard. She was working as a servant to help her mother out financially." That had been the lie they'd agreed on. Elle had eventually admitted she'd gone there to spy on Kipling. From what he'd seen of the vampire, he wouldn't be surprised if the man *had* been targeting Graceds. Kipling was…cold. That was the best way to describe him.

"A guard? Of my own city." The king was shaking his head.

"Yes. I'm sorry the idea offends you."

Johan flinched. "I know it shouldn't. But I always took comfort in the thought that you never really wanted anyone, so not wanting me was okay."

"I told you then, and I'll tell you now, I don't swing that way."

Johan's eyes hardened, became lavender flints. "You never even tried."

"I tried it," Clay said. "Thousands of years ago. Wasn't for me." Most of the older weres and vamps swung both ways, but not Clay. He'd just never been able to get into guys. They had cocks. He had a cock. There only needed to be one cock.

The king slumped back in his chair. "I never had a chance."

"No." Clay couldn't believe he was having this conversation. Again. Johan's obsession is what had kept him away from this city – and why he'd kept an almost invisible profile when he'd traveled through the last few times. Elle had wound him up so tight he'd forgotten.

"I want to punish your fiancée, but I can't."

"Punish her?" Clay asked, raising an eyebrow. He wouldn't put it past the child-Johan, but the adult had matured. He'd heard nothing but good things about the king, which was unusual for a vamp.

Johan waved a ringed hand through the air. "She's been Chosen, but not registered with the palace. That is a punishable crime."

"Not her fault," Clay said. "Wintermere said she was dead, gave her back to her family and they were going to cremate her." He'd managed to piece it all together, finally, after listening to her rant and Kipling muse aloud. Then he'd gotten Dante and Elle to confirm it. The male vampire really was a bit odd, even for one of his kind.

"But she's with Kipling now?" Johan asked.

"Right this minute? I'm not sure. But when I left, they were together."

"That has caused a lot of gossip. People assume that Kipling loved your fiancée and that's why he Chose her. Which confuses the rumor that he tried to Choose Greystoke's fiancée and killed her."

Clay shook his head and thought quickly. Kipling was a trouble magnet, that was for sure.

"Kipling tried to Choose Greystoke's fiancée, but she died. I think he thought that Elle would be happy to be Chosen, since she was going to be Bitten, and did it to her to prove he could."

"He didn't get consent?" Johan spluttered.

Clay decided no answer was the best solution. He couldn't risk Kipling being executed for a more than justifiable reason, because it would destroy Elle, whether she knew it or not. Especially because of their…unusual…link.

Johan frowned and asked, "Why haven't you killed him, since he took the chance of children from you?"

"It would have been exceedingly unlikely that Elle and I could have had children, even if she had been Bitten."

"But she was Graced," the king said, puzzled.

Clay swallowed. He'd always suspected that Johan knew

about them – he was too astute to have not worked it out, and he had all those old records – but to have it confirmed so easily…

"Graced?"

"Don't tell me you don't know what they are. And if you didn't before, you should now. Her eyes are remarkable. The only one of her kind. And she's my subject. I want to see how she…evolves. But to return to my earlier comment: the chance of children *was* a possibility."

So Elle was an experiment to Johan. Clay wanted to hate that, but he couldn't. Most rulers would have killed Elle rather than take the risk she could become more powerful. And the fact he knew about Graceds… Did he know what was going on in his city with Olive?

He couldn't.

It was one thing to have an oddity like Elle occur…but to have the Graceds actively try to become immortal and stronger than vampires was something no vampire king could ignore.

"I had thought about killing Kipling. But I can't, because of the bond between him and Elle," Clay admitted. "It's…stronger than normal."

"Really?" Johan fingered his chin. "But then, I wouldn't know what it is like anyway; it's not like I can Choose whoever I want."

No, Johan had never Chosen anyone that Clay was aware of. He couldn't. Favoritism. Nepotism. Angry courtiers as a result.

Johan looked at him, something cunning glinting in his lavender eyes. "You're worried if one dies, the other will, too."

Clay shifted on his chair. "It's a possibility."

"So, what am I going to do about this situation, Clay? The aristos are going to be unhappy, just because they can be, and I am aware who Elle's grandmother is."

"I'm sure you have ideas."

"I do, but I want to hear *yours*. After all, you seem to be involved in all of this."

And suddenly, Clay wondered if Johan had known he'd been here all along. Things had just gotten tricky.

Again.

CHAPTER FORTY-EIGHT

Anton's home was in chaos, utter chaos.

He had gone to the palace to spend a day in the counsel chambers – so his father wouldn't have to come to town – and he'd come home to *this*. *This* had been his fault, but he hadn't known it would be a problem. He'd assumed Dante had *known*.

When he'd been at the counsel chambers, he'd stopped by the hall of records, to add Elle's name to his family's register. It had seemed logical. Then he'd double-checked the reference, after the librarian had made the amendment, and had noticed that Dante had *two* sisters. And that his mother hadn't been the Countess of Wintermere.

So when he'd arrived home, he'd asked Dante where his other sister was, since he'd only ever heard mention of Mistique. Dante hadn't known what Anton was talking about.

Now, Anton's mother was in a panic, saying that poor, poor Dante was beside himself with the news he had just heard: he had a twin sister that he'd never known about. Some *foreign* woman had sired Dante and taken his sibling away. And oh, she just *knew* Anton would be upset with having *foreigners* in the family, but he shouldn't be because *poor, dear* Dante was just hysterical.

Thankfully, Dante had known the countess wasn't his mother. Some aristo children never knew they were the product of a breeding contract until they had to sign a legal document. "She's the countess," he had said. "She's Misty's mother and my stepmother, but she tends to drop by from time to time to lecture me on propriety before leaving for another world tour. Misty says it's how she shows her love." Dante hadn't looked like he believed the latter statement, however.

Like Anton cared that Dante had a *foreign* mother; he hadn't married the mother. And Beatrice's theory that Dante was upset was just pure idiocy. He'd never met anyone who was *less* prone to hysterics than Dante. And Dante looked no different to normal; Anton had studied Dante's "normal" appearance quite thoroughly.

Elle, it seemed, had decided that she didn't quite hate Dante as much as before, because of the revelation, and so she was trying to "help him out" by cracking hugely inappropriate jokes that had Anton's mother alternating between laughter and horror, which didn't help the situation. He'd had to send Darla to her room, because her eyes welled with tears every time she even spotted Dante, and since she was sitting next to him in the drawing room, that was about every two seconds. She had been doing a rather remarkable imitation of a fountain, sounds and all.

Dante was, just, well, Dante. "Hysterics" seemed to leave him calm.

The only time he'd shown any expression was when Anton had sent Darla to her room.

"Better for everyone if she goes and calms down," Anton had said.

But now *he* was sitting next to the vampire, because his mother had insisted that *poor, dear* Dante would need the support of his husband through such a *trying* time.

"At least that means the countess is not *my* Chosen grandmama. Imagine the horror!" Elle shuddered dramatically at Dante. When had Elle ever met the countess? Another joke?

"She never was," Dante muttered.

"No, but *my* mother is," Anton said over Dante.

"And it is so lovely to have a granddaughter." Beatrice went over to Elle.

"I wouldn't do that," Dante said. The third thing he'd said since Anton had arrived home.

Beatrice stopped her movement, her body bent halfway to give Elle a hug. Anton could see Elle sniffing the air between them.

Dante leaped forward just as Elle moved. He snatched Beatrice away and deposited Anton's blinking mother next to him. Dante then turned to Elle and tapped her on the nose with a finger. "Bad baby vampire."

Elle snarled.

"Sorry," Dante said to Beatrice and Anton. He grabbed Elle's arm, although she didn't seem to be diving across the room after Beatrice. "New vampires have trouble controlling their hunger."

Anton looked over at his mother, who had wide eyes and a hand clutched to her throat. She shook herself. "No, no. It is quite all right. It has been such a stressful afternoon. I forgot that Elle would be hungry."

Typical Mother, Anton thought, always taking the blame for everything.

A deep voice rolled through the room then. "Why are you touching my fiancée?"

Anton hung his head. Not him, too.

Could the day get *any* worse?

"Because she was trying to bite my mother-in-law's neck," Dante replied.

The werewolf, Clay, stalked into the room. The expression on his unshaven face was not kind. In his buckskins and loose white shirt, he looked like sex on a stick. *Angry* sex on a stick.

Anton felt Elle's eyes flash to him, but then they moved to Beatrice. "She's my grandma-in-law, too. I'm sorry, I didn't mean to try and bite you."

She hadn't even flashed her teeth, Anton thought. But he was glad Dante had decided on prevention.

"Quite all right, dear." His mother's hands were fluttering through the air.

"You're *still* touching my fiancée," Clay said to Dante.

"I don't want to risk her losing control again."

Anton saw Elle look down at the pale hand gripping her arm and then back up at Dante. He towered over the tall woman.

"How did you know I wanted to bite the countess?" she asked.

Dante frowned. "I could feel it."

Anton blinked, and the next thing he knew, Clay was standing in Dante's face. "Let her go or I'll hurt you."

"Oh, I'm scared of the big bad wolf," Dante taunted.

"You should be."

"Be still my racing heart!" Dante placed a hand over his chest. Anton figured his husband was being sarcastic. Which was odd.

Clay's fist shot out, but Dante was gone. Standing on the other side of Elle, holding her other arm. Anton hadn't even seen him move. Clay was staring at his fist with a frown on his face.

"That was lucky," Clay said and looked like he was going to try and punch Dante again.

"Not in the Rose room!" Beatrice cried.

Everyone turned to stare at Anton's mother. "If you *must* degenerate into violence," she raised her chin high, as if she scolded vampires and werewolves every other day, "do it outside."

Grumbling, Clay stalked to the door. Over his shoulder, he snapped to Dante and Elle, "Are you coming or not?"

Anton saw Elle start to walk forward, only to stop and glare at the hand Dante was using to restrain her. "Hey, I don't want to miss Clay kicking your ass. Let's go."

Muttering something Anton couldn't hear, Dante walked past him and his mother. At the door, he released Elle's arm. She continued after Clay, calling out encouragement.

"Why are you going outside?" Anton blurted.

"Werewolves like to show their dominance. I can't let him think he has rights over me and my role as Elle's Chooser. Things could turn…nasty, if I do."

Anton wasn't sure he wanted to know what "nasty" entailed.

Dante took two steps outside the Rose room, then turned back to look inside at Beatrice and Anton. "Stay inside."

Since Anton wasn't sure if that was directed at him or his mother – although he had a feeling it was for both of them – he decided to follow him out. "You'd better stay here, Mother."

Anton emerged onto the terrace and blinked in the weak sunlight. Clay and Dante were down in the garden below, and Clay had stripped off his shirt. The werewolf was rolling his shoulders. Anton's mouth went dry at the sight.

"Stop drooling," Elle said from next to him.

Anton flicked a glance over at her. "I don't know what you're talking about."

"Uh-huh. That's *my* wolf, so eyes off."

"I'm a married man."

"Yeah, but you're married to *Dante*." He thought he heard her add, "Sucks to be you," but he wasn't sure.

"You have any uncontrollable urges to bite me?" Anton asked.

"Not right now."

Anton turned back to the garden below the terrace. Dante was standing there, in his breeches and shirt, jacket gone. He looked almost delicate next to Clay, but that was only because the werewolf was so muscled. Dante wasn't exactly skin and bones, he was in fact lithely built; he'd seen it before by accident when the vamp had been coming from the bathroom.

Realizing he *was* drooling, but over a memory, Anton said, "In case you hadn't noticed, Dante isn't exactly a trial to look at either."

"He's creepy," Elle said. "Hard to find that hot."

"You're going to fight in that?" Clay called to Dante, his voice carrying to Anton.

The vampire shrugged. He was leaning against an ivy-covered stone wall near the side of the garden. Dante crossed his arms. "I don't need to strip off to fight. Or did you want this to have a happy ending?"

Anton's jaw dropped. He'd never heard Dante speak like that before. Out the corner of his eye, he saw that Elle wore the same expression. Then she turned a slight greenish hue.

"You fucking wish. Fight or not?" Clay called.

Quick as a flash, Dante moved to stand in the middle of the courtyard.

CHAPTER FORTY-NINE

Dante wondered what had gotten into him. He was outside, without a jacket – something the Countess Maerylina would have fits about – and was preparing to have a fight with a werewolf. And not just any werewolf. Dante could tell an old dog when he saw one, which meant that Clay would be stronger than him. Maybe even faster, although he wasn't sure about that. Dante was *really* fast.

"You don't have to do this," Anton called.

Shaking his head, Dante looked up onto the terrace. "Thought I told you to wait inside."

"Aww, is the baron being a bad wifey?" Elle snorted.

Dante frowned. Actually, Anton was being a rather *good* husband. Surprisingly so. No stakes, no anger, just acceptance. Even about Dante's lack of…needs.

"Keep your teeth to yourself while we're busy," Dante said to Elle.

Clay paused his fist cracking to add, "Don't bite him!" Then the werewolf turned to Dante. "You ready to fight or you going to just stand there and daydream?"

Dante blinked. Warm sunshine drifted down over him, and the strong floral scent of the garden wound around him. Maybe he should spend more time out here. When he wasn't about to get beaten up. Although, he was hoping to avoid that.

Better get this over with, he thought. Quicker than the time it took to blink, Dante was behind Clay, poking him in the back with a finger. "Too slow."

Clay spun around, but Dante was gone. He'd never really been able to enjoy this; his speed, his senses. To his father, anything that marked him as different had meant that he was "delicate." Although how being super fast was fragile, Dante didn't know.

He could hear the whoosh of air as Clay lunged for him, so Dante ran. He was in another spot by the time Clay arrived. But Clay was fast, Dante realized. Really fast. The wolf had only just missed him.

A shout from the terrace reached them – "Go Clay!" – and it distracted him for a moment. Next thing he knew, he was being thrown back against the garden wall. Stone crumbled behind him, and a bone broke.

Elle yelped.

"No biting!" Dante and Clay yelled at her.

Clay was in his face in the next second, yellow eyes glowing, teeth bared. He wrapped a hand around Dante's throat and squeezed before letting go. "Pay attention, leech."

Dante hissed in a breath as his shoulder blade began to knit itself together again. Then Dante was gone; he ran through the sweet-smelling garden until he was standing on the other side of the terrace. "Come get me, dog."

He landed a few punches here and there, but mostly, Clay chased, Dante ran. Dante hit, Clay chased. It was a game of cat and mouse, with very few hits landed. It was almost...fun.

Dante leaped over a stone wall and heard Clay curse and follow. "We're meant to be fighting, leech."

"Gotta catch me first," Dante yelled over his now-healed shoulder.

"Enough!" Anton's voice thundered through the courtyard.

Dante stopped, Clay slamming into his back, both of them spinning to the ground in a cloud of torn flowers and dust. He landed against the roots of a woody honeysuckle vine. Thankfully, he thought, it wasn't the rose bush, or Dante's life may have been in danger.

Winded, Dante tried to suck air in through resisting lungs.

"Get off," he hissed at Clay, who hadn't moved.

"Slight problem here," Clay said.

Craning his neck at an awkward angle, he saw and smelled blood dripping from a cut. Which was odd. Frowning, Dante tried to get a better look and then understood why he couldn't. Elle was lying on top of Clay.

"What the – ?" Dante gasped.

"Elle, get your teeth out of my neck," Clay snapped.

Ahh, the dripping blood. Elle was biting Clay. Dante wheezed a laugh.

"Shut up," Clay said. "Elle, if you don't stop now, I'm going to stop you. You won't like it."

Dante wondered why Elle had launched herself on them in the first place. Clay must have been cut at some point.

She's *fast*, Dante realized. For her to have made it here when they spilled to the ground… *Almost as fast as me.*

Anton's voice was cold as it said, "Eleanor Greystoke, remove your fangs from your fiancé this instant."

"Get Anton away from here," Dante hissed.

"Little busy. I don't think she'll bite him since she's got her fangs in me," Clay said.

Dante shut his eyes then opened them to find Anton's boots and cane planted on the ground in front of Dante's face. At least they hadn't landed on his head. Anton set the cane against the crumpled honeysuckle and then grabbed the back of Elle's neck, like she was a naughty kitten.

Elle hissed.

"Do not make me pick you up," Anton said.

Clay grunted, then heaved himself up. Not before he shoved a hand on Dante's back and used it to lever himself upright. Dante could barely breathe.

A second later, the weight had lifted off Dante and he managed to draw in a proper breath. Sitting up, Dante turned and saw Clay standing, wearing a rather thunderous frown, while he pried Elle from his neck. Anton reached over and picked up his cane.

"*Elle.*"

Something about Clay's voice seemed to penetrate her haze, and she let go. She stared at Clay's neck for a few seconds, hunger warping her face, before a warm tint spread up her neck and into her cheeks. She wiped her mouth with the back of her sleeve. "I'm sorry," she muttered.

"Did you drink the pig's blood I left for you this morning?" Clay demanded.

"No."

"Why not?"

"It tastes bad."

Dante had to screw his face up in sympathy. It *did* taste bad. In comparison. But most vampires never noticed the difference. He'd figured once again it was due to his "sensitivity." Looked like Elle had inherited that, too. But he was also living on pig's blood at the moment. He hadn't wanted to drink from any of the servants, didn't want to risk making them bit-ridden.

"I don't mind you drinking from me if you absolutely have to; better me than the countess or Darla," Clay said. "But you were putting *their* lives in danger by not drinking what I left for you. What if the leech here *hadn't* stopped you? Maybe it was *your* ass I should have been kicking, rather than his."

Dante hauled himself to his feet. Now he was going to have to drink more of that awful stuff as well, to make up for the healing his body had just done.

He heard Anton come to stand beside him. The gentle scent of the human's aftershave wreathed in the air around him, adding to the garden's fragrance. Dante flicked a glance at him, but part of him was fascinated by the argument unfolding in front of him.

"They don't sound so lover-like, huh?" Anton said.

Dante shook his head. Clay had squared off against Elle and they were standing almost nose to nose, growling at each other. "You're not the boss of me. I can make my own choices," Elle almost hissed.

"Bad ones," Clay snapped back.

"How did Elle manage to get the drop on you when she arrived here? You know, that first day," Anton asked Dante.

Dante turned to look at his husband and frowned. "I thought it wouldn't be polite to fight back. And she surprised me."

It had been a bit embarrassing, Elle flattening him that first day. But she *was* fast as well. And she'd been trained as a guard before he'd Chosen her. Add her previous knowledge, body's fitness and his blood, and it seemed you got a very quick vampire.

Anton's lips were thinned and he looked fatigued. Dante quickly glanced down at the hand that was holding the cane and saw it was white-knuckled. Again. Humans shouldn't be allowed to get too tired, he thought. That had been one of the lessons he'd learned. "Come on, let's go inside. They can argue out here without us."

Grabbing the arm that was cane-free, Dante led Anton up the porch steps and back inside to the drawing room. Beatrice wasn't there, which was probably a good thing right now. He forced Anton to sit on a chair in the delicate pink-tinged room, and then rang the bell for a servant.

"Do you want a drink?"

Anton grunted.

When the servant arrived, Dante asked for a decanter of brandy and a pitcher of pig's blood. The servant tried to keep the disgust from their face, but even Dante noticed it. In fact, Dante thought, he was generally improving on reading expressions. He'd try to work out why later.

"Mother will have a heart attack if she sees you sitting on her furniture in clothes like that," Anton said.

Dante looked down at himself and noticed he was covered in mud and scratches. "Do you mean literally or figuratively?" Dante asked.

"Figuratively. Probably."

He rang the bell for another servant and sent them off for a rug, so he could throw it over the chair. He couldn't be bothered getting changed. He had to do that too many times a day as it was. Breakfast clothing, lunch clothing, dinner clothing, going-out clothing. It was all too much.

Anton sat and Dante stood in silence until the servant returned with the rug, which Dante arranged on the chaise next to Anton. Another servant arrived shortly after, bringing the alcohol and the blood.

"Thank you, Amy," Anton said.

Dante blinked. After the servant was gone, he asked, "How do you tell them apart?"

Anton poured some brandy into a tumbler. "What?"

"How do you tell them apart? The servants? They all look the same." Dante picked up the black glass he'd been given and poured blood into it. Obviously the servants assumed that his drinking blood would be off-putting for the humans. He hadn't thought of that before. Anton had a clear crystal tumbler.

"Servants or humans?"

"Both, I guess. Although some humans stand out." Dante took a sip. They'd warmed it. It didn't taste half so horrible as a result.

"Good thing you know what address to come home to then," Anton said.

Dante thought he was being sarcastic. "I can tell you and your family apart from everyone else."

"How lucky for us."

Now that was definitely sarcasm.

"Why are you annoyed?" He figured that was a safe question.

Anton put his now empty glass down on the silver tray that it had been brought in on.

"Why do you think?"

Dante thought fast. "Because I had a fight with Clay? We didn't really hurt each other."

"Guess again."

Dante shrugged and downed the rest of his beverage. "I don't know."

Anton opened his mouth, but Elle and Clay stormed into the room just then.

"Fine!" Elle snarled.

"I just want you to make sure you don't get too hungry. You can't put the Greystokes at risk – or Emmie."

Dante wondered who Emmie was. "Is Emmie a servant?" he

asked Anton.

Anton glanced at him. "Not that I know of."

"Fine. Get me some of that muck." Elle plopped down onto a chair and folded her arms. Dante was about to tell her not to dirty the cushions, but didn't manage to slip a word in between the rising domestic feud.

"You need more now? After you tried to suck me dry?" Clay looked incredulous.

Elle rolled her eyes. "Prevention, idiot."

"You shouldn't sit on the chair, you're dirty," Dante said quickly.

"You!" Elle pointed a finger at him.

He looked around, but her finger was aimed firmly in his direction. "Me?"

"This is all *your* fault."

He couldn't really deny that.

"Will everyone just shut up!"

They all turned to stare at Anton. His face was white and he was massaging the muscles in his bad leg. His human really wasn't doing very well, Dante gathered. He reached over and went to massage the limb for him, but Anton slapped his hand away.

"I can do it myself." Anton glared at him.

"Not hard enough," Dante returned.

Elle snickered.

"What?" Dante snapped at her, surprising himself. He never snapped. Well, rarely. Only lately.

"Nothing," she said with a close-mouthed smile.

Dante turned back to Anton. "You are in pain, let me help you."

"Why do you insist on this?" Anton said, voice low.

"It's my job to help you," Dante said, confused.

"Job."

"Yes?"

"Fine, but don't do it in public. Leave me some dignity."

Dante frowned, trying to work out what Anton wasn't saying,

because he was sure there was a message there.

"It makes him horny, you idiot."

"What?" Dante turned to Elle.

"I didn't say anything," she said, but her face was whiter than normal.

"Yes, you did. I heard you."

"No, she didn't," Anton and Clay said.

"I heard her, she said…" Dante grasped he probably shouldn't repeat it. Not if it would make Anton uncomfortable, which he assumed it would. "She said something," he finished lamely.

"What did I say?" Elle demanded.

"I don't want to repeat it," Dante said.

"We all would have heard it then, if I said it," Elle said. She looked smug.

Dante shook his head. "I heard you say it, loud and clear. It was your voice."

"You imagined it," Elle insisted.

"No, it's not something I would have thought of."

Elle's face had a pinched expression. "You just imagined it. Let's move on."

Cornered, not wanting to appear like he was deranged, he said, "You said it makes him horny when I massage his leg."

A gasp, a choking sound and a chuckle emerged. The laugh was from Clay. Dante guessed Elle was the gasper, since Anton was still choking.

Clutching his brandy tumbler, Anton edged toward the end of the seat; almost climbing onto the arm of the chair to get away from him. For some reason, Dante found that he didn't like that.

"I did *not* say that out loud," Elle muttered.

"But you did say it, or thought it. I heard it," Dante insisted.

Elle looked at Clay, then at Dante.

"Aww, shit."

CHAPTER FIFTY

Elle had managed to put her foot in it this time. With a royal-sized shoe covered in horse shit.

"I'm sorry, I'm not following," Anton said.

The four of them were still seated in the Rose drawing room, and Elle realized belatedly that the servants were probably going to have to scrub the seat she was sitting on. When she'd lost control and jumped Clay – he'd been cut and then she'd been there in a flash, mouth fastened, teeth biting, biting, biting – she'd managed to get herself covered in dirt and blood. She hated making a mess that other people would have to clean up. When would she learn? Her mother had been fussy about this stuff, as well.

"I think that Elle *thought* it and I heard it," Dante said.

Elle felt her jaw fall open, and noticed Clay's had done the same. How had Dante managed to deduce *that* from their conversation?

Dante swung his violet stare to her, and seemed to answer her thought. "I spent a number of years trying to work out why you people were different. I had a lot of theories. Psychic powers were in the top three."

"You heard that, too?" she asked Dante. She turned to Clay. "I'm not even thinking at him like I have to for you."

"You knew about it?" Dante looked at Clay.

Elle swung back to look at him. She hadn't wanted Dante to know. She'd gathered that he really *had* been hunting Graceds.

Worse, she'd just given away the lifelong secret she'd been charged with keeping.

She really sucked.

"Maybe it's the bond," Clay said. "Makes it easier for your thoughts to slip into his mind."

"The bond is not meant to be telepathic," Dante said.

"Wait just a second," Anton was saying. "You seriously believe she can project her thoughts?"

Elle, Clay and Dante said in unison, "Yes."

Anton scoffed. "Impossible."

"Haven't you ever noticed that humans with eye colors other than brown are…different?" Dante asked his husband.

"No, that's ridiculous!"

Elle sighed.

Clay's hand gently touched her shoulder. She guessed he'd gotten over his pique at her for biting him. *"I will get you back for it later,"* he thought at her.

"Yay."

She felt, rather than heard, him chuckle.

Dante pinched the bridge of his nose for a few seconds before dropping his hand to his side. "I spent years studying the ones with colored eyes; this makes sense. It couldn't be something too obvious."

"Studying us?" Elle's skin prickled.

Dante eyed her like she was a snake about to strike. "Uh, watching you?"

Her eyes narrowed.

"So, what are these powers then?" Anton asked, defusing some of the tension. Doubt laced his every word.

"I don't want to talk about it," Elle said.

"Well, telepathy is definitely one," Dante said at the same time.

Anton looked from Dante to her and back again. "So you really can read minds?" he asked, then paled.

Lie, lie, lie, she thought. But Dante was staring at her and something made her say, "Yes."

The bloody bond.

That had been his plan all along, she realized. Choose her and then get all the answers afterward. The cunning little bastard. Even though she wanted to rip him apart for his deception, part of her admired him for it.

"Great," Anton said hollowly. "What am I thinking now?"

She didn't want to, but she lowered her mental shields. She'd had to rely on them a lot since moving to Greystoke House. The people here were actually genuinely nice. She'd worked that out without the benefit of her new ability, but had used it to confirm her knowledge. Beatrice and Darla were happy to have her here. They thought that Dante must have loved her – to some extent; they'd settled on like a daughter – to Choose her. And so they loved her. That simple. She felt like she was eavesdropping when she heard Beatrice's and Darla's thoughts; she didn't like it.

They didn't know that Dante hadn't wanted to marry Anton, or that Anton certainly hadn't wanted to marry his former fiancée's murderer. There were so many lies and undercurrents running through this house – mostly between Anton and Dante – that sometimes she listened into their thoughts just for fun. Which made her feel horrible. It was sick of her, she knew.

It was made even worse by the fact that Anton secretly lusted after his husband, and hated himself for it. She didn't like hearing those thoughts, either.

Remembering that she was meant to be reading Anton's mind, she focused on him and his unique mental signature. Whenever she looked at his thoughts, she was reminded of the scent of brandy and the fragrance of sandalwood. Strange.

Images began swirling from him to her. Pictures of Annabel – she fought a sneer – and of his family and then finally, the one he tried *not* to think about; Dante three-quarters naked. Even though she still didn't like Dante much, her mouth went dry at the image, because she could *feel* Anton's desire for all that pale, smooth skin coated over firm muscle.

Feeling a little nauseated, she quickly slipped from his mind.

"You were thinking of Annabel and your mother and sister." She decided not to mention Dante – Anton had already been embarrassed enough. She'd seen that in the red-purple tinge of his outer thoughts.

Anton's mouth dropped open and then he flushed, sending her a grateful look, as if he knew she'd deliberately kept her mouth shut about his last thought.

"I take it you were thinking those things, from your expression?" Dante asked.

"Uh, yeah, he was," Elle said.

Anton nodded.

Dante really was an oddity in comparison to his husband, Elle reflected. Or, well, to anyone. He wasn't as much of a creep as she'd originally thought, and he did actually seem to feel some emotions, although his range was limited. He also didn't understand facial expressions and had no social skills. No wonder Annabel had had no luck with him; no luck escaping him, anyway. You can't manipulate a person's emotions when they had next to none.

"So, what other things can you do? Can other people with colored eyes do other things?" Anton asked her, drawing her away from her thoughts.

"I can just read minds," Elle said, hedging.

"Yes, but anything else?"

"No, not really." Not that she knew of. But she did have a little Gray in her eyes, which meant she might be able to move things with a flick of a thought. One day.

Dante stared hard at her. "What do the colors mean?"

"Mean?"

Even though her shields were up, she could *hear* his mind ticking away. Adding this, changing that, sorting this, deducing that. It was almost giving her a headache.

"Yes, what can green-eyed and blue-eyed humans do?" He was sitting forward on his chair, eager almost.

"What makes you think that the colors mean anything?" Elle hedged.

"Because they have to," Dante replied.

Elle wanted to hit her head against a nearby wall.

"Greens are telepaths," Clay said from behind her shoulder.

Elle swung around and glared at him. "Clay!"

"What? He may as well know. It will help us, I think."

She didn't lower her glare.

"That's all they can do?" Dante asked.

Clay nodded.

Elle turned back to face Dante and Anton, growling low in her throat.

"What about blue eyes or gray eyes?"

"Grays can move things with their minds. Blues are empaths," Clay answered.

"What's an empath?" Anton asked.

Elle shut her eyes. Oh boy, she didn't want to go where they were about to go.

"They can control emotions," Clay said.

"C-control emotions?" There was a slight tremble in Anton's voice.

Dante reached out and took hold of the other man's hand. She doubted he knew he was doing it. For some reason, the vampire didn't like it when his human was upset. Elle had a feeling it was because somewhere deep inside the murky nothingness of Dante's existence, there actually was a *something* for Anton.

Lucky Anton.

"Yes, Blues control emotions." Elle met Anton's eyes.

"Annabel had blue eyes. Beautiful, bright blue eyes," Anton said, but he didn't seem to appreciate he was speaking out loud.

Since Elle had hated Annabel, she didn't feel any guilt about saying, "Annabel was very strong. She could...control people with her ability."

Stricken Brown eyes met hers. "Control people?"

"She could make them love her. Could make them lose their minds for her. It was like an addiction for them."

She'd always assumed that was how it worked, but she'd seen the confirmation in Anton's mind last night. His recent withdrawal from nothing, which reminded him of the time when he actually *had* been addicted. She hadn't wanted to see it, but she'd stumbled on him musing about Annabel and his betrayal of her through his lust for Dante.

"No," Anton said.

"No?" Elle wondered what the no was in response to.

"No, Annabel wouldn't have done that." Anton almost moaned the words, but Elle had a feeling he was consoling himself.

"She was a whore," Dante said, something sharp in his voice.

Elle quickly speared a thought his way and grasped that the Creep was *feeling* something, but he didn't know what it was. He couldn't identify the rolling sensation that was whirling through his mind, but she could.

Jealousy.

Wow, Elle thought, *Dante really likes his human.*

He looked at her. *"No, I don't."*

"Yeah, you do." She really had to learn to shut this bond-link thing off. She didn't like Dante hearing *her* thoughts.

"I know plenty of whores who don't control people," Clay said. "Nice women."

"Of course you do," Elle muttered.

Clay chuckled again.

"But why would she do that?" the baron asked, almost whispering, his face ashen.

Tightening her mental barriers a bit more, Elle decided she wasn't going to announce the real reason. She'd already failed her heritage as much as she was willing to do in a single day. "Why wouldn't she? You're a baron," she said instead.

"She made me love her for my *title*?"

"Don't you aristos marry for titles every day?" She looked at them both and Dante nodded. Anton appeared numb. "Plus, Annabel was a mercenary bitch," Elle said, trying to be helpful.

Anton spluttered.

"So that's why she kept wondering why I didn't feel guilty or upset for her," Dante said.

Elle froze. "Why would you have needed to feel like that?"

A faint red tinge crept up his cheeks. "She, uh, didn't exactly say yes to being Chosen."

Anton leaped to his feet, his bad leg nearly buckling under him. Only quick use of his cane seemed to keep him upright. He spun to Dante and then poked the vampire in the chest, hard. "You did it against her will!"

"I thought she would have wanted it!" Dante said, arms raised, as if to defend himself.

Elle shook her head. "She wouldn't have, because she knew she wouldn't make it. Graceds don't."

Anton raised his cane, as if to bludgeon Dante with it.

Go Anton, she thought.

"You're upset with me when she *made* you love her? Your relationship wasn't even real." Dante almost snarled it, his voice lower than his normal almost-monotone.

Anton's cane didn't waver. He brought it down hard on Dante's shoulder. The vampire recoiled and stared up at him in shock. "That *hurt*."

Elle knew that Dante was fast, that he could have avoided that bashing, but he'd sat there and taken it. Which meant he hadn't actually believed Anton would do it, or that it would be painful.

Her shoulder twinged in sympathy.

Dipping into Dante's mind, she figured out that Dante felt that he deserved the wallop. He didn't like the fact he'd upset Anton and took the caning as punishment.

"I loved her anyway!" Anton yelled, raising the cane again.

Deciding that enough was enough – which was odd, her being the one to normally incite violence – Elle stood and quickly stepped over to grab the raised cane. "Anton, you didn't really love her. She made you."

He looked at her, eyes showing the broken and bleeding man just as well as his thoughts did. "You don't know that."

"I do," Elle said softly, lowering the cane.

"Get out of my fucking head." His shoulders dropped. Almost everything about him did.

Dante stood and went to touch Anton, to offer him comfort, but the man shrugged his hand away. "Don't touch me, murderer."

"I didn't know she wouldn't survive! She never said anything."

Anton looked at her.

Elle shook her head. "Dante didn't know. He really did think she'd make it." As he'd hoped she would, she realized. As he'd been *convinced* Elle would. It was only his father and her gran that had almost resulted in her being burned alive.

Her gran owed her so fucking much. Emmie was at the top of that list, though.

"I should report you to the king," Anton said, but there was no heat in his threat.

"If I'd known she wouldn't have survived, I wouldn't have done it," Dante said.

Would have been a waste of my time, she thought she heard Dante think.

"Sounds to me like he saved your life," Clay said, the first time he'd spoken in a while.

"What?" all three of them blurted simultaneously.

"I have heard of people being strong enough to control others – Greens and Blues doing it," Clay said. "Rarer for Greens, because they have to force someone to *think* in a certain way, rather than *feel*. But eventually, their will takes over the person. The…subject…becomes addicted to the high, the need for that stimulation. A love that isn't love, one that turns to obsession, and then sometimes, hate. But they need that person, that stimulation. Love so strong that it can never be replicated in real life. Greens and Blues can turn people into puppets."

Elle's jaw dropped. She snapped it shut. She'd been doing that enough lately.

"You're saying Annabel was like that?" Anton asked, his expression still ravaged.

Clay shrugged. "Sounds like it."

Yeah, Elle thought, staring at the broken man in front of her. Annabel had been like that.

Dante looked at her, as if he'd heard her thought. Then he gave her a smile, a small one, but one that looked like he was pleased with himself.

Why?

Dante's voice entered her mind, low and calm and creepy. *"Completely by accident, I managed to save someone's life. Can't say I've done that before."*

"What, too busy taking them?"

"No," he replied. *"Too busy not caring about it one way or another."*

Wasn't that the truth.

CHAPTER FIFTY-ONE

Melissande didn't know what to do. Emmie was barely eating and she had nightmares every single night. Screams were heard more often than conversation. As Melissande set a plate of bacon and eggs down in front of her youngest daughter, she was stunned by the purple marks under Emmie's eyes. They were like slashing bruises, as if someone had got their fingers and dug them in deep.

"Emmie, what's wrong?" Melissande asked. She felt useless, a pathetic excuse for a mother.

"I miss Elle," Emmie said, her baby voice a whisper.

Melissande slumped down at the kitchen table, her butt hitting the seat hard. She gripped one of Emmie's brown hands in a pale one of her own. "I do too, baby."

Emmie looked at her, those bright Teal eyes almost glittering. But not with tears, with something else. "Gran doesn't. She's happy Elle's gone."

Since Elle's death, Melissande hadn't really tapped into her empathy; had shut herself away from everyone, not wanting to feel their pain, greed and lust. She had enough of her own anguish to deal with. But Emmie needed her, and she needed to know what was wrong with her daughter.

Opening herself up, she exposed herself to the world and encountered…anger. Rage, even. No sadness, no grief, just burning, white-hot fury. And it came from Emmie, her seven-year-old daughter.

Eyes wide, she looked at Emmie, letting her hand drop.

"You don't feel any grief." Melissande couldn't keep the accusatory tone from her voice.

"Elle's gone," Emmie said, her sharp little chin jutting. "But she's not gone for good."

Sincerity beat through to her. Emmie truly believed Elle wasn't gone forever. "Wh-what?"

Didn't her daughter understand the concept of death?

"You know how Graceds can't be Chosen or Bitten?" Emmie asked. The little girl picked up a fork and stared down at the mound of food Melissande had cooked. She still wasn't used to preparing for just two.

Melissande nodded.

Emmie jabbed the fork down and brought up a piece of egg, yolk running over the tines and dripping onto the plate. Emmie looked at her. "Well, what if you're not fully Graced?" She popped the egg into her mouth and chewed.

"You die," Melissande said.

Emmie put her fork down and looked at her, hard. "Do you?"

"I've always been told that–"

"By who?" Emmie asked.

"Everyone."

Emmie scooped up another forkful of egg. "Who is everyone?"

Melissande wondered when her youngest had become so cynical. So bitter.

"Well, Mother said so." Her eyes tracked Emmie's eating.

In between mouthfuls, Emmie said, "Gran is a mean old hag."

Melissande nearly choked on her own saliva.

"What–"

"Gran wanted Elle dead. She was an embarrassment." Emmie jutted that chin out again. "I heard her say so."

"Because she was a Hazel," Melissande agreed. How many times had she been railed at for wasting her reproductive abilities on Elle? It was why she'd agreed to birth Emmie. For her mother. She'd hoped that meant Olive would allow her to marry Simeon, but that hadn't happened. He'd moved on, was married now to a Brown woman, although they had no children of their own.

But Melissande loved Emmie, no matter what. No matter that she'd almost vomited from the act of conception; that she'd felt forced into it by her mother. That she'd almost been *compelled*, even.

"But Mom, Elle was a Hazel...she had a lot of Brown. Not much Green or Gray. She could have survived."

Melissande rubbed at her cheek, feeling worn out, washed out. "She couldn't have survived the cremation."

Something like satisfaction burned through her from Emmie. "Not unless she got out before."

Staring at her daughter, deep into those unusual eyes – eyes that she'd had to whore herself for – she began to feel a small spark of hope. Her own hope.

"Do you think she did?" Melissande asked, whispering.

"We will have to wait and see." But Emmie was smiling, a small, secretive expression.

CHAPTER FIFTY-TWO

"Whatcha doing here?" Anton asked. He was lying in bed, worn out, feeling like he'd been beaten all over with his cane. Which he may have been, he couldn't really remember. The afternoon was a nice fuzzy blur, and he intended to keep it that way.

Dante took a step closer to the bed and frowned down at him. "I am not a murderer."

Anton waved an arm through the dim light at him. "Whatever."

Where was that brandy?

A second later, Dante's face hovered over his own. Strange, how'd it get there?

"Are you drunk?"

Anton could feel Dante's breath moving over him, almost like a caress. *Not a caress*, his mind slurred. *Don't think like that. Bad, bad, bad. Dante's bad for you. Like a virus.*

"Maybe," Anton replied.

How was he meant to get more alcohol if he was lying down? Anton really hadn't thought this situation through. He needed to get up. Propping himself on his elbows, he groaned when the room started to spin. He didn't mind the sensation, but it was a bit exhausting, so he flopped back.

Ah, he thought, *this is how I ended up on the bed with no brandy.*

"There isn't a maybe about it," Dante said.

It sounded like he was a bit...annoyed?

"So?"

Who cared if Dante was peeved, anyway. He deserved to be. He's the one who took away Anton's one true love.

"She wasn't your true love," Dante snapped.

"Who wasn't?" Anton wasn't sure he was following. He opened his eyes and turned his head to the right. The almost empty bottle of brandy stood on the bedside table, taunting him, cut crystal glinting mockingly. It thought it was safe.

Dante sounded like he was gritting his teeth. "Annabel."

"Yeah, she was. Loved her." Anton stretched an arm out to see if he could reach the glittering bottle. "Lots."

"She made you think that," Dante said and took the bottle away.

Anton groaned.

"No more, you are well past three sheets to the wind. Any further away in the wind and you'd be blown all the way to Brahma."

As if he'd make it that far. Thousands of leagues away, it was, and he was too drunk to even stand. He thought over Dante's phrasing and snickered.

Dante appeared in his field of vision again. It was prettier than the top of the bed frame. "What?"

"You said blown."

"What's so funny about that?"

Anton giggled. "Bllooowww."

"I don't understand."

He held his hand up in front of his mouth, and then poked his tongue into the side of his cheek, so it protruded.

Dante turned a dull red. "Oh, *that*."

"What's wrong with *that*?" Anton demanded. He was rather fond of it himself.

"It's a bit embarrassing," Dante said.

Embarrassing wasn't a word Anton normally used to describe a blowjob.

"Why? Can't get it up?"

Dante seemed to go even redder, which for a vampire, was akin to a human's full-body humiliation. "Not normally, no."

Anton's head lolled back against his pillows. "Ahhh. Poor Dante."

He felt the mattress sag as Dante sat next to him. "How much did you drink, exactly?"

"Dunno," Anton said. "How much is left in the bottle?"

"It's almost gone."

He thought for a few moments. "More than that, then."

"Thought I said I didn't want to be married to a drunk," Dante muttered.

Anton rolled his head to look at the vampire. Too pretty, blast him. "Didn't want to be married to a murderer, either. But we all can't have what we want, eh?"

"I didn't deliberately kill her."

"Fine. Didn't want to be married to someone who doesn't want sex." Anton shut his eyes. He felt like he was flying.

Something made him rattle. Anton squinted an eye open and realized Dante was shaking him. The vampire stopped and muttered something that sounded like "not dead."

"You *said* you didn't want it either," the vampire ground out.

Anton rolled his eyes. Who wouldn't want sex?

"Must've lied."

"You *want* to have sex with me?" Dante sounded stunned.

"Why not?" Anton looked Dante up and down with his one open eye.

"You hate me."

He sighed. "Not so much, want to hate you more." It was hard to hate someone so pretty. No, that was a lie. It was hard to hate someone who kept trying to be helpful, even when it wasn't helpful at all. It was hard to see Dante try so, well, hard.

"Why don't you hate me as much?" Dante was frowning. Even that was pretty.

Anton shut his eye. "Because you try to be nice."

"Well, yes. Doesn't everyone?" He sounded bewildered.

Probably was, Anton gathered. Dante wasn't the sharpest stake in the woodpile at times.

He folded his arms behind his head. Made the flying sensation dim a little. "Yeah, but you actually *mean* it."

"Anton," Dante said.

He cracked open one eye. The vampire was a little fuzzy.

"Do you want to have sex now?" Dante seemed to swallow a lump in his throat.

Thinking about it, Anton said, "No."

Dante seemed to slump in relief. "I would, if you wanted to."

"I don't want pity sex," Anton said, although, if he wasn't so drunk and annoyed, he might have said yes. Shame on him.

"It wouldn't be pity sex," Dante said slowly.

Anton stared at him, then at the vampire's groin. "Get back to me when you get an erection. Then we'll talk."

CHAPTER FIFTY-THREE

"When are we going to *do* something?" Elle asked. She was sharpening one of her favorite knives, since her stake was already nicely pointy. The sound of the whetstone was soothing. By the blood, she missed Emmie. It was like a constant toothache.

"When I work out what to do," Clay snapped.

She turned around in her window seat and faced him, one knee tucked under her other leg. The werewolf was standing next to the closet and was holding up a pair of socks.

"What's with the attitude?" she asked.

"Things are getting much more complicated than I'd hoped they would."

Elle snorted. "Vampires are involved. Things always end up complicated."

When she'd been a guard, that had been the rule. A vampire caught causing a bar fight, the human was blamed if there was one involved. If no human was around, then the least aristo vampire was fined. And the excuses…always so many of those. Some days her job had been a real head fuck.

"I was hoping to ask Johan to grant us custody of Emmie, but I don't know if that's possible anymore," Clay said.

Elle stood and walked over to the chest that she kept by the bed. She opened it and began looking for the whetstone's leather case. It should have been on the top, but she had a tendency to throw things in and not look where they landed. "Why not?"

"The meeting didn't go so well," Clay replied.

Elle put the stone away and shut the lid of the chest. It had no decoration, was sharp corners and simple lines. Rather like her, she thought.

She sat on the edge of the bed and looked at him. "How come?"

Clay sat down next to her, hands clasped between his knees, shoulders slumped, socks now on his feet. "Johan doesn't really believe we're engaged."

Elle brought her knees up and hugged them to her chest. The topaz on her "engagement" ring winked in the light. It felt like a brand on her finger. "Why?"

"Because I've never been married and he knows it."

She started twisting the ring. "Doesn't think I'm special enough?"

"No."

Elle tried not to feel offended. "What's wrong with me?"

"You aren't him," Clay said, staring at his hands.

Elle stopped turning the ring. "Wait – what?"

Clay sighed. "Johan had a bit of a crush on me when he was growing up. I thought he'd grown out of it."

"So he's jealous of your fake fiancée?" Elle asked, eyebrows high on her forehead. The *king* had wanted Clay?

Well, why not? She had wanted him and she'd been taught to hate weres from the cradle.

"Well, he doesn't *believe* that you're my fiancée because I've never settled down. Why would I pick a guard when I could have had a king?"

"But, you don't like guys, right?" Elle certainly hoped not. She didn't think she could cope with two sexes worth of competition. And she *knew* Anton – and now Johan – thought that Clay was hot. Who wouldn't?

"No. That doesn't seem to matter to Johan, though. I never tried it with him, so how would I know?" Clay rolled his eyes.

"Sounds like it was a fun meeting," Elle said.

"Oh yeah."

"So he won't help us?" Elle asked.

"I doubt it; but he might surprise me. He needs to get used to the idea that I *do* want to settle down. We might even have to get married first." The latter he said with a wince.

"Gee, thanks."

"It is a fake engagement, Elle." His voice was stern.

"Wow. Really?"

He tilted his head and looked at her. "If we marry, it's for life."

"Ever heard of divorce?" Elle said.

"It'd have to be for at *least* Emmie's life. That's over eighty years, minimum."

"Once we legally get her out of Pinton, there's not much they can do. We can divorce then."

"I don't want to."

Elle frowned. "Get divorced?"

"No."

"I don't follow; we wouldn't really be married."

"I've never married because I don't want to get a divorce. When I marry, it's for life. And for me, that's basically forever." Clay looked uncomfortable.

Elle gasped. "You're a romantic!"

"Shut up."

She burst into laughter.

"What! It's not funny." Clay grabbed her and shook her.

Elle laughed harder.

"Stop!" He threw her back on the bed and pinned her down. "It's not funny, okay? I want to get married and I want it to mean something."

Elle stared up at him, at his fierce yellow eyes that glowed like molten gold. He had stubble on his cheeks and his shaggy hair hung low, touching her face. He was yummy. Yummier than ever, really. Since she'd been Chosen, she'd noticed so much more about him. Like the fact that his teeth really were super white and straight, that his eyes were more gold than yellow, that his skin was really warm and he smelled great…much to her chagrin.

"Sorry," Elle said. "My parents were never married. In fact, Mother never got married. Neither did Gran. Wasn't important to them; it was about breeding, not love."

Clay leaned back a little. "That's how most aristos think. Wolves are a little different."

"Explain to me again why there aren't many around Pinton?"

Clay did an odd movement, which she gathered was a shrug. "We don't love leeches, so it's easier to just avoid them. We have different values, tend to live in packs."

"So you're a lone wolf?" Elle asked with a grin.

"Mostly." Clay didn't seem inclined to add any more than that.

"Should we try and see if the baron's father will help us?" Elle asked.

Clay stared over her head at the pillow for a few seconds. "Could be worth a try." Then he kissed her and she forgot what they were talking about, his tongue warm and firm in her mouth.

Chapter Fifty-Four

Dante was feeling rather like someone had come and jabbed a stake in his stomach. Well, not the pain part, but the shocked and numb part. He'd been right. For the latter part of his adult life, he'd been convinced that there was something different about a small percentage of the humans that surrounded him. He'd been called crazy; he'd been labeled a freak by his own family.

And he'd been *right*.

But he couldn't tell anyone. That was a kicker. Elle had cornered him after their conversation and had said that if he dared tell anyone anything, she'd gut him and let him watch his intestines being pulled out as far as they'd go. It wouldn't kill him, so the bond should be fine.

He believed her.

And he had a sister. Another one. A *twin*. He wasn't even ready to confront that new addendum to his life.

So after his day of shocks, he'd gone to gloat to Anton, as much as he could, and found him drunk and sprawled on his bed. The human had been wearing a shirt and pants, but the shirt had been unbuttoned and had left an expanse of smooth, light brown skin exposed. Dante had confiscated Anton's alcohol supply and had wanted to make sure his husband wouldn't choke on his own vomit, but Anton had been feeling chatty. About sex, of all things.

So now Dante was feeling something akin to embarrassment as well as shock, because Anton thought him a murderer and *impotent*. He wasn't unable, he just wasn't interested. Well, not normally. But all Anton's talk of sex had gotten Dante thinking that it might not be such a bad thing after all.

"What's got you in a tizz?"

Dante looked up from his worktable and saw that Elle was standing in front of him, watching him.

"I'm not in a tizz," Dante replied.

Elle seemed to be examining his room. They were in the western part of the townhouse, in his study. Her strange eyes landed back on him. "For you, you're in a tizz. It's annoying."

Dante frowned. "Why? I was *alone* in my study."

"Yeah, but I could hear your thoughts squirreling around. It's giving *me* a headache. So I thought I'd come and see what's up, so you can shut up."

"You hate me, what would you care about what's going on?"

He watched as Elle seemed to scout around for a second, looking for a chair, before giving up and hoisting herself on the table. He frowned. Where *had* the other two chairs gone? Dante moved his hands out of the way.

"I don't hate you as much as I used to. Having you hot-wired into my skull is helping that." She started swinging her legs.

Wasn't he becoming popular. Both Elle and Anton had managed to "hate him less."

"Maybe that's why I feel so out of it lately," Dante mused aloud.

Elle's legs stopped for a heartbeat or two. "What do you mean? The fact you're feeling at all?"

He thought about it. "Well, yeah."

Dante hadn't really ever felt anything. Resentment, he guessed, for the relationship Misty had with his father. Annoyance at his sister, fear maybe for his own safety at the hands of an enraged parent. But that was about it and nothing particularly worth breaking into a sweat over. That had been the gamut of his emotional experience.

Until after he'd Chosen Elle. Then he'd started to experience worry, insecurity, even a bit of happiness.

Her legs started moving again. "Interesting. I'm not a Blue, so it shouldn't work like that; me giving you emotions or the ability to feel. But, my mother is one. Maybe it was something latent in me."

He blinked at her unusual amount of candor. "It sounds like you stress the color. Is that how you refer to yourselves?"

"Yeah. Blue, Green, Gray. Colors, not the abilities."

Dante frowned. "Do you consider yourselves human or different?"

She was silent for a long time, so he thought she wasn't going to answer. Turning back to his notes, he began reading them in the dim light.

"We call ourselves Graceds."

Dante glanced up at her, shuffled some papers. "Why?"

"Why do you call yourselves vampires?"

He tilted his head in acknowledgment. Some words were so old their origins were lost. Some things just *were*.

"So, what's caused the tizz?"

Sighing, Dante moved his notes out of the way. He guessed he didn't really need them anymore. "Nothing."

"Now, now. No one likes a liar."

"You lie all the time," Dante said.

Elle's eyes went wide. "I don't!"

"Do so." He leaned away from her on his chair, but not very far, since it didn't have a back. "I have good hearing. I can hear you talking in your room even when I'm on the other side of the house."

Elle blinked. "Doesn't that drive you mad?"

"Well, yeah. I don't like listening to people having sex or whispering or complaining about this, telling secrets about that. But I can't help it."

"That sounds awfully familiar." Elle tapped her skull, so he figured she was talking about her telepathy. "So what have you heard, exactly?" Elle asked.

"I wasn't listening in, not until after your revelation, otherwise I would have worked it all out a lot sooner."

"I'm surprised you hadn't found out years ago."

Dante shrugged. "I didn't tend to leave the estate because of my 'difficulty.'"

"As in your sociopathy?"

"As in I can *hear everything*."

"Right. So what did you hear?"

She was persistent, his Chosen. "That you have someone you want to get custody of and that you aren't really engaged to the wolf. But you *do* like him, I know that."

Elle leaned forward, hands gripping the edge of the table. "You aren't going to tell anyone, are you? Because the gutting threat stands for that, too."

"I was going to tell Anton, but I can avoid doing so, if you want," Dante said. He rubbed his stomach absently.

"Good. So, back to the original topic, why is your brain doing an imitation of a rat in a running wheel?"

Dante felt like rolling his eyes. She was worse than Misty, since she could actually *hear* what he was thinking. "Can you turn it on and off?" he asked.

"What?"

"The telepathy."

"Kind of. Now answer my question."

"Why don't you just look and see?" Dante snapped.

She smiled, one corner of her mouth lifting higher than the other, but no sign of teeth. "More fun this way."

"Sure it is."

"Well?"

Dante sighed. "Anton wants to have sex."

"So? Aren't you married to him?"

He scrunched his eyes shut. "Yes, but I don't like sex."

"Not at all?" She whistled. "That's...very *you*."

"That's nicer than what other people say."

She winced. "Sorry."

"You aren't, but that's okay."

Elle frowned at him. "No, really. I am sorry. If you don't like it, you don't like it. Each to their own. But, can't you just be on the bottom or something?"

"I could, and I said I *would* have sex if he wanted it – which I didn't think he'd ever want, because I took Annabel from him."

Dante had thought he'd be safe from that, had thought Anton would seek relief outside of their marriage, but even though he couldn't read people very well, he knew enough now to realize Anton was honorable. And so his hopes had always been in vain, even though he hadn't understood it until recently.

"Anton thinks you're hot." The way Elle said it though, it was clear even to him that she thought that was strange.

Although, Dante did feel…flattered? Happy? He wasn't sure, but it was positive.

Elle's legs were swinging, back and forth, back and forth, rather like a pendulum. It distracted him. "So just let him do his thing," she said.

"But, he said I had to get back to him when I…well…when…"

"When what?"

Dante could feel heat rising up his cheeks. "When I got an erection. I assume for him."

"Well, Anton is good-looking. Can't be that hard. No pun intended." Her eyes widened. "You aren't hetero are you?"

"Well, no. But that's because I'm asexual."

"What?"

"It means–"

"I know what the word means, moron." She was glaring at him. "How did you ever manage to have sex before, then? You *have* had sex before, right?"

"Yes."

"So you had to get hard for that, right?"

"Yes."

"Then how?"

Dante felt his teeth grinding against each other. This was growing beyond humiliating, and now he could feel it, it was really bad. "By nearly giving someone lock-jaw."

"Lock – right." Now she was blushing. "So you can't get hard for Anton? Have you tried? Why are you so worried, anyway? Just tell him you will put out and let him do the work."

This was the most embarrassing part of all. "I want to please him."

Dante actually *liked* Anton. He'd never really liked anyone before. And last night, when he'd seen Anton sprawled over his bed, firm stomach exposed, it had, well, caused a stirring in his pants. Not an erection, but perhaps the start of one.

"Okay. So…I don't know. Maybe try kissing him or something. See where it goes."

Dante guessed that was good advice. It couldn't hurt. And people liked kissing. Maybe it wouldn't be so bad with Anton?

"Thanks."

Elle gave him a half smile and stood. "Uh, no problem. But, let's not do this again."

Dante returned the expression. "Agreed."

CHAPTER FIFTY-FIVE

"Eleanor is not dead."

Melissande glanced up from her cup of tea, surprised to see her mother standing in the doorway to her kitchen. "How did you get in?"

"Didn't you hear what I said? Eleanor *is not dead.*"

Blinking, Melissande felt her stomach do a funny flip-flop. "Have you seen her, or have you just decided this?"

Melissande had always worried – hoped – that because Olive could read minds so easily, she would eventually go senile. Maybe today was the day? Although a senile Green was a dangerous one, and her mother was hazardous enough as she was.

Olive folded her arms across her bony chest. "I haven't seen her, but Bjorn has."

At the mention of his name, Bjorn filled the space in the doorway behind Olive. Well, Melissande thought, that explains how Mother got inside. Locks weren't really a bother for Grays.

Bjorn inclined his head. "I saw her, near Lord Row."

Lord Row?

"Why would Elle have been there? Are you sure it was her? After all, she was *cremated.*"

"She must have escaped," Olive muttered, looking over at the sink and then back at Melissande.

"Escaped?" Melissande laughed. "I tended to my daughter, washed her cold body before she was sent to the crematorium.

She was dead. You think she just up and climbed out of her coffin?"

Green eyes snapped and snared Melissande's. "She might not have been dead."

Shaking her head, trying to clear it of a sudden fuzzy feeling, Melissande looked down at her chipped mug. The one Elle had made for her all those years ago. "What are you saying?"

"I think you already know. What did Emmie tell you? What does the child know?"

"Nothing," Melissande said.

"Mel–"

"What is Gran doing here?" The small, piping voice came from Emmie, who must have been stuck in the hallway behind Bjorn.

She wanted to lie to Emmie, make up some half-truth, but from the expression on her mother's face, she knew she wouldn't be so lucky. "Gran says Elle is still alive."

Emmie's voice was flat as it floated to her in the kitchen. "Elle's dead."

"She might have survived, and I think you know about it." Olive turned around and motioned for Bjorn to get out of her way. She disappeared into the hallway and Emmie shouted, "Ow! Let me go!"

Melissande stood and rushed to the hallway, in time to see her mother's white-knuckled grip on Emmie's arm.

"Let her go!" Melissande grabbed her mother's arm and shook it. Emmie whimpered.

"Leave me," Olive barked, and Melissande almost let go; her fingers loosened to do so, but Emmie's new cry of pain had her tightening her grip and jerking her mother from Emmie.

"Don't hurt my daughter," Melissande growled. She quickly stood in front of Emmie.

"Get out of the way, Melissande."

"You are in *my* home, Mother. You will *not* hurt my daughter." Melissande felt anger, blessed anger, rising up through her. It cleared the cobwebs from her mind, burned through her fear and doubt, washed away the need to give in.

"So how is it that you miraculously saw Elle?" she asked Bjorn, ignoring her mother who was sputtering in the hallway between her and the hulking bodyguard.

"I was – uh, in the area."

Melissande glared at him. "You need to learn to lie better. Why were you in the area?"

She let go of her mental shield to sample the emotional currents in the hall. As normal, her mother was a mixture of indignation and annoyance. It never varied, excepting the occasional bout of smugness. Emmie was scared. Bjorn was feeling upset and angry. Betrayed, almost. Melissande frowned.

"I was asked to have a look around, to follow a werewolf."

She felt Emmie's fear spike, which was strange. Her daughter normally didn't fear wolves or vampires, even though she should.

"And?"

"Elle was with him."

"*Elle* was with a *werewolf*?" Melissande felt a bubble of laughter erupt. "Elle? Who hated vampires and weres almost more than anyone I know?"

"Well, Elle probably doesn't hate 'em as much anymore since she is now a leech."

Her laughter died as suddenly as it was born. "Not possible." Melissande deliberately kept her mind blank, refusing to remember a certain conversation. She looked at her mother.

Olive shrugged. "It happens from time to time."

"Graceds becoming vampires? Isn't the first rule of being Graced don't get Bitten and don't get Chosen?"

Olive frowned. "She wasn't a full-blood. She had enough Brown to survive."

"By the blood, you're serious, aren't you?" She looked from Bjorn to Olive and back again. "You really think Elle is still alive? And you're telling me *now*? How did she survive the cremation? Why didn't you do something then?"

"We think the werewolf let her out before the cremation," Bjorn said, pronouncing "werewolf" like it was a curse.

Like Elle surviving was a bad thing.

If it was true, she wanted to kiss whoever it was who'd helped Elle escape. Thinking back, she remembered that there'd been a wolf at the funeral. A tall, hulking fellow who looked like he'd spent most of his life on a farm. "That's, well, that's–" Melissande said.

"Disgusting, I know. It's why I wanted to see the body before it was cremated. But the wolf convinced me it wasn't necessary." Olive was annoyed, more so than normal.

"Wait – what?" Melissande blinked twice. "You're saying you *thought* she might survive and you wanted to cremate her anyway?"

"She shouldn't have gotten away," Olive said.

"You're horrible!" Emmie yelled. "You want Elle dead. You want to kill her!"

Melissande froze. "You want to kill Elle?"

Olive's jaw set. "She's an abomination. She has to die."

CHAPTER FIFTY-SIX

"Explain to me again why I can't go and knock on my mother's door and say hello?" Elle plucked a blossom off a nearby honeysuckle vine and twirled it between her fingers. The light, sweet scent tickled her nose, but she didn't mind. It smelled better than the dimly lit streets outside the townhouse.

Clay sighed. He was sitting next to her on a stone bench in the Greystokes' garden. It was a nice space, Elle decided, and she hadn't really appreciated it before, since the previous two occasions she'd spent any length of time in the quiet green space had been during fights. It had a really relaxing quality to it, and she felt her shoulders droop, in a good way. The invisible stake that she'd felt aimed between her shoulder blades even seemed to vanish.

"If your grandmother learns of your, uh, unlife, she'll try to kill you," Clay said.

"I get that. But, I kinda already announced my presence in the receiving room at the Crystal Palace. Gossip gets around. *Especially* to Gran."

Always to Gran. When you could hear what everyone around you thought, there wasn't much gossip you didn't know. Elle knew that firsthand, now. Add to that Gran's propensity for placing Graceds in high-ranking positions in the palace, and well, it was only a matter of time before she worked out that Elle had escaped her coffin.

Lifting the flower up, Elle breathed in the scent again. Darla, sweet kid that she was, had announced they were going to plant some night-blooming flowers in the garden. Because even though Elle and Dante could hang out in the courtyard during the daytime, it wasn't comfortable for them unless it was cloudy. Like today.

Stupid sensitive skin, she thought.

It wasn't all that bad, she supposed, but bright light hurt her eyes, and her skin *felt* sunburned, even if it didn't look it.

Clay spoke, interrupting her thoughts. "It's why the baron is petitioning the king today for your sister's custody. If he fails, he'll bring his father to town to try. An earl should have more sway."

"How is he going to convince them to give her to me?" Elle asked.

"By proving that your mother isn't competent as a guardian."

Elle flinched. Her mother was able, just vague. She'd never really taken a strong interest in her children's upbringing, leaving most of it to Gran, until Gran had kicked her out in a fit of fury when Elle was little. Rather than beg to come back – which Elle thought had been Gran's intention – Melissande had decided to get a place of her own. She liked to think it was because her mother finally realized the ill treatment Elle had been receiving at her gran's hands. But she didn't know for sure. Then it had been up to Elle to look after Emmie.

"But wouldn't Emmie go to Gran if that was the case?"

Clay plucked the flower from her hands. "Normally, yes. But you're of age, you're engaged, you're the stepdaughter to a baron *and* you're step-granddaughter of an earl. Rules of society say that *you're* able to better provide for her."

"But Gran is rich."

Clay frowned. "I know. But I'm sure if we were to dig, we'd find something about her that we could use in our favor."

It all seemed too wishy-washy to Elle. "There're so many maybes in this plan. We should have just taken Emmie and run."

Clay groaned and ran a hand over his hair. "Want some blood?"

Fine, she thought, change the topic. They'd only discuss it

again later when it all fell apart and they'd have to try something new. If she didn't get results soon though, she'd just go with her gut, grab her sister and vanish. Screw Clay and fuck his politics.

"Yes, please."

Clay nodded and stood. She watched his back as he meandered down the stone path of the garden toward the terrace. Her annoyance at him disappeared and her mouth went dry. Blood, she liked the way his butt looked in those pants.

"Elle?"

And his back. *Gee*, Clay did know how to fill a shirt…

"Elle?"

Maybe she'd rip it off him later. Make him buy a new one.

"Elle?"

Jolting, Elle sat upright and stared into the distance. Someone was calling her name from *outside* the garden?

"Elle!"

Standing, she quickly followed the sound, the voice sending shivers down her spine. Looking either side of her, she noticed that no one was around. Throwing the gate open, her jaw dropped at the sight on the other side.

"Mother?"

"Elle, darling!" Melissande opened her arms and rushed at Elle, crushing her in a hug. "Sweetheart, they said you weren't dead…"

"How did you know I was here?" Elle asked, gut sinking. She pushed her mother back and held her by the shoulders, staring into those clear Blue eyes. Tears sparkled there. She tried to get a grab onto her mother's thoughts, but they were jumbled, swirling, moving faster than Elle's inexperience could handle.

Melissande turned and started tugging on Elle's arm. It didn't move her. "You need to come with me. Emmie will be so pleased to see you. She's been missing you like crazy."

Instant concern. "Is she okay?" Elle asked.

Her mother turned back to her, eyes darkening. "No."

"What? What's wrong?" Elle took a step forward, through the gate and into the alley behind Greystoke House. She tried to reach her mother's thoughts again, but had no luck. She hadn't realized her mother was so good at evading Greens. Elle had always thought Gran had easy access.

Unless, Elle thought, *Mother is so upset I just can't get a grip on her mind.* Which she guessed was possible.

Melissande's eyes darkened even more. "You need to come with me. She'll be so happy to see you."

"But, Mother, is Emmie okay?" Fear and worry pounded through her. Her mother was acting weird, weirder than normal. Had something happened to Emmie? Had all this time Elle had been wasting, living it up in a baron's household, been detrimental to her sister?

Melissande shook her head, tugging on Elle's arm. "No, but she will be."

Frowning, Elle followed her, down the alley. A sharp, stinging feeling exploded on her neck and she slapped at it, as if it was a mosquito. She rubbed at the pain and her hand came away, splotched in blood. What kind of a mosquito bit vampires and then exploded in a bubble of blood?

Feeling a little dizzy – what kind of a fucking mosquito *was* that? – she shook her head. Elle followed her mother, her non-bloody hand tightening around Melissande's. A shadow stepped into her path and she tried to dodge it, but she was knocked to the ground. Her vision blurred.

Something large landed on top of her, and she was too giddy to do anything about it. Elle batted at it with her hands, feebly, and heard a grunt in complaint. Then something gripped her head like a vice and twisted. Sickening, roaring pain ripped through her neck, accompanied by a loud crunching noise.

Then everything went black.

CHAPTER FIFTY-SEVEN

Dante's neck hurt. Really hurt.

I mean, he thought, *it* really *fucking hurts*. Rubbing the joint in question, he couldn't stop the frown that spread across his face. It was like someone had punched him right in the back of his skull. Shaking his head, wincing as he did so, he held his book up higher, trying to prevent moving any more than he had to. He *should* have been reading his notes, but had figured that there wasn't really much point now. He was surreptitiously keeping a record of everything Elle had told him and what he'd been able to monitor, but he was being careful. He assumed his father's threat still stood.

So rather than pursue his studies, or be social in the drawing room, Dante was hiding in his study reading a romance novel. If only Misty could see him now, he thought, she would laugh her head off. But he had to *try* and understand how love worked. And he was too embarrassed to speak to Elle or Anton.

The door to his study burst open and Dante hastily shoved the book under the table. Clay stood in the doorway, panting, as if he'd been running. Sighing to himself, Dante realized that was just a sign of how distracted he was. He should have heard Clay's approach, and he may have, had he been paying any attention to anything other than the pain in his neck or his soon-to-be new obsession: romance novels.

"Have you seen Elle?" Clay almost growled at him.

Standing, sliding the book onto his empty chair, Dante went to shake his head and almost lost his balance from pain. "No."

Clay went to leave the room, but stopped. He turned and focused on Dante with those bright yellow eyes.

"What?" Dante asked.

"What's wrong with your neck, leech?"

"I don't know, but it hurts like, well, shit." Dante rubbed it. He began walking to the door. Maybe Beatrice would have something he could take for the pain? Although, vampires didn't normally *need* anything to relieve pain, since they healed so fast it didn't really matter.

Clay was looking at him strangely. "When did your neck start hurting?"

Dante thought about it and then checked his watch. "Thirty minutes and nineteen seconds ago."

The werewolf rolled his eyes. "You're a freak, you know that?"

"So I'm told," Dante replied.

"Can you sense Elle?" Clay asked him.

He didn't have to think about it. "No."

Clay took a step closer to Dante, almost like he was trying to threaten him, Dante gathered. "You should be able to, with the bond. You sure you can't?"

Shutting his eyes, still rubbing his neck, Dante tried to think about Elle. About the annoying, infuriating person that she was. And he felt nothing. Not a single thing. "No?"

Clay let out a gush of air. "You're coming with me."

Dante let go of his neck. "What?"

Clay started walking and when he realized Dante wasn't right behind him, he stormed back into the room and grabbed his arm. If he wasn't in so much pain, Dante would have resisted. As it was, he tagged along behind the wolf.

"I think someone's taken Elle," Clay said.

"Why?"

"I was outside with her, then went in to grab her some pig's blood, and when I came back, she was gone."

"I would be too," Dante muttered.

Clay snorted. "But she wasn't anywhere in the house or the

garden afterward; I searched."

"Did you check to see if she went for a walk?" Dante asked, back to rubbing his neck.

Clay shook his head. "No one saw her leave."

"Doesn't mean much. If I wanted to – or you either, for that matter – no one would see us leave."

The wolf nodded slowly. "Let's go back to the garden and check. This time, we'll follow our noses."

◆

Melissande fought the hands that were holding her. She couldn't see anything, it was so dark. Something was wrong, something was *very* wrong, but she couldn't remember what it was. Something about her daughter?

"Where's Emmie?" she asked.

"Ssshhh, Mel, you're okay. You had a fit, but you're okay now." Olive's voice.

Wait…she'd had a fit? Melissande had never had a fit in her life. Why couldn't she *see*?

"Sometimes these things can happen. I need you to rest." Olive again.

"Where am I?" she asked.

"You're at my house. You'll be okay."

"Where's Emmie?" Melissande tried to get up, but strong hands were holding her down. She was on a bed, she realized.

"She's here too. Sshh, now. Just sleep."

Her eyes heavy, Melissande gave in.

CHAPTER FIFTY-EIGHT

Dante didn't like where they were going. Clay had dragged him down past King's Park and toward the river, only to lead them through the docks and back up to Court Road. They were standing on an intersection that would lead them back over the river and into the industrial area of the city.

"Where are we going?" Dante asked. It was such a circular route.

"They hired a hack or something, and they've actually gone a lot further afield than this," Clay said. "But I'm following the scent, and it crossed here."

"How can you do that?" Dante asked. He had "delicate" senses, but even he was struggling to tail the cab in the stench of the city.

"I'm that good," Clay said with a brief toothy grin.

Dante just looked at him.

"Come on, I *think* they're heading back toward the cit area."

Following behind the werewolf, Dante tried to ignore the stares that were coming their way. For once, he knew why he was receiving them. Clay was wandering around in a loose shirt and buckskins, and the day was chilly. And Dante was following – a were and a vampire hanging out together? – in formal pants and shirtsleeves. Aristo vampires they passed had actually gasped at his appearance. How dare he walk outside without a cravat or jacket?

Idiots, he thought.

"*Dante?*" someone said.

"What?" Dante replied.

Clay stopped walking and Dante almost slammed into the werewolf. "What?"

"I dunno. You said something," Dante replied, shrugging. His neck was starting to feel a bit better.

"*Dante?*"

Looking around, Dante frowned. He said to Clay, "Will you quit saying my name, you've got my attention."

Clay raised an eyebrow. "Uh, I didn't say anything. Did I mention you're a freak?"

"*Dante, it's not Clay, you idiot. It's me. Elle.*"

"Oh."

"*Moron, don't speak out loud. Think your reply to me. Do you see what I have to work with here?*"

"*Where are you?*" Dante thought back, ignoring the insults. At least it meant Elle wasn't dying.

"*I can't see anything, my eyes haven't adjusted yet.*"

"*Okay, give it a few seconds.*" He nodded to himself.

"Who the fuck are you nodding at?" Clay asked, making Dante jump.

Realizing that he'd stopped in the middle of Court Road, Dante quickly pulled Clay to the side, near a doorway that led to an apartment above two shops.

"Elle is talking to me." He tapped his head.

Rather than calling him a freak again, Clay said, "Where is she?"

"Says she doesn't know yet."

"*Hellloooo, are you paying attention to me?*"

"Yes!"

Clay was right up in his face. "What? Did she say where she was?"

"No, sorry, replying to her."

"Well, ask her. And ask her why she doesn't know where she is." Although from the look in Clay's eyes, the wolf probably already knew the answer.

"*Hellooo, need a little help here.*"

"Just shut up for a sec!" Dante snapped.

"Me?"

"*Me?*" Annoyance radiated from Elle to him.

"Both of you! I can't carry on two conversations at once."

Silence.

Thank the blood.

Taking a deep breath, feeling completely adrift, Dante said, "Now Clay, I'm going to talk to Elle. Keep quiet, okay?"

"Okay."

"*Finally.*"

"*Why did you pick me, rather than Clay?*"

"*You were easier to find. Dunno why. Maybe the bond?*"

That stupid fucking bond.

"*Hey! It's working for me now. Don't knock it.*"

"*Okay. So why are you chatting like this rather than just coming to find us?*"

"*I was kidnapped, moron.*"

"*How'd you manage that?*"

"*I thought I was bitten by a bug—*"

"*Not likely. Bugs don't bite vampires.*"

"*—but it was a dart. And it would have been nice if my Chooser had actually told me about bugs.*"

Dante winced. Scorn hurt when it was delivered straight into your mind.

"*What did they poison you with?*"

"*Dunno. Then they snapped my fucking neck.*"

"Shit." He couldn't stop saying that aloud.

"What?" Clay jumped on it.

Dante ignored him. "*Guess that's why my neck aches.*"

"*Your neck hurts, too?*"

"*Yes.*"

"*Good.*"

"*Hey!*"

"*Life's a bitch. Either way, my neck is starting to heal, faster than I think they thought it would.*"

"Do you know who took you?"

Radio silence, then, *"I think it was my mother and grandmother."*

"Why did they take you?"

"Graceds shouldn't become vampires; at least, that's what my gran reckons."

He could *feel* her rage and…fear. Finally, he knew what they felt like. And he didn't like them, not one bit.

"We're coming to get you."

If his neck hurt like this from *her* having her neck broken, imagine what he'd feel like if she died?

"You better fucking be. Hurry, before they stake me."

"On our way."

Dante turned to Clay, locking his gaze. "She was kidnapped and she thinks it was her grandmother."

Clay licked his lips, eyes blazing. "I know where she is then."

CHAPTER FIFTY-NINE

Feeling was slow to come back to her torso, arms and legs. Fucking assholes, she thought.

At first, she hadn't known if it had been her grandmother who'd taken her or if she'd been a victim of a mugging, but then she'd remembered seeing her mother. After speaking with Dante – while waiting for her vision to return – she'd figured out that she'd been dropped in the corner of her gran's green room. There hadn't been much light, but she hadn't needed it, not once her eyes started behaving again. Green walls, green floor, her gran's favorite chair. It had been pretty obvious.

And why, for blood's sake, hadn't Gran just killed her already?

Elle had been lying in her corner, mentally abusing Dante for what felt like ages, and yet there'd been no sign of Gran or anyone. And there wasn't really anyone close enough for her to spy on effectively. The most she could hear were random thoughts.

"How far away are you?" Elle shot at Dante.

"We're trying to work out a way of getting in without being detected."

"Good luck, moron. You're in a telepath's *home. She'll sense you."*

"Us?"

"You. Clay has got something funky going on where Greens can't hear him."

"Lucky him."

"Watch it."

When she got out of here – *if* she got out of here – she was going to smack Dante upside the head. Even if it gave her a headache. The vamp had a lot of attitude stored away under that creepy exterior.

"Hey! I'm not creepy."

Oops, she must have sent that last bit.

"No…you're not creepy at all.*"*

She smiled when she realized he didn't have a comeback for her. If he and Clay managed to save her ass, she might even hug Dante. Then smack him.

Footsteps began winding down the stairs toward the green room. At least two pairs, she heard. One slow, one heavy. Muffled voices reached her, but she couldn't hear them well. The room had been soundproofed. The door opened and light entered, causing the figures to be silhouetted, but she didn't need to see their faces to know who they were.

Gran and Bjorn.

She wondered when Bjorn had gotten involved in this shit. He was meant to be a bodyguard, just muscle.

She still owed the bastard for dislocating her shoulder.

"That should keep Melissande out of the way," Gran was saying.

"I didn't think she'd fight it so hard."

Olive walked into the room, her footsteps slow and sure. "She's always been protective of those girls. Who knows why? Wastes of space, both of them."

What. A. Bitch.

Elle hated her gran, but that feeling had just spiked past rational and off the scale.

"You should check on Elle to see if she is awake," Gran said.

She quickly shut her eyes as she heard Bjorn turn and walk in her direction. "Maybe turn up the light?" Bjorn asked.

Perhaps they wouldn't stake her until they thought she was conscious? Not that she knew why they hadn't staked her already. If she'd been them, she wouldn't have kept her alive, that was for sure.

"It's too bad she got Chosen," Bjorn said as he walked up to her. "I would have married her, half-blood though she was."

Elle had to fight to keep relaxed.

"I said you could have her, although I would have preferred someone else, someone fully Graced."

Marry *Bjorn*? Even a leech would have been better. Blood, she'd have taken *Dante* over Bjorn.

"Sure I can't keep her now?" Bjorn asked.

Elle thought she vomited a little into her mouth.

"Even after she's fucked a werewolf and is now a vampire?" There was a pause. Elle could picture the sneer on her gran's face. "She'd be dead by now if you hadn't begged me to spare her."

Bjorn touched her neck, checking her pulse. Did she even still have a noticeable one? She was going to kick Dante's butt when she got out of here. He had to give her a list of "100 Things About Being A Vampire You Should Know."

Bjorn moved away from her. "She's just confused from being Chosen. And we need to know if she told anyone about Graceds."

Elle wanted to wriggle her toes, to confirm that feeling had returned to them, but she couldn't risk it.

"She can't give you children. And if she did, imagine what monstrosities they'd be."

She could hear Bjorn walking away from her. "You wanted to breed Emmie with that wolf, Clay."

What!

"Oh good, she's awake."

She heard her gran walking toward her, but all she could think about was Clay having sex with Emmie. She *did* vomit in her mouth. Sour, rotten blood.

"What the fuck! Dante, ask Clay if he was going to rape my sister."

"Uh, okay?" Silence. *"He says no, with a few expletives."*

"Ask him if he'd planned on siring a child on her."

"He says your gran asked him to."

"Just get the fuck down here. I don't care how much noise you make or who you hurt, but leave my mother and sister alone." Elle flashed the vampire images of the woman and girl, so he'd know to avoid them.

Elle's eyes snapped open, causing her gran to jump back a little. The woman had been right in her face.

"Abomination," she hissed.

"Says *you*." Elle spat in her gran's face.

The woman, hand shaking from what Elle presumed was rage, wiped Elle's blood-stained saliva away.

"You risk everything we are by being alive!" Olive yelled.

Elle was seething with fury, her gut burning. Feeling had definitely returned to her torso. If only she knew her arms would work properly…

"And you don't risk us every day? By trying to control aristos through emotional addiction? Through controlling people's minds?"

"I do it for the good of my people!"

"You do it for *your* good. What about trying to breed a half-blood off a little girl?" Elle was yelling now. "Emmie's a fucking *child*."

Olive jerked back, affronted. "He said he would wait for her to grow up."

Oh Clay, Elle thought, *you have some explaining to do.*

Launching herself up, she tried to grab her gran by the throat, but her arms weren't quite hers to control, and her clumsily thrusting hands merely managed to push the old woman off balance. Olive landed with a thump on her backside. *Hope you broke a hip*, Elle thought.

Before Elle could kick her grandmother while she was down, she was thrown against the wall as Bjorn rushed her. Elle felt something pop. Her shoulder. *Again.* She tried to move, but it was as if she were jammed between two concrete walls. Bjorn was using his TK.

"Your sister is good for nothing!" Olive shouted from the floor. "She has developed no abilities and she's a drain on my time and resources. She has to do *something* to prove her worth. Breeding is all she can do."

Like your mother.

Elle blinked. That hadn't been her thought; it had been Gran's.

Swooping down with her mind, she began battering at Gran's mental shield, clawing it, ripping at it. She saw snatches of images – the freshest one a burning brand: Gran hiding in the shadows, forcing Melissande to knock on the gate at Greystoke House. Like a master with their puppet.

With a scream, she threw herself off the wall, not even stopping to think how she'd managed it. Bjorn looked up, alarm spreading across his features as Elle dove for the old woman. He blocked her, throwing her with his shoulder. She landed on the arm of a couch with a painful crack. *There goes my spine.* Forcing herself to move her arms, since her legs had gone numb again, she shoved herself off the chair, just in time for a stake to come slashing down where she had been.

"You *are* a monster! Trying to attack your own grandmother." Bjorn was panting, stake poised again.

Bjorn held the weapon high above his head while shouts and thumps sounded from the hall. As he drove the wooden spike down, Elle rolled, screaming as the wood pierced her shoulder. An answering yell emerged from the hall.

Dante, she realized.

The doorway was suddenly filled with men. Some fighting, one grabbing his shoulder yelling, "Mother fucker!"

Elle felt a half smile form, even through the pain. *"Great entrance,"* she thought at Dante.

Seeing Clay, she could finally lock onto his mind. She thought one thing: *"Kill Bjorn."*

CHAPTER SIXTY

Clay watched Dante as he gripped his shoulder and howled, "Mother fucker!" Seeing no wound on him, he realized what had happened. Elle had been stabbed.

Fighting his way past a group of Grays, jabbing with elbows and knees and throwing punches whenever he could, he made it through the door. Dante wasn't doing too badly, either, despite the shoulder. With his uncanny speed and ability with a blade, men fell in bloody heaps, and when Clay looked at the leech, Dante merely looked back, fangs out.

"Elle's hurt," Dante said, between his teeth.

"No shit."

Clay froze when he saw the Gray bastard, Bjorn, with a bloody stake poised over Elle. Dimly, he heard Elle scream into his mind, *"Kill Bjorn."*

He didn't think, he just rushed him. Next thing he knew, he was flying back against a wall. As he struggled against the invisible force pushing against him, a sharp pain dug into his shoulder. *A dart.* He began to feel dizzy.

He met Bjorn's eyes. "Tipped with silver nitrate, dog. Won't kill you, but it *will* fucking hurt."

Idiot, Clay snarled at himself. He should have thought they'd do something like this. Fucking Grays. Pain began burning its way from his shoulder and down his arm.

Eyes never leaving the Graced man, he watched in horror as Bjorn raised his stake again, and then stared in shock as a knife slammed into the Graced's chest.

He shook his head. Was the poison making him see things? It was certainly making him feel things. Bad things.

Bjorn was staring down at the blade, a look of surprise etched across his face. "Who the blood are you?" he gasped.

Clay followed his stare. Dante stood inside the doorway, bodies littered around him. The man was a machine. Clay realized that it was Dante's knife in Bjorn's chest.

Dante smiled then, and it was one of the scariest things Clay had seen in a long time. The vampire nodded at Elle. "Her very pissed off daddy."

Bjorn toppled over, the lock on Clay slipping, but not easing, which meant the Graced was still alive. But Clay couldn't move anyway with the poison roaring through his limbs, turning them leaden.

Dante was about to step into the room, but he froze, eyes locking on Olive, who was lying on the floor near the far corner. Clay could see her Green eyes blazing even from this distance. Sweat dotted her brow.

Dante walked past Bjorn over to Elle. He picked her up and began dragging her toward her grandmother.

"Let her go!" Clay shouted, helpless.

"What are you…doing?" Elle gasped. She was trying to move her good arm, but nothing else. Had something not healed?

Dante's face was strained. It was like he was trying to resist…

"Olive's in his head!" Clay yelled.

Elle's eyes closed and she seemed to go limp. Dante's movements slowed.

Olive screamed, "No!"

Dante started moving again. Moaning, Elle's eyes clenched tighter and the vampire's movements slowed once more, but it wasn't enough. Elle was almost at her gran.

Leaning down, Dante dropped Elle, mere feet from Olive. Elle was panting, her skin clammy, blood still oozing from the wound in her shoulder. Dante screamed. Forcing his sweat-drenched stare back to the vampire, Clay saw a stake jutting from between the man's shoulder blades.

Elle was keening.

What the blood?

Eyes snapping back to her, Clay saw no stake, but she was arched, as if it had been slammed into her. Dante slumped to the ground next to her.

Bjorn. It had to be. There were no other Grays in the room and stakes just didn't move on their own.

"You are an abomination." Olive's words reached his ears, even though they were softly spoken and directed at Elle.

A movement caught his attention then, something small, child-sized, running into the room, tracking blood across the carpet. "ELLE!"

Shit, Clay thought, *it's the kid. Emmie.*

"Emmie?" Elle gasped, trying to lift her head. She stopped her movement, her head turning to stare at Olive. Clay felt his stomach drop even as his muscles clenched in pain and more sweat dripped over him.

Olive was hauling herself up, a stake clenched in a bony fist. The old woman pulled herself to her knees, and held the stake over Elle's heart.

Emmie stopped running, skidding to a stop. "No!" the girl was screaming. "No!"

Olive snapped her eyes to her other granddaughter. "She has to die. She's a threat to everything we are."

His gut dropped and his vision almost went black. Elle could not die. She *couldn't*. The pain around his chest intensified.

"No!" Emmie didn't seem to hear her grandmother.

Blinking, his body fighting against the poison, Clay's vision returned. He could see the child's eyes locked on the stake, on where it was going to land. Without thinking, the little girl leaped forward, her skinny hand locking on her gran's wrinkled one.

"I can make you let me go," Olive growled, those wrinkled features maniacal.

"And I can stop your heart," Emmie spat.

"Really? You can't throw a ball, let alone do anything

productive."

The little girl's face was set. "I can *heal*."

"Emmie, no!" Elle yelled.

The little girl didn't look at her sister, her eyes focused on the stake.

"Lies! I would have known if you had an ability. *Any* ability."

Clay saw Emmie flick her gaze to her gran's. Then those bright Teal orbs met his for a brief second. They were old beyond their years.

"You know nothing!" the girl yelled.

The stake began to fall. Clay's heart was pounding, his fury at being trapped in his own body, unable to help, overpowering him. But the weapon stopped. Olive gave a gasp and then…she stopped breathing. Clay could hear her heart thud to a sudden stop, as if it had just been switched off.

The girl dropped her gran's arm, and watched as the old woman toppled over, dead.

Elle was crying. "Emmie, baby, you shouldn't have done it."

The little girl dropped to her knees and Clay could see blood seeping up into the cloth of her gown. "She was going to kill you."

"I know, but baby, you didn't have to do it. I would have worked something out." Elle lifted her good arm and Emmie reached down, hugging her sister. Elle let out a startled scream, her body bowing.

"Elle!" Clay shouted.

When Emmie moved away, Elle sat up, eyes wide, touching the shoulder where she'd been staked. Emmie looked…peaky.

Clay wanted to rub his eyes, but he couldn't move his arms, so he blinked. Had Emmie just *healed* Elle?

Those Teal eyes swept the room. "Elle, I only have enough energy left to heal one more person. There are three injured ones here."

Elle had tears trekking down her cheeks, but Clay wasn't sure if it was from pain, shock or worry. "Which one is closest to death?"

He wanted to comfort her, but he couldn't move. But he'd heal himself, he was sure.

Emmie quickly moved through the room, touching Dante, Bjorn and Clay.

"Bjorn."

Hatred filled her voice as Elle said, "Leave him."

Emmie said nothing, just looked at her sister. "Then it's the werewolf or vampire." Emmie started walking toward Clay.

Elle stared at him, and he could feel her reaching for his mind. "Wait! Clay, will you survive this? Can you heal?"

He nodded. It would take weeks, but yes, he could.

"Dante, then."

"Is he the one who Chose you?" Emmie asked, staying where she was in the middle of the room, blood covering her feet and knees.

Elle nodded.

Emmie took a step closer to Clay.

"Emmie, if Dante dies, it might kill me."

Without looking at him, her apparent need to save Clay gone with those words, Emmie turned on her heel and marched back to the vampire. "Pretty," he thought he heard the girl mutter before she touched Dante. Then, with surprising strength, she ripped the stake from his back.

The vampire let out a loud groan.

Minutes later and panting, Emmie dropped her hands from him. "I can't do any more. But he should heal the rest on his own."

Elle stood and swept her sister into a hug. "Thank you."

"I hate to break this up," Clay said from his slump against the wall. "But, can someone pull out the dart? And what are we going to do now?"

CHAPTER SIXTY-ONE

Dante watched as Anton wiped down Melissande's forehead. The woman was lying still as death – her thrashing had quietened – in one of the spare rooms at Greystoke House. She was suffering withdrawal.

If Dante hadn't experienced it himself, he would never have believed that someone could control another's thoughts to the extent it would leave them like this. But he had. He'd had *two* people fighting for control of his mind, and he'd hated it. He knew that Elle had been trying to save herself – and him – but it didn't make it any easier to accept.

Anton placed the sponge in a bowl that perched on a table next to the bed and turned, pausing when he saw Dante in the doorway. He walked to the door, shooing Dante out of the way, before softly closing the wooden panel.

"Shouldn't you be resting?" Anton asked him.

Dante shook his head. "It healed up a day ago."

Anton crossed his arms over his chest. "Let me see it."

It might have healed, but it was still a rough, puckered piece of scarring. "No."

"I am going to check it tonight anyway." Anton glared at him. "Uh-huh."

Anton had *tried* to tend Dante's wounds, but Beatrice had constantly shoved him out of the way. No place for a man, she said, the sickroom. Little did she know how much time Anton spent with Melissande; he was probably the only person who truly understood what the poor woman was going through.

Or at least could begin to understand – she'd been controlled like a puppet for almost her whole life.

Elle had assured Dante that most Greens weren't like her gran, that they weren't that strong. But Dante didn't like knowing there might be *more* Graceds out there who were like that. It was bloody scary.

"Has your sister left?" Anton asked him.

Dante nodded. He wondered why they were still standing in the hallway, but didn't comment on it. Anton had been moody of late. Snapping at him, then being almost too nice…it was bizarre. Elle said it was because the human was worried. Which was silly. Dante should be the one worrying about Dante.

"Will she be returning?" Anton asked.

"Hopefully not anytime soon." Misty had stayed during the initial stages of his recovery. When he'd been well enough to stand, she'd smacked him over the head and yelled at him for getting staked. To get her off his back, he'd told her about his "missing" twin sister. She'd then smacked him for not telling her as soon as he'd found out. At least he hadn't been the only one kept in the dark about it. But it had given her something else to think about. He almost pitied his missing twin.

"Good," Anton said.

Dante raised an eyebrow. "Good?"

"Your sister was scaring the staff and tormenting Clay."

Dante gave a small half smile. Scaring them, having sex with them, it was all the same to his sister.

"She scares me half the time," Dante admitted.

Anton shook his head. "I can see why."

There were a few moments of uncomfortable silence. "Thank you for not staking me when I was weak," Dante said.

"*What?*" Anton's eyes almost bulged.

"I said–"

"I know what you said. But *why* would you say that? I'd never do that!"

Dante shrugged. "You hate me."

"Not so much." Anton was staring at him. He took a step closer, and Dante realized they were almost nose-to-nose.

"No?" Dante was confused.

Rolling his eyes, Anton closed the distance between them. His mouth settled over Dante's and it was warm, spicy, like brandy.

And it was…nice.

As Anton's tongue swept over his lips, causing Dante's mouth to open, he worked out that it was better than nice.

♦

Emmie was running through the garden at Greystoke House, laughing. She wore a new dress, this one a pretty blue color, and Darla was chasing her, carrying a bright pink ribbon in her hand. Elle watched them from the terrace above with a small smile on her face.

Part of her was worried, though.

Emmie had been able to kill *with a touch*. Her own grandmother. Sure, Emmie had hated Gran and the old bitch had been about to stake Elle, but what could Elle do? Something like that traumatized people, and Emmie was only seven.

She sensed and heard Clay walk up to her side. He tucked her in against himself, hand at her waist. He dropped his chin on her head. He was still shaky after his poisoning, but had rebounded quickly. Faster than he'd thought he would.

That the king had been furious when he'd heard about the incident was an understatement. Having the king lust after you had its benefits, Elle decided. Clay was apparently a "royal guest" and the attack had been taken as a personal affront to the crown.

And then there'd been the fact that Dante and Elle had been staked, albeit unsuccessfully. There'd been a massive uproar in aristo circles over it, according to Anton. So much so that Choosing anyone had been temporarily banned across the city – until emotions calmed, apparently.

In other words, until the perceived outbreak of anti-vampire sentiment had been quietly taken care of.

It meant that the Graced community was lying *very* low at the moment, so at least Elle didn't have to fear another stake to the heart, for now.

And Elle's mother…well, Melissande had basically handed Emmie to her. She had to "sort things out," which Elle took to mean she had to come to terms with the fact that Gran had been controlling her most of her life.

Right now though, Melissande was in a bedroom upstairs physically withdrawing from the addiction of having her mind watched for years. Just like Anton had had to do when Annabel died. The baron had spent a lot of time helping Melissande through it, since he'd experienced it himself.

"She seems to be coping," Clay said, waving his free hand at Emmie.

Elle nodded and wrapped an arm around his middle. "I don't know for how long, though."

Clay's voice was warm and soothing against her. "We'll help her. Once your mother improves, she can help her, too."

"Everything's changed, but everything's almost the same," Elle said softly.

"Tell me about it," Clay said, almost conversationally. "How does it feel to be rich?"

Elle laughed, but it was a hollow sound. She'd inherited Gran's fortune, since Melissande *was* incompetent at the moment and the king wasn't sure she'd recover to his satisfaction. It was unnerving that King Jo had taken a personal interest in them. And that he clearly knew about Graceds. So much for Gran's big secret. "Shitty."

"Oh?"

"Gran's main source of income was human flesh."

Clay frowned. "Thought that was illegal?"

"Not dead human flesh. As in slaves. I knew she traded in them…but she'd deliberately bankrupt people or get them into compromising positions where she could sell them to vampires and weres."

Elle may have thought of herself as Graced, rather than a Non, but she'd had plenty of them who were her friends. Gran would lend them money, and when they couldn't pay her back, she'd send them to the estates at top dollar. No wonder she'd managed to get Elle into Kipling House.

Hearing a noise behind her, Elle turned her head and saw Dante standing in the doorway. He leaned casually against the frame. The bastard was healed and grinning. Wait, grinning?

"Did you get lucky, Daddy Vamp?" Elle asked with a snicker.

Dante's grin widened. She'd never seen him so...normal.

"Maybe."

Elle gagged.

"What are you two chatting about?" Clay asked. He'd gotten used to Elle and Dante talking mind-to-mind. They'd done it a lot during their recovery. She'd felt bad that he'd almost died trying to save her. She'd still smacked him though, but she'd been pissed off to learn that his sister had gotten in before her.

"Dante reckons he got lucky."

"With who?" Anton asked. The man was standing behind Dante in the doorway, leaning heavily on his cane.

"His hand?" Elle suggested with a smirk.

Dante blushed.

Ewww.

"How's your leg?" Dante asked Anton.

"Fine."

"You're leaning on your cane."

"I need the bloody thing to walk."

"Need a massage?"

"Not right now."

"Later then," Dante said and it sounded like a promise.

"You're making me feel sick," Elle said.

Anton grinned. By the blood, maybe Dante really had put out. Good for Anton. It was still gross though.

Emmie squealed and went running by the terrace, a laughing Darla still in pursuit.

"Found out something interesting yesterday," Anton said, eyes following his sister and Emmie through the garden.

"Oh?" Elle asked. She didn't pry, she didn't want to.

"Mother was still upset about your missing twin sister, Dante. And she was convinced you wouldn't heal properly until you found out where she was."

One of Dante's black eyebrows rose.

"I know. Anyway, to keep her happy, I went and checked out the counsel records, this time with a special request. Your sister's name is Hannah Romanov. She's never come back to the city, but I can probably track her now I have her surname. Your birth mother was Skarvan nobility."

Dante didn't say anything.

"Well, are you going to look for her?" Clay asked.

"I don't know. Not now. Misty will want to know."

She felt Dante's complete *lack* of curiosity. He had his answers, and while he wanted to know more about Graceds, his need for knowledge had been temporarily quieted. But she knew him. He would need to learn more information from her about Graceds. And would one day track down his sister.

Laughter trilled through the garden, but it wasn't Emmie's. Darla must have caught Elle's sister.

"Maybe Emmie needs a holiday," Clay said.

"Where could we go, though?" Elle asked.

"We could visit my sister."

"Didn't you say she was dead?"

"Uh, no. I may have implied it, though."

"Right."

"Well, you'll get to meet her if we go. I might even tell you about her."

Elle narrowed her eyes at the wolf. "What's there to know?"

"You'll just have to wait and see."

She humphed and turned back to the chase in the garden. It seemed Emmie had escaped Darla's clutches.

"Plus," Clay said, "I want her to meet my fiancée."

"Pretend one, you mean," Elle said privately.

"Not anymore."

"Uhh, don't you need me to agree to that?" Elle asked.

"So, will you agree to end the pretend engagement and start a real

one?" Clay asked, his eyes twinkling down at her.

"Oh my, I think my heart is all aflutter." Elle smirked. But it was. Clay really wanted to marry her? She looked up at him.

"The suspense is killing me."

From the tightening grip around her waist, she guessed it might be. Warmth blossomed out from her heart, flooding her. Her sexy wolf wanted to marry her. *"Why not? It isn't every day a man almost dies trying to save your life."*

"By those standards, you'd be marrying Dante next."

"Nah," Elle said with a grin. "He's married."

"Who is?" Dante asked.

Clay and Elle laughed.

EPILOGUE

Ralia, or Lia to her mostly absent friends, smiled as she wiggled her fingers through the finely grained white sand that ran across Limpinto Beach. After dotting a seemingly random spot on her work, she took a few steps back and brushed the sand from her knees. Yes, that would do it.

There were boxes and lines and waves and dots. Animal heads too, just for good measure. All drawn into the sand to be left there overnight. If any of the signs were altered – blown away or brushed over by the feet of an animal – it would be considered a sign. A foretelling.

Not that she needed help.

But the dark-skinned people who lived near Limpinto Beach didn't know that. They thought her a future-teller, who could read signs and speak tongues no one knew. They thought from that, she could divine the answers only the gods could know. Except there were no gods and she needed no signs.

Footsteps sounded on the sand and she smiled. "Clay!" she called, before she turned.

The big werewolf rushed over to her, wrapped her in his arms and swung her around. From the top of her spin, she spotted two other people standing under a palm at the edge of the beach. Clay almost stepped on her carefully constructed design as he pirouetted her around, and she said, "Stop! Be careful."

Eyes following her pointed finger, he looked at the designs and stepped away from them, closer to the water, where he set her down. "Lia, it's good to see you." He didn't ask about the signs, maybe he understood. She never used to do them, back when they'd lived together.

"And you, brother."

"How'd you know it was me?" he asked.

She smiled and ignored his question. Walking forward, her hands outstretched, she approached his friends. One was a tall vampire woman with a large straw hat, and the other was a young girl, who'd pushed her hat off to hang down her back on its string.

"You must be Elle and Emmie. It's so good to see you. And you had a pleasant trip through the Turquoise Sea? Yes, I see you did," Lia said with a warm smile. She clasped their hands and squeezed gently.

"What are you?" the little girl whispered.

"Ssssh," Elle hushed.

"It's okay," Lia said. She'd heard this question a lot, over her life. With her pale white skin, and whiter than white hair, it was a natural curiosity. It didn't help matters that Lia had woven string and beads and bones into her hair as well, and had even dyed bits different colors. Right now, her hair had purple and pink in it, amongst all the baubles. And then there were her eyes.

"Elle, Emmie, this is Lia. She's my sister."

Elle looked over at Clay and rolled her eyes. Which were just as Lia had known they would be: dark purple with specks of Gray and flares of Green. Lovely.

"I figured that one out. How'd she know our names? Did you send a letter ahead?"

"No," Clay said. He sounded uncomfortable.

Lia smiled. "He never needs to. I always know when he's going to visit me."

"Are you Graced?" The girl – Emmie – asked. Her eyes were the brightest Teal Lia had ever seen. Well, equal brightest.

"Emmie!" Elle sounded scandalized.

Lia spun in a circle, raising her hands to the sky. When she turned back to them, she was grinning, the bones and beads in her hair clinking. "Yes."

"Well, she's half-Graced, half-were," Clay said.

Lia tilted her head to the side and looked at him. "More Graced than wolf, brother." She leaned down next to Emmie's ear and mock-whispered, "I've never been able to change form."

The little girl's eyes were wide. "No?"

"No. But I don't age, so it's all wonderful." Lia plopped onto the sand and patted the vacant space next to her. Elle, Clay and Emmie all sat, as she'd known they would.

"What can you do? Your eyes are…Pink."

Red, Lia liked to think, but on the days she was being honest with herself, she did admit that they were pink. Today wasn't one of them.

"Red," she said.

Emmie shook her head, but didn't correct her.

Lia clapped. Oh, she was going to like her! Just as she'd known she would.

"Lia, I have something to tell you…" Clay started.

"Which bit?" Lia asked, excited. Oh, she'd been waiting for their arrival for months. She'd been so happy. Even the local people had caught on to her upbeat mood. But they thought it meant there was going to be good fishing. She'd have to apologize to them later.

Lia didn't wait for Clay to elaborate, but rushed to speak. "The part where you're engaged to Elle – yay! A new sister – or the bit where Emmie is a healer?"

Elle and Emmie stared at her, slack-jawed. Clay just gave her a half smile. "Both?"

Lia laughed and clapped. "It's so wonderful!"

"If you hadn't guessed," Clay said to the others, "Lia can see the future."

The vampire and healer both gaped at Lia, and she saw images flash through her mind. Years and years they'd have together. But Emmie didn't know that yet. Didn't understand that she could heal herself of age damage. The things Lia could tell her…

"Oh, we're going to have so much fun!"

ACKNOWLEDGMENTS

Graced is my first published novel, and I owe some very special people some very large thank yous. First, I'd like to thank my husband Tom, for listening to me develop my ideas and reading over the very first draft, and my wonderful beta readers: Liz Grzyb, Marty Young, Stephanie Gunn, and Joanne Danton. All your thoughts and comments – even the painful ones! – made this book better.

I also want to send out a huge thanks to my amazing and persistent agent, Jenny Darling. Her belief in this book has been absolutely invaluable in it reaching your bookshelves. And then there's the team at Momentum, where the book was originally published: Haylee Nash, Tara Goedjen, Michelle Cameron and Julia Knapman: you have been an absolute delight to work with.

Amanda Pillar is an award-winning editor and author who lives in Victoria, Australia, with her husband and two cats.

Amanda is the author of the Graced series, and has had numerous short stories published. She has co-edited six fiction anthologies and solo-edited two: *Bloodstones* and *Bloodlines*, published by Ticonderoga Publications.

In her day job, she works as an archaeologist.

www.ingramcontent.com/pod-product-compliance
Lightning Source LLC
Chambersburg PA
CBHW021456110726
47899CB00001BA/178